surface tension

surface
tension

CHRISTINE KLING

ballantine books • new york

A Ballantine Book
Published by The Ballantine Publishing Group

Copyright © 2002 by Christine Kling

All rights reserved under International and
Pan-American Copyright Conventions. Published in the
United States by The Ballantine Publishing Group, a division
of Random House, Inc., New York, and simultaneously in
Canada by Random House of Canada Limited, Toronto.

Ballantine and colophon are registered trademarks of Random House, Inc.

www.ballantinebooks.com

Library of Congress Cataloging-in-Publication Data
is available from the publisher upon request.

ISBN 0-345-44828-6

Text design by Holly Johnson

Manufactured in the United States of America

First Edition: December 2002

10 9 8 7 6 5 4 3 2 1

Tim, this one's for your dad.

I would like to thank the following people:
Tracy Brown, Ballantine Books; Judith Weber,
Sobel/Weber Associates; Red Koch, tug *Hero*; Marcia
Trice and Clio, dancers at Tootsie's; Mike Springstun,
Hollywood Police Department; Mark Meyers,
Deerfield Beach Fire Department; Ed Magno, DEA;
R. C. White, Fort Lauderdale Police Department;
James W. Hall, Lynne Barrett, and Les Standiford,
Florida International University; Laurie Foster, Barbara
Lichter, Elaine Vannostrand, Carole Lytle, Pat and J. J. Gray,
Cindy Gray, Steve Gray, my readers, my family and friends,
and finally, my son, Tim Kling.

1

THE MAYDAY CALL BROKE THROUGH SOME FISHERMEN'S chatter on channel sixteen. Brushing stray hairs back toward my ponytail, I quieted my breathing and listened. I always left the tug's wheelhouse VHF radio turned up extra loud so that I wouldn't have to feel guilty about missing any calls. Let's face it, towing and salvage is a tough business, and if any calls for tows came in, I needed to get on the horn and make the deal before the competition.

I was down in the head compartment, wedged in alongside the Royal Flusher whose display model had operated so beautifully at the boat show, but once installed, it plugged up regularly every time I allowed someone else to use the head. B.J. was supposed to have been here this morning to fix the damn thing, and instead I found myself scrunched up in the tiny compartment, trying to make sense of an exploded diagram of a toilet.

The radio finally squawked again. "Mayday, mayday, this is the *Top Ten*."

I dropped a washer under the shower grate and banged my head on the porcelain bowl. The *Top Ten*. Neal's boat. And it had been a woman's voice.

I straightened out my legs and tried to extricate myself from the pretzel-like position required to get at the bolts on the base of the Flusher. Please let him be all right, I thought. He should be the one making that radio call; the fact that he wasn't was causing the hairs on my arms to lift in spite of the Florida heat. Where was he? Yet, in the midst of my worry, I couldn't help but wonder who the woman was. Neal didn't actually own the *Top Ten*; she was a ninety-two-foot private motor yacht, and Neal Garrett, all five feet eleven inches of sunny, brown-skinned, blue-eyed smiles, was her hired skipper and my former lover.

I backed out of the head and made it up to the wheelhouse in three long strides. Coast Guard Station Fort Lauderdale was already on the air trying to get the woman to state the vessel's position. Several times their transmission got stepped on by local traffic, and she became more hysterical by the minute. You weren't supposed to call mayday unless someone's life was in danger. The question was, did she know that? I didn't recognize her voice, but I had heard in the Downtowner that Neal had teamed up with some young girl he met there in the bar. Where was Neal?

I wiped my hands on my cutoff jeans and kicked the toolbox closed with the toe of my deck shoe. I wanted to break in on her transmission with the Coasties to ask about Neal, but, of course, that would be against regulations. The Coast Guard radio operators could be so exasperating sometimes. It seemed like they had to know everybody's mother's maiden name before they could determine the nature of an emergency.

"How many persons are on board?"

"Nobody," she said, "at least not now. I don't know what to do. Please, we're getting closer."

He finally asked her what was wrong. The boat was drifting, she said, toward some tall white buildings. Then she broke off, and he couldn't get her to respond.

Now, that's a big help, I thought as I clicked on the VHF radio direction finder, turned up the radio, and slipped out of the wheelhouse. From her description, she could be anywhere along the hundred miles of tall white buildings from Palm Beach to Coconut Grove.

I jumped the gap from the gunwale of my tug to the seawall and then trotted across the lawn to my little cottage to lock up. I looked around for B.J., usually both my mechanic and the best deckhand I knew. The storm shutters were all closed on the big house, where he had been working in the library the day before. I trotted around the side of the house.

I had met B.J. when I used to work as a lifeguard down on Lauderdale beach. A big Samoan, he often surfed after work with a couple of the other lifeguards. When they introduced us one afternoon, he was one of the few people who had recognized something in my name.

"Hey . . . Seychelle," he said. "Isn't that the name for some islands?"

When I explained my dad had named all us kids after islands, he wanted to know if I had a sister named Pago Pago.

I walked out to the gate, but his truck wasn't in the drive. Taking a megayacht like the *Top Ten* under tow would certainly not be easy as a one-man job, but I didn't have time to chase around anymore.

Locking the door to my cottage, I whistled for Abaco, my black Lab. She crawled out from under her bougainvillea bush at the side of the cottage and jumped through the gate in the bulwarks.

The noise of *Gorda's* Caterpillar diesel grumbling to life rolled across the river like nearby thunder. I threw the dock lines onto the grass just beyond the seawall and adjusted the throttle to achieve maximum speed with the least amount of wake. I noted in the log that we were under way at 9:18 A.M., Thursday, March 18. Abaco took up her position at the bow, ears blowing back, tongue lolling out of the corner of her mouth.

I hoped Neal had surfaced from wherever he was and the emergency was over, but until I heard otherwise, I'd keep the steam on. The *Top Ten*, at ninety-two feet, was a custom Broward yacht, replacement value somewhere near five million. In today's market, unfortunately, her new owner would be lucky to get two to three for her. But if she were in danger of going on the beach, the salvage claim could be in numbers *I* hadn't seen in a long time.

I had not heard any radio transmissions since I cast off and got under way, but I knew very well that even at nine in the morning, Perry Greene had been sitting in Flossie's Bar and Grill with his handheld VHF on the bar next to his can of Bud. Just as I was pushing the speed limit down the New River, Perry was headed down the Dania Cutoff Canal in *Little Bitt*, his twenty-eight-foot towboat.

Perry Greene wore greasy T-shirts and ripped blue jeans that showed off the fact that he never wore underwear. He had an IQ about as high as the winter temperature after a cold front, and he'd beaten me out of too many jobs lately. The *Little Bitt* was always piled high with slimy lines, old hemp fenders, and various broken engine parts, but Perry knew how to get the most out of an engine, and she was fast. I tapped the throttle forward a notch. Marine salvage was a no-cure, no-pay business; whoever got there first would get the job. No way Perry was going to beat me out of this one.

Coast Guard Station Lauderdale came back on the air and began calling the *Top Ten*. For the longest time the girl's voice didn't answer their call. Then her voice broke in sounding weak, but the transmission was so clear, I would have thought she was within a few hundred yards of me.

"Oh, God, help me . . . please . . ."

Then nothing. The transmission ended and the radio remained silent for several long seconds. When the Coast Guardsman's voice came back on, calling the name of the boat in his monotone, I jumped, but *her* voice never came back on the air. I wished I could just climb into my fifteen-foot Whaler and fly on out there to see what was going on. While *Gorda* had plenty of raw power in her diesel, she would never get up and plane over the waves like a dinghy. But then again, I wouldn't be able to do much good in the Whaler if that ninety-two-footer was in the surf line.

The run down the river had never taken quite as long as it did that morning. At best, with the current with me, my dock was a good twenty minutes from the harbor entrance, but because I was fighting the incoming tide, the harbor markers seemed to crawl past even more slowly. Early as it was, the river stink was already overpowering the smell of the newly cut grass and flowering trees of the multimillion-dollar homes on either side of us. It hadn't always been that way along Fort Lauderdale's New River—the smell, I mean. Even I could remember when kids caught tarpon off the Davie Bridge, and the crabs the locals pulled up in their traps didn't have a deadly dose of mercury in them. But nowadays, between the agriculture runoff and the hundreds of live-aboard yachts dumping all their sewage overboard, there were days, quiet mornings like this one, when the river was a real bacteria bath.

Finally, I turned south at the mouth of the New River and headed for the entrance to Port Everglades. For a Monday, there was a fair amount of traffic on the Intracoastal Waterway, and I got a break at the Seventeenth Street Bridge. Though *Gorda* could get through without a bridge opening, the traffic jostling for position often forced me to slow way down. This morning I joined the line of sailboats and sportfishermen and steamed straight on through without touching the throttle.

When I'd almost cleared the last inner harbor beacon and was ready to turn out the cut, I looked to seaward and saw, three-quarters of a mile offshore, a gigantic, gray, V-shaped ship lined up on the channel markers, a tiny pilot boat bobbing next to it like a remora attached to a shark.

"Goddamn!" I cut back the throttle and started to make a wide turn back into the ship turning basin. No way did I want to share the channel with an aircraft carrier. Two big harbor tugs churned past me, headed out to the ship.

Gorda slowly lost way and began to drift toward the south side of the harbor entrance. I checked down the Intracoastal toward the Dania Cutoff Canal, and sure enough, there was Perry Greene's blond hair flying around his head, just visible over the windscreen of *Little Bitt*. His boat was throwing up a three-foot wake, and as I saw it, I had a choice: pray for the harbor police to stop him for speeding in a manatee zone, or try to beat him out the cut.

"Come on, baby!" I pushed the throttle forward all the way to the stops. I couldn't remember ever running *Gorda* flat out at max RPM. I turned her around and lined up, midchannel, head on and closing with the carrier. As *Gorda* picked up speed, her stern started to squat in the water, and the wake we were throwing up made Perry's look like bathtub play. The fishermen on the rock jetties grabbed for their bait coolers and scrambled for higher ground.

"*Securité, securité*," the radio crackled, "this is Port Everglades Harbor Pilot. All traffic please clear Port Everglades entrance channel, this is Port Everglades Harbor Pilot, clear." The pilot's voice on the radio sounded convincing, but I could barely hear him over *Gorda*'s screaming engine. And if the growing vision out my windshield didn't stop me, nothing would.

It just didn't look like it could stay upright. The damn thing looked like a skyscraper, and it narrowed down to this knifelike bow that dwarfed the harbor tugs I knew to be more than twice *Gorda*'s size. Fortunately, the massive ship was moving at no more than two or three knots. I'd read somewhere just how many miles out those babies had to start slowing before they could come to a complete stop. They'd probably throttled down somewhere off Bimini.

I glanced at the oil pressure and temperature gauges; the engine seemed to be handling it.

"*Securité, securité*, attention all vessels . . ." I tuned the radio out and tried my best to ignore the five-story-high, thousand-man floating city that was bearing down on me.

Water color. I concentrated on the color of the water and the size of the wind chop as I cleared the towering condos at Point of Americas and edged over as close as I dared to the north side of the channel. The end of the breakwater came into view surrounded by pale yellow-green water. Shallow, sand bottom. Six feet of water was what *Gorda* needed: aquamarine. While there was plenty of depth in the channel, on either side the bottom shallowed up quickly. We were hitting the wind chop now, and waves were exploding into rainbow-tinted mist off *Gorda's* bow. Abaco deserted the bow and stationed herself in a corner of the wheelhouse, watching me with big black doubting eyes.

I nearly tripped on the doorframe when the carrier blew her deep, deafening horn. What, did they think I couldn't see them?

Then there it was. Turquoise water. Twelve feet or better.

They blew their horn again and again. Five blasts in all, signaling "get the hell out of the way." I couldn't see the deck of the ship now, only this titanic gray wall of steel closing the narrow band of water that separated us. Although fine at the bow, the ship fattened amidships to fill the channel. And both in the air and through the deck, I could feel the throb and bite of her screws as they idled into harbor: *thunk, thunk, thunk.*

I turned the wheel and *Gorda* slipped around the end of the jetty, from the dark blue channel into the turquoise water. The tug's squatting stern lifted up and began to surf on the swell of displaced water the carrier pushed in front of her. I eased off the throttle and watched the gray wall slide past. I stepped out of the wheelhouse and squinted up at the deck where small white-capped faces peered over the side. One sailor waved as the great ship filled the harbor entrance behind me. Perry hadn't followed, thank God.

Now I had a tow to locate.

It was early in the day, but once offshore and clear of the tall stucco windbreaks, the wind was blowing a good ten to fifteen knots out of the southeast. High, clean-looking trade-wind clouds chased each other off toward the Glades. I slid the binoculars out of the case attached to the bulkhead and, steadying the wheel with one hip, I scanned the horizon, first to the north out the wheelhouse window.

I got lucky. It was not difficult to make out the distant bright outline of the *Top Ten*, apparently adrift. Looked like they'd made it no farther north than the Galt Ocean Mile before trouble stalled them. She was too close to shore. The *Top Ten* drew over seven feet, and with the onshore breeze, I figured she'd hit bottom within the hour. The problem was, it would take me half that time just to reach her.

I pushed the throttle back up to fourteen hundred RPM and checked around for any of the other boats from the local towing services. Off to the east the *Cape Coral* was towing a water barge back from Bimini, but this wasn't her kind of job even if she were free. Perry was still the one I had to worry about.

When my father, Red Sullivan, built *Gorda* over twenty-five years ago, his was the only boat to enter the business of towing luxury megayachts between the boatyards and marinas of Miami and Fort Lauderdale's New River. Our next-door neighbor, a harbor pilot down in Port Everglades, told my father about the new regulations that would require every motor yacht with a draft greater than seven feet to be assisted by a tug. So when Red retired from the navy, he started building the aluminum hull over in a corner at Summerfield Boatworks. Mother often told us how thrilled she was to get him out of her house. She had grown accustomed to her life as a navy wife, to his long absences, and she was chafing at having him home all the time. Red had never intended the forty-foot tug to be an oceangoing salvage vessel, but as the luxury yachts grew bigger and more numerous, more towing companies jumped into the business. Eventually, he started taking *Gorda* out on breakdowns and salvage jobs just to stay busy.

The Fathometer registered twelve feet when I pulled alongside the big slab-sided yacht. The brisk wind was throwing up quite a chop and, just drifting as she was, it put the *Top Ten* broadside to the slop. That, with the easterly swell, had *Gorda* rolling the rails down as we circled the ninety-two-footer. I blew the air horn a couple of times, but I couldn't raise anyone on deck. There was an inexplicable stillness about the ship.

I drew in close to the swim step aft. Abaco tilted her head up and sniffed the air, then looked at me quizzically.

"I don't know where Neal is, girl. I wish I did."

One hundred feet of three-quarter-inch nylon line lay coiled on the foredeck. Backing off from the megayacht, I dashed out of the wheelhouse, threaded one end of the line through the hawser hole in the bulwark, and tied it securely with several hitches around the large aluminum post on the foredeck. The other end of the line I wrapped in a loose bowline around my waist, and I made it back to the wheel before we'd drifted too far.

When I'd eased *Gorda*'s bow up to within a few feet of the *Top Ten*'s swim step, a squirt in reverse stopped the tug from colliding with the motor yacht. I shoved the throttle into neutral and ran out of the wheelhouse, climbed up on the bow bulwark, coiled some slack line in my hand, and leaped down onto the swim step at the stern of the big yacht.

I lost my balance and collapsed in an awkward heap, slamming my shoulder into the gold-leaf *T* painted on the yacht's transom. My heart felt like it was trying to break out of my rib cage, and it was several seconds before I drew a normal breath. Great landing, Sullivan, I thought. *Gorda* was drifting back rapidly, and if I didn't hurry, the line around my waist would soon pull me right into the sea. Quickly I stood and untied myself. Apparently the only one who had seen my bumbling arrival was Abaco, her head cocked to one side and her legs spread for balance, watching me from the tug's bow.

I climbed up the ladder to the aft deck and secured the line, adjusting the slack so that *Gorda* drifted angling off downwind, about forty feet off the big yacht's stern. Then I called out, "Hello. Hello. *Top Ten*." Neither the engines nor the generators were running, and in the shallow water, beam on to the wind, I could hear the vessel creaking and groaning as the hull wallowed in the swell. Yet even with that noise, the utter lifelessness seemed even more oppressive now that I was actually aboard.

Stepping over a puddle of water, I made my way forward up the starboard side. I hadn't been aboard the *Top Ten* since Neal and I broke up, and every detail I observed kindled a small memory.

I cupped my hands to the glass on my left to try to see through the glare. The main salon was empty; a half-eaten sandwich on a paper plate and a romance novel with a gaudy cover rested on the glass table. Neal had served us charbroiled dolphin on that table the first night he came aboard as captain. That night we'd been so happy about his new job, and we celebrated on the huge bunk in the owner's stateroom, blissfully unaware that it was that job that would be the end of us.

A stainless ladder led to the bridge on the upper deck. I held tight to the rungs as the boat rolled, and I swung out, the water visible beneath my back. I used the momentum when the boat rolled back to pull myself up through the bulwarks, grabbing hold of the speedboat in chocks on the upper deck, but my sweaty hands slid across the smooth fiberglass. I dropped to a crouch to regain my balance.

The voice of the Coast Guardsman calling on the bridge VHF radio startled me at the same time I saw the hand at the base of the companionway door. The fingers were curved upward in a distinctly feminine curl, soft and relaxed. As the yacht rolled, the hand rocked slightly, showing a flash of red nail polish on the thumb.

"Hello," I called out, feeling stupid as I did. Clearly, she wasn't going to answer me.

11

"COAST GUARD STATION FORT LAUDERDALE. THIS is the *Top Ten.*" My throat tightened. I couldn't, shouldn't look down. I'd had to step over the body to reach the dangling microphone, and it had taken every ounce of willpower I had not to run straight back to *Gorda* and get the hell out of there. The girl was on her side, resting in a pool of dark blood, the stainless-steel hilt of the dive knife showing below her left shoulder blade. Her long blond hair fanned out across the teak cabin sole and hid her face. She was wearing a thong bathing suit, and her exposed white buttocks looked more like smooth latex than flesh. I kept myself from looking down again, but the picture had been burned into my inner eyelids, and my mind kept flashing the snapshot over and over again.

The sour taste crept up the back of my throat again.

The Coastie's radioman sounded almost excited when he came back on the air with his mundane questions. I didn't want to spend any more time than was necessary on the radio. It was possible the killer was still aboard. The very thought made me swivel my head around and check out the windows on all sides of the bridge. I felt so exposed. I kept glancing over my shoulder as I listened to the Coast Guard. The killer must be gone, I told myself. If he had wanted to kill me, there had been plenty of opportunity as I'd wandered around shouting earlier.

Besides, the big boat *felt* utterly empty. Maybe it was stupid to trust a gut feeling like that, but my intuition and instincts had kept me alive before. Finally I interrupted the Coast Guardsman, identified myself, and got straight to the point.

"Coast Guard Lauderdale, there is a fatality here." At the time I said it, I wondered at my own words. They sounded official and self-assured even if they were at a slightly higher-than-normal, breathy pitch, and yet I felt everything but. The girl was dead, as in cold, white, plastic-looking, no longer a human being. Is that why cops withdraw into that silly techno-speak on the TV news all the time? Because to use the real words conjures up that slide show on the mind's big screen, and it doesn't matter if you looked only once, it's going to replay over and over again.

I had seen dead bodies before. In six years working as a lifeguard on Fort Lauderdale's city beach, I'd pulled one heart attack victim out of the surf, there had been several drownings, and I'd found that girl who overdosed, sitting up, back to a palm tree, facing the sunrise. And long before any of that, there had been my mother. But seeing it doesn't make you get used to it. Besides, this one was different. This was no accident. Someone had intentionally thrust that blade through her skin. Although the hot sun shone brightly through the bridge windows, I shivered.

The boat rolled almost thirty degrees on an oversized swell, and a Heineken bottle crashed over on the console. I jumped back, my hand at the neck of my T-shirt, as the amber liquid spilled across the teak, wetting a chart folded back to reveal about a ten-mile stretch of coast. Weighting the chart down was a copy of Bowditch's *Practical Navigator*. I looked more closely at the blue clothbound book, and I realized it was *my* copy of Bowditch—I'd loaned it to Neal several months before.

That was when I noticed the gun for the first time. It was on the console next to the depth sounder: a black handgun. I had no idea what kind it was. There were some holes in the instruments on the console, too. Obviously the gun had been fired. Then my ankle rubbed against cool flesh.

"Shit!" The sound of my own voice frightened me, and I knew I had to start doing something to get both myself and the *Top Ten* under control. The yacht was rolling worse, which meant she was getting into shallower water. While *Gorda* drew only four feet, the draft of a yacht like the *Top Ten* was closer to eight feet. I couldn't let either boat touch bottom. Out the port-side windows, the morning sun reflected off the glass and white plaster of the condominiums several thousand yards away. A crowd was gathering at the water's edge, retirees out for their morning walk and swim, now delighted at the prospect of their daily ritual being livened up by the chance to see a multimillion-dollar yacht about to go into the surf line.

I reached for the engines' starter switch, but nothing happened. Either the engines needed to be started down in the engine room, or the damage here on the bridge had shorted out some necessary connection. I wished B.J. were here. He would probably be able to get these engines started. If not, at least he would have helped me get a line on this boat. Hell, it felt more like a ship. There was no more time to take the chance that the engines might not start.

I didn't want to have to step over the body again. Dropping the mike onto the dashboard, I slipped out the port side of the bridge. My boat shoe slid on the deck, and a quick glance down revealed a red smear. I'd slipped on blood. More droplets led aft, and there was a good-sized dark puddle in front of the port ladder. Beyond, I could see the line of breakers, now no more than a couple of hundred yards off.

On the bow I found some yacht braid dock lines. I tied several of them together with hasty bowlines and ran the line from the *Top Ten*'s bow, outside everything, back to the stern. Abaco yelped and wiggled like a pup when she saw me. I could tell from the tension on the line between the two boats that there was no way I could pull up the *Gorda* by hand. Fortunately, the *Top Ten* had an Ideal warping capstan on the stern. I assumed the winch was hardwired directly to the ship's batteries, but I still breathed a soft "thank you" when I hit the button and the drum started turning. I was able to winch the line in until the two boats were banging together. *Gorda's* aluminum bow was munching the big yacht's teak swim step a bit, but it was nothing compared to what a few hours in the surf might do.

I tossed the *Top Ten's* bowline onto *Gorda's* foredeck and pulled myself up onto the tug. Abaco licked my face once as I came aboard, and then she stood back, out of the way. After untying the line that secured us to the big yacht's stern, I tossed that line into the water. I wasn't going to have to worry about *Top Ten's* props getting tangled on the line; her engines were out of commission.

I walked the line that was tied to *Top Ten's* bow back to the stern of *Gorda* and tied it to the tow bit. From the wheelhouse, I brought the tug around in a half circle to the seaward side of the *Top Ten's* bow, careful not to foul the towline on my own prop. If the *Top Ten* didn't touch bottom before I swung the bow around, she must have been missing by just inches. As we pounded our way offshore, away from the breakers, I noticed Perry circling in *Little Bitt*, probably praying my towline would bust. Then I heard the siren and saw the blue flashing lights of the Fort Lauderdale Marine Police Unit and, behind them, the Coast Guard cutter.

I smiled to myself. A little late, boys.

3

"YOU'RE THE ONE WHO FOUND HER."

I wasn't sure whether he was asking me or telling me, or even if he meant the girl or the boat.

"Yes." I stuck out my hand. "Seychelle Sullivan."

He looked at my hand for a moment as though he were being offered a dead fish. Then he reached out and shook it in one brisk stroke.

"Detective Victor Collazo, Fort Lauderdale Police." Long black hairs curled out from the cuffs of his white shirt, and though it was only midday, his face was already darkened by coarse black stubble. "Tell me about it," he said.

"When I got there, the boat was unmanned and adrift. No captain, no helmsman, nobody. Nobody alive, at least. The vessel just missed going on the beach by minutes, but then I got a line on her and towed her in."

"You just happened by."

"No. I heard the mayday call on the radio. Towing is what I do." I handed him a business card from my shoulder bag. "Sullivan Towing and Salvage. I've always got the radio on."

We were sitting on the bright tropical-print sofa in the *Top Ten*'s main salon. With no generators and no air, the atmosphere in the boat was like an overheated engine room. He glanced at my card and dropped it in his coat pocket.

"And the victim," he said.

"I didn't touch a thing." I nodded toward the upper deck. "That's how she was when I found her."

The Coasties had swarmed aboard as soon as *Gorda* nudged the *Top Ten* alongside the Port Everglades Coast Guard dock. Once I'd tied up the tug, I went back to tell them my side of the story, and they ushered me aboard, telling me to wait. Not too much later, the cops showed up, some in uniforms, others in plain clothes. There was a regular parade heading up and down from the bridge deck carrying suitcases, flash cameras, even video cameras. They all seemed to ignore me. Finally I got up and asked a uniformed policewoman what they wanted me to do. She, too, told me to sit and wait. At that point, the last thing I wanted was to sit there with nothing to do, allowing my mind to replay the dead-girl slide show in my brain. Over and over, I watched myself approach the bridge, spot the hand, and then slowly, as I come around the corner, see the knife and the blood.

Only this time, I was suddenly on a beach, and there was no blood. The sun was so bright, it leached the color out of everything, and there was the overpowering coconut-sweet smell of suntan lotion. I heard hushed voices as I pushed my way through the crowd, but I couldn't make out what they were saying. The only word I could hear was the last word I'd said to my mother. I was eleven years old again when I reached down and turned her head, brushing the sea grass from pale sandy skin; I knew that face.

Shaking my head as though to pry loose the memories, I refocused my eyes and my brain on the scene at hand. What was taking so long? What were they doing to find Neal? Were they thoroughly searching the boat? The sea? They surely wouldn't know where to look. They didn't know him like I did.

I remembered the book then, Bowditch's *Practical Navigator*, and those days when we were down in the Keys aboard his little wooden sailboat, and he was teaching me celestial navigation. He was a lousy teacher; he carried it all around inside his head, and he didn't know how to share it. He recommended I bring the Bowditch along and read it. I tried, but I was always getting lost, because the teacher was more interested in getting his student off the subject (and on to studying human anatomy) than in teaching navigation. Now, maybe that man I once loved was hurt and lost, and I was stuck in that hot salon, waiting.

I'd been sitting there trying hard to turn off the memories for over an hour when Collazo finally showed up. I was feeling irritable, hot, and sweaty. But the few drops on my upper lip were nothing compared to the sweat on that cop. Within minutes he was pressing a linen handkerchief to his face and neck, trying to mop up the rivulets of sweat, but no sooner had he wiped his face and neck dry than more droplets popped out of his skin. The man was an honest-to-God sweat machine. Immaculately dressed, he had taken off his jacket when he first sat down, revealing his perfectly pressed, custom-fitted shirt, but he never loosened his tie. Even so, above his collar, I could see the tufts of hair peeking out. I figured he had to be a regular gorilla underneath all his clothes. Maybe, since some women don't react too well to hairy guys, he tried to keep himself covered, no matter how miserable he might be.

"Did you recognize the victim?"

"No."

"The captain wasn't aboard when you arrived."

His voice was a monotone, unaccented and almost without inflection, and he had this weird way of asking questions by making statements and then waiting for me to agree or disagree.

"No, I didn't see him, and I never heard him on the radio on my way out there. Does anybody know if Neal was even aboard?"

Collazo gazed up at one of the uniformed officers searching the boat. He watched the man as he rifled through the drawer of CDs under the stereo system. Then he turned back to me, sizing me up. Given my height, I was used to it. I could tell he was trying to guess how tall I was. I'd been five foot ten ever since junior high school, and generally I could classify men into two categories: those who found it intimidating and those who didn't. I figured Collazo fell in the latter category.

"You knew Neal Garrett."

The way he said it, it sounded almost like an accusation.

"In my business, I know most of the professional captains."

"You heard the mayday call."

We'd been over this part already. It seemed like a detective should be better at asking questions and getting the story straight. I knew I didn't want to stay in that heat any longer than necessary, so I told him the story exactly as it had happened. He nodded as I spoke, and sometimes wrote in a little notebook he had. His handwriting was small, neat, and precise. When I got to the part about the girl, he stopped writing and our eyes met. I explained about the knife, and I saw her all over again reflected in the detective's dark eyes. Then when I'd finished, he had me go over several parts and repeat them.

"You started out there on your tugboat after the girl started calling for help."

"That's right."

"And someone saw you leave your dock."

"No, nobody was around. I tried to find my mechanic, B.J. Moana, to help me out, but I couldn't locate him. Time was running out. The Seventeenth Street Bridge tender might remember me going through, though."

He wrote in his book.

"You knew the captain"—he glanced down at his book—"Neal Garrett."

I sighed. There probably wasn't any way to avoid talking about it. He'd find out soon enough if he asked around.

When Neal and I had finally agreed that it was time for him to move his wet suits, weight belts, dive tanks, and precious few clothes out of my cottage, we had both grown tired of the yelling. It seemed we were arguing more often than not, and he accused me of ruining our relationship by "asking too many questions." I'd watched him undergo a transformation in two years from a shaggy-haired boat bum (a refugee from a long stint as a Navy Seal) who wanted nothing more than to sail naked, dive for conch and lobster, and make love under the forepeak hatch of his lovely H-28, *Wind Dancer,* to a driven, gold-epaulettes-type captain of a boat right out of *Lifestyles of the Rich and Famous.* He began to forget that the boat he was driving wasn't really his. He wanted me to give up my boat and the business I'd inherited from my dad so I could become his first mate and stewardess. We'd had some great times together, especially in bed, and I admit I was tempted briefly—long nights in that queen-size bed in the *Top Ten*'s master stateroom and no more struggling to pay bills. But Neal brought that same passion to our arguments, and there was no way I was ready to take orders from him. I knew we were finished the night his rage took over; he was totally out of control, screaming at me and cursing, and he lifted his arm, threatening to hit me. I stood up to him, staring silently into the eyes I no longer recognized, fighting hard inside not to let him see just how much those eyes frightened me. By the time he moved out, I didn't think his leaving would matter much to me anymore. But two days later I was balled up in a soggy robe, clutching a bottle of Mount Gay, burying myself in the sofa behind closed drapes.

"Neal and I lived together for a bit over a year. He moved out several months ago. We hadn't seen much of each other lately."

He wrote in his book. Then he watched me expectantly.

I tried hard not to volunteer anything more, but the silence was just so empty. "I heard he had a new girlfriend." I pointed overhead with my index finger. "That may be her."

"And you know who owns the vessel, then," he said.

"Not really. I used to know who the old owner was, but the boat was sold last summer. Neal said it was some corporation that bought it. It used to belong to the guy that owns those topless clubs, you know, the ones with the Top Ten Girls. That's how the boat got its name."

He looked up at me. "Benjamin Crystal."

"Yeah, that guy."

"You know him."

"Not really. I know of him. You'd just about have to be living in a hut out in the Everglades to not hear about him. He's always on TV or in the newspapers in some exposé about this poor guy from the Dominican Republic who struck it rich building his strip joints. Anyway, he sold the boat. It was right after that that he got arrested."

Whenever I get the feeling that someone doesn't believe me, I start feeling guilty even though I know I'm telling the truth. I kept seeing that flash of red fingernail and those porcelain-smooth buttocks. I glanced at Collazo, certain I must have looked guilty as hell.

"You seem to know a great deal about Crystal."

"Neal talked about him. It was like he was fascinated with his boss."

Then he asked me again if I knew where Neal might be.

"I can guarantee you Neal would never have let that girl take the boat out by herself. I doubt she even could. He had to have been on board. Now, maybe somebody held a gun to his head and made him do something he didn't want to do, maybe there was another boat involved, maybe he went overboard, I don't know. None of it makes any sense at this point."

I wasn't sure anymore what to call the feelings I had for Neal. But the thought of his ending up like the girl on the bridge made my throat start closing involuntarily.

"I don't know where he is now," I said, "but you could check that he was aboard the boat this morning. Just call over to Pier 66 and ask some of the guys around there."

Collazo nodded at a plainclothes policewoman who had been standing nearby throughout most of the questioning. She disappeared through the side door of the main salon.

Collazo stood. "Come with me."

We climbed up the interior stairs leading to the bridge. I'd been up those stairs dozens of times, but they seemed shorter this time—we got there too fast. There were two men working the crime scene, one examining bullet holes, the other doing something to the bloodstains on the teak doorframe. The body was still there, but covered.

"Look around, Miss Sullivan. You know boats. Everything here looks normal to you, as it should on this ship."

The last time I'd been up here, a few hours earlier, it had been as though I had tunnel vision, noticing little other than a dead woman and a gun. I forced myself to ignore both those now, and, starting from the port side, I scanned the bridge, looking for something out of place. From the high-tech electronics instrument panel that looked more like it belonged in a jet than a boat to the small charting and plotting area and over to the helm, everything looked as it should to me.

"Other than a dead body and a bullet hole, it looks pretty normal to me." I tried smiling at Collazo, but he didn't smile back.

I pointed to the copy of Bowditch's *Practical Navigator.* "That book, it belongs to me. I loaned it to Neal. Don't suppose I could take it back, could I?"

"It's evidence now, miss. But as soon as we're finished, I'll see to it you get it back."

Then he thanked me for my time and took down my address and phone number.

"Go to the station downtown, and they will take your formal statement," he said, standing and heading toward the door. I followed after him. I couldn't wait to get out into the fresh air.

Collazo accompanied me to the top of the gangway. We met the policewoman coming up. She looked questioningly at me, and he nodded.

"The dockmaster at Pier 66"—she looked down at her notebook—"Bill Heller, helped them get the boat out when they left the slip at approximately seven-thirty A.M. He says Garrett was definitely aboard when they left the dock, but it was just the two of them, Garrett and the girl."

The detective nodded, took hold of my elbow, and steered me down to the dock. At the base of the gangway, he turned seaward, the direction where it all had happened.

"They *are* out there searching for him, aren't they?" I said.

Collazo nodded. My eyes met his, and I didn't like the way he was staring at me.

"Is there anything else I can do to help?" I asked.

He shook his head and handed me his card, looking at me as though he just knew I was lying about everything I'd said.

"Call me if there's anything *more* you want to tell me," he said.

IV

BY THE TIME I TIED *GORDA* TO THE SEAWALL BACK AT THE
estate, and Abaco leaped off and ran into the bushes to pee,
it was almost two o'clock. All the way back up the river I
had tried to put things together. I refused to consider the possibility
that Neal was dead. As I'd untied *Gorda* down at the Coast Guard
dock, I overheard the police discussing the search that was taking
place offshore; as far as they were concerned, it was a search for another dead body. But it simply couldn't be, no way, not Neal. Not
that former Seal trained in self-defense, trained to kill. Not the man
who had once lain next to me on the foredeck of his sailboat and
pointed out Orion's Belt and Ursa Minor and tried to educate me,
the celestial illiterate. I knew it didn't make any sense, but he just
seemed too alive to be dead.

But if he wasn't dead, then what had happened out there this
morning? Where was he? Was he capable of doing that to that girl?
I knew the answer to that question, and I didn't want to think
about it.

I walked the brick path to my cottage, and even after the
events of the morning, I felt some of the tension leave me. It had
been almost two years since I first moved into the old boathouse on
the Larsen estate, and I still marveled at how lucky I was to have

found the place. The location, in the Rio Vista section of Lauderdale, was convenient for me, because it was close to both the inlet and downtown. The main house was a big two-story Moorish mansion originally built in the 1930s, with multiple turrets and towers, all topped by red barrel tile, and it was set about sixty feet back from the New River. My cottage, on the other hand, had the best river view. The tiny wood-frame structure had once been a boathouse, a storage outbuilding for some past owner's collection of sailing dinghies and sculls. At some time in the sixties the place had been refurbished as a guest house and was now topped with a matching barrel-tile roof and divided inside into a small bedroom, with a combined living area and kitchen all built over varnished Dade County pine floors. The Larsens gave me a break on the rent because I kept an eye on the house, the grounds, and their toys, like the garaged Jaguar and the Jet Ski they kept on the dock. There had been a number of break-ins in this neighborhood of snowbird owners these past few years, and my comings and goings made the big house look lived in as well. What made the place perfect for me was that I could sleep just a few steps away from where I kept *Gorda* tied up.

When I unlocked the front door, I saw that the red light was blinking on my answering machine. I punched the button on my way to the fridge and listened while gulping straight from the jug of cold orange juice—just one of the benefits of living alone. It was Galen Hightower, the owner of the *Ruby Yacht*, a seventy-two-foot steel ketch, reminding me that I had to be at Pier 66 at "eleven on the dot" Saturday morning. He'd had this tow booked for weeks, but he was the nervous type who needed his hand held all the time.

The machine beeped and clicked to the next message. I immediately recognized the voice—my older brother, Maddy, who throughout my childhood had threatened to beat me up if I ever called him Madagascar in public.

"Look, uh, we gotta talk. I got some problems, money problems, and you still haven't paid your February payment. It's not working, Seychelle. *Gorda's* gotta go. I want out, now . . . Call me."

The dial tone sounded. I jammed my index finger down on the stop button, rewound the machine, and listened to the message again.

"You bastard, Maddy," I said out loud and rewound the machine one more time. I thought somehow if I kept on listening to it, maybe I'd hear something in his voice that indicated it was all some kind of a cruel joke.

It was skin cancer from all those years with the sun shining down on his fair freckled skin that had finally taken my dad. During the years that I was lifeguarding and taking a few classes at the local community college, when I'd moved out into my own apartment, leaving Red alone in the big house, the doctors kept cutting off big chunks of him. When I'd call him every few weeks, just to see how he was doing, I didn't want to hear about his most recent trip to the doctors. Red and I never talked about the important things, not about Mother's death, not about what his illness might mean. Toward the end, I moved back home, quit school, cut back on my hours lifeguarding. I did what I could, tried to make him comfortable, even though I didn't want to remember him like that, but rather like the big barrel-chested man with the red suspenders, blazing beard, and mischievous grin I'd looked up to as a little girl.

Red's will had left everything to the three of us equally. I was surprised he even had a will; as sick as he was at the end, he never let on that he considered his own death a possibility. The doctors' bills and taxes ate up most of what we got out of the house. After Red's funeral, my brothers and I sat down and tried to figure out what to do with the *Gorda*. Maddy already had his own boat business going, running a charter sportfisherman out of Haulover down in Miami. He'd developed a reputation as a fishing guide—he even gave the morning fishing report on a local AM sports radio station—and he wasn't about to give up his charter business to go into towing and salvage work.

Pitcairn was the nomad in the family. Maddy and I couldn't figure out how he supported himself, but he had fallen in love, first with surfing and then, when he grew taller, with windsurfing. We received his postcards from Maui, Costa Rica, the Columbia River Gorge, and when he came to Red's funeral, it was the first time either of us had seen him in over three years. He said he didn't care about the money, he'd leave any decisions to us. He just didn't want to give up his life on the pro windsurfing circuit to settle in Lauderdale.

They both laughed when I said I'd like to take over Red's business. Maddy said most of the yacht captains wouldn't want to hire a woman, that I'd never make enough to pay the maintenance on the boat, much less support myself. But I was twenty-seven years old, and although I was still in good shape, I didn't want to be a lifeguard in my thirties. I didn't want to have to sit out there in a tank suit when the flesh started to sag and my reactions started to slow. I was ready for a career change.

Besides, most of the old-timers knew me, I'd argued. I practically grew up aboard *Gorda*, and I had worked for Red off and on ever since I was a kid. He was a great teacher, and he loved showing off how well his little girl could handle a boat. I'd spent so much more time on the boat than Maddy had; I knew I was the most experienced of the three of us, and probably the only one who could qualify for the commercial towing captain's license. My brother Pit was all for me from the start, and finally Maddy relented. Although I ran the boat, we were still three-way partners in Sullivan Towing.

I made mistakes at first, but eventually I got back most of Red's river and waterway business. I hoped to be able to buy my brothers out in a few years' time. I had a little nest egg—it wasn't much, just a couple of thousand dollars, but it was my emergency money. I'd vowed not to touch it unless it was a serious emergency—something like a blown engine. It was my security fund, and I knew that once I started to dip into it to pay the bills, those thousands would become hundreds in a flash. Neither of my brothers had seemed to be in any particular hurry to get their money out of the boat, and I paid them each a small percentage of the business every month. Sure, things had been a little slow lately, but it would pick up. That was the nature of the business. And now I had a salvage claim to pursue against a multimillion-dollar vessel.

I was about to shut the machine off when a familiar voice started speaking on the third message.

"Hey, Seychelle, I just heard about the *Top Ten*." B.J.'s voice sounded unusually subdued. "I stopped in down at Sailorman to buy a rebuild kit for that head of yours, and everybody's talking about it." He paused, and in my mind I could see the way his eyes must have wrinkled as he tried to figure out what to say next.

"Sey, I know it must have been pretty bad out there." I blinked back the pictures. "If you want to talk, I'll be at the Downtowner around six. We could grab a bite. Later."

For some reason that did it, hearing the sympathy in his voice. He was the first person who seemed to realize that the events of that morning had hurt. Suddenly I was overwhelmed by memories of Neal, alive, there in my cottage, making love on the floor, sitting up in bed talking all night, drinking beer and eating pizza by the window over there, listening to him whistle in the shower. I remembered that night we had slept in a sleeping bag on a little sandy cay down in the Dry Tortugas, swimming in the phosphorescent water at midnight and making love as the velvety trade winds dried the seawater on our skin. When we woke at dawn, Neal held me and kissed me, his tongue tracing the shape of my lips. His blue eyes glistened with unshed tears when he told me I tasted like rain.

The pressure inside my chest was building to the breaking point, and sour-tasting muscles pulled at the corners of my mouth, the back of my throat. I forced it back inside and blinked away the blurriness. Picking up my keys, I headed out the door.

First I locked up the boat and set the alarm from the electronic keypad I'd installed on the side of the wheelhouse. I checked to make sure Abaco had water, and then I crossed the grounds and passed through the side gate that led to the street side of the Larsens' house, where my old white Jeep was parked in the gravel drive. Neal had nicknamed her "Lightnin' " because she wasn't any ball of fire. I'd bought her in my lifeguarding days, and since I usually didn't drive a whole lot, she'd served me well in spite of her ever-growing collection of rust patches. Her original owner, back in '72, had seen fit to put a Jesus on the dashboard, and none of the rest of us who'd owned her had been brazen enough to remove the thing. Now faded and cracked from years in the Florida sun, the pale pink figure stood in mute testimony to the effectiveness of '70s adhesives.

I just wanted to get out of the cottage as much as anything else, but as soon as I got behind the wheel, I realized I had better get over to see Jeannie Black, my lawyer. If Maddy had made up his mind that we were selling *Gorda*, I needed a cash infusion right now. Somebody did own the *Top Ten*, and that somebody should be very grateful that I just pulled his megayacht out of imminent peril. Just how grateful, in terms of dollars and cents, was for the lawyers to figure out, but I certainly had not gone through all that out of the goodness of my heart. I intended to get every dollar I could out of it.

Jeannie didn't look like much; actually, at well over 250 pounds, she looked like too much, but she had served me well in the past. She'd been a lawyer on the fast track in a high-powered firm when her twin boys were born. She never even told her boyfriend, who she knew had no interest in fatherhood, that she was pregnant, believing she could handle it all herself. But single motherhood turned out to be far more difficult than law school. She eventually decided to quit the firm, stay at home with the twins, and work out of her own house. Though her office was no longer of the high-powered sort, any opponents who judged her to be soft in the courtroom soon learned not to evaluate her on her appearance.

I'd met Jeannie in Winn-Dixie in the frozen-food aisle when one of her boys pitched a box of frozen waffles at my backside as I bent down to reach for a can of orange juice. Jeannie was totally unfazed by the incident. She just flashed me a boys-will-be-boys smile and introduced herself. She gave me her card. Later, when Red died and I needed a lawyer, I gave her a call.

Jeannie lived in the neighborhood known as Sailboat Bend, an interesting blend of million-dollar waterfront homes right across the street from low-rent apartment buildings. Thrown in among these were some of the oldest homes in Lauderdale, old Conch cottages built by Bahamian carpenters in the '20s and '30s. Jeannie's place was in a '50s-vintage two-story concrete block and stucco house that had been divided into two apartments. She lived in the upstairs half of the building, and when I drove into the dirt yard, Andrew and Adair were up in the branches of a live oak tree, complete with eye patches, bandanas, and clip-on gold hoop earrings. I waved at the boys and climbed the outside staircase to the porch in front of Jeannie's apartment.

Peering through the screen, I called out, "Hello! Jeannie?"

The dark shadow of her bulky silhouette completely blocked out the light coming from the kitchen at the end of the hall.

"Seychelle!" she called out in her contralto voice as she burst through the screen door. Her bright tentlike muumuu surrounded me with folds of parrot-and-bamboo-print fabric. A squeeze from her arms threatened my air supply, and she smacked a wet kiss just in front of my right ear.

"It's so good to see you. I take it you made it past the pirate patrol out there."

I nodded and started to speak, but she held open the door and jerked her head in the direction of the interior. With a meaty hand in the small of my back, she propelled me into the small living room of her two-bedroom apartment.

There was always a homelike feeling to being with Jeannie. Although physically she was nothing like my mother, her housekeeping reminded me of my childhood. Every level surface in the room was covered with papers, files, and books, and the local public radio station played classical music in the background.

I knew better than to share the couch with Jeannie. I'd made that mistake once before and had ended up perched on a forty-five-degree slope, trying to keep myself from tumbling downhill into Jeannie's lap during the whole visit. I cleared a dining room chair, pulled it over by the couch, and sat.

"So, you must be in some kind of trouble again. I swear, girl,

I never see you unless you need my help. Like that last time when you towed that Bertram charter boat, and it turned out the brokers had repoed the wrong boat, and everybody tried to hang it on you . . ." She chuckled.

Compared to the uncontested divorces, guardianship cases, and real estate closings that were her mainstay, Jeannie thought the work she did for me was interesting, and she loved to go back over the cases, gossiping about the "glamorous" world of yachts.

"You're right, in a way."

She grabbed a bag of blue corn tortilla chips off the pile of paperwork on the coffee table, propped open the bag, and offered it to me.

I shook my head and offered a thin smile at another of her attempts to eat healthy. "I don't know as I would call this trouble exactly, but I would like you to look into something for me."

"Fire away."

"I towed the *Top Ten* in this morning."

"Ha! Neal run out of gas or something and have to beg you for a lift?"

When Jeannie saw I wasn't smiling anymore, she dropped the joking tone and reached for my hand. I stared for several seconds at the wrinkles of fat around her wrist. Her small gold watch almost disappeared in a fold.

"Seychelle, just seeing that man again can make you go all droopy like this? Lord, I thought you were through with him."

"I didn't see him."

"But I thought you said . . ."

"That's just it." I proceeded then to tell her the whole story, about the mayday call, and how I'd found the boat, and the girl, dead in the water.

"Oh, my God." Jeannie shuddered. She heaved herself up in a big bounce to inch forward on the couch. "Was there much blood?"

I guess most attorneys are really ambulance chasers at heart, I thought.

"I did my best not to look."

"And there was no sign of Neal?"

I shook my head, not trusting my voice to keep steady if we got off on that. Business, stick to business, I told myself. "Jeannie, the boat was sold shortly after Neal took over as captain, about a year ago. Neal said some big corporation owns her now. I don't think he ever did tell me the name, or if he did I don't remember, but it shouldn't be that hard to find out. That's what I'm here for. I need you to find the owner and get him to sign a copy of Lloyd's Open Form. Obviously, I am entitled to a salvage claim, and to own a yacht like that, there ought to be some deep pockets there."

"The kind I like."

"You find out who owns her and start the paperwork rolling. Since she was nearly aground when I got to her, I risked the safety of *Gorda* and myself . . . you know the line to take. Figuring possible replacement cost of *Gorda*, my livelihood that I risked, and my fair wages for the effort I put in, we ought to ask for fifty thousand and settle for around twenty-five."

"Don't get your heart set on numbers like those, girl. It's not that easy."

"And it's not every day that you find a multimillion-dollar yacht floating around completely unmanned. Besides, I've got the best damned attorney in Fort Lauderdale." I grinned.

"Ha, well, I always knew you were a smart kid." She returned the smile. "Okay, tomorrow's Friday. I'll see what I can get started, but there won't be too much I can do on the weekend."

"I know. Just do what you can. Unfortunately, business hasn't been great lately. I'm not desperate . . . yet. But faster is better." I stood up and started to walk to the screen door. I stopped and turned. "There's something else, Jeannie." The boys' voices drifted up to the outside porch. Their little-boy voices strained for deeper pitches as they threw around "avasts" and "ahoys" aplenty. "I had a message from Maddy on the machine when I got back to the cottage. He wants me to buy him out of his portion of *Gorda*. I don't have that kind of money, and he knows it. So he wants me to sell the boat."

"What? Did this just come out of the blue?"

"Yeah. I don't really understand where it's coming from. I have my suspicions, but I'm going to talk to him about it. Once he makes his mind up about something, though, he usually doesn't change it. Anyway, this salvage claim is now doubly important."

Jeannie got up and followed me to the door. When we stepped outside, she glanced toward her boys with unseeing eyes. Her mind was already at work, mapping out strategies. "What do the cops think happened to Neal?" she asked.

I watched as Andrew leaned far out on a branch and tried to impale his brother with his plastic sword. I remembered Neal's smile: the white teeth set in a brown leathery face, the deep cleft in his chin, the intricate patterns of crisscrossing lines around the corners of his eyes. "The cops? They're out there now with divers, helicopters, the works, searching for a body. That's what they think."

V

WHEN I LEFT JEANNIE'S IT WAS STILL TOO EARLY to meet B.J. at the Downtowner, so I drove down Las Olas to the beach. As I crossed over the Intracoastal drawbridge I could see a helicopter working a search pattern offshore.

I turned south at A1A and cruised slowly down the beachfront. The tourist season was nearly over, and the only people out at the beach midweek were the old and the unemployed. They walked A1A checking the trash for aluminum cans and rattling the coin returns at the pay phones. I supposed it was better than the days when I first started lifeguarding, and the spring-breakers came down from the north and tore up the town. Those were the days before the city commissioners decided, in all their wisdom, that no tourists were better than the drunken, debauching variety. They used the cops to drive away the spring-breakers, and with their business gone, slowly the small mom-and-pop motels closed, nailing plywood over the windows and putting up For Sale signs in the dry, unkempt grass. Corporate America went on a buying spree then, with the beach looking like a ghost town, and now the big chain hotels, franchise restaurants, and chic boutiques were popping up all along the newly redesigned beachfront. The Fort Lauderdale

Strip would soon have as much character as any middle-America shopping mall.

When I was a teenager we used to come down to the Lauderdale Strip and cruise, six or seven kids packed into my brother Pit's old Ford Galaxy with the surfboard rack on the roof. Pit would oblige us, though he wasn't really into the hooting and hollering and acting crazy like the rest of us. He'd scrimped and saved to get his car so he could get to the beach to surf after school. That boy just lived to surf, and sometimes, when we were cruising like that, with the bright neon-lit crowds on one side of the street and the glowing, foaming surf on the other, I would watch my brother from the backseat, where I was wedged between pimply-faced boys. He would completely ignore the scantily clad crowds the other kids found so enticing. Instead, Pit's eyes measured the breaking waves as he surfed down them in his mind, a half smile dancing around his lips. I remembered how I envied him his distance, his independence, and how I wanted to get to the point where I would not be hurt by every teasing remark about my height or the breadth of my shoulders.

I drove up Seventeenth toward U.S. 1 and passed the Top Ten Club, the flagship of Crystal's fleet of strip joints. The club was sandwiched between a luxury auto rental store and a mirrored office building. From the outside, the place looked pretty posh with a modern, multilevel design, gold trim, and neon. The grounds were beautifully landscaped to fit right in with the yacht brokerages and the high-end restaurants elsewhere on the street. It was a case of sleaze trying to go classy. An innocent observer would never guess it was a girlie joint, that day and night they had ten women dancing nude. The club motto was "All our girls are tens on top."

THE DOWNTOWNER WAS THE KIND OF PLACE I KNEW WOULDN'T be around much longer, given the way waterfront property values were mounting along the river, but I hoped it could somehow hold out against the twin demons of taxes and gentrification.

Both a bar and a restaurant, the memorabilia that covered the walls was not fake junk collected by a professional decorator, but rather old life preservers with real boat names that the old-timers still remembered, street-name signs from the days when people earned a street instead of buying one, old dinghies and ancient outboards, black-and-white photos and stuffed fish and wild-pig heads with yellowed tusks, all collected during the past fifty years from river folk coming and going through the doors of this place. The dark varnished wood interior had been built by boat builders and still retained that well-fitted feeling in spite of years of abuse. Behind the bartender's back, plate glass windows ran the length of the bar and provided a view of the constant parade of river traffic, an ever-changing tableau of motor yachts, shrimpers, sailboats, barges, dinghies, and water taxis.

When I arrived, the place was abuzz with the gossip of the murder or murders, and Jake, Nestor, Wally, and a bunch of the others crowded around me when I came in. I told them an abbreviated version of my part in the morning's events so they would leave me alone. I told them nobody knew what had happened to Neal, but the Coasties and the cops seemed to think he was dead.

Nestor, another of the charter captains, said, "You know, Sey, I'm not surprised that something strange like this happened to Neal."

"What do you mean?"

"Well, he's just been acting weird lately."

"That's right, Sey," Wally said. "He's changed since he got that job on the *Top Ten*. He doesn't much talk to his old pals anymore, keeps to himself more."

Suddenly I found myself very conscious of the language they were using. They were talking about him in the present tense, and I was glad. "Why do you think he's acting like that?"

"Some of the other guys think his head's got as big as that boat he's driving," Nestor said, "but me, I think he's into something, something he doesn't want anybody to know about."

"Like what, Nestor?"

"Last time I talked to him, I felt like Neal was hiding something. Kinda reminded me of how the guys used to act back in the eighties when pretty near every captain on the water was in the drug trade. People didn't get real friendly with each other in those days. They kept their mouths shut."

"Come on, Nestor, I can't see Neal involved in drugs. How could he? I mean, the *Top Ten* almost never went out except for the occasional charter up and down the waterway or for a sunset cruise offshore."

"I don't know, Sey. I'm just saying it's something he's keeping a secret. I tell you, he's been acting weird lately. That's all. I guess the cops will figure it out."

I told them then that I needed some time alone, so they bought me a draft and moved down to the far end of the bar. I figured they wanted to discuss what they thought really happened out there. The Lauderdale waterfront community was a tightly knit group that loved nothing more than gossip, intrigue, and conspiracy theories. I remembered one time a local captain had taken off to the Bahamas for a couple of weeks with a charter group, and gossip flew round the Downtowner that the captain had died of a heart attack as he took his first dive into the aqua Bahamian waters. A week later the same fellow came driving his sailboat up the New River past the Downtowner's windows, and several of the regulars nearly had heart attacks, believing they'd seen a ghost. Turned out it was a charter guest who died, and the waterfront gossip machine had twisted the facts once again. By evening, they surely would have found Neal guilty of smuggling drugs, illegal aliens, exotic animals, or God knows what.

I'd been thinking ever since leaving Jeannie's about how good a beer would taste, but now, somehow, I found it couldn't wash away the bad taste in my mouth.

As soon as I emptied the first glass, Pete brought me a fresh one on the house. He leaned across the bar.

"She seemed like a nice girl," he said.

"You knew her?" I asked.

"Yeah, she filled in here a couple of times when Lil's kid was out sick."

"Who was she? What was she like?"

"Patty Krix was her name. Pretty girl, too, though mighty headstrong. Once she set her sights on Neal, he didn't have a chance."

I smiled at him. I'd known Pete a long time. He was an ex-single-hander. On his way up from the Virgins, he'd gone to sleep one night on watch. His autopilot had driven his pretty little Swedish-built cutter right up on the beach in front of the Fountainbleu in Miami. The boat was holed, and he lost everything. He'd been tending bar in the Downtowner back in the days when Red used to bring me in for Shirley Temples and regale the other regulars with his stories about the great little boat handler his daughter was turning out to be.

"Don't worry about trying to make me feel better, Pete. I knew Neal had been seeing somebody else. He and I broke it off a while ago. He was free to do as he pleased."

"It wasn't that, Seychelle, honest. It just seemed kinda strange at the time. She came in here all alone one afternoon, about three weeks ago. I carded her, so I know for a fact she was just barely twenty-one, but she looked mighty at home in a bar. A bunch of the guys hit on her, and they all struck out. Then Neal came in and sat at the bar. He was thinking about something, keeping to himself, and didn't hardly seem to notice her. She called me over and asked me his name. Then before I knew it, she was over there sitting by him, laughing at his jokes, staring up at him with those big blue eyes. Like I said, he didn't have a chance."

Another customer called Pete over, and I was left to wonder why such a gorgeous girl would have singled him out. Neal was an attractive guy, all right, but why would he have appealed to a girl like Patty Krix? Really beautiful people were a different breed, and they always made me slightly uncomfortable.

Hiking my purse onto my shoulder, I slid off my stool and walked back to the corridor where the bathroom was. The beer was making me sleepy. I splashed cold water on my face and looked at myself in the mirror. What a mess. I hadn't changed clothes since I'd thrown on shorts and a worn T-shirt in order to work on the damn broken marine head. Loose, windblown hairs stood out around my head in a sort of sun-bleached halo. I pulled the rubber band out of my shoulder-length light brown hair, used my fingers to comb out the snarls, and decided to leave my hair down. Although I usually sport a fairly dark tan from working outdoors, my skin looked pale, as though it were drawn too tightly over my cheekbones. Evidently, discovering dead bodies is not a recommended beauty treatment.

When I returned to the bar I was surprised to see that Collazo had come in and was sitting on my stool. He leaned across the bar talking to Pete, his notebook open, gold pen in hand.

"*Buenas tardes,* Detective. What brings you to this place?" I slid onto the stool next to him and reached across for my beer.

"Miss Sullivan." He nodded at me, something like a little bow, but ignored my question.

I tried another question. "Any word on Neal yet?"

"No. It doesn't look likely we'll find anything at this point. The Gulf Stream, you know." He tapped his pen on the cover of his notebook. "But we'll give it one more day. You haven't gone downtown to sign your statement yet."

"No. I had some personal business to do take care of this afternoon. You didn't say I had to do it today."

He nodded. "Tomorrow morning, then, first thing."

I reached for my glass and took a long drink. "Care for a beer, Detective?"

Pete shot me a look that told me to shut up. He'd had a strong distrust of cops ever since the Miami Beach police had stood by and watched as looters stripped his boat of everything he owned.

Collazo dismissed my question with a wave of his hand. "I understand from this gentleman," he said, indicating Pete, "that

Patty Krix used to work as a barmaid here. And he tells me that you are quite a regular. Yet this afternoon you claimed not to know her."

"Hey," Pete jumped in, "I never said Seychelle knew Patty. She only worked here a couple of times."

He leaned his chest against the bar and focused his full attention on Pete. "They'd never met, then."

"How should I know? I'm running a bar here." Pete tossed his damp towel on the bar.

"It's okay, Pete." I set my glass on the bar. Two beers on an empty stomach, and I felt a surge of alcohol-induced confidence. "Detective, I'd never seen that girl before today when I found her dead on the *Top Ten.*"

He swung his head around and focused his dark eyes on me. In spite of the beer, my mouth felt dry. "You are absolutely certain of this."

"Of course I'm certain. I'd remember if I'd met her."

"Because she was Garrett's *new* girlfriend."

"What are you fishing for, Collazo? Just exactly what do you think happened out there?"

"I don't know, Miss Sullivan, but I have been considering a possible scenario. I'd like you to tell me what you think of it. Yesterday morning, Garrett gave the ship's engineer the day off. I am told it is very irregular to take out a boat of that size with only two people aboard. Apparently, the captain wanted a day alone with his new lady friend. His former lady friend was not happy about the new relationship. Garrett goes down for a dive, leaving his current girlfriend on the boat, but the fuel pumps malfunctioned and all the engines shut down. The girl got scared. She called for help. She didn't know when Garrett would surface.

"You happened to be nearby when you heard this mayday call. When you came aboard, you saw your chance. You killed the girl, and when Garrett surfaced, you shot him, pushed his body overboard, and pressed the gun into the girl's hand to mark it with her prints. Given the Gulf Stream, I assume the body will eventually wash up somewhere north of Pompano. Not even weight belts hold them down for long, Miss Sullivan."

I wasn't sure if it was the beer or Collazo's little scenario, but suddenly I was feeling a little woozy and nauseous. "You're joking, right?"

"I've been a cop a long time. We know you always start looking close and then work your way out: family, ex-lovers, friends. We rarely get to strangers."

It was happening again, that guilty thing. I knew I hadn't done anything, but I could feel my heart racing, my face burning, and worst of all, I knew without looking just how intently Collazo was watching my reaction.

"You haven't told me yet what you think of my little scenario, Miss Sullivan."

I looked up, and over the detective's shoulder I saw a familiar figure enter the bar. His sleek black hair was pulled back in a ponytail, and backlit as he was, his white teeth glowed almost neon white against his brown skin. He walked around Collazo, ignoring him, and wrapped me up in his huge arms, squeezing me tight in a warm bear hug. A little shiver ran up my body as the tension left me, and I kissed B.J. just at the hairline on his neck. He held me at arm's length. "Are you okay?"

"I'm fine." I turned my head toward the detective. "Detective Collazo, this is B.J. Moana."

B.J. extended his hand, smiling. Collazo took it reluctantly, squinting at the big Samoan.

Turning back to face me, B.J. said, "Sey, I'm so sorry." He brushed fingers along the side of my head, attempting to tame some of my wilder hair. "We both know Neal would not go gentle. . . . I'm sure there's reason to be positive, to hope." He shook his head slowly, never taking his eyes off mine.

I closed my eyes for a few seconds and swallowed. "The detective here has certainly put his positive spin on things. He has just been telling me his theory about how I killed Neal and his girlfriend."

B.J. turned to stare at the detective, inspecting him with those penetrating dark eyes. "A girl's dead. That's not something to joke about."

Collazo held his stare longer than most can. "I'm not laughing."

"You don't seriously consider that a possibility, do you?"

Collazo looked up at B.J., at his six feet two inches of lean, surf-hardened muscle.

"I consider all possibilities, Mr. Moana."

"Well, consider this, then." He took a step toward Collazo. "Seychelle Sullivan has devoted her life to *saving* people. She would no more hurt somebody than Mother Teresa would." He moved in closer, his nose not three inches from the detective's. "There's a real killer out there. I suggest you get out there and find out who really did this, and stop hassling Seychelle."

The detective stood and adjusted his tie, never breaking eye contact with B.J. I could practically smell the testosterone in the air. Then Collazo smiled. It was the first time I had seen him smile, and I couldn't help but notice the huge gap between his front teeth. He could have slid his gold pen in there without touching enamel.

"Oh, I'll do that, all right." He looked straight at me. "We will be waiting for your statement, Miss Sullivan. Tomorrow." He picked up his jacket, turned, and walked out of the bar.

When the door closed behind him, Wally called over, "I think you scared him off, B.J." All the guys, including Pete, laughed.

Jake said, "You beat the hell out of his karma there, man."

"Yeah," Nestor shouted, "I think you threatened to meditate him to death and scared the shit out of him."

"Okay, guys, that's enough." I swiveled around on my barstool to face him. "I'm surprised at you, B.J. Bullying him like that." I tried very hard to look stern, but my face broke into a grin. "Mother Teresa?"

He shrugged and smiled. "A much sexier version."

I shook my head at him.

We moved to a booth along the back wall. B.J. ordered grilled dolphin with rice and vegetables, and he shook his head in disgust when I asked for a basket of fried shrimp and chips. Normally, he would have told me that I was going to die of a heart attack by the time I was forty because I lived on beer, fried food, and takeout, but after the day I'd had, apparently he was going to give me a break.

"I looked for you today before going out on this job," I said. "I thought you were going to work on repairing that head. Where were you?"

"Jimmy St. Clair came by on the river in his Sea Ray. He asked me to go down with him to Bahia Mar to give him a price on a boat he's rebuilding. He's got a nice old Chris Craft right there on A dock. A classic. You can see her when you're driving by on A1A. She's got a bad case of dry rot—enough to keep me busy into the summer." He unfolded his napkin and carefully spread it on his lap. "But I wish I had been at the estate today. Do you want to tell me about it?"

Pete brought a couple more beers over at that point, and as we drank, I told the story again. I was beginning to find it therapeutic to repeat the tale so many times.

"And then when I finally made it back to the cottage, I had a message on my machine from Maddy. He wants me to sell *Gorda* so he can get his money out of the boat."

"Whoa! That's kind of sudden, isn't it?"

"Yeah. But Maddy can lose money fast. He used to be a regular at the track."

I hadn't realized how hungry I was until Lil set the plate down and I inhaled the tangy sea smell of the fried shrimp. B.J. wrinkled his nose when I drowned my fries in catsup, but he didn't slow down his eating. He'd always been ultrapicky about food. He insisted on healthy food, but when it came time to eat, he was like a machine. He didn't shovel it in or look gross, but he ate with an incredible economy of movement. I would look up and suddenly realize that he had cleaned his entire plate. I always had to concentrate to keep up with him. I didn't dare try to talk while eating, and we'd been friends long enough that silence at the table didn't feel uncomfortable to either one of us.

When he finished, he wiped his mouth with his napkin and leaned back, spreading his arms on the back of the booth. Unlike most Samoans, he didn't have wavy hair. His was straight and shiny, nearly the same length as mine. Because of his hair, his lean, muscular build, and his almond-shaped brown eyes, I suspected there was some Chinese or Japanese somewhere in his family tree.

"I'd met her," B.J. said.

For a minute I wasn't sure who he was talking about. He must have seen the blank look on my face.

"The girl, Patty Krix. One night a couple of weeks ago, I came into the Downtowner, and she was here with Neal."

I pushed away my basket of soggy fries. He'd conjured up that picture of her again, with the knife and the pool of congealing blood. I couldn't face catsup anymore.

"Did you talk to her?"

He shrugged. "A little. She told me there was some girl at her other job that she would like to introduce me to."

It was always that way with B.J. Women were drawn to him like flies to a bug zapper, always flitting about him and trying to get closer to the source of the heat. Luckily, attraction to B.J. was never fatal. There were no broken hearts. In the years I'd known him there had been lots of short-term girlfriends who became long-term friends. I'd never known one of them to go away bitter, but they always went away. They seemed to understand that they would never play a larger part in B.J.'s life.

I, too, was thankful for our friendship, but in a different way. Ever since I had shot up in height in the fifth grade, I'd felt awkward around incredibly handsome guys. This made it a challenge just talking to B.J. He worked for me as a handyman and mechanic, yet he had a couple of degrees in classical lit and Asian studies, so not only was he gorgeous, but he was damn smart. Being *friends* with B.J. put us on a different level; sometimes he made me feel like a complete idiot, but at least I didn't need to play any boy/girl games with him.

Apparently, even though Patty Krix had already teamed up with Neal, she couldn't let irresistible B.J. be. She figured she'd fix him up with her friend. I was beginning to get an idea of who Patty was.

"But I thought Pete said she used to work here."

"That was just part-time. She was also a dancer at that Top Ten Club." B.J. smiled. "I'd have liked to see that."

I felt my jaw sag. "What? You're kidding."

"No. She was really built."

I tapped my forehead with my fingertips and shook my head at him. "I mean, I had no idea she worked at the Top Ten Club. Don't you think that's kind of odd?"

"I've never understood why a woman would want to dance around naked for a lot of strange men." I could tell by the sparkle in his eyes that he was teasing me, pretending not to understand. But it still made me mad.

"According to Pete," I said, "the day she met Neal, it was almost as if she was looking for him. And she worked for the same outfit that used to own the boat she died on."

"What, you mean you think she might have been some kind of Mata Hari or something?"

"I don't know. Neal was the one who was more likely to see conspiracies everywhere, not me. You should have heard him carry on about that Crystal character he worked for. I'd mostly just tune it out, attribute it to too many years in the big-government machine. But now . . . I don't know."

It hurt to think about it. I wanted to talk about something else, anything—the weather, the sea conditions, the job B.J. was working on this week. But Neal's absence loomed between us, and I could feel myself dancing around the periphery of this big dark place. Like a scuba diver's blue hole, the depths gaped invitingly, taunting me with the unknown, daring my curiosity. It was too dark down there to see what lurked in the depths, but I knew somehow that I wasn't ready to go there yet.

By the time we walked out to the parking lot together, it was nearly eight o'clock. The lot backed onto a street across from which rose the high, nearly windowless walls of the big new Broward County Jail. There were no lights working in the lot. B.J.'s perfectly restored jet-black El Camino was parked in the pale light that was cast by the restaurant's bathroom windows. We stopped next to his truck, and he asked if I wanted him to follow me home.

"Thanks, but I'll be fine."

We stood for several seconds facing each other, neither of us certain what to do next. I was intensely aware of the way his royal blue T-shirt was stretched taut across his pecs and then fell loosely around his narrow waist. He smelled faintly of coconut soap. Buddies though we were, I couldn't not be aware of B.J.'s sexiness. Part of me wanted to bury my face in that chest, wrap my arms around his waist, and hope the events of the day would vanish. Another part of me wanted to be sure I never depended on a man again the way I had depended on Neal.

"When you didn't show up this morning, I took the head apart myself. It doesn't seem like just this morning—more like days ago."

B.J. leaned down and gave me a brotherly kiss on the cheek. "I'll take care of that tomorrow. And please, don't hesitate to call me for *anything* else."

I turned, ready to climb into the Jeep, but I paused, my hand resting on the door handle. "I wonder if he's out there somewhere in the dark, hurt and wondering when they're going to find him." I didn't want to cry. It was too soon. We didn't know anything yet. That would be like giving up. "You're right about one thing, though, B.J.—he's a tough one, that's for sure. He won't go easy. But I just keep thinking, if only I'd got there sooner . . . maybe none of this would have happened."

"This is not your fault, Seychelle."

I turned halfway and tried to smile at him over my shoulder. "Easy for you to say."

WHEN I PULLED LIGHTNIN' INTO THE DRIVE AT THE ESTATE, I shut off the engine and just sat there in the Jeep for a few minutes listening to the slow ticking noises of the cooling engine. I felt achingly tired, like some kind of big vacuum had just sucked every ounce of energy out of my body. Collazo's words—"We know where to look: family, friends, ex-lovers"—kept replaying in my head. The way he told the story did make a certain amount of sense. I was certain that if I had ever seen that gorgeous body alive and draped across Neal, I'd have *wanted* to kill her.

It took an effort to open the Jeep door, go through the gate, and walk back to my cottage. Abaco met me at the gate and danced up the path ahead of me, turning to look back as though wondering why I wouldn't stop to pet her. I just wanted to fall into bed. When I tried to push my key into the doorknob, the door swung ajar, and although I thought it a bit odd, no alarms went off in my head. I pushed open the door and switched on the overhead light, and my brain was so fuzzy, it still didn't register the mess that was all that was left of the inside of my cottage.

I stood and stared, confused, wondering for just a second if I had somehow come home to the wrong place. Then I saw the photo of my mother with all three of us kids, a picture that was taken when I was eleven, the summer she died. It rested on a pile of books that had been pulled off the shelves, and there were several shards of broken glass remaining in the frame.

I stepped into the room, dropping my keys to the floor, and gravelly bits of glass and pottery ground into the soles of my shoes. In the center of the room, I surprised myself when I let out an audible little gasp as I turned around surveying the damage. My cottage was really only two rooms: the front room, a combined living room, kitchen and dining room, and a small bedroom with bath in the back. A bar separated the kitchen from the living area, and now all the contents of the kitchen drawers—utensils, pot holders, towels, and toothpicks—had been spilled across the counter. There wasn't much food in the place, but what little was there—a few cans of Campbell's soup, fruit cocktail, catsup and other condiments—had been dragged out of the cupboards and tossed onto the floor, in many cases breaking on the white tile. I had kept an easel in a corner of the living room that generally had a work in progress on it. Painting was something I'd learned from my mother, one of the few happy memories I had of her. I normally had my watercolors and brushes set up on the TV tray next to the easel. Now the easel lay broken like kindling, the paints were probably somewhere in the mess, and the intruder had taken the time to tear my painting of the historic old Stranahan House into pieces.

Stepping carefully around the broken dishes, papers, clothes, and trash, I squatted down and reached for the photograph. The frame hung loose from one side. I slid the print out of the frame. We looked so happy, the three of us kids mugging for the camera, and my mother's lovely slim body in a white one-piece suit. I wondered what she would have looked like if she'd had a chance to grow old. Thankful the photo had not been damaged, I slid it into the zippered side pocket of my shoulder bag. My brothers and I had very few photos of her or of Red.

From the center of the room I could see, through the open bedroom door, that the chaos was no less in the other room. Standing, I started to step across the debris and into the bedroom, and then I noticed that the seat tops were missing off the bolted-down marine barstools on the far side of the living room.

"No!" I trampled across my possessions and peered down into the hollow pipe that served as the base for one of the stools.

"Shit!" I picked up a spatula off the bar and threw it at the wall. It fell soundlessly onto a pile of file folders. Somehow, somebody had figured out where I kept my cash, in a hollow compartment in the base of one of the stools. The stools had come off a fancy sportfisherman B.J. did a remodel on, and aside from the fact that they were free, they took up less space in the little cottage. Sometimes I worked for folks who owned big custom boats and preferred to pay in cash. I didn't ask any questions, and I didn't always deposit it in my bank account. What a mistake. My emergency money, two thousand dollars, was gone.

I shoved aside several corkscrews and linen dish towels and pressed my forehead against the cool Formica of the bar. Shit. Why me? Here I lived in one of the richest neighborhoods in the country in what is obviously the littlest, cheapest, poorest house in the neighborhood. Why would a thief think there would be anything to steal in here? Two thousand dollars was nothing in this neighborhood. But it had been my safety net. I stared into the empty hole. I'd always been convinced that most burglars wouldn't even know that that type of marine chair base *could* come apart. I looked around the room. The TV and VCR were still there. That didn't make sense. No crackhead or petty thief would have left them. Leaning against the side of my desk, I could see the laptop computer Neal bought me as a gift was still there in its carrying case. Curious.

There was only one other person who knew where I kept that cash stash.

Cleaning up was something I just could not contemplate at that point. Stepping over the food and debris on the kitchen floor, I opened the refrigerator door and reached for a cold beer. At least he hadn't trashed the little bit of food and drink in there. As I pulled a can out of the plastic ring on the six-pack holder, it occurred to me that one beer was missing. When you're single, the only one in the house doing any eating or drinking, you remember these things. I had bought that six-pack yesterday. I hadn't drunk a single beer. But somebody had.

It was that beer that was the clincher. That and the fact that whoever had trashed my place didn't really seem to be searching for anything, but rather had destroyed my property purely out of anger and meanness—a passion of sorts. That sort of angry passion was familiar to me, too familiar.

I fished around in my pocket for the card Detective Collazo had given me earlier, and I reached for the phone. At first I hadn't intended to call the cops, since I'd already spent hours with cops that day, and I didn't really see what good they'd do. On most break-ins in the neighborhood, they as much as told folks not to go on hoping they would ever see any of their stuff again. But this was different . . . apparently my home had just been trashed by somebody the cops thought I had killed.

"OF COURSE. IT HAD TO BE HIM, DETECTIVE."
Collazo stood in the center of my living room looking around at the mess with a slack, almost bored expression on his face.

"Miss Sullivan, we will take your report, and we will investigate, and we will draw our own conclusions."

I walked over to the laptop computer, picked it up, and held it in front of his face.

"Does this make any sense to you? Or the TV there, or any of the other stuff in here that would be so easy to sell?" He turned his back to me and walked over to the easel and my torn painting.

"This is your work."

"Well, it was. It's garbage now."

"Such a shame."

Neal had always admired and encouraged my painting. He was forever telling me to take a few paintings to this gallery owner friend of his over on Las Olas. "Yeah. I *am* surprised he would do that."

"He . . . you mean Garrett."

"Of course. I mean, what about the money? What other possible answer could there be?"

"You claim he tossed the place just to cover the fact that he was stealing your money."

"Obviously. That's the only thing missing."

"Garrett was a reasonably intelligent man."

"In a street-smart kind of way, yes."

"Yet you are saying that he wanted you to believe a stranger trashed and robbed your cottage here, but he did not take these valuables."

"Maybe I surprised him and he wasn't able to take everything he wanted to take. Maybe he was still in here when I pulled into the driveway, and he had to run when he heard my Jeep." Or just maybe, I thought, he wanted to make it look like a burglary, and then that anger of his took over again.

"Perhaps you surprised some other burglar, or kids, vandals, or—"

"But it had to be somebody who knew where that money was, don't you think?"

He didn't speak at first, and I was determined to wait, to make him answer that. When he did finally speak, he did so without turning around. His voice was so soft, I could barely make out the words. "Perhaps you overestimate the cleverness of your hiding place, Miss Sullivan. Many of the criminals in this town have worked in the marine industry at some point. Or yes, perhaps it was someone who knew where that money was." He turned slowly and looked at me with those black eyes. "You knew where the money was."

"Oh, come on, you don't think I would do this to my own place?"

"I consider all possibilities."

"Seems to me like you've only been considering one possibility ever since this whole mess started, Detective."

"Garrett is gone, Miss Sullivan. The blood on the boat, the distance to shore . . . how could he have made it?"

"Detective, Neal used to be a Navy Seal. He was probably wearing scuba gear. If you don't think he could have swum that distance underwater, you don't know the Seals."

"I see no evidence to convince me the man is still alive, and"—he waved his arm to indicate my cottage—"a little event like this is not going to change my mind on that count."

"Little event? What are you talking about? Neal was in here tonight, I'd bet my life on it."

"I see." He slipped his gold pen from his pocket and began to write in those tiny letters on the pages of his notepad.

I pointed at the officer taking photos of the mess. "Have them check for fingerprints. I know you'll find Neal's prints in here."

He looked up at me and squinted his eyes. "Yes, you're quite correct there, I'm sure. You said earlier that Garrett lived with you. This place will still be covered with his prints." He picked up my torn canvas of the Stranahan House painting. "It would take a very desperate person to destroy things just to try to throw suspicion off himself." He walked up very close to me and said, almost into my ear, "Or herself."

"Jesus." I stepped back from him, putting distance between us to give me some measure of comfort. "Wait a minute. Hold on. Somebody breaks into my home, and when I call you guys for help, you come in here accusing me?"

"There is no sign of any forced entry."

"Well, Neal had a key to this place at one time. Maybe he made a copy. Or hid one out in the yard somewhere." My voice was getting higher and more strained. I sounded guilty to myself. But it was Neal, dammit, I knew it. I had to make him understand, but I wasn't willing just yet to tell him about the rage I had seen in Neal that one time. "Detective, I don't care what you think about all this," I told him, waving my arm at the mess in the room, "but the truth is I did not kill that girl or Neal. She was dead when I got aboard the *Top Ten*, and somehow, Neal got off alive. He was here tonight in my cottage. You've got to believe that."

"No, Miss Sullivan, *you've* got to think about the kind of trouble you're in. If you don't have an attorney, I suggest you get one, and I expect to see you at the station tomorrow morning, first thing."

After they'd left, I sat on the stool top I had replaced and finished my now warm beer, staring across the room, seeing nothing.

How had this happened? How, in the course of one day, had I

become a suspect, apparently the only suspect, in a murder case? This didn't happen to people like me. Innocent people didn't go to prison for crimes they didn't commit, did they? I was not that naive. Of course they did; innocent people had been found to have spent years in prison, in solitary confinement, even on death row. The thought of prison terrified me. I had to come up with a plan, because if the police weren't looking for other suspects, someone had better start.

But just then, I wanted to sleep, and I knew I couldn't do it in the cottage. I turned off the light, left the porch light on, and locked up. Collazo was right about one thing: I couldn't see any sign of the lock having been jimmied. I figured there was one place I could sleep safely without having to worry about whether or not anybody was coming back.

Abaco rubbed up against my thighs.

"Some watchdog you are." I rubbed her ears. She seemed very pleased with herself.

I looked around the beautifully manicured yard with its large live oak tree blocking the view of the stars. It was dark in among the hedges and shrubs, the butterfly garden, and the shed on the far side of the house where the Larsens stored their recreational toys. The night sounds of crickets and the brush rustlings of the creatures who survived in suburbia sounded natural and soothing. Nothing out of the ordinary. Had he really been here? If so, how did he get from the *Top Ten* offshore to here in the past fifteen hours? Or did I just want so much for him to be alive that I was stretching the evidence to make myself believe it? Maybe it was just a thief, and something—Abaco or a boat or even my returning— scared him off before he could take all the goods. I put my hands under Abaco's chin and lifted her face. "God, I wish you could talk. It was him, wasn't it? You'd have torn up anybody else. It's the only thing that makes sense." Angry as I was about my trashed house, I was more relieved by the evidence that the son of a bitch was still around. Wrapping my arms around the dog's neck, I whispered, "He's alive, isn't he, girl?"

I walked down the dock and climbed aboard *Gorda*. Abaco looked at me as though asking permission to come aboard. "All right, you useless dog." I would feel better with company.

When Red built *Gorda*, he knew there would be times he would have to take her down to Miami or up to Palm Beach, and he wanted to be able to sleep aboard. The main wheelhouse had three windows across the front, with the wheel and all the engine instruments on the console below. To starboard, aft of the wheelhouse door, was a chart table with a swing-out stool, and aft of that was a narrow bunk stretched across the bulkhead. To port, through the bulkhead aft, steps led down to the engine room with the tiny enclosed head in a corner, while in the center sat the single 220-horsepower CAT D342 six-cylinder diesel that powered the tug. In spite of the engine room insulation, sleeping on the little aluminum shelf over the engine was nearly impossible due to the heat and noise when under way. But tonight, I knew I'd feel far safer sleeping there than in the mess that was my cottage. I reactivated the alarm system and fell into the bunk without bothering to undress. I wasn't awake long enough to realize how uncomfortable I was.

VI

ABACO'S BARKING BLENDED RIGHT IN WITH MY DREAM. I was running, running hard and scared in total darkness. I was barefoot, struggling to run in sand, then mud, deep thick muck that sucked at my feet. The darkness was so complete I couldn't even see my body, but I knew something was back there, getting closer. I opened my mouth to try to scream for help, but no sound came out. My voice was gone. As I started to crawl up to the surface, out of my dream, the first thing I became aware of was a distant muffled voice calling, "Hello, hello, is anybody home?"

I opened one eye, and blazing sunlight assaulted my retina. Gradually, my eyes began to make out shapes in the glare. This wasn't my cottage. There wasn't a bare aluminum ceiling in my cottage. When I saw the instruments and the helm, I remembered where I was and why I was there. I groaned and pulled the pillow over my head.

Abaco stopped barking briefly, growled a low throaty rumble, and scratched at the wheelhouse door. She wanted to get out and protect her territory.

"Hello? Miss Sullivan?"

Whoever it was didn't seem to want to go away. Apparently I had no choice but to get up and deal with him, whoever he was. It was beastly hot in the closed wheelhouse, as the sun had been up for quite a while, beating on and heating up the aluminum super-structure. I disentangled my legs from the damp, knotted sheet and stood up. My mouth tasted like bilge water from too much beer the night before, and I knew I smelled even worse. Through the wheel-house window I could see a man standing at my cottage, pounding on the door. It was unusual for anyone to come back here. It re-quired entering private property through a closed gate. He was wearing what looked like a very expensive suit and fancy tasseled loafers. He exuded power and confidence. In the hand that wasn't beating on the door, he held a briefcase.

"Persistent fellow," I said aloud. When I attempted to comb my fingers through my hair, the strands seemed hopelessly tangled. Giving up, I slid my fingers under Abaco's collar, unlocked the wheelhouse door and slid it open. The dog barked, and the man spun around at the sound, a startled expression on his face. When he saw me struggling to hold on to the dog, a fleeting expression of distaste passed over his face. I guessed I looked about as bad as I felt.

I leaned down. "Abaco, stay." She sat down obediently, sur-prising the hell out of me.

"Miss Sullivan?"

"Yeah, that's me. Sorry about my appearance." I gave another futile swipe at my hair. "Things were a bit of a mess last night, and I slept on the boat." For some reason I could not define, I found myself not wanting him to know just what the inside of my cottage actually looked like at that moment. "I guess I kinda slept in." I slid the wheelhouse door closed. "What time is it, anyway?"

He raised his wrist and glanced at his watch. It looked ex-pensive. "It's nearly nine-thirty. I apologize for waking you." He walked across the grass and extended his hand to me. "My name is Hamilton Burns, and I would like to talk to you if you have a few minutes. It's about the *Top Ten*."

He had my attention then. I stepped onto the seawall and shook his hand.

"Seychelle Sullivan, but I guess you know that already."

He nodded.

"Look, it's so hot inside, why don't we just sit over here?" I led him over to the picnic table in the shade of a big live oak tree.

He took a handkerchief from his breast pocket and brushed away the leaves and seeds on the rough wood bench. He explained, "I am an attorney, and I represent the owners of the motor yacht the *Top Ten.*" He set his briefcase on the table and snapped the catches. Raising the lid, he removed some half glasses and put them on. "They appreciate very much the efforts that you went to yesterday to secure the yacht after the unfortunate events that occurred aboard the vessel."

Unfortunate? I thought. I'm not sure that's the way Neal or Patty Krix would have described the events.

"My clients have enlisted me to present you with this check." With a flourish, he produced a cashier's check from behind the lid of his briefcase. "I think you will find it represents a very fair sum, and upon your acceptance, we will ask you to sign this document certifying your receipt of the check."

I looked down at the check. It was made out to me in the sum of ten thousand dollars. I'd never seen a check that big with my name on the "pay to the order of" line before. Unless you count those fake sweepstakes ones you get in the mail all the time, but, of course, they don't count. No, this one was real, and since it was a cashier's check, I could exchange it for cash that very afternoon. The check impressed me, and Burns could undoubtedly see that on my face.

That must have been what he was counting on. The document he was pushing at me was several pages long, and he had all the top pages folded back. Only the last page, which required my signature, was showing. Obviously, he was so certain I would jump at the ten grand, he didn't think I'd worry about little things like reading the document he was asking me to sign.

What he wasn't counting on was the fact that I knew perfectly well that this was a pittance compared to what that boat was worth and what I was entitled to as the salvor. And as much as I needed money at that point, ten thousand dollars wouldn't do me a bit of good when it came to buying out Maddy. I needed more than twice that amount. And what I resented most of all was the assumption that he could just come traipsing in here with his fancy clothes and take advantage of me.

I picked up the salvage documents. "Do you mind if I read this?"

"It really isn't necessary. It's just the standard form for this sort of thing."

"Mmm." I glanced through the contract, the heavy paper crackling as I folded back each page. "I see. And since I'd have trouble understanding all these great big words, I really shouldn't worry my pretty little head about it, isn't that right, Mr. Burns?"

From the look on his face, I could tell he knew something had gone wrong. The odd thing was, it made him look frightened.

"Miss Sullivan, I assure you—"

"No, Mr. Burns, I assure *you* that this is not the standard form for this sort of thing. That would be Lloyd's Open Form, the standard salvage document that entitles us both to arbitration in London to determine what the fair award should be. That's the document the owner of the *Top Ten* should be signing right now. Who is the owner, Mr. Burns?"

"I'm not at liberty to disclose that to you."

"I see. Well, look." I pushed the document back across the picnic table. "The amount you're offering me is an insult. How much do you figure the *Top Ten* is worth, anyway? Three, four million? What's she insured for? You go back and tell the owner to think about that. I found her floating around out there completely unmanned. She was very nearly lost on that beach, and there are those who would consider me crazy to have taken my tug into water that shallow and that close to the surf line. The idea in marine salvage is no cure, no pay. That was the chance I took. Well, I cured their problem, and they now have to pay me for my services. You tell them they're lucky I didn't just say finders keepers." I tossed his contract down on the table.

"Really, you should reconsider. This is a very fair offer." His face was reddening, and the man looked like he was having an anxiety attack. What a change from the cool, confident guy who had been banging on my cottage door.

"This is bullshit, Burns, and you know it. You go back and tell the owner that I resent this offer, especially your thinking that I would be fool enough to sign something without even reading it first. My attorney is Jean Black. She will need to contact the vessel's owner, and we will present our bill for my services. If that's not satisfactory, we'll be happy to ask Lloyd's arbitrators to decide what's fair." I stood with my arms folded across my chest and watched him pack up his papers. The cashier's check disappeared into the briefcase. I hoped I was making the right decision and would win this round. Ten grand was a lot better than nothing.

He snapped the case closed, lifted it up on end, and leaned on it. Maybe he thought he was smiling, but it was an ugly sneer. "You will regret this. These are powerful people, Miss Sullivan. You don't fuck with them."

Wow, I thought, interesting. Uptown suit and gutter mouth. I couldn't resist. As he walked out along the path, I stuck out my tongue and crossed my eyes at his back.

Unfortunately, no magical elves had appeared overnight to clean up the mess inside the cottage. When I unlocked the door, the sight of all my belongings trashed in heaps on the floor didn't exactly cheer me up. Robberies and break-ins were not uncommon in South Florida, and I'd often heard people talk about how violated they felt after their homes had been entered. I just felt pure, seething anger. A girl was dead, and while the Coast Guard was out there spending tens of thousands on a search-and-rescue operation and the cops were looking for some kind of evidence to hang the whole thing on me, Neal Garrett was apparently alive and well enough to toss my cottage. The jerk. In the bright light of morning, it seemed so obvious. I wasn't ready to believe some dumb thief just got lucky.

I picked my way into the bedroom and found a reasonably presentable pair of jeans and one blouse that remained hanging half on, half off a hanger in the closet.

The bathroom had scarcely been touched. Some of the bedroom debris had fallen in there, but it seemed almost as if he had run out of steam. Had he been looking for something in particular, something besides the cash?

After a long, hot shower and lathering my hair three times, I finally started to feel human again. Clean clothes felt great, though rumpled. I combed out my wet hair, stepped into my Top-Siders, grabbed my shoulder bag, and went out the front door. I knew I couldn't go on living this way; eventually I would have to face the prospect of an entire day spent putting my house back in order, but right now, more than anything, I wanted to see what my brother Maddy would say face-to-face.

Maddy lived in a townhouse in Surfside, and he kept his boat in Haulover Marina. Since they were close together, I figured I'd swing by the boat first, and if he wasn't there, I'd check the house. I hoped he wasn't out on an all-day trip. Maddy's truck wasn't in the marina parking lot, and his boat, the *Lady Jane*, was securely tied up in her slip, so I didn't even bother turning into the marina parking lot.

They had inherited the townhouse from Jane's dad. It was in a very nice neighborhood in Surfside, full of retirees and escalating property values. It hadn't quite developed the South Beach coolness, but you could see it was coming. I was pretty sure they were mortgaged up to their eyeballs, and while they could sell the place, the top of the market would be a few more years in the future; undoubtedly, they intended to hold out for that.

My eight-year-old nephew, Freddie, answered the door, and without even saying hello, he screamed, "It's Auntie Seychelle!" Then he turned and headed back to the Nintendo hooked up to the big-screen color TV in the living room. I closed the front door behind me, and Jane appeared out of the kitchen wearing a flowered housecoat. Though she was only about six years older than me, she looked old and tired already.

"Hi, Seychelle," she said, up on tiptoe and delivering an air kiss next to my cheek. She didn't look particularly happy to see me. From the kitchen I heard a wail. "Oh, Annie's in the high chair. I'm feeding her. Maddy's up in our room, at the office." She pointed to the carpeted stairs and disappeared back down the hall.

Such a warm family welcome.

Maddy had an old rolltop desk that he kept in his bedroom, and that's where he sat to pay all his bills. He called it "the office." I guess he wanted his kids to be able to say, "My daddy goes to his office," instead of "My daddy baits dead ballyhoo on rich people's hooks."

I climbed the stairs.

"I thought you might show up." He didn't look up from the check he was writing. One thing about his townhouse, it wasn't exactly soundproof.

"I guess you would expect it after that bombshell you dropped yesterday." I sat down on the quilted bedspread. A can of Old Milwaukee was making a wet ring on the desk. It wasn't even noon yet, and he was already sucking up the beer.

"You shouldn't be so surprised, Seychelle. There's a lot of capital tied up in that boat. I can't afford to keep on being sentimental over its being Red's boat."

On the far side of the room, a sliding glass door opened onto a balcony overlooking a canal. The view looked nice, but he'd discovered the first time he tried to bring the *Lady Jane* up to the house that the water was less than two feet deep.

I couldn't believe what he was saying. My brother had never been sentimental a day in his life. He had agreed to let me run *Gorda* because he thought it was a good investment. "Maddy, that's my business. It's my life. It would be like my asking you to sell the *Lady Jane*."

"No. It wouldn't. You don't own a third of the *Lady Jane.*"

I looked out the window across the canal at the townhouse opposite theirs. A white-haired man in bright golf-green polyester pants was sitting in a wrought-iron chair reaching for a young girl's hand. The child looked about ten years old, and she was wearing a frilly, going-to-see-Grampa special dress. He pulled her to him and sat her on his lap.

"I thought we all agreed to let me have a go at it for two years, Maddy."

"Seychelle, we also agreed that you were going to make payments to me and Pit." He consulted his watch. "Today is March nineteenth. I haven't seen the February payment yet. You're getting behind, and I don't think we should let the business go all to hell."

It was true, things had been slow lately, but I didn't know how I was going to eat if I paid Maddy. I had been late before, and he had never said anything about it. Maybe it had been bothering him all along, or maybe something had changed.

I looked back out the window and watched the girl and the old man. He was talking to her, and her face looked slack and vacant, as though she wasn't hearing a word the old man said.

I took my checkbook out of my shoulder bag and began writing. "Here." I tore off the check. I wasn't sure I had enough in the bank to cover the five hundred bucks, but I sure as hell didn't want Maddy to know that. "February and March. I didn't think my own brother would try to shut me down if I let one month's payment ride for a couple of weeks."

"I'm not a banker. I got bills to pay, too, you know."

Maddy and I had never gotten along, and there was no way in hell I was going to admit I was wrong even if I was. It always took Pit, the middle child, to keep us from erupting and really hurting each other. "Have you talked to Pit lately?" I asked him.

"No. But you know he could use the money. I don't know what he lives on as it is."

I felt fairly confident Pit would side with me if it came down to it. He'd never cared very much about money and somehow seemed to live quite happily with very little of it. He supported himself with sponsorships and cash prizes, and he gave windsurfing lessons at various resorts in exchange for free room and board. The problem would be contacting him. I deposited his check in a bank account in Fort Lauderdale, and he used an ATM card to access it from wherever he happened to be. I was certain the bank would not release any information. And I knew next to nothing about the World Cup Windsurfing Tour. He could be anywhere from St. Thomas to Maui.

"I guess, until we hear from Pit, it's just between you and me, Maddy."

He lifted the can, chugalugged the rest of his beer, and belched loudly.

"Maddy, look at me," I said, raising my voice. His desk chair was one of those swivel jobs, and he eased around to face me. I noticed the bags in the flesh under his eyes, and the paunch that pulled his T-shirt tight. God, it looked like he had a basketball under there. "Are you in some kind of trouble? Is that what brought this on?"

He looked away. "No, nothing like that. I just want out. That's all."

"I don't think you're telling me the whole truth."

Maddy was known in our family for his terrific temper. Pit and I used to harass him just to watch his face turn bright red. Maddy had always been chunky, even as a kid, and though he was the oldest, both Pit and I could outrun him by the time we were ten or twelve. As his face flushed, I could tell he didn't take kindly to me calling him a liar.

"It doesn't matter what you think," he yelled, waving his arm in a dismissive gesture. "I knew this would never work. Face the facts, Seychelle. Guys don't like to trust the safety of their big yachts to a woman. That's the bottom line. You're not getting the business, and you're going to sell the goddamn boat." He belched again and looked toward the bedroom door. "Either that or buy me out." He tried to laugh, but it sounded more like a croak.

"You know I can't do that right away."

He shrugged. "Okay, so sell."

"Maddy, you're a shitheel." He was goading me into name-calling, like he always used to do. "Just give me a few days and I might be able to buy you out. I've got something working."

"This have something to do with the *Top Ten*?"

"How'd you know about that?"

"It's in today's paper. I figure the reason Neal didn't show up is either he killed the girl and he's running, or else he's shark food."

"Thanks for your sensitivity, big brother."

"Well, I wouldn't expect to get much out of that deal." Instead of anger, Maddy's face took on a calculating look. "I say take whatever they offer and get out of the towing business. Maybe you saved this boat this time. But you're not always gonna have that kind of luck. We both know that. You can't fool me, Seychelle, remember? I know you never ever talk about it, but refusing to talk about it won't make it go away. You were there, but you didn't do a goddamn thing for her."

I couldn't trust myself to speak. The anger that had been building up in my chest against Collazo, Burns, Maddy, and especially Neal, for being stupid enough to get into this mess and dragging me into it with him, all threatened to explode. I wanted to bury my fist in Maddy's basketball belly, but instead I took the stairs two at a time, slammed the door on my way out, and ground the gears on my Jeep trying to get far, far away from there.

I DROVE BLINDLY UP A1A, OVER THE HAULOVER BRIDGE, AND on Collins Avenue into North Miami. Cars honked at me, and I honked back, a dangerous practice on the streets of South Florida, where over half the drivers surveyed confess to carrying a gun in their vehicles. Maddy would always blame me for what had happened that day on Hollywood Beach when we were kids.

Up until yesterday morning, I'd been reasonably content with my life—I'd thought I had moved beyond all that. I had mourned the many losses in my life, including the death of my relationship with Neal. I loved my job, and I'd discovered how much I enjoyed solitary life. I had gone from college roommates to taking care of Red and then to moving in with Neal. Now, coming home to an empty cottage and open evenings had grown to feel luxurious. No one expecting conversation, dinner, or clean laundry. No one leaving the toilet seat up or the cap off the milk jug. I would never be the domestic type, and after Neal left, I no longer needed to pretend. But now my cottage was a mess, I was broke, my livelihood was being threatened, and at least one more person was dead because I hadn't gotten there in time.

When I got to Hollywood Beach, I pulled off into one of the side streets and parked next to a meter. I fed it a couple of quarters and walked up toward the beach. Ever since that summer when I was eleven years old, I have always been drawn back to this beach when I'm sad, or need to think, or just want to sit on a bench, alone, watching the freighters on the horizon. By now, the season was starting to slow down a little, but most of the people I passed on the Broadwalk were speaking French—Canadians fleeing the frozen north. This was the beach we had come to most often as children. This was where my brothers taught me to bodysurf, where we'd held birthdays and come for holidays dragging beach chairs, picnic baskets, coolers, and inflatable rafts. And this was the beach where my mother had drowned.

Kicking off my Top-Siders, I dug my toes into the cool, damp sand. The beach had changed very little in the eighteen years since it happened. There were still the funky low-rise family hotels along the Broadwalk and the hundred-yard-wide stretch of sable-colored sand that dropped down to the pale blue-green shallows. Now, after a long winter of northerly storms, much of the sand had washed away, leaving only a narrow band of aqua before the water turned deep Gulf Stream blue. To the south, in the direction of Johnson Street, the hotels gave way to pizza places, ice cream shops, and Greek takeouts with salads and falafel, and the beachfront always hummed with happy humanity like a carnival midway.

My mother and father probably never should have married in the first place. As an adult, trying to look at them objectively, it was clear that they were not well suited to each other. Red once told me that he had met Mother in a bar on the Intracoastal. His ship was berthed in Port Everglades, and he and some buddies met this group of girls up in the old Crow's Nest Bar over at Bahia Mar, at the time a hangout for sailors and charter captains. Annie was the wild one, he said, talkative, vivacious, daringly throwing back shots of tequila to compete with the navy guys. She was a third-generation Floridian, the daughter of a prominent Fort Lauderdale doctor, majoring in art at the University of Miami, artistic, flighty, and wildly impractical. Red, thirteen years her senior, was a navy lifer and a sensible, orderly, dependable, entirely practical man. He had already done a tour in Southeast Asia and would probably play out the remainder of his twenty years on ships in the Atlantic.

They honeymooned on Staniel Cay in the Bahamas, and it was then they vowed to visit new islands throughout their married life. Eventually Red was able to buy a very modest little cinder-block canal-front home in the Shady Banks neighborhood of Fort Lauderdale. First it was finances that prevented them from ever carrying out their traveling dreams, and later babies, so they named each of us for the islands they'd intended to visit someday.

In the early years Red was gone in the navy, and then he spent all his time on *Gorda*, and Mother never managed well alone. Her wealthy family had turned their backs on her when she married a penniless navy man, and she struggled to manage a household without servants. Her books were scattered around the house and her art covered the walls, and if there were dust bunnies the size of jackrabbits roaming the house, it mattered little to her. She could be so fun and laughing, so shining and beautiful, and then suddenly plummet into the depths of a depression that closed out everyone else. Maddy, Pit, and I did our best to avoid her when she was having one of her "bad days."

She wanted me to go with her to the beach that day. It was a Saturday, and I wanted to stay home and play with Pit and our friend Molly, who lived next door. They were planning on taking Pit's skiff across the river and up what we called Mosquito Creek to a spot where there were lots of polliwogs and baby frogs. But my mother insisted I go with her. She was having one of her bad days, and often when she was depressed, she just wanted to get out of the house. Once away, either she wouldn't talk or she would complain. I hadn't wanted to listen to her go on about my brothers or Red, so I sulked but went along.

In the car, I sat in the backseat. I'd relived that day so many times in my mind, tried to take it back, do it differently. But on that day, I wouldn't look at her as we walked out onto the beach.

We settled on our blanket, and I stretched out on the farthest edge.

"Will you swim with me?" she asked after several minutes.

I shook my head. She was talking to me, but I wouldn't listen.

"Honey," she said, taking off her sunglasses, revealing the dark circles beneath her penetrating eyes. "Sey, please try to understand." I buried my nose in my book and flipped my hair over my shoulder.

She reached out and touched the part at the crown of my head, then gently slid her fingers down the strands to rest on the bare brown skin of my shoulder. Her voice was quiet when she spoke.

"Seychelle, will you ever forgive me?"

Getting it all wrong, thinking she meant just that day and making me leave Pit and Molly, I stared at her, wrapping myself in preadolescent self-righteousness, and said, "No."

I pretended to ignore her when she stood and walked into the water. I remember noticing, though, that she was wearing her beach shoes, purple sandals with garish pink plastic flowers over the toes, which she usually kicked off onto the blanket. I knew there was something wrong about that, and I remembered thinking, I don't care.

I didn't see her again until the people on the beach started running down to the tide line and I got up to see what the commotion was all about. I pushed my way through the crowd, already feeling the coldness staving off the sun's warmth. The first thing I saw was the white foot beneath the pink plastic flowers, then this blond lifeguard trying to blow life back into her body.

Yesterday I hadn't been there for Neal or Patty Krix. Not in time. And just like Maddy said, I'd never ever spoken about what happened that day because even though everyone kept telling me that it wasn't my fault, I always felt deep down inside that Maddy was right.

W HEN I GOT BACK TO LIGHTNIN', I PULLED OUT ONTO A1A and headed north toward Lauderdale. The more I turned things over in my mind, the more questions I came up with. I couldn't just let it alone. It was like one of those persistent little leaks in the boat that would continue to nag me until I solved the problem of where it was coming from. Much as I was ticked off about the mess that had been made of my cottage, I knew that Neal had to be in a hell of a bad fix if he didn't think he could come to me and just ask for my help. Was he that hurt, scared, angry? In fact, maybe it was a signal; maybe he was asking for help in his own way. I was determined not to miss any more signals. I wasn't really conscious of having made a decision when I turned onto Seventeenth, but when I pulled into the parking lot of the Top Ten Club, I figured that if I asked around, found out a little more about Patty Krix, I might understand what had happened out there and help both Neal and me out of this mess.

It was lunchtime, and the parking lot was about half full. The cars were much fancier than I would have guessed: Lincolns, BMWs, Infinitis. I'd always thought these places were full of frat boys and solitary raincoat wearers. Did businessmen have power lunches while looking at naked women? The idea made me laugh out loud.

I waved off the valet parking attendant and parked my Jeep

out back by the Dumpsters, where I didn't think anybody would notice the clearly out-of-place vehicle. I walked around to the front door feeling the eyes of the jocular, hail-fellow-well-met business guys in dark suits taking in my casual dress and my aloneness. I squared my shoulders, which after years of competition swimming and lifeguard paddling were rather broad, stood at my full height, and dared the little parking attendant with my eyes. He didn't say a word as I passed.

Aside from the fact that there were ten stark-naked women around on brilliantly lit stages, dancing to an old Bee Gees tune, the restaurant didn't really look much different from other franchise restaurants across America. It had the standard booths, tables, and bar. The tacky decor, in red and gold, was supposed to look better in the subdued lighting. Oversize lava lamps graced either end of the bar, looking like elongated, transparent female torsos. Lots of reproductions of oil paintings hung on the walls from the days when painters liked their models to have a bit more meat on their bones, when round bellies and fleshy thighs were thought as lovely as big breasts. The waitresses wore gold lamé bodices that revealed plenty of cleavage, frilly tutulike skirts, and fishnet stockings. The lunch rush was over, and no more than half the tables were occupied. Every single customer in the place was male.

A short, muscular Latino guy wearing a gold tank top stood just inside the door. His black hair stood up in a spiky crew cut, shiny with gel, and though his eyes were hidden behind dark shades, I could feel him looking me over. I headed straight for the bar, feeling awkward, but none of the customers paid the least attention to me. The tables were clustered in groups of four around the raised stages, and the men sat transfixed. Most of the dancers wore nothing but garters, under which they had bunches of bills. Periodically, one of the men would reach out and add to their collections. If there was conversation going on among the patrons, it was indicated only by heads cocked to the side. The men didn't look at one another.

At the bar I ordered a Corona from the bartender, who had the most enormous bosom I had ever seen. Her metallic bodice looked stiff as fiberglass, like it had been molded over a couple of Patriot missiles. I was sure it took some pretty advanced engineering to provide support for that. When she brought me the beer, I waved off the glass and squeezed the lime straight into the cold bottle.

"So what brings you in here?" she asked as she replaced the glass in the rack overhead. "I guess it's not the entertainment."

I smiled. "No, you're right there. I'm looking for anybody who knew a girl named Patty Krix."

She squinted at me. "Well, now, I don't think you're a cop. Besides, they've already been here. Sent over some gorilla. Wanted to know about both Patty and the boss." She shivered, and her cleavage undulated the way a dead jellyfish does when you poke it with a stick. "Like I can tell them anything on him they don't already have in their files."

"You know Crystal?"

"He's the boss."

"He sold his boat, the *Top Ten*, a few months ago. Do you have any idea who he sold it to?"

She chuckled and slapped her hand down on the bar. "That's a good one. He used to come in here sometimes and drink a cuba libre, but honey, he didn't talk business with the likes of me. Of course, that's all before he took this little retreat of his."

"You mean before he went to jail."

She laughed again, and the sound seemed to rise out of her in deep bubbles. "Smart girl. You some friend or relative of Patty's?"

I was tempted to lie, but I never was very good at it. I gave myself away half the time just by looking guilty. "No, my name's Seychelle Sullivan. I run a boat towing service. I'm the one who found her out there, and I'm an old friend of Neal's."

"That's the guy who's missing, right? I met him once. Not bad-looking, but Patty coulda done better. There were guys both good-looking *and* rich who were interested in her." A waitress came and gave an order, and when the bartender had lined up the glasses and begun pouring, she said, "My name's Teenie, by the way."

I didn't want to ask how she'd got the name. "Had Patty worked here long?"

" 'Bout a year. I didn't really know her, though. I don't talk much to the dancers. Don't have time. But you might try Alexis. Seems they knew each other from before or something. That's her dancin' over there in front of the dude with the Bulls hat on."

The young woman she pointed to wore a long black wig, too-heavy black eyeliner, and deep purple lipstick. Her body looked hard, not from exercise but from life. Her right nipple was pierced with a stud, and a tinkling silver chain dangled from the stud and danced as she did. More chains were wrapped around her waist and supported the tiny patch at her crotch. When she spun around and waggled her behind, I saw the chains disappear between her cheeks. I'm always amazed at the level of discomfort some women are willing to put up with in the attempt to look sexy.

Drinking from the icy bottle, I wondered how I was going to pry Alexis away from the Bulls guy. His head bobbed in cadence with the music and her thrusting pelvis. She began to undo the chains of her G-string, and he reached up and slipped a twenty-dollar bill under the leather thong on her thigh.

"Okay," Teenie said. "I figure that about taps him out." She shouted over the music, "Hey, Lex, come here a minute."

The dancer nodded in Teenie's direction and stepped down from the stage. The Bulls guy reached for her buttocks as she passed, but she deftly swatted his hand away as though it were an annoying insect. The man got up and left as she shrugged into a shimmering golden robe. The stage was then taken by a tiny Asian girl, who began to dance for the mostly empty tables.

"What's up, Teenie?"

The bartender jerked her head in my direction. "She wants to talk to somebody who knew Patty."

Lex turned to look at me. Her heavy makeup was not able to hide the fact that her skin was scarred from a severe case of acne, and she had a dark bruise on the left side of her face. Her eyes looked like two black crab holes in the sand. "Who're you?"

"My name is Seychelle Sullivan."

"What's it to you?"

"Neal Garrett, the guy she was with, well, we're good friends, and I'm trying to find out what happened out there."

"Cop who was here thinks he's dead."

"Well, I have reason to believe he's alive. I've got to have faith in that right now," I said.

"I don't know nothin' about that." She pulled a pack of Marlboros out of a pocket in her robe and lit one with a purple disposable lighter. Her fingernails were a good inch long and painted purple, too.

"How long did you know Patty?"

"First met her at Harbor House a couple of years ago."

"You mean that place for runaways?"

"It ain't no hotel. We was both crashing there for a while."

I knew the place, and I knew they didn't take in anyone over eighteen. I couldn't believe that this woman had qualified as a teenager only a few years before.

"Somebody told me Patty was twenty-one. How could she have been at Harbor House two years ago?"

She looked at me like I was incredibly stupid. "Fake ID," she said, and stuck out her lower lip as she exhaled blue smoke toward the ceiling.

I wondered whether she meant they faked being younger then or older now. I suspected Patty had not even been twenty-one.

"Do you still know anybody over at Harbor House?"

She watched the smoke curl off the end of her cigarette, and a slight smirk of a smile passed across her face. "Yeah, I still know 'em over there." She turned to face me. "It's no place for somebody like you."

Her eyes shifted to focus on something over my shoulder, then she jerked her head to the side suddenly, as though she'd been slapped by an invisible hand. "Fuck," she muttered at the floor, all the bravado suddenly gone, and she looked like a scared kid for a brief moment.

I looked behind me, across the restaurant, in time to see the muscular Latino bouncer lowering his arms to his sides and attempting to assume a very casual-looking pose at the door. His shades were pushed to the top of his head, balancing atop the stiff hair spikes. He glanced at us out of the corner of his eye and quickly looked away.

Alexis continued to hurl a barrage of curse words at the floor, then bit at one of her purple nails. She looked up finally and stuck out her chin defiantly. "You done?" The cigarette she held in her right hand was trembling slightly.

"Can you think of any reason why somebody would have wanted to kill Patty?"

"Shit, who needs a reason? Hey, look, it was just her time. When your time's up, it's up, and there's not shit you can do about it." Her eyes went unfocused again as she glanced over my shoulder and then lightly touched the bruised side of her face with the two fingers that held the burning cigarette. Suddenly she stood and stubbed out the butt in a plastic ashtray. "I gotta get back to work."

Teenie reached across the bar and patted the back of my hand. It was an odd gesture, comforting in a motherly sort of way.

"What was that all about?"

"Don't mind her. It wasn't nothing. She acts that way 'round everybody. Thinks 'cause she's had a hard time of it, it gives her the right to be rude. She's too young to realize that everybody's got a story, not just her."

I watched Alexis walk across the floor, then turned back to the bartender. "Thanks, Teenie." After paying for my beer, I headed for the door. Alexis had tossed off her robe and taken the empty stage. She was facing the far side of the room, as though deliberately avoiding the bouncer's gaze. I had intended to look him straight in the eye on my way out, but there was something about him, about his dark shades, that made me change my mind. Lowering my eyes as I walked out into the blinding sunshine, I felt as though I'd been challenged, and lost.

VII

I'D FIRST HEARD OF HARBOR HOUSE WHEN I WAS WORKING as a lifeguard on Fort Lauderdale Beach over two years ago. The lifeguards took to the towers at nine o'clock every morning, and we often found people sleeping inside our posts. Usually they were winos, homeless men, most of whom we knew because they were regulars along the beach. We'd roust them, chew them out, explain that they weren't supposed to sleep on county property. The thing that bothered me the most was when they peed in the towers. I mean, there you have a whole wide beach, nobody can see you from the street at night if you go down by the water's edge, but no, they'd pee in a corner of the tower, and I'd have to sit there all day as the hot sun cooked up an intense, pissy smell.

A couple of years ago, on a morning two days before Christmas, a cold front passed through overnight, and the temperature dropped down into the low forties. I wore sneakers with two pairs of socks, a heavy sweat suit, and gloves. I'd brought my little pocket set of watercolors to pass the time. The shades of green and gray found in a windswept sea were always the hardest to capture on paper. I figured no one would be going into the water that day unless one of the hotels had booked a bunch of Scandinavian tourists. I was assigned tower twelve, which put me way down at the far north end of the beach. I rode a three-wheeled ATV down the sand, the cold wind making my nose run. When I pulled up to the tower, a pile of newspapers and cardboard made it obvious that the structure had a tenant already. At the top of the ladder I looked down into the sleepy green eyes of a fifteen-year-old girl. Her trembling was caused both by the cold and her fear that I was going to turn her over to the cops.

Her name was Elysia, and she was from Frostproof, a small town in central Florida. She stayed with me my whole shift. Nobody tried to go swimming that December day, so we had eight hours to watch the sea and talk. I wrapped her up in the gray county-issued blanket usually reserved for victims of near-drowning.

She told me why she couldn't go back home. She said she and her mom just couldn't get along ever since her mom had married this bum. Even before she told me, I knew what was coming. I could see the horror and disgust building in her eyes as she worked up the courage to talk about it out loud. When she finally told it, her voice remained emotionless. Her face went slack. It was as though it had happened to someone else, not her. Her stepfather had been sexually molesting her for six months, and according to Elysia, her mom deliberately chose to remain blind to the situation, to keep her man at the expense of her child. Elysia felt she had no recourse but to run away.

In a few weeks on the streets in Lauderdale she'd gone from being a teenager who smoked a little weed now and again to an addict who was turning twenty-dollar tricks for crack. At five in the afternoon I drove her to Lester's Diner and watched her, a tiny thing at about five feet two inches and a hundred pounds, put away a mountain of meat loaf, mashed potatoes, salad, and pecan pie. That night was my first visit to Harbor House, but I'd gone back several times in the last few years, to visit Elysia and to drop off a few others I'd picked up along the beach.

Harbor House had helped her kick the crack and given her a place to stay while she pulled herself back together. Jeannie had assisted with the legal stuff, and Elysia became an emancipated minor.

Not needing to go to a foster home, she just stayed on at Harbor House where she worked part-time as a peer counselor and office clerk. Last year, I convinced her to get her GED, and then B.J. helped her get a job as a hostess at the Bahia Cabana, a nice little patio restaurant on the Intracoastal. She was hoping to become a waitress soon, so she could start making the big tips and get out of Harbor House and into her own apartment. Just recently she'd started talking about maybe taking a class at the community college. I drove over the causeway to the beach and found a parking space a couple of blocks from the restaurant.

She was working the front when I walked in, past the outdoor Jacuzzi, up to the little sign that said Please Wait to Be Seated. She started to turn on the canned spiel for a couple of seconds, then her eyes lit up with recognition, and she ran up and hugged me, standing on her tiptoes.

"Seychelle! What are you doing here?" She pushed the unruly curls of redwood-colored hair back from her face.

"I came to see how you're getting along, kiddo." She looked great, and I noticed she was still wearing the little golden angel around her neck that I had given her for her birthday the year before.

Her eyes darted down and she reached for the charm. "My guardian angel's checking up on me, huh?" Elysia smiled. She pretended not to like it when I watched out for her.

"Well, somebody's got to, Ely. Look there. See, that couple just walked in, and here's the hostess flapping her jaw with some friend of hers."

She scooped up a couple of menus from her little podium and strode confidently up to the new arrivals. Her pleated white slacks and high-heeled sandals made even *her* legs look long, and combined with the required blue-and-white-striped sweater, she looked like a shorter version of those models in the classy nautical clothing catalogues. She maneuvered the couple through the inside tables and out on to the deck overlooking the marina. Watching her filled me with a sense of wonder. She had fought her way back from a despair so black I couldn't imagine it, and she had grown into this stunning, self-assured young woman.

When she returned, she explained she couldn't talk and work, so she pointed me in the direction of the bar and told me her shift would be over at five, in about twenty minutes. I sat down to wait, deciding against a beer. After looking at Maddy's beer gut that morning, I knew I'd been doing too much drinking lately.

The couples coming in for the early-bird dinner tended to be older people, but many of them entered arm in arm, smiling. The husbands joked and flirted with Ely. They were tanned from days spent sunning themselves like lizards on the beach. I wondered if it had been any of them standing on the beach yesterday morning watching hopefully as the *Top Ten* nearly went aground. They didn't have to wonder if someone they once loved was either underwater, providing food for the fishes, or a murderer on the run.

Finally Elysia appeared at my shoulder with her purse tucked under her arm. "Let's get out of here," she said.

Once we were outside on the street, she pointed toward the beach. "Do you mind if we just walk for a while? That's what I usually do after my shift, before I catch the bus back to Harbor House. I need the fresh air."

"Sounds good to me," I said.

We dodged cars, jaywalking across A1A in front of the *Jungle Queen* tour boat dock at the Bahia Mar Marina, and zigzagging through the parked cars in the city parking lot. When we hit the sand I slipped out of my boat shoes, and Elysia pulled off her white spike-heeled sandals with little red anchors embroidered on them. Now about three inches shorter, she looked younger but more familiar to me. The tall buildings along the Intracoastal cast long shadows across the beach as the sun dropped behind the city. The sand between my toes felt warmer than the evening air. We walked down to the waterline, where small waves broke into golden foam in the last of the day's sunlight.

"So, how you been doing?"

"Not bad. The money's adding up. I think I'll have enough for first and last months' rent on a furnished studio soon."

"All right. You've come far, you know. I'm proud of you."

She didn't say anything at first. Then finally she said, "Seychelle, I know you didn't come down here just to tell me that. I mean, you tell me how proud you are every time you see me these days."

I smiled at her. In some ways she was wise way beyond her teenage years. "Something happened yesterday, and I wanted to talk to you about it."

"I heard about Neal. Some guys at the bar were talking about what happened on this big yacht, and when they said the name of the boat, I knew it had to be Neal." She ran her fingers through her hair and bit her lower lip. "I didn't really know how to bring it up when you walked into the restaurant like that. I'm sorry."

My throat constricted, and I couldn't say anything for several seconds. A fancy sportfisherman raced toward the inlet, throwing up a huge, creamy bow wave, the hired skipper hunched over the wheel high up on the flybridge while his paying customers drank their liquor in the air-conditioned cabin below.

"You know, Ely, I thought I had been through it all with Neal. I thought I had finally got him out of my system for good. And then this happens, and suddenly he's thrust back into my life. I can't believe he's dead, Ely. In fact, I don't believe it. And I've got my reasons." I shook my head and stared out to sea. "Life's so strange sometimes."

"Yeah, I know. I mean, look at me." She did a little pirouette in the sand. "Who'd have thought, after all the shit I've been through, that I'd end up like some little debutante in a sailor suit?" We both laughed loud and hard. It didn't matter that it wasn't all that funny.

"Did you know the girl, Ely? The one who was with him. I found out she used to stay out at Harbor House."

"What was her name?"

"Patty Krix." As soon as I said the name, I saw the recognition in her eyes.

"Patty was with Neal?"

"Yeah. I guess they'd been seeing each other for a while. When I found out she'd lived at Harbor House, I thought maybe you could tell me something about her. Did you know her?"

We walked past a surf fisherman wearing hip waders, casting his line into the waves. He had white hair and a fluffy white mustache. He looked a little like Einstein.

She took a while to answer, as though she was choosing her words carefully. It seemed so out of character for this impetuous girl. I watched her face closely to see if she was telling the truth. One of the first skills learned in a life on the streets was the ability to lie without any trace whatsoever of moral conflict. Elysia was an artist.

"Yeah, I knew Patty. Not real well, but I knew of her. I saw her around."

"What kind of girl was she?"

She shrugged. "I don't know." Her face seemed to close down, and she turned away from me to stare at the sea.

The last of the sunlight was gone now. The sky inland had gone patchwork with swatches of pink and red and bronze, while the sea had already turned the blue-black color of a bruise.

We walked together for quite a while without talking, enjoying the fresh, moist air as night closed in around us. In the past, I had found it useless to try to force Elysia to talk. So I just waited, watching the stars winking their way into the darkening sky, knowing that, like any seventeen-year-old, she would eventually fill the silence.

"I can't believe she's dead," Ely said at last. "I mean, she's like the last one I would have expected."

"Why's that?"

"Patty's like, or *was* like, somebody who was always in charge. If you were going to go somewhere or do something with her, you'd always have to do it her way."

"Mmm," I said, convinced that the less I said, the more she would explain.

"I didn't like her at all when she first came to the House. She'd been there less than a week, and she had everybody doing things for her, trying to be her friend. Even James fell for it."

"Who's James?"

"He's the director at the House. You know him, don't you?"

"No, I don't think so. I know that lady, the one who's always at the front desk. Minerva's her name, I think."

"Yeah, she really runs the place. James isn't really there all that much. You don't see him around too often, but he is the one who's well known—he's in the papers and on TV and stuff, he does all the charity events and fund-raisers, and he handles the money side, and, well, he's just involved in lots of other things." She turned away and shut down again. It was too dark now to see her face, but I knew the look by heart.

"What do you mean, 'James fell for it'?"

She didn't answer for a long time. I was afraid I had pushed her too far. But then her voice started again, with a higher-pitched, childlike quality to it. It sounded like she was afraid. "Patty was one of those kinds of people who just always thought she was right about everything. And she was wild; she always needed excitement. She wasn't afraid to try anything 'cuz nothing scared her." She paused for a moment, looking down at the sand. When she spoke again, I could barely make out the words. "There are things that go on there, Seychelle, things you don't know anything about."

Before I could find out what she was talking about, a large hand appeared out of the semidarkness, grabbed my left arm just above the elbow, and jerked me back and sideways. I could tell from the little yelp that Elysia had been grabbed, too. My attacker was a big guy wearing a Florida Marlins baseball cap pulled down low on his forehead. He seemed to tower over me—he must have been at least six feet four, but it was too dark to make out any features on his face.

"We just want to talk to you. Don't scream." His voice

sounded Anglo, oddly high-pitched and gravelly, but I could barely hear him over the loud rasp of my own rapid breathing.

"Where's Garrett?"

I stared at him openmouthed, frightened, but still not quite able to comprehend what was going on.

He shook me, and I felt like a rag doll as I flopped around at the end of his arm. "Come on, where's he at?"

At first, it didn't even register what he was asking me. I tried to twist around to see what was going on with Elysia. Another guy had her by the arm. He was much shorter, but extremely wide, undoubtedly a bodybuilder, and he wore a cap pulled down low over his face. He was holding his hand over Ely's mouth.

"Hey, bitch, talk to me. We ain't gonna hurt ya." Big Guy squeezed my arm tighter, and my fingers started tingling.

"You're already hurting me."

The shorter guy holding on to Elysia laughed at that, an incongruously deep chuckle given his height, which only seemed to make the big guy madder.

"Shut up, man."

At that, Shorty took his hand from Ely's face and pointed his index finger at Big Guy. He started to say, "You—" but then Ely screamed. He swung his arm, backhanding her in the face, and the force of the blow caused her head to snap back. Again he started cursing in that weird deep voice, and clamped his hand over her mouth.

Big Guy turned back to me.

"We ain't gonna buy no bullshit disappearing act. We wanna have a little talk with him." He tightened his grip, and I winced, my eyes damp from the pain. "Where the fuck is Garrett?" He twisted my arm, nearly lifting me off the ground.

Until then, I'd felt afraid, and I'd been sucking for air as though there weren't enough oxygen in the atmosphere. But between Ely's slap and my arm nearly getting twisted off, my gut changed from Jell-O to fire.

"I don't know what you're talking about, asshole. I don't

know anybody named Garrett," I said as I dug the toes of my right foot deep into the sand.

"I don't have time for this shit."

"Ely, I think these guys have mistaken us for someone else. I think we'd better be leaving."

"You know who I'm talking about."

"I do?" I tried to look innocent as I loosened a mound of sand on top of my foot.

"Garrett. Your boyfriend. We just want to ask him a few questions."

All at once I bent forward from the waist, pulling his upper body down with me. At the same time I flipped a footful of sand right up into his face. I turned my face aside, avoiding getting any grit in my own eyes, but Big Guy let out a bellow, released my arm, and began pawing at his eyes. Straightening up, I glanced over at Ely in time to see her swing those spike-heeled sandals into the crotch of Shorty's nylon board shorts, hook them, and then yank upward with all her might. He let out a noise that sounded inhuman; more like a cat losing a fight.

We took off running as fast as we could toward the lights and crowds of A1A. Apparently we hadn't done any permanent damage, as I could soon hear labored panting a distance behind us, mixed with assorted curse words. It seemed to take us forever to get to the highway. I could hear them coming, closer now.

We ran between the rows of parked cars in the beach lot, but the cars soon ran out, and we were exposed.

"Bahia Mar," I gasped, and we took off running across the traffic, avoiding cars that cruised down the beach doing forty miles an hour. Seconds after we hit the sidewalk on the far side, I heard a horn and the screech of tires as Big Guy and Shorty crossed the street. The back of my throat burned, and I felt like I couldn't get enough air, but my bare feet kept slapping the pavement. I didn't know how Ely was keeping up with her short little legs. It probably helped being more than ten years younger than me.

As I ran, I scanned the boats in the north basin through the chain-link fence. I was looking for a classic old Chris Craft, and if I was lucky, B.J. would be working late on his new job. My eyes teared from the wind and the strands of hair that whipped across my face. I blinked and squinted and searched the line of sport-fishermen. Finally I saw the varnished hull, the tarps, and the pile of raw lumber on the afterdeck. It was very clear from the padlock hanging on the companionway door that the boat was closed up for the day.

"Shit!" I wheezed.

I could see the security guard's booth at the entrance to the Bahia Mar Hotel and Marina. He was really just a glorified parking attendant, and I didn't even know if the guy carried a gun, but surely if we threw ourselves into his little guard hut, those assholes wouldn't be able to drag us out of there. I didn't know where else to turn. I knew I couldn't keep up this pace any longer, and Ely was falling farther and farther behind me.

A vehicle pulled up on the outbound side of the guardhouse. The guard stepped out to the curb and leaned down to talk to the person in the car. Don't leave, I thought, willing the guard to stay put. I couldn't make out the whereabouts of the security man any-more, but when the car nosed out to check on the traffic, I saw that it was a black El Camino.

"B.J.!" I yelled. "Hey, B.J.! Hold up!" I leaped the center di-vider and rolled over the side and into the El Camino's truck bed. B.J.'s face jerked around in the window, looking fierce, but he arched his eyebrows and shook his head when he saw me. He obvi-ously thought it was all a big joke. I sat up in time to see Big Guy and Shorty no more than a hundred feet behind Ely, who was just crossing the grass divider. Then she jumped at the truck and crooked one leg up over the top.

I banged on the roof of the cab. "Go, go, go. Move it. Go!"

B.J. burned rubber taking off toward the north in front of the oncoming traffic, nearly getting in a wreck in the process. For the first fifty feet he drove on the wrong side of the road. Horns blared. I looked behind us and saw the broad backs and shoulders of Big Guy and Shorty. They both wore tank tops, and under the fluorescent streetlights, their enormous sculptured arms were pressed against their knees as they struggled to catch the only thing left to them: their breaths.

$\mathcal{VIII}$

B J. TURNED THE EL CAMINO INLAND AT SUNRISE BOULE-
vard, and after crossing the Intracoastal Waterway, he pulled
into the parking lot at the Galleria Mall. He stopped under
a light, far from the boxy building, and parked amid the empty rows
of painted white lines. When the engine stopped, he slowly opened
his door and climbed out of the truck. He was wearing a plain white
T-shirt tucked into navy cargo shorts. He leaned his back against the
door and rested his head on the roof staring up at the stars.

"I've never driven like that in my life."

"It showed," I said.

He lifted his head and looked at me, ready to be angry.

I grinned at him, and he started laughing out loud. Then
Elysia started laughing, too.

"You should have seen your face when you turned around and
looked through your window," I said, gasping.

He rested his arms on the top of the vehicle. "What about
you? Flopping around in the back of my truck like a boated bass?"

"Seychelle," Ely said, "did you see the look on that guy's face
when I got him with my shoes?" She rolled onto her back in the
truck bed and kicked her feet in the air, laughing so hard she got
the hiccups. And that set us all off again.

"Whooee," B.J. said finally, getting himself under control. He pressed his forehead against his bent arms for a few seconds, then looked straight at me. "What was that all about?"

I ignored his question. "I was so glad you hadn't left yet, B.J. I was looking for the Chris Craft, and when I saw she was all buttoned up, I thought you'd gone."

"Seychelle, are you ready to explain any of this to me?" he asked.

I stood up, straddled the side of the truck, and sat just behind the cab. "Okay, okay. You know, I'm not sure I understand what happened myself." At that moment, the full impact of what the two muscle men had been asking finally hit me. It sobered me up fast. "I came by the restaurant to see Elysia, and we went for a walk on the beach. And then when it got dark, these guys came up and grabbed us."

"Did they hurt you?"

"No. But this wasn't just random violence, B.J. They started asking me where Neal is."

He didn't say anything right away. "Those guys knew who you were?"

"Apparently."

He rubbed his hand across his chin. "They must have been following you. You didn't notice anything?"

I shook my head.

"Maybe they don't know about what happened on the *Top Ten*. Maybe these guys just wanted Neal for something else," he said.

"I don't think so. The big guy who had hold of me did most of the talking, and he said something about not believing in disappearing acts. They think he's alive, B.J., and they seem to think I know where he is."

W E ALL THREE CRAMMED OURSELVES INTO THE TRUCK cab with me in the middle, Elysia by the window. I tucked my shoulder down so B.J. could reach over me to shift.

"Where to?" he asked. His breath smelled like spearmint gum.

"Let's take Ely home. Harbor House."

We doubled back along Sunrise Boulevard to A1A and turned north at the beach. B.J. swung left on Bimini Lane, next to the Flamingo Motor Lodge. One block back from the ocean stood Harbor House. Once upon a time it had been a typical dumpy little beach hotel, but when they turned it into a house for runaway girls, they actually made it look better. There was an elegance to the place, with its whitewashed walls and teal trim. The windows were covered with heavy, wood Bahama shutters. The mirrored glass front door and the classy carved wood sign made the place look more like a high-tech firm than a halfway house for runaway teens.

We dropped Elysia off at the curb out front.

"God, I'm exhausted," she said, opening the truck door. "At least I don't have to work tomorrow. I'm going to sleep in till noon and then go apartment hunting."

"Some people have all the luck." I reached around and gave her a swift hug. "Are you okay?"

"Yeah, I'm always fine, you know that."

"Ely, I know you're tired, but I need to know anything more you can tell me about Patty."

She glanced over at the mirrored glass door. "Seychelle, don't ask too many questions, okay? Take it from a survivor. Know when to leave things alone."

"Hey, worrying is *my* job. I'll call you. Take care of yourself. Now"—I pointed to the house—"to bed."

"Bye," she called. She waved goodbye, barefoot, swinging her sandals, then she turned and walked into the house. I watched through the back window as B.J. pulled away from the curb. Ely practically bounced up to the door. The buzzer sounded, and she passed inside. I saw her bending over talking to the person behind the counter as the door swung closed.

I settled myself on the seat next to the door.

We drove up Sunrise, past the strip malls and the fast-food joints. Groups of men loitered outside the convenience stores drinking out of paper bags in the glare of the fluorescent lights. Young women in skintight miniskirts stood talking in groups outside a package store. In the very next block, a brilliantly lit showroom displayed dozens of exotic Jaguars, Rolls-Royces, and Maseratis. I'd grown up in South Florida, and most of the time I loved my home, but there was a squalor, a tackiness that lived right next door to the palatial homes of the rich and famous. Just down the street from the oceanfront million-dollar condos we were passing prostitutes, drug dealers, adult bookstores. The neon lights bathed the street-level ugliness with a day-bright glow and lit the overhead tangle of telephone and electrical wires. I imagined for a moment that if alien spaceships ever hovered over this part of South Florida, they might think the earth's inhabitants were a mutant form of spiders waiting to catch them in their wire webs.

"Where's your Jeep?"

B.J. startled me with his question.

"It's still down by Bahia Cabana."

"Would you rather I take you back to pick up Lightnin', or straight home?"

I thought about the mess in my cottage, and I groaned. "Damn, I'd almost forgotten."

"What do you mean?"

"Somebody broke into the cottage last night while I was having dinner with you at the Downtowner. They really trashed the place. It's still a mess. I didn't feel like cleaning up, so I slept on the boat last night."

"Did they take anything?"

"Only my rainy-day fund—about two grand."

He let out a long, low whistle. "Would you feel more comfortable sleeping on the couch at my place tonight?"

I didn't want to explain to him that I thought Neal had tossed my place, and that he might have killed that girl, and that both thoughts scared the hell out of me. I needed a good night's sleep. If Big Guy and Shorty knew who I was, then they could easily find out where I lived and come back at night. The thought of sleeping with B.J. just in the other room sounded mighty appealing.

"I don't want to put you to any kind of trouble."

"It's no problem," he said in the fake South Pacific accent he sometimes used. In a matter of seconds he could switch from *Masterpiece Theatre* to *Hawaii 5-0*.

"I guess it would be better, then. Maybe you could run me over to pick up Lightnin' in the morning?"

"Sure, my pleasure."

B.J.'S APARTMENT WAS A ONE-BEDROOM UNIT IN A MOTEL down near Dania Beach. A short section of the beach was backed with older vacation homes and run-down motels that had long been out of favor with any but the most tight-fisted tourists. Martha's Restaurant and the Intracoastal Waterway were along one side of A1A, and the aging tourist traps were on the other. The older motels were slowly being bought up a few at a time, and the developers were building high-end townhouses or, more recently, posh beach condo towers. The Sands Motel (B.J. referred to the place as the "Shiftless Sands") remained tucked back on a narrow street nestled in the shadows of the derricks building the high-rises. The bungalows were arranged around a sand and weed courtyard that harbored a motley collection of broken patio furniture and sunbleached plastic toys. Several cement sea horses were stuck to the sides of buildings, and round concrete picnic tables were arranged around an old gas grill.

B.J. jingled his keys as we crossed the dark courtyard, and a black cat streaked out from under an ixora bush. It threaded its way between B.J.'s legs, leaning against his ankle and purring loudly.

"Okay, Savai'i, I know you're hungry. You smell the moo shu pork."

"I don't believe it, B.J. You have a cat?" I looked up at him over the top of the white bags in my arms. We had stopped at

Chinese Moon for takeout. "You might end up with cat hair on your clothes." He was always disgustedly picking Abaco's black hairs off my clothes.

Balancing the aluminum screen door open with his foot, he put the key in the lock. "She adopted me. I had no choice in the matter."

"Oh, brother, even female *cats* can't resist you."

He pushed open the door and stepped into the dark room, but before he turned on the lights, I saw his teeth flash in a white grin.

I'd only been inside his apartment once before, but I remembered the decor. It was a strange combination of tacky Florida transient and refined tastes. It had been a furnished apartment when he rented it, but it was now personalized with B.J.'s eclectic collection of personal belongings. On the chipped and dented gray terrazzo floors rested a thin blue-and-white hand-tied Oriental rug. The kitchenette consisted of a single-burner propane camp stove next to the sink on what had once been the suite's minibar. A huge brown-and-white Samoan tapa cloth adorned one wall, while the remaining walls were covered with books neatly arranged in stacks of wooden orange crates. A small collection of exquisite jade and brass Buddha figurines was arranged atop one of the crates.

When he'd finished eating, B.J. washed up his plate, and I scraped the last of the shrimp fried rice out of the carton onto my fork. I refuse to eat Chinese food on a plate. It just doesn't taste the same, and besides, it gets cold. I walked to the sink, gave him my fork, and dropped the empty white box into the trash.

He hung the terry dish towel on a cabinet door handle and handed me a cup of strong black tea. He had left the front door open, and through the screen I could hear the pounding surf on the beach half a block away. The air smelled tangy. I didn't need to see it to know that the high-water mark was piled with dark seaweed, pushed ashore by the north swells.

Padding in his bare feet to the low table in the center of the room, he sat cross-legged on the floor and began to read the newspaper. A small transistor radio tuned to NPR played soft Brazilian jazz. B.J.'s hair, pulled tight against his scalp, shone in the light from the rice paper globe overhead. He looked so completely relaxed. I imagined that he would have done exactly the same things whether or not I was there. It was pretty decent of him to give me plenty of breathing room.

I looked up at the blue-and-green surfboard on a rack high on the wall. I had first met B.J. when I was still with the beach patrol. I knew quite a few surfers then. My brother Pit had been one. Several of the guys told me that B.J. was good enough to compete as a pro but that he would never do it. They said surfing was a spiritual thing to him.

Silently I mouthed the names on some of the books in the crates against the wall: Plato, Ezra Pound, Edmund Spenser, Krishnamurti, Mark Twain, Immanuel Kant. I didn't know them all, but I knew of enough of them to know that I didn't want to go up against him in a game of *Jeopardy*. There were both hardcovers and paperbacks, and most of them looked old and well thumbed.

He was still engrossed in his paper. I'd meant it when I said I didn't want to put him out. I sat down on the tropical-print futon folded up against the wall, nearly spilling my tea in the process. How could he sit so still? Granted, he was extremely limber from practicing aikido most of his life, but even so, I found his state of total relaxation unnerving sometimes. I studied the way he had his legs crossed. He had a lot less hair on his inner thighs. It was amazing that he managed to keep his back so straight. Setting my teacup down on the floor, I tried to pull my left foot up on top of my right thigh. My knee made a loud popping noise, and something along the back of my leg hurt like hell. B.J. didn't even look up. I guessed he was still giving me that breathing room. But on the other hand, it would be nice to be noticed.

Almost as though he had heard my thoughts, he lifted his head and looked at me. Our eyes locked for several seconds before he spoke. I felt as though he were seeing things in me that even I didn't know existed. As a child, I was always afraid that other people possessed the ability to read my mind—not really read, exactly, more like listen in on the constant banter in my brain. The idea terrified me. Then they would really know what silly things I thought about, and I wouldn't be able to fool the world anymore.

For the first time, I noticed there were tiny flecks of gold in B.J.'s brown eyes, and yet I felt I had always known that.

"Have you read today's paper?" He nodded at the pages spread out before him.

I forced my eyes down to the print. "No." I could make out the name *Top Ten* in the headline.

"They don't seem to hold out much hope for Neal." He turned back to the front page. "Listen to this. 'The *Top Ten*'s hired skipper, Neal Garrett, was aboard when the vessel left harbor Thursday morning, March eighteenth. According to police reports, he was not aboard at the time the vessel was found adrift. In addition, there were large quantities of blood on deck that could not have come from Krix, the female victim. The officer in charge of the case, Detective Victor Collazo, surmised that a third party was aboard the *Top Ten* and may have killed both members of her crew. Police are searching offshore for any sign of Garrett. They did indicate that chances of his surviving decrease the longer he remains missing.' "

B.J. stood up and carried the paper over to the futon. He sat down next to me and spread the newsprint across both our laps.

"And look at this," he said. " 'Although he would not reveal any possible motives, Collazo did say the police have several suspects under investigation.' " B.J. grinned. "I guess they're talking about you, huh?"

I leaned back against the flowered futon and closed my eyes. I had to shut some of it out. Too many things were happening at once. Collazo was probably really pissed and even more suspicious since I hadn't gone to give my statement that day.

The air seemed to swirl with the sweet coconut smell of B.J.'s skin, and I felt the feathery tickle where the hairs on his legs brushed against my thighs. Part of me was wondering what it would feel like to reach out and touch those legs, and then I felt ashamed for think-

ing about sex when he was telling me that Neal, the last man I had
slept with, was possibly dead.

Neal dead? I refused to believe it, but my only proof was the
fact that he had robbed me of my life's savings and then rather vi-
ciously trashed my home. If my version of what happened these
past couple of days was true, it also looked like he was a killer as
well as a thief. What had happened out there? The girl had the gun.
Had he killed her in self-defense?

"There wasn't that much blood on the deck . . . I saw it. I
could smell the blood in the wheelhouse. I never knew what blood
smelled like before."

"Seychelle, I think you need some rest."

"But see, even if it was his blood, he could still be alive, and I
don't know which is worse, thinking that he's dead, or believing
that this guy, this guy I'd really loved . . . could do that to that girl."
I shivered suddenly and saw the hairs on my forearms lifting off the
flesh. "Am I that bad a judge of character, B.J., that I was in love
with a murderer?" I rubbed my hands hard across the skin on my
forearms. "He's out there, B.J., I know he is. He probably doesn't
know where to turn. . . . Maybe, if guys like those creeps Ely and I
met tonight are after him, he wants to stay 'dead,' to disappear. You
know, living with Neal had become impossible. God knows, there
were a few times I swore I'd like to kill him myself. Don't tell Collazo that. But even after we'd split up, after it had gotten real ugly
between us, I'd always felt he would be there for me if I needed
him." B.J.'s eyes seemed to draw the words out of me. No matter
how much I wanted to stop talking and forget, each time I looked
at B.J., I began again. "It's like he's two people, B.J. On one hand,
he's this gentle, wonderful man who's funny and fun and a great
sailor, but sometimes there is this jet of anger that spurts out of him
like one of those cheap fireworks. It scared me, but I never stopped
caring for him. You can't just turn that off. It was enough, though,
to make me know I had to leave him. That was the hardest thing.
I'd hear all the gossip about him and that girl down at the Downtowner. I mean, I was the one who pushed him away, the one who

wanted it over, so why did it hurt so damn much to think of him with somebody else?" I asked the question of the walls, afraid to look at B.J., afraid of what was welling up inside. "Now, no matter which way this turns out, I'm afraid I've lost him, and living in a world without him in it would hurt even more."

I tried rolling my eyes up, looking at the ceiling so the tears wouldn't spill out and give me away, but I had to blink finally and my eyes overflowed.

"Seychelle, you're tired, you—"

"No, no, it's not that, it's just . . ." Just what? I didn't even know myself, only that I was suddenly overcome with such a profound sadness, I couldn't control my sobs. B.J. wrapped his arms around me, but all I was aware of for what seemed like hours was the wet T-shirt fabric pressing against my face and the gut-wrenching sobs that racked my body. I was snorting and gulping and hiccuping, trying to get air as I released this huge black ball of emotion that I didn't even know had been inside me.

Finally I peeled my face off B.J.'s soaked shirt and took a couple of swipes at my eyes. I had felt so warm leaning against his body; as long as I'd known him, he had radiated heat as though he glowed with a perpetual sunburn.

"It's a good thing I don't wear any makeup or I would have made a worse mess of that shirt." I pushed the fabric around a little on his chest. I suddenly felt intensely aware of a familiar achy squeeze between my legs.

He pushed some stray hairs back from my face and just looked at me without saying a word. No wonder every woman goes nuts over this guy, I thought. And I'd always been so convinced I'd never be one of them.

"I guess I've looked better, huh?"

He smiled. "Yeah."

Oh, thanks, I thought. That's what I get for being friends, buddies with the guy. Instead of romance, I get honesty. What truly aroused woman wants that?

Then with his fingers he lightly traced the features on my

face, his feathery touch gliding over my nose, eyebrows, cheeks, and lips. Our eyes remained locked, the corners of his eyes crinkled in a playful smile. When his touch reached my neck and slid down, then back up to my hairline, I couldn't suppress the shudder.

And then he kissed me. It was no just-between-buddies kiss on the cheek. It was one of those you-don't-even-remember-what-planet-you're-on kisses.

Suddenly, a high-pitched yowl filled my ears and claws dug into the back of my head and neck. I cried out and swatted with my right arm at the thing that was attacking me. My hand struck soft fur, and then claws raked the back of my hand.

"Savai'i," B.J. said softly, "stop that, you silly cat." He stood and lifted the animal off my back. She immediately started purring in his arms.

I cradled my right hand. Three long lines oozed red. B.J. stroked the top of the cat's head.

"*Silly* cat? That's it? Aren't you even going to throw her out of the house or anything?" I held out my hand for him to see. "She attacked me, B.J."

He laughed softly. "You can't blame a cat for being a cat. We'd better get some antibiotic cream on that."

"But she . . ." I knew I was being unreasonable, but it made me mad as hell that he was stroking the cat's head instead of mine.

B.J. dropped Savai'i to the ground outside the front door, closed and latched the screen door, and turned to me. "Relax, Seychelle, she's just a cat. You're tired." He disappeared into the bathroom, and I could hear him rummaging around in the medicine cabinet. He came out a few moments later with a small white tube.

I knew I was blowing this out of proportion, but a part of me had been afraid. He rubbed the cream into the back of my hand. I knew he was smiling, probably even laughing at me, but I refused to meet his eyes.

He went into the back bedroom and came out with a pile of linens. "Do you want some help pulling out the futon?" he asked.

I shook my head.

"Good night." He disappeared into his bedroom and closed the door. I heard him moving around in there, then he went into the bathroom, and I could hear him brushing his teeth, humming to himself.

I didn't pull out the futon and make up the bed until it had grown quiet back there. I turned out the light and undressed, wearing only panties as I slipped between the cool sheets. I felt hot and lifted my hair so my neck could press against the smooth pillow. The curtainless window faced north into the little courtyard. Between two Australian pines, I could see a three-quarter moon already angling toward the western sky. I was exhausted, but I felt I'd never fall asleep. Every nerve in my body felt like it had OD'd on No-Doz. The surf sounds pounded and hissed outside the screen door, and I wondered for a while if that was what it sounded like to an unborn child floating in her mother's womb. *Boom. Sshh. Boom. Sshh.*

I listened, trying to hear something, any kind of sound, from B.J.'s room. I fell asleep, finally, still listening.

IX

WHEN I OPENED MY EYES, THE BEDROOM DOOR WAS open and the apartment felt empty. From the angle of the sunlight, I judged I'd slept past eight. I got up and pulled on my clothes. Then I realized the surfboard was missing. I wandered out to look for B.J.

I expected the sunlight to be bright, and I was prepared to squint, but the sight of the Sands Motel in daylight was not something I could have prepared for. Apparently, since my last visit, the owner had decided to paint the place. It looked like he'd chosen his color scheme from a canvas in a Little Haiti art gallery. The walls were bright pink, the eaves and the plaster sea horses orange, and the balcony banisters around the sundeck turquoise. The rest of the concrete, the picnic tables, and the piles of coral rock around the empty planters had been left natural gray, mottled with black mildew spots.

The breeze was light out of the east and the sky nearly cloudless. The walk from the Shiftless Sands to the beach was less than a block, past the other motel and efficiency apartment rentals with names like the Oceanside Hideaway and California Dream Inn. None of them was nearly as tacky as the Sands, and their parking lots were filled with traveling cars. The narrow asphalt lane dead-ended at the beach, and a vacant lot filled with tangled sea grape trees was echoing with the competing songs of mockingbirds, green parrots, and finches.

When I reached the sand, it was easy to pick out B.J. in the handful of surfers sitting on their boards, floating over the smaller swells, waiting for the perfect wave. His sleek but muscled brown body and black hair stood out among the slight and slender blond boys. He was the only one without a rash guard or wet suit, even in the March water that most Floridians found quite chilly. The other surfers seemed to watch him, taking their cues from him. When he started to paddle, selecting a certain wave, the others followed, trusting his judgment, but keeping out of his way.

I walked down to the water's edge, arriving just as B.J. kicked out, abandoning his wave to the sharp shore break, and he waved at me. I nodded in return, then turned south, heading toward the Dania pier. I hadn't exercised in days, and my leg muscles felt tight and resistant when I started to jog. I sucked the sea air deep into my lungs and tried to flush out all the accumulated stress and craziness of the last couple of days.

I needed some time to think. Especially about B.J. Something about the status of our friendship had changed last night. I wasn't sure I liked the change, but it was irrevocable.

He was fresh out of the shower and the surfboard was back in its rack when I returned to the apartment.

"Would you like some tea, something to eat?"

I shook my head.

"Feel free to shower if you want."

"No, I've got to get back and clean up my place. I'll shower at home. I've got a job at eleven."

"I can take you right now if you want."

I didn't understand why, but I felt like being as uncooperative and disagreeable as I could.

"I think that would be best."

We didn't talk in his truck at all. I felt him looking at me several times. I was afraid to return his glances, afraid he would see something in my eyes to let him know that I was just like all those other girls who lusted after him. I didn't want to join the ranks of B.J.'s ex-girlfriends. What had made me think that I could have something different with him? It was about a fifteen-minute drive to Bahia Cabana, where I had left Lightnin', but in that silence it seemed much longer.

We pulled up alongside my Jeep. "Oh great." There was a ticket tucked under the windshield wiper.

"Things could be worse," B.J. said.

"Yeah, right." I climbed out of the El Camino and leaned back in through the open passenger window. Bouncing the palm of my hand against the side of the El Camino's window frame, I said, "Thanks, man," and turned away. From the corner of my eye, I watched the truck pull out onto A1A.

Me and B.J.? I had to put it out of my mind. There was no way that could ever work out.

ON MY WAY HOME, I STOPPED OFF AT MY FAVORITE BREAKFAST spot, a drive-through gourmet coffee place, and ordered an onion bagel and a big café con leche. I drove to a little park overlooking the river and ate my breakfast in the Jeep. It was a hot morning for March, and the coffee brought a mist of sweat to my upper lip. The usual Saturday morning parade of pleasure boats putt-putted down the river carrying throngs of white, lotion-smeared bodies from the western edges of the county. Many folks who lived out in the suburbs spent their whole lives inside their air-conditioned homes on treeless landfill lots. There were places out there where Red used to take us back when we were kids, places where we could launch our old Sears aluminum skiff along the side of the road and pole our way through the sawgrass, fishing for bass. Those places don't exist anymore, the land's changed so much. Bulldozers and truckloads of fill have made driveways where folks now park their boats so they can drive fifteen miles east on weekends and launch their boats at one of the ramps along the river.

Back at the cottage, Abaco greeted me like I had been gone weeks. She had a doghouse on the grounds of the Larsen place, but usually I let her inside for the night. After a thorough belly rub, I opened the door to the mess, determined not to be discouraged. Nothing had changed. I scooped up some dry dog food from the torn bag on the floor, put it in Abaco's dish outside, and filled her water bowl.

I decided I'd work first, shower later. Taking several big lawn-size garbage bags and spreading them around the cottage, I told myself to throw away everything I could live without, to clean out the debris that was cluttering up my life.

I got my easel set back up and found my paints, which were intact. I found my telephone answering machine under a pile of books and papers and plugged it back in. I cursed myself for not having thought of it sooner. It was possible I'd lost a job or two because a client had been unable to reach me. I also dug my handheld VHF out of the debris and turned it on to monitor channel sixteen. With that payment to Maddy, I'd pretty well cleaned out my checking account, Neal had cleaned out my reserves, and basically, I was broke. I wondered how Jeannie was making out with the salvage claim. I picked up the telephone receiver and dialed her number.

"I tried to call you last night, but there was no answer right up to midnight," she said.

I brought her up to date on the break-in, Burns, the guys on the beach, and Maddy's unforgiving stance.

"Jeannie, only one person on earth knew where I kept that money. I think he tried to make it look like a break-in and maybe got a little carried away, but I'm pretty sure Neal was the one who made this mess. It looks like he's in trouble, and I'd like to think he'd help me out if things were reversed."

"You said those muscleheads on the beach thought he was alive, too."

"Yeah, and they seemed to think Neal would contact me."

"These guys are playing a rough game. I just wish we knew what it was. No wonder you're not answering your phone."

"Actually, I spent last night on B.J.'s couch," I said. I felt like I needed to talk to somebody about it. "I think I even messed up my friendship with him."

"Why do you say that?"

"I kissed him."

"So?"

"Well, he's B.J.! And this wasn't just a hello-goodbye kiss. I mean, Jeannie, he works for me."

She didn't say anything.

"Jeannie, B.J. and I have always just been friends. Buddies. I don't know what the hell I was thinking."

"Maybe you were just thinking about being lonely. How long has it been since you and Neal split up? Six months?"

"Closer to seven." I didn't let on that I knew the exact number of weeks, down to the day, since the last time I'd made love to a man. "I'm just not ready for another relationship, Jeannie. I like living alone. And B.J.—has he ever lasted more than a month or two with one woman? I don't have any desire to join the ever-growing club of B.J.'s old girlfriends."

Jeannie chuckled. "The lady doth protest too much. I don't think you know what you want. And as for B.J., my guess is that he hasn't met the right woman. Well, I'm afraid I don't have any better news for you. I haven't been able to find out who owns the *Top Ten*. I traced it as far as an offshore corporation in the Cayman Islands, but I can't find out anything from those goddamned island bankers. That attorney you said visited you, though, what was his name again?"

"Hamilton Burns. A real blue-blood type."

"Let me see what I can find out through him, and I'll see if I can get them to sign a salvage form. Then we'll present them with *our* settlement offer."

"I need the money, Jeannie. As soon as possible."

"Don't worry about my end. You just watch your back, girl."

"There's one more slight little problem, Jeannie."

"I get worried when you talk about slight problems."

"Well, it's just this cop, Collazo. I did say I would go give a statement yesterday, but with everything that happened, I didn't have time."

"So get your butt over there, girl."

"I've got a job this morning, I can't. And it's a little more complicated. He said I should have my attorney present. He thinks I killed Neal and Patty."

"What?"

"I know, it's crazy, right?"

Jeannie didn't say anything at first. I could almost hear her thinking. "Seychelle, listen to me. Whatever you do, don't talk to the cops without me. As soon as you're finished with that job, we'll go over there together. Do you hear me?"

We said our goodbyes, and I got back to work. Soon the front room started to look habitable again. But the bedroom was another story. I didn't own enough clothes as it was, so I couldn't just throw all that stuff out. I sorted and folded and hung things back up in the closet. When I went to hang up my one and only long formal-type dress, I noticed something was missing. Normally, when I slid that dress—actually a bridesmaid gown I'd had to wear to the wedding of a fellow lifeguard—into the closet, I usually had to make sure I didn't snag its lace on the valve on top of my scuba gear. But there was no tank in the closet, nor in the bedroom anywhere. I went out into the front room and looked all around again, thinking maybe I had somehow overlooked the gear out there. Nothing.

I was standing in the middle of the room in that sort of dreamy far-off space of deep contemplation when the phone rang. The noise startled me back to the here and now. I had to reach across three fat black trash bags in the kitchen to pick up the phone.

I was beginning to think that maybe everybody should get their home ransacked periodically—it forced you to do a really good spring cleaning.

"Hello."

"Miss Sullivan. Detective Collazo. I've been trying to get in touch with you."

This guy sure was persistent. "Look, Detective, I'll go in and make a statement as soon as I have the time."

"Today. You will make the time."

"I'm getting ready to do a job this morning, and—"

"But that is not the main reason I called this morning."

"Okay. So?"

He paused. "You knew a young woman by the name of Elysia Daggett."

I drew in my breath sharply and felt a prickly sensation creep up my spine. He had used the past tense. No.

"Yes," I said. "I know her."

"This morning, at approximately six-thirty A.M. . . ." I could hear the sound of paper rustling as he flipped through the pages of his notebook. When he began again, it was clear he was reading directly from his notes. "A Fort Lauderdale resident, riverfront home, raised an anchor used to prevent his boat from damaging itself against the dock. Lodged in the prongs of a—" I heard the rustling of paper as he turned a page in his notebook. "—Danforth-type anchor was the upper right arm of a nude body. Female. Body was partially wrapped in a blanket. Rope binding the ankles attached to a broken piece of cinder block." He coughed, and I could hear the sound of him snapping the notebook closed. "We won't know the exact cause of death until we get the M.E.'s report."

No, no, no. I just kept chanting the same word over and over in my head. I was hearing what he was saying, but it wasn't registering in my mind. The words were searing straight through to my guts.

"Miss Sullivan, are you still there?"

"Yes." No, no, no.

"We ran the prints and made the ID. She had a record. The

brick tied to her ankles was not heavy enough to prevent the body from moving in the current. We assume it was dumped somewhere upriver and the outgoing tide carried it down until she snagged on this anchor. We checked with her last known residence, a facility called Harbor House, and they gave us the name of her employer. I am here at the Bahia Cabana at this moment, and the manager tells us she left work with you yesterday."

I couldn't speak. My hands were shaking so, I could feel the phone vibrating against the side of my head.

"Miss Sullivan."

She was so beautiful. The little sailor suit. The white heels that clicked so authoritatively on the tile floors. I could see her laughing, laughing at being alive, her auburn curls splayed out in the back of B.J.'s El Camino, kicking her bare feet in the air. Stop shaking, Seychelle. This isn't so. It can't be. Oh, child, Ely. No.

"At Harbor House, they say she never returned last night. You were the last one seen with her, Miss Sullivan."

"No." The word finally seemed to explode out of my mouth.

"Start with when you left the restaurant."

"No. I wasn't the last one to see her." Finally, something I could focus on. "We dropped her off at Harbor House last night. We waited until she went inside. She got home. I saw her go inside." I was gulping air. My lungs couldn't seem to process the oxygen, and my chest hurt. "It must be someone else. It can't be Elysia." Maybe if I kept talking, didn't give him a chance to say any more, it would all turn out to be a big mistake.

"The body has been identified." There was more paper crinkling. "A James Long, executive director of Harbor House. Said he'd known Miss Daggett more than two years."

"There has got to be a mistake," I said. Elysia had mentioned that name just last night. What had she said?

"No mistake. At this point we are unable to determine if it was an accidental overdose or intentional. We haven't ruled out suicide, but due to the marks on the body, it appears unlikely at this point. And I doubt very much she tied the brick to her own ankles."

"Overdose? Ely wasn't an addict, Detective. Not anymore."

"Whoever dumped her probably assumed it would be a long time before anyone even missed her."

"She's not like that."

"You did see her last night. You left her work with her."

"Yes. And the last time I saw Elysia, B.J. and I dropped her off in front of Harbor House and watched her walk in the door. Somebody buzzed her in around, oh, I don't know, eight o'clock last night. I *know* she made it home last night."

"You are coming in to make a statement today about the Krix case."

I stared at the phone, my stomach suddenly nauseated, the remains of my morning bagel threatening to revisit.

"Miss Sullivan?"

"Yes." My voice sounded to me like that of a ten-year-old.

"You are coming to the station today."

"Yes, okay."

"We'll speak more about the Daggett girl then. And Miss Sullivan . . ."

"Yes?"

"The Coast Guard has suspended the search for Neal Garrett's body. It has been over forty-eight hours."

I didn't say anything at first. The silence dragged on, broken only by the occasion pops and crackles from the phone line. "What do you want from me, Collazo?"

"I want to know what really happened out there." He paused expectantly, but I just let the silence drag on. "And perhaps you will be able to explain something to me: Why are so many people connected to you turning up dead?" He hung up the phone.

I slowly settled the receiver back in its cradle.

It didn't feel real. Surely I could get in Lightnin' and drive over to Harbor House and she would be there, laughing, telling me that it was all a goofy mistake. Her curls would be bouncing, her eyes sparkling.

In the distance, the *Jungle Queen*, a popular tourist cruise boat, tooted her horn for one of the bridges. I stared out the window at the estate across the river. The main house was shuttered and blind-looking. Closed up against the ravages of weather and crime and time. I wanted to close my own shutters, block out the world. I shut my eyes, and fat tears dropped to my cheeks. It was real, wasn't it? And it seemed Collazo had finally asked me a real question. This time, I wanted to know the answer, too.

X

GALEN HIGHTOWER BOUGHT THE *RUBY YACHT* SIX YEARS ago when the seventy-five-year-old ketch lay abandoned and half sunk in an estuary in Rhode Island. A podiatrist, Hightower had come up with the idea for the Happy Feet franchises. He was hoping his name would push Dr. Scholl's off the map, and he was making more money than a person that tacky had a right to make. Granted, he didn't pay much for the seventy-two-foot steel hulk when he bought her, but he had sunk over half a million into the boat since. He thought she was gorgeous, and there was some dubious connection to Errol Flynn and a few other 1920s film stars that he was using to make his investment in "historical preservation" tax deductible. He talked on and on about the history of the boat, and I had a tendency to tune him out because there was no avoiding the fact that, historical or not, the boat was just plain ugly. Squat and tubby with a ridiculously high wheelhouse and short, stubby masts, she didn't even look like a sailboat. The interior boasted two claw-footed bathtubs and several carved teak cherubs, and Hightower had added garish orange-red velvet upholstery. The whole thing was a case of too much money and far too little taste colliding on the waterfront.

I had agreed to tow the *Ruby Yacht* up to River Bend Boatyard for Hightower's annual haul-out at eleven that morning. The boat had a dangerously small rudder, and the first time he had tried to take her upriver himself, the incoming tide had carried him right into the Andrews Avenue Bridge; he lay there listening to his mast and rigging scrape and grind against the steel bridge for ten minutes before the irritated bridge keeper finally opened the span.

I pulled myself together by showering and dressing in clean blue jeans, a T-shirt, and sockless deck shoes. I didn't have time to wash my hair, so I just tucked it inside a black baseball cap.

The ride down the river seemed different; the colors of the broad lawns, empty swimming pools, and barrel-tiled roofs were less vibrant, less alive, but I knew that what had really changed was me. I piloted the *Gorda* through the bridges and the turns, past the buoys and the traffic of the waterway, but I saw little of it. The world had become a dull and empty place, and I felt a certain numbness inside. Keeping busy might keep the tears at bay, but it didn't fill the hollowness in my heart.

I could not believe that Elysia had intentionally used drugs. Someone had done this to her. Someone had decided that she needed to die. I didn't understand how or why anyone could have taken the life of such an innocent kid. She deserved so much more. She had worked so hard to pull herself together, for this? Collazo had said her death was either suicide, accidental overdose, or homicide. And he thought somebody had either killed her or tried to hide the fact that she'd killed herself. Me? Surely he didn't really suspect me on this one, too. He was just fishing, but he always seemed to be headed in the wrong direction. He believed them over at the Harbor House, and he evidently thought I was the one who was covering up. I owed it to Elysia to find out what really happened.

The *Ruby Yacht* was normally tied up near the end of Pier C, and when I saw the T-pier open, I pulled alongside and tied up *Gorda* at a couple of minutes after eleven. I was surprised that

Galen Hightower wasn't out pacing the deck looking for me. He was usually so tense whenever his boat had to leave the dock, and he panicked at the slightest deviation from routine. I walked down to *Ruby Yacht*'s slip, and there, tied to the aft quarter of the steel ketch, was Perry Greene's twenty-eight-foot open towboat, *Little Bitt*. I couldn't miss Perry's white-blond hair in the cockpit of the big yacht. He was handing a clipboard down the companionway, no doubt with a towing contract on it.

"Hey, Perry, where's Hightower? What's going on?"

Perry looked up and squinted through the smoke coming from the butt hanging between his thin lips. When he recognized me, he plucked the cigarette from his mouth and walked over to my side of the cockpit. He was wearing his trademark hole-ridden and paint-stained cutoff jeans and a too-tight faded Florida Marlins T-shirt.

"Hey, baby," he said.

He was trying to irritate me, I knew. I was determined to remain professional, although I couldn't repress a shudder. "What are you doing here, Perry?"

Dr. Hightower climbed out of the companionway at that point, glancing at his watch. He stood several inches taller than Perry. "You finally decided to get here, eh, Sullivan?"

"What's going on here, Dr. Hightower? What's he doing here?" I pointed toward Perry as I spoke. Perry leaned back out of the doctor's peripheral vision and puckered up, making like he was kissing me as Hightower spoke.

"I tried to contact you all day yesterday, Seychelle, but no one answered your telephone. I sent you e-mails, but you never replied. I was afraid you would be late again, as usual, and this time I took precautions against such a problem."

"Late? You've never said anything about having a problem with my being late. I tied up *Gorda* here at two minutes after eleven. The tide won't shift until twelve-thirty. We've still got plenty of time."

"I'm dealing with Mr. Greene now, Seychelle. I found his Web page when I was searching for your e-mail address, and it was very impressive."

"Perry has a Web page?"

"You better believe it, baby," Perry said. "That's the way to go these days. You know, Seychelle, you can find *anything* your little heart desires on the Internet."

"And when you're looking, I'm sure that *desire* and *little* are the key words, Perry."

"That's enough, boys and girls. I've signed a contract with Mr. Greene. End of story." He turned his back to me and busied himself at the helm in the wheelhouse.

I spread my hands wide. "Just like that? You've hired this redneck pervert and I'm fired?"

Hightower reached down and turned the key. The old boat's diesel rumbled to life. He walked out and around the deckhouse and jumped to the dock. He looked like an idiot in his pale blue polyester slacks, white shirt with epaulettes, brand-new Top-Siders, and Greek fisherman's cap.

"Miss Sullivan," he said, raising himself up to his full six feet and trying to look down at me, "I made the effort to contact you after I spoke to your brother."

"What do you mean, after you spoke to my brother?"

"I happened to see your brother at Gulf Stream yesterday."

"Oh, great. My brother was at the track?"

He nodded. "We got into a casual conversation, and when I mentioned that you were going to be towing the *Ruby Yacht* today, he told me that you had been having financial difficulties. You hadn't been meeting your responsibilities, he said, and I would be well advised to find myself another towing company. Well, I've done that, Miss Sullivan."

"What? Maddy said what?" I couldn't believe what I was hearing. I blocked the finger pier, and Hightower couldn't get past me to untie his bowlines.

"Move aside, Seychelle. This is business. If you can't play with the big boys, then get out of the business."

He started to brush me aside.

"Perry is one of the big boys? He's nothing but a slimy—"

I was suddenly grabbed from behind. Perry had jumped off the bow, and he took me by the forearms and marched me off the finger pier. I looked down at the hands that held my arms. The thick, callused fingers were topped by half crescents of black grease.

"Now, be a good girl and go on home, honey pie." He swatted me on the behind and cackled. "Perry's in charge now."

Collazo suspected I was capable of murder, and at that moment I realized I could kill. If I'd had any kind of weapon at hand, anything to wipe that goddam smirk off Perry's face, I would have been seriously tempted to use it.

"This isn't over, Perry." I looked over his shoulder at Galen Hightower, standing with his hands on his hips, watching us with a look of disgust, as though we were a lower order of mammal. "Dr. Hightower, I would say what you've got here"—I jerked my head toward Perry—"is exactly what you deserve."

I threw off the lines before I started the engine. The old cat purred to life when I turned the key, and I jockeyed her around in her own length, hotdogging it just a little to show Hightower that he had given up the better captain.

As I headed back up the Intracoastal, just off the Fort Lauderdale Yacht Club, Nestor Frias pulled up alongside in the thirty-eight-foot Bertram sportfisherman *My Way*. Aside from casual hellos at the Downtowner, I hadn't seen Nestor very much since Neal and I had gone our separate ways. He ran the charter sportfisherman out of Pier 66, and he was looking to break into a job as captain of one of the big luxury yachts like the *Top Ten*. He was always hanging around Neal hoping for news of some big job.

He waved me out of the wheelhouse. I throttled back and stepped out to the side decks.

He shouted down at me from his flybridge. "Hey, Seychelle. Sorry about Neal."

I closed my eyes for a few seconds and nodded. "Thanks, Nestor."

"A bunch of us are going to have a little service at dawn tomorrow, just outside the inlet. You know."

"He's missing, Nestor. Nobody knows what happened to him at this point."

"It's been forty-eight hours, Seychelle. There'd be no reason for him to just disappear." I thought of Big Guy and Shorty on the beach and what happened to Ely. He could have very good reasons, and I was quickly learning that I didn't know who to trust.

"Neal's never been very reasonable, you know," I said.

"I just thought maybe you would like to be there."

For the first time I found myself thinking about what people would see in my actions. If I didn't show, would I look guilty? In my business, reputation was everything. "Yeah, okay, I guess I would."

He waved a hand in the air and pulled away from *Gorda*.

I waved back. "Thanks, Nestor."

On the aft deck of his boat a couple sat together in the fighting chair, an older man with graying hair and a young, firm blonde in a thong bikini on his lap. She was probably five foot two and a size three. And definitely not his wife.

"OUTTA THE BLUE, OUTTA THE BLUE, THIS IS THE *GORDA*." When he didn't answer, I hung the microphone back on the side of the VHF and pushed the throttle forward to prevent the boat from drifting onto the sandbar at the mouth of the river. Just when I was about to give up, figuring that either Mike didn't have his radio on or else he wasn't monitoring channel sixteen, I finally got an answer.

"*Gorda, Gorda,* this is *Outta the Blue.* You want to switch to channel zero nine?"

"Roger that, zero nine."

Mike Beesting was a former Fort Lauderdale cop who had quit the force four or five years before and now lived aboard and ran sunset charter cruises on his Irwin 54, *Outta the Blue*. I wasn't sure of all the details, but I knew that back when he was on the force, he had heard a call for help and walked into a situation in progress where some disgruntled city maintenance worker had decided to use a shotgun to pay back his boss and coworkers for all his perceived ills. After it was over, two people were dead and Mike's leg had to be amputated at the knee. He was feted as a hero for taking down the guy, but when they offered him a desk job, he said no thanks and walked away from the department for good.

Mike knew nothing about boats at first, and especially about diesel mechanics, but he always attempted to work on his own engine. More often than not, he screwed things up and it ended up costing him more than if he had just called a mechanic in the first place. However, his settlement with the city had been quite generous, allowing him to buy his sailboat outright and still have enough to feed his daily need for generous amounts of Pusser's Rum. The net result was I'd towed him home more than a couple of times when his engine quit with guests aboard.

I punched the numbers onto the keypad of the VHF radio and changed channels. Mike was already there, and I just caught the tail end of his sentence.

". . . thinking about you as I've been watching the TV. How are you holding up?"

"I'm managing, but I'll be honest, things aren't good. I need your help with something, over."

"Sey, you know we are on an open channel here, over."

"Roger that. A young girl, a friend of mine, drowned in the river last night. I'm really feeling lousy about it. Is it okay if I come over a little later? I sure could use a friend like you."

"Say no more. I have a charter at four-thirty, but I'll be here with shoulders to cry on until then, over."

"Thanks, Mike. I'll be seeing you. This is *Gorda* clear and going back to sixteen."

Whether or not Mike understood what I was really asking of him remained to be seen.

I CURSED MY BROTHER, ALL THE WAY BACK UP THE RIVER. SO he was back at the track again. That explained a lot. Not that I hadn't expected as much. Maddy was a compulsive gambler, and Jane had finally got him to agree to join Gamblers Anonymous a couple of years ago. They had started to work off all those credit card balances, and I thought he had overcome this handicap, so to speak. Obviously not. So Maddy needed money immediately, and he knew where to get it. There had been offers for *Gorda* in the past, and Maddy knew several people who would be happy to buy her if the price was right. I was tempted to drive right down to his place to have it out with him. How dare he sabotage my business to make sure that I wouldn't be able to make my payments? Typical of my brother. He was going to get his way no matter what.

As I was ranting and raving out loud in the wheelhouse, I suddenly saw in my mind the image of Ely walking across the dining room at the Bahia Cabana, her green eyes flashing with recognition and joy. Things had finally been going right for her. Last night she'd told us she planned to go apartment hunting in the morning. Whoever had "dumped her," as Collazo called it, was wrong. Somebody did miss her. Maddy would have to wait.

I HAD DRIVEN BY THE FORT LAUDERDALE POLICE STATION hundreds, probably thousands of times, but I'd never been inside. I parked in a visitor's spot and fed a handful of quarters and nickels into the meter: not a good spot to let your meter expire. At the pay phone in the parking lot, I dialed Jeannie's number. She lived only a few blocks away, and I figured I'd go back, sit in the Jeep, and wait until she arrived so we could go in together. The phone continued to ring until finally her answering machine picked up.

"Great," I said aloud as I replaced the receiver. I wasn't willing to sit around waiting for Jeannie to get home. She would be furious with me, but I needed to talk to Collazo about this now.

Beyond the door, a receptionist sat inside a tinted glass booth and pointed to a telephone on the counter as I approached. I picked up the handset as she picked up hers. I told her I was there to make a statement about the murder of the Krix girl. She told me to have a seat, someone would be with me shortly.

Two young women wearing miniskirts and tube tops sat at the end of the row of red plastic chairs. I nodded to them, but they ignored me. They sat slack-jawed, bored, staring into space. They looked like extras for some Hollywood version of life on the streets. The smaller of the two, a Hispanic girl with black hair teased high on her head, walked over to the gumball machine and put a dime inside. She opened the little metal door.

"Aw, shit. I hate green ones." She turned to her friend. "You want it?"

The other girl, a blonde with a serious case of crusty acne and extremely red, bloodshot eyes, took the gum and popped it into her mouth.

On her second try, the Hispanic girl got a red one, and for the next few minutes they sat there blowing little pink bubbles. In spite of the makeup and the clothes, I doubted either girl was over sixteen.

I thought about how easy it was to dislike girls like them, to turn away from them and not see them, and yet how similar they were to Ely in many ways. She could have been them at the same age.

"Do you girls go to school?" I asked.

"Nah," said the blonde. "I quit when I had my baby. They acted all hinky 'bout it. Dumb-ass teachers. I didn't need that shit."

If one of them vanished tomorrow, would she be missed?

The other girl blew a huge bubble that popped all over her face. They both burst into giggles.

A woman came through the glass door at the far end of the lobby. "Seychelle Sullivan."

"Here." I got up and followed her through the door and into an office off the hallway just beyond. She was very friendly and efficient, and I was beginning to think better of the Lauderdale cops. She fired questions at me, typing the answers on her keyboard nearly as fast as I spoke them. We got the preliminary stuff out of the way first. Name, address, birth date.

"You've got a birthday coming soon, then," she said.

"Yeah. The big three-oh."

She smiled. "It's not so bad."

That was what everybody always said to me, but I didn't believe them.

"Okay, just tell me, slowly, exactly what happened that day." I had repeated the story so many times that the telling went quickly. I didn't have to pause or search for words to describe the horror, as I had the first time. Just as we were finishing up, the phone rang on the woman's desk.

"That was Detective Collazo," she said after hanging up. "He wants to speak to you. I'll show you the way."

She led me upstairs to the homicide squad room. Collazo was the only one there, sitting at one of the desks back in the corner of the large room. The air-conditioning must have been set as cool as it would go. My hands felt icy, but I could see the sweat rings under the sleeves of Collazo's neatly pressed white shirt.

He looked up from the papers on his desk, nodded to me, and pointed to the chair opposite his desk. "Miss Sullivan, I wanted to talk to you about Elysia Daggett."

"Good, because I want to talk to you about her, too. What happened?"

"Miss Sullivan. Start with your version of what happened last night."

I told him the story then about my meeting Elysia at her work, walking on the beach, the two guys who jumped us, and the strange questions they were asking. He took notes and asked me to go over my descriptions of the two men several times. I once thought I was a fairly observant person, but I soon realized I wasn't able to give lots of details, just more of an overall impression. It was what they were asking that had attracted my attention.

"You see, Detective, they didn't ask me if I knew anything about if or how Neal got off the boat. They just assumed he was still alive, and that I somehow knew where he was."

Collazo narrowed his eyes and stared at me, clearly thinking about what I'd said. His stare made me uncomfortable. Finally he lowered his eyes to the papers on his desk.

"There are certain factors in common with this Daggett girl and the Krix girl. They both lived at Harbor House at some point, and they both were connected to you."

"Come on, I'd never met Patty Krix."

"I can't verify that. You were there at, or around, the time the Krix girl was murdered, and you were with the Daggett girl just before she died."

His words should have made me nervous. He was telling me I was a suspect, but I couldn't get past the questions in my mind. "It just doesn't make any sense to me. Why would anybody want to kill Elysia? She made it home safely last night, I swear to God. How can she be dead?" I stared at Collazo, fighting the pressure that was building up in my throat again, wanting him to give me some understandable answer to this incomprehensible act.

He was shaking his head. Now his eyes refused to meet mine. "It looks very probable, Miss Sullivan, that Garrett is also dead." He flipped through the pages of his notebook and sucked on the end of his gold pen. "According to the forensics report, the blood on the deck matched the type listed in his military records."

I wiped my eyes with the back of my hand. "So where's his body?"

He shrugged. "It's a big ocean. Sharks, currents, you name it. We don't always find them all."

"Okay." My other hand hurt. I forced myself to relax my grip on my shoulder bag. "Even if you *assume* he's dead, it doesn't tell us why, or what happened to Elysia."

"True. Nor does it tell us who fired the gun on the *Top Ten*. I thought perhaps you would enlighten me on that one, Miss Sullivan."

"I've told you everything I know. I feel like I've been over and over it so many times." I ran my fingers back through my hair at my temples. I was developing one of those behind-the-eyeballs headaches. "Detective Collazo, please, just tell me what happened to my friend."

"I'm not at liberty to share certain details with you."

"That's bullshit. I'm the closest thing to family that girl had. I have a right to know what happened to her. She wouldn't do drugs. What makes you think she was doing drugs?"

He ignored my question and let the silence drag out. I refused to let him win this one. I wasn't going to volunteer anything more until he asked.

"These men who were questioning you, they left you alone finally."

I finished the story up to our dropping Elysia off at Harbor House, glad to be able to fill the uncomfortable silence.

"Miss Sullivan, what you're telling me is in direct conflict with what Mr. Long at Harbor House asserts."

"I'm just telling you what happened."

"That is precisely the problem." He grasped the edge of his desk and leaned forward. "You are not telling me *everything* that happened." Then he raised his voice, loud but not quite shouting, enunciating each word clearly and never taking his eyes off me. "You think you're smart. You think I don't know and I'll never find out what went on out there, that I'll never find your connection to all this. But I will, Miss Sullivan. You can count on it. I'll be there watching your every move. There's a great deal more to your story than what's on the surface."

"I've been straight with you. I've told you what I know." My voice sounded thin and whiny.

"Right, Miss Sullivan," he said, his voice heavy with sarcasm. Sliding his chair back, he stood over me. "Long says the Daggett girl never arrived last night, that they have a curfew. She had never been late before, much less stayed out all night. He says he questioned all the staff and no one saw her. They have a sign-in log by the door, and she never signed in."

"No way. I saw her walk in the door, and there was a person sitting there at the desk. Someone over there's lying."

"I quite agree with you," he said, leaning over his desk, speaking in a hushed tone now and staring down at me, "that *someone* is not telling the truth."

A S I DROVE UP FEDERAL HIGHWAY TO SUNRISE ON MY WAY to Mike's dock, I went over in my mind all the things I wished I'd said, all the clever comebacks, the questions that would have thrown Collazo off guard.

"Goddammit!" I slammed my hand against the steering wheel. I hated the way I'd reacted to Collazo's insinuations. The man's eyes were like laser beams. Why did I get all whiny and act guilty as hell?

I parked Lightnin' in the half-empty lot of a pizza restaurant and crossed the street to the waterfront apartment building where Mike kept *Outta the Blue*. I passed through the first-floor parking garage and went out to the boat slips on the Middle River. The boat was all closed up, with the telltale water discharge indicating he had the air-conditioning running below. I pounded extra hard on the hull, and the main hatch slid open almost immediately.

Mike's salt-and-pepper hair and straggly beard were barely visible through the translucent plastic of the spray dodger. "Who's there? Oh, hey, Seychelle, come on down."

After climbing through the gate in the lifelines and making my way around the bimini supports, I followed Mike down the companionway ladder, closing the hatch behind me.

"Have a seat." He pointed to one of the two swivel captain's chairs in the main salon. He hopped comfortably about without his prosthesis, his scarred stump protruding from his shorts. He hardly ever wore the artificial leg on board, claiming his balance wasn't good enough yet with it on. "Would you like a piña colada?" He motioned toward the full blender on the galley counter.

Down below, one could see that this boat was the home of a dock-bound bachelor who wasn't really interested in any distance sailing. Judging from the nineteen-inch TV, VCR, CD player, desktop computer, and humidor filled with cigars, I was surprised Mike hadn't fried the wiring in the boat already.

"No thanks, I don't have much time. Mike, I don't know if you understood what I wanted from you, but I hope you can help me with some information."

"Hey, look, I know I seem pretty stupid when it comes to boats, but there was a time folks thought I was a pretty smart cop. Still got lots of cop friends, too. I've already made a few phone calls." He poured himself a coffee mug full of the yellow slush and hopped over to the other captain's chair. "Hope you don't mind. Cheers." He took a long drink, then licked the ice off his mustache.

"This girl, Mike, she was just a kid, a great kid. I'd seen Ely come through some really bad stuff, but she was a survivor. She was going to make it. I don't understand what happened. Neal's missing, Ely's dead, and this cop thinks I'm involved."

"Give me a quick overview. What happened yesterday?"

I told him about meeting Ely, walking on the beach, and all the rest of it, up to dropping her off. "Mike, this detective, he's making me crazy with his weird questions that aren't even questions. I don't mean to tell him things, but then I do."

"What's his name?"

"Collazo."

"Shit, Collazo's on this case? You haven't been talking to him without a lawyer, have you?"

"I couldn't reach my lawyer, and I'm trying to find out what's going on, how an innocent girl who went home to bed could end up in the river the next morning."

"Listen to me, Seychelle. Never, and I mean *never*, talk to the cops without your lawyer. Especially to him. Man, he's a bit of a strange one, I've heard, but good, damn good. He pounds a suspect with details, making it sound like the case is all but wrapped up, scaring 'em shitless, but actually he just throws out little bits and then goes all silent and just waits till they can't take it anymore. They start to fill in the silence. Then he throws 'em off guard by coming at 'em from another direction."

"Exactly. God, he made me feel like such an idiot."

Mike shrugged. "It's his job, and he's good at it. Too good. They say he's one of those overachievers who tracks down every little shred of evidence . . . even working on his time off sometimes. If he thinks you had something to do with any of this, you're in deep shit. You'd better have a damn good lawyer."

"But I didn't do anything, Mike."

"Seychelle, get real. Do you think that matters? Cops are too damn busy today to worry about whether they've got the right person for the crime. They just need a person. They need to make the arrest. If the evidence points to you right now, they don't have the time to be out there looking for any other suspects. There'll probably be another couple of murders tonight to add to Collazo's caseload."

"You're scaring me."

"What I found out about this Daggett girl scares me."

"You know something about Ely?"

"Like I said, I made a few calls. Asked for a few favors. The whole thing was really stupid and sloppy. These guys were total fuck-ups when it came to trying to hide a body in the river. Stupid assholes like these scare me worse than smart ones." He slapped his hand on the stub of leg that protruded from his cutoff jeans. "They're unpredictable. Too often they just can't control their impulses."

He stared at his leg for several seconds, then seemed to shake off the memory.

"They're pretty sure it was heroin. We'll know for sure when the report comes in, and my friend's gonna call me."

"Heroin? No way."

"The M.E. at the scene found the injection site."

"No way. She'd never do that. Even when Ely was on the streets, she wasn't into anything that involved sticking needles in herself. If she could smoke it, yeah. Grass, crack. But injecting heroin? No way."

"That's not all of it. She didn't die of an overdose. It was strangulation . . . there were marks. It may not have been intentional."

"What the . . ." I struggled to comprehend what he was saying to me. "How do you strangle someone accidentally?"

"She was probably so out of it from the drugs, they didn't know she was dying. The people who are sexually stimulated by that sort of thing sometimes get carried away."

"Mike, what are you talking about?"

"There was evidence of sexual activity, Sey. Nasty, rough, ritualistic stuff. There were rope marks on her wrists, and she was tore up pretty bad—inside and out. Probably gonna find semen from several partners. The people who enjoy bondage are like addicts. They need more and more. This time your friend's extracurricular activities went too far."

"Elysia?" I knew she hadn't had a boyfriend since she'd come off the streets and cleaned up her act. "No way. She'd never—"

"My sources said she'd had one prior arrest for prostitution in ninety-seven."

"Yeah, but that was before she got cleaned up. Her life had changed. Totally. She had a job. She was clean."

Elysia into bondage? Tough as she was in other ways, the girl cried if she got a paper cut.

"Mike, if what you're saying is true, she didn't do any of it voluntarily. I know that for sure. She was forced. Shot full of drugs like that, she probably didn't know what the hell was happening.

But why? And how did she get back out on the street without anybody over at Harbor House noticing anything?"

"She couldn't have. Not from how you describe their check-in procedures at Harbor House. Either you're lying or they are. Simple as that. That's how the cops see it. Question they'll ask themselves is, which of you stands to gain by telling a lie? Which one of you is already under suspicion for another crime?"

XI

EVERYTHING KEPT COMING BACK AROUND TO HARBOR House. As I drove down Sunrise, headed for the beach, I told myself that my real reason for going over there was to find out what sort of funeral arrangements were being made for Ely. If nobody else was going to step forward, I'd figure out a way to take care of it somehow. At least that's what I'd tell them over at Harbor House. But at the same time, I tried to remember exactly what Elysia had said about James Long. She'd said something about how Patty had fooled even James. What had she meant by that? I wanted to find out if he was the one doing the lying or if he was being lied to.

The door buzzed when I was still several steps away, and I hustled to grab it. Inside the lobby area, I was struck by the similarities to the police station: the glass booth, reception desk, locked doors leading to the inner areas. I wondered, briefly, if they were trying to keep people out or in.

Behind the reception desk, a young woman sat in the chair and an older woman was looking over her shoulder at a paper.

"Can I help you?" the older woman asked looking up at me.

"Yes, I don't know if you remember me, but I used to come

here to visit Elysia Daggett, and I spoke to you several times about her. You are Minerva, right?"

Her face took on a practiced expression of grief. "Oh, yes, I remember you. Yes. We're just devastated here. Really, we're so sorry, and we want you to know we share your grief. She had been doing so well. It's doubly hard to lose them when they've been doing so well."

She wore her long, gray-streaked hair pulled back in a tight bun. She looked the epitome of the spinster schoolmarm, and I wondered how she could possibly strike up a rapport with these street-hardened girls. As she spoke, I made the appropriate nods and sad smiles, but her words didn't convey any of the true heart-rending ache that I felt. There was a void in my life where Ely had been, but it was more than just emptiness. I couldn't stop asking myself if I had done something wrong. Could I have visited her yesterday or taken her home with me last night? Could I have changed the course of events?

"I was wondering if I could talk to the director about her. I'd like to know what arrangements are being made, and I have some questions about her actions last night."

"Well, Mr. Long is a very busy man. He's in a staff meeting this afternoon."

"Minerva, this is very important to me." I was not about to give up easily. "Ely was like a sister to me. She told me *everything* about her life." I tried to look very knowing, though I hadn't a clue what it was I was pretending to know. But someone in this place was lying and had made me look like both a fool and a liar. I was determined to find out why.

"Well." She sighed loudly. "I'll see what I can do." She picked up the phone and dialed an extension. I wandered across the lobby and gazed at the photos, press clippings, and posters on the far wall. Across the lobby, Minerva turned her back to me and spoke in hushed tones. I couldn't understand much, but I did hear Elysia's name.

There was a framed clipping on the wall from the Fort Lauderdale *Sun-Sentinel* with the headline "Runaways Find a Safe Harbor." A large color photo showed three girls clustered around a tall black man outside the building, standing next to a wood sign that read Harbor House. They were gazing up adoringly at him, and it was understandable; he had the high cheekbones, strong jaw, and cleft chin of a professional model.

He appeared again in the next photo, a color glossy taken the night of a fund-raising ball. There were three couples in the picture, and it almost looked like a put-up job to demonstrate the multiethnic South Florida population: a black couple, a white couple, and a Hispanic couple. The handsome black man stood next to a woman with a gracefully long neck and big dark exotic eyes. The white couple looked like the typical old Florida monied socialites, big hair and a bad toupee, whose pictures always grace the society pages. The Hispanic man was just plain ugly. With a big nose, small eyes, and bad skin, he was several inches shorter than the brassily beautiful Cuban on his arm. The bronze plate at the bottom of the glass read Harbor House Gala 1997.

At that moment, the door leading to the inner sanctum opened, and the tall black man I had been admiring in the photos walked through the door.

"Good afternoon," he said, extending his hand to shake mine. He bowed his head a bit to get his eyes closer to mine. I gauged his height at somewhere near six foot four. "My name is James Long." His hair was cut very short, accentuating the shape of his head and his long jawline. In his left ear he wore a fine gold wire hoop, and his voice carried the musical lilt of Caribbean roots. As he spoke, his eyes darted down for an instant in an assessing glance.

"Seychelle Sullivan." He continued to hold my hand several seconds longer than was usual. Then he gave my hand an extra squeeze, and it felt almost as though electricity coursed up my arm and through my body. Whoa! Whatever it was this guy had, he had lots of it.

"Let's go find a more private place to talk."

He used a plastic card key to open the locked door. I followed him down a long hallway lined with closed doors. Tall and slender, he was wearing black pleated slacks and a coral-colored short-sleeved shirt that complemented his light brown skin. The legs in those soft black slacks seemed to go on forever. He was very high-waisted, and the view from behind as we walked down that corridor was memorable, to say the least.

Halfway down the corridor, one of the side doors opened and a blond teenage girl flounced out and ran into Mr. Long. She was wearing little pink running shorts and a midriff-showing, spaghetti-strapped knit camisole that did little to contain her considerable bust. A huge grin spread over her face when she recognized James, and she looked like she was about to launch herself into his arms, "Ja—," she started, then she looked up at his face. From behind, I couldn't see his expression, but she immediately backed down and looked at me. She crossed her arms in front of her body and her eyes went blank.

"Sunny, this is Ms. Sullivan. I'm giving her a tour of our facility."

She nodded at me, mumbled something that sounded like "Excuse me," and disappeared back into the room.

James turned to me. "Some of the girls here teeter on the edge of holding things together. They feel secure at Harbor House, but outsiders frighten them."

As we continued down the corridor, I thought about what Ely had been saying just before we got jumped. There were things going on here at Harbor House, things I wouldn't understand.

At the end of the hall we passed through a living room where a couple of girls sat watching Oprah. James pointed to a corridor leading off the far side of the TV room.

"We take in boys as well as girls. The boys' dorms are down that hall."

The girls ignored us as James slid open a glass door and led me out into the courtyard. He pulled out a white wrought-iron chair for me beneath the canopy of a large royal poinciana tree that was just beginning to bloom. James sat down on the opposite side and folded his hands on the table. His eyes slid all over me like little feathery flicks of a tongue. So this is what they mean when they talk about animal magnetism, I said to myself. I can't say that it was all that unpleasant. My feminine ego had taken a bit of a blow at B.J.'s last night, and it was reassuring to know someone found me interesting.

James squeezed his lips together and looked up at the lacy green overhead. "Elysia," he said, then paused. "I still can't believe she's gone." He shook his head.

"I know."

"Did you know she'd lived here more than two years?"

"Yeah." I'd get into that later. "Have you tried to contact her family?" I asked.

"Yes," he said, and blew out his breath in an expression of disgust. "I called this morning. Do you know what her stepfather said? He said he didn't have a daughter."

"You're kidding. What about the mother?"

"He wouldn't let me talk to her."

"I've never understood how a woman could side with a man and decide to leave her own daughter out on the streets. Did you ask them about funeral arrangements?"

"I didn't have time to. The man hung up on me." He flexed his fingers. "Normally, I don't consider myself a combative person, but I would like just a few minutes alone with that man. For Ely's sake." He sat for several seconds staring at his fist, then suddenly looked up. "Anyway, if the family doesn't claim the body, I think I could talk the board here into giving her a modest funeral."

"Let me know, please." We sat in silence for several long minutes.

The house and royal poinciana tree shaded the cool courtyard where we sat. It was obvious a great deal of money had been spent on the landscaping surrounding us. There were dozens of varieties of orchids, heliconias, bromeliads. So much effort to cultivate such a lovely appearance, such a genteel surface. It was amazing in this little jungly enclave to think of the traffic and the crime of the city just outside the walls.

"I was the one who brought her here."

"Really? I didn't know that," he said. There was in his voice a quality that made you want to tell him more.

"I'd heard about this place, but this is the first time I've been beyond the lobby. It's lovely." I waved my hand at our surroundings. "And you seem to do good things for the girls. She seemed to be happy here."

He smiled. "Oh, yes. She was one I often used as an example when I'd go out begging for money. You see, fund-raising's my primary job around here. Minerva really runs the place. I don't get to spend as much time here as I would like because trying to keep these doors open is a full-time job. Yes, Elysia Daggett. Our great success story." He pressed his fist against his lips. I could certainly see how he could be very successful convincing rich widows to donate to the cause.

"Are there many who don't succeed?" I asked.

"Unfortunately, yes, there are. They come in here as runaways, and then they run away from here. They seem to be doing so well, and then poof—they just vanish." He noticed a piece of lint on his slacks, and he picked it off and flicked it at the underbrush.

"Had you seen any indication at all that Ely was back on drugs?" I asked.

He shook his head. "No. Nothing." The denial was not as vehement as it should have been. He sat up straighter in his chair and rested his forearms on the table. "So you and Elysia were quite good friends."

"Yes, I suppose you could say that. She was younger by quite a bit, and she used to laughingly call me her guardian angel. You know, I tried to look out for her. In the end, I guess I didn't do so well."

"I suppose she confided in you, then."

From every bit of body language James Long was giving off, one would assume this was still a casual conversation, but whether it was just my vivid imagination or not, I sensed we had suddenly moved onto slippery ground.

"Yes, you could say that." I flicked my eyes at him quickly, then away. My palms felt cold and damp. Even as my face began to feel flushed, I was determined not to let him be the one to gain the upper hand here. "Especially when we first met a couple of years ago. But you know how it is—when you don't have much to complain about, there's not much to say. Whatever you do here, it was working out for her."

He smiled. "Did she ever talk to you about what we do here?"

I paused and made a showy pretense of trying to remember. "Let's see. No, not really. Nothing specific." I smiled at him. "Oh, sometimes she sort of complained about curfews and security measures around here. She was a teenager, after all. But, you know, Mr. Long, there is something that doesn't make any sense to me. I've dropped Ely off here lots of times before, and it's always been the same. I wait until she gets buzzed in before I leave. I've always appreciated that part of your security. It was the same last night: My friend and I dropped her off right outside the front door at around eight o'clock, but this morning your people told the police that Ely never came home last night. I saw her go in. Something doesn't fit."

His face registered surprise, the brown eyes wide, the eyebrows lifted. I watched closely for any signs that he was faking it. It was hard to tell. "I checked the logs myself," he said. "She never signed in. We have residents who work the door at night, as a sort of job training. Sonya was on the door last night. She's a friend of Elysia's, as a matter of fact, so she would remember."

"Then how do you explain it? I know I saw her go inside."

He didn't say anything for quite a long time. He just gazed into the distance with unfocused eyes. "Perhaps," he said finally, "perhaps Sonya took a break. They do that sometimes and have a friend sit in for them for a few minutes. I'll ask Sonya."

"Could you do that now?"

"I'm afraid not, Ms. Sullivan. She's at work." Those high

cheekbones, full lips, jutting chin. It was so difficult not to be taken by his looks.

"Just call me Seychelle," I said. "I hate Ms. Sullivan."

He smiled then, and turned on about ten thousand watts of dazzle. You could not *not* smile back. "And I'm James, okay?"

"That's a deal," I said, grinning like an idiot.

B Y THE TIME I LEFT HARBOR HOUSE I HAD AGREED THAT James Long would pick me up for dinner at seven. He was so smooth, the date was set before I really had time to think about it.

I was on the verge of losing my business, I seemed to have screwed up the friendship I valued with B.J., and people were dying all around me. So what was I doing? Going on a date with some gorgeous guy I'd just met, a smooth operator who either played very fast and loose with the truth or was unaware of what was going on in the establishment he managed. James Long didn't seem unaware of anything. I didn't completely understand why I'd said yes, except that I hadn't found any real information to explain what had happened last night after we'd dropped off Ely. Maybe, relaxing over a drink or two, James Long would tell me a little more about those things that went on here, those things that Ely had insisted I would never understand. And maybe, given the sting of a certain recent rejection, I'd feel what it was like to be out in public on the arm of an incredibly handsome man.

And, of course, given my financial state, a free meal wasn't a bad deal, either.

That left me with at least an hour to kill before trying to put on a "girl suit." Red used to say that whenever he saw me get dressed up. Working as a lifeguard or helping him out on the *Gorda*, I lived in shorts and T-shirts, so he had always been surprised to see me looking like a woman.

When I turned into the Larsens' drive and there was no sign of B.J.'s El Camino, I wasn't sure whether I was relieved or disappointed.

I hopped out of the Jeep and walked out to the street to get the mail. Bills, bills, and more bills. The only stuff for the Larsens was some third-class junk the post office wouldn't forward. There was also a note from FedEx that they'd left a package under the mat at the Larsens' front door. I collected the package and walked around to their back door, took the key from under the rock and left the package on their kitchen table along with the rest of their mail. Since we were heading into summer, I didn't expect them to show up anytime soon, but it was so typical of rich people like the Larsens, having their stuff sent FedEx just because they could afford to.

I showered and sorted through my clothes, trying to find something appropriate. Judging from appearances, James would choose a formal dining spot, and my wardrobe was sorely lacking in that department. I finally decided that since I wasn't big on chiffon, I'd have to be original. I took a hand-painted silk pareu I'd once bought on a lark and tied it as a sort of off-the-shoulder sarong. I blow-dried my hair and pulled back one side with a small barrette, then rubbed vanilla-scented lotion on my freshly shaved legs and put on some low-heeled leather sandals. That was it. I stood in front of the mirror, turning to look at my profile. No, braless was not the way to go when one was nearly thirty. I dug around in my underwear drawer and found an old strapless swimsuit top with an under-wire. Presto—cleavage. I checked the mirror again. Good enough. I wasn't about to trowel on makeup just because I had a date with a guy who looked like he belonged in a cafe on South Beach surrounded by gorgeous models.

I had given James directions to my place, but I'd told him to ring the buzzer outside the fence. Abaco didn't particularly like strange men, and I didn't want to start my date off with a dog bite.

The buzzer rang at seven on the dot. I locked the cottage door and hurried out to the gate.

"You look great," James whispered as he brushed his lips across my cheek. He was wearing a crisp, original Guy Harvey shirt with a picture of a leaping marlin painted on the back, khaki pants, and Top-Siders. I was pleased to see I wasn't too underdressed.

Looking past him at the car in the Larsens' driveway, I let loose a loud "Wow!" I walked around the silver Jaguar convertible making all kinds of unintelligible, appreciative noises. He opened the door, smiling, but without saying a word. I liked the fact that he didn't launch into a big lecture about the car. Most guys who drive hot cars like nothing better than to talk about them all the time.

I sank into the soft leather seats and decided I would be perfectly happy if he took me to a drive-in. I could have stayed in that car all night.

We headed north on Federal Highway, making the usual small talk. I laughed when he told me we were going to the Mai Kai Restaurant.

"You don't like it?" he asked

"No, it's not that, it's just that I have a friend who has several family members who work there. He's always complaining about the place. See, he's Samoan, and he thinks the shows are far from authentic—*demeaning* is the word he uses. Now I'll have a chance to tell him what I think."

It felt rotten talking about B.J. like that. Talking about him was making me feel the heat of his kiss all over again.

Fort Lauderdale's Mai Kai really belongs in Orlando. It was as fake and touristy a place as I'd ever seen, full of vacationing New Yorkers, French Canadians, and Germans. Although we had no reservations, James was taken to a table right away. Several of the waiting tourists glared at us as we were led to a spot near the stage, but there were nods and acknowledgments as James walked past the tables of better-dressed patrons. James explained to me that we would eat first and watch the famed Polynesian revue afterward.

He pulled out my bamboo chair, and before I sat, he brushed away imaginary crumbs with a cloth napkin from one of the extra place settings. He did the same to his own seat. I looked around at the carved tikis, flower leis, fake rock waterfalls, live orchids, and lush palms. No wonder B.J. was irked at his culture being reduced to Disney proportions.

James lifted his glass after the waiter poured us each some Pouilly-Fuissé. "To Elysia. We'll keep her alive in our memories." We were seated not across from each another, but rather at an angle so we would both have a good view of the stage. We clinked our glasses.

I sipped a little of the wine. I would have preferred a beer.

"You really look lovely, Seychelle," James said, resting his chin sideways on his interlaced fingers and staring at me. "It's quite a treat for me to be out with a beautiful young woman instead of a wealthy, wrinkly widow with a large estate."

"Thank you." It embarrassed me when men complimented me, but it was a pleasant embarrassment.

"How is it that a beautiful and accomplished young woman like you is not involved with a man at the present?"

I didn't really want to go into this tonight. I tried for the short version. "I was in a relationship, but that ended a few months ago. I don't want to jump into anything on the rebound."

"Hmmm. Tell me about him. Have you two remained friends?"

It seemed like a slightly odd turn for the conversation, but I soon forgot it as our waiter showed up. Though I protested that it was really too expensive, James insisted we both order the lobster Bora Bora. At least we didn't have to drink any of those silly colorful drinks with the umbrellas in them. The food arrived quickly, and I gave myself over to the succulent flesh. Soon my chin was dripping butter, but I was ecstatic.

I let James do all the talking. I watched as he meticulously dug out nearly every piece of meat without once ever touching the lobster's shell. He said he was originally from Jamaica, but came to Miami at age six, grew up in Overtown, and had attended Ringling School of Design on an art scholarship. His grandmother, who had raised him, died in a house fire during his third year, and he quit school to take guardianship of his younger brothers and sisters. In need of money, he had started working in clubs in the city, and eventually went back to school for a degree in business administration.

"Art is still my first love, but it just doesn't pay the bills," he said.

There was an earnestness as he talked about himself that was charming. He was neither too boastful nor too modest. There was very little not to like about the man, except for the fact that he (I was finding it more difficult to believe it could have been him) or someone else at Harbor House had played some part I didn't understand in Ely's death.

I hadn't yet said a word to James about the *Top Ten* and Patty Krix.

"There's something I keep wondering about," I said, taking off the plastic bib with a picture of a cartoon lobster on the front.

"What's that?"

"I keep wondering if there isn't some kind of a connection between Elysia's death and Patty's."

James looked puzzled. "Patty?" he asked. Again, I couldn't read his reaction. Either he was an exceptionally good actor or he really didn't know what I was talking about.

"Patty Krix. You remember her? Ely told me she was a resident of Harbor House for a while."

"Oh, yes, yes, I remember her now. What happened to her?"

"You didn't read about it in the papers or see it on TV? That big yacht, the *Top Ten*, found offshore with a dead girl aboard? That girl was Patty Krix."

"What? Patty? I did hear something about that, but I never heard the girl's name." He shook his head. "Oh, my God . . ." He was wearing the same expression that he had worn in the courtyard discussing Elysia. Either Collazo hadn't asked him about Patty Krix—which, given Collazo's reputation for thoroughness, was rather surprising—or James Long was getting himself caught in a rather peculiar little lie.

BEFORE THE COFFEE AND RUM PINEAPPLE CHEESECAKE, James had the waiter bring us finger bowls with lemon and warm towels. He scrubbed each and every finger with his towel as I told him about my business, the *Gorda*, and how I had come to tow the *Top Ten*. I conveniently skipped over the fact that Neal had been my lover.

"I had no idea I was out with a lady captain," he said, setting aside his towel with that smile that eclipsed every tiki torch in the room.

Once the Polynesian revue began, conversation became impossible. Okay, it's touristy and hokey, but hey, I enjoyed it. It was fabulous to watch the men, their hard, oiled bodies undulating to the pounding rhythms. As I watched, I thought about how few opportunities women have to watch men's bodies. I don't mean checking out a guy's butt in tight pants, but rather the chance to stare at and drink in the full curve of his bicep, the rippling of his abdomen, or the deep shadowed groove down his back. It didn't mean that I wanted to bed them, but they moved in a manner so foreign and yet so familiar, the skin swelling over the flexing muscles, that watching them was pure sensual pleasure.

Our table was off to the right of the stage in an intimate, dark corner. As we watched the show, I was intensely aware of the proximity of James's knee under the table. My head was telling me not to trust him, but all the while that deep animal part of me was reacting to his sexuality, his maleness. His knee brushed against mine, and I felt weak and foolish when I looked up and smiled at him. I forced myself to look away. We had a good view of the opposite side of the stage, where a door led to a backstage entrance. I tried to put some distance between us as I watched a group of dancers leaving the stage.

Suddenly, I was startled to see B.J. standing there among the dancers, staring straight at me. When our eyes met, he smiled and gave a barely perceptible nod, and my stomach, full though it was, suddenly felt like it was doing its own Tahitian dancing. Then he turned, put his arm around the narrow brown shoulders of one of the lovelier women dancers, and vanished into the throng of brightly costumed performers. I glanced at James to see if he'd noticed, but he was concentrating on the other female Tahitian dancers onstage.

What was that all about? I wondered for a moment if I had even seen B.J. In my mind, I again saw his hand touching the girl's skin, and I shifted in my chair, brushing my knee up hard against James's and leaving it there. His head turned and his eyes flicked down, then back up with one eyebrow raised. I smiled, and James put his arm around my shoulder. I hoped to hell B.J. was watching.

After the show, I excused myself and walked across the dining room to the ladies' room. On my way back to the table, I passed by some tall potted palms near the front cash register. A large, dark figure stepped out into my path.

I heard my own gasp over the general din of the dining room before I recognized him.

"B.J.?" I felt a bit sheepish at taking fright so easily, but after the past few days, I'd grown very jumpy.

"Hey, Seychelle." He smiled. "Don't you look nice."

I held my hand to my throat. "God, you scared me. What are you doing here?" I had been genuinely frightened.

"I came by to speak to my uncle Aunu'u. He wants me to help his son with his application for a scholarship to the University of Miami."

"Here at work?"

"They get an hour or so between sets, and that's when Vanu does his homework. He's the fire walker you just saw."

In my mind I saw him again, the barely clothed young man walking across the hot coals.

"They give athletic scholarships in fire walking now?"

B.J. grinned at me. "No, it's an academic scholarship. A few Samoans are more than just big muscles, brown skin, and white teeth."

I realized I had been caught in my own prejudice, and B.J. seemed to think it was funny. I knew what I was about to tell him would take the smile away.

"Collazo, the cop, called me this morning. Have you heard from him?"

"No, I've been working on the Chris Craft at Bahia Mar all day, surfed an hour around sunset, then came straight here."

"Elysia died last night."

The smile disappeared. "What?"

"They said she was on heroin."

"Wait a minute." He shook his head as though trying to clear out his ears. "What did you just say? That's crazy. We saw her last night."

"I know. I didn't believe it at first, either. They found her in the river this morning. And the people at Harbor House are saying she never got home last night, making us look like liars."

He opened his mouth as though to speak, but instead exhaled with a soft groan. He wrapped his big arms around me and leaned his weight against my body. After last night, I didn't know what to think about B.J., and I felt awkward.

"How did she . . . ?" he half whispered, half moaned into my ear.

I bit my lower lip to control the trembling. "I don't know. But I will find out."

"Sey . . ." He held me tighter.

"I've got to get back," I said.

B.J.'s body tensed.

I pulled away from him and looked at his face. He was frowning and staring across the room.

"It looks to me like your friend keeps some bad company," he said, his voice, now deep and strong, completely changed from seconds before.

When I turned to look, I saw a short, powerfully built man leaning over my vacant chair. James was speaking fast and gesturing wildly, the whites of his eyes showing brightly in the darkened dining room. He no longer looked like the calm, sophisticated man I had left at the table. The other man wore a bright, flowered Hawaiian shirt, and from his black hair and broad, flat nose, I guessed he might be one of the dancers from the show. His right hand grasped the back of my chair, and on the back of his hand was a tattoo that from that distance looked like a coiled snake. There was something familiar about him, but I couldn't place where I had seen him.

"You know him?" I asked B.J.

"Yeah, Cesar Espinosa." He seemed to spit out the name. "He used to work here for a while as one of the walk-on torchbearers in the show. He's not Polynesian, he's Mexican, but he sort of appointed himself as bouncer. He liked to get into it with customers who'd had too much to drink—you know, roughed them up for the fun of it, acted like he owned the place."

"I take it you don't like him much."

"That's an understatement. There was this girl working here. One of Vanu's friends. She wasn't Polynesian either, she was Chinese-Jamaican, an amazing exotic beauty. Her parents owned a convenience store, and her father was shot and killed there. She was only sixteen when she started here, still in high school, a bright, really nice girl, but she started dating Cesar right after her dad died, and she changed—quit school, ran away from home, got into drugs and prostitution. She still used to call Vanu sometimes, told him she wanted out, and then we heard she'd been found dead. They called it an accidental overdose, but Vanu always thought it was intentional, that that had been her way out. Cesar used her and then just threw her aside. She could not take the shame."

"You said he used to work here?"

"Yeah, he quit about six months ago. I haven't seen him around here since."

"I wonder what the two of them are talking about."

"It can't be good. If your friend is a buddy of Cesar's, be careful, Seychelle."

"B.J., my 'friend,' James Long, is the director of a very reputable charitable organization. He wouldn't be in that position if he was a lowlife or crook of some kind. This man's in the limelight. They write stories about him in the newspaper, for crissakes."

"And you say I'm the one who is naive. Just promise me you'll be careful."

"Okay, okay." I wondered if his distrust of James could have anything to do with his having seen James's hand on my shoulder.

He placed a quick peck on my cheek. "Tomorrow, we need to talk."

For an instant I felt a kind of hope rise inside me, a hope that maybe things could be different.

"You take care of yourself."

He turned and passed through a side door into the backstage area.

When I returned to the table, Cesar Espinosa was halfway across the dining room, headed for the exit.

"Sorry I took so long," I said, settling into my seat.

"That's all right." James smiled. He looked completely calm; there was no trace left of the wildly animated speaker of a few moments ago.

"That man you were speaking to. Was he a friend?"

He looked surprised. "Him? No way. He's an unsavory character who has dated some of the girls at the Harbor House. I try to warn them, but some young girls are just attracted to bad men. You know the saying 'Good guys can't win.' " He flashed those perfect white teeth and shrugged.

I nodded and grinned back at him like a smitten teen.

"Apparently he wants to see one of our girls now, and Minerva won't put his phone calls through. Sometimes I can't help feeling paternal about the girls. I want them to get their lives back on track. He's not going to help them out in that direction."

I nodded. It made sense. For now.

THE NIGHT WAS CLOUDLESS WHEN WE LEFT THE MAI KAI, and James asked if he could put the top down. I told him I would have asked if he hadn't, that I wasn't exactly the sort to mind wind-whipped hair. We drove down to A1A and along the beach, and I felt like purring, nestled into that buttery leather, admiring the few stars that could overpower the city lights and the velvet night wind that was teasing my face with loose wisps of hair. He put a Louis Armstrong CD in and we cruised to "What a Wonderful World." I felt more than a little woozy from the wine, and it was only when we cruised past Bimini Lane and I looked down at the darkened outline of Harbor House that I started to sort through my confusion about what I was doing in a Jaguar cruising the beach with James Long.

James left me to my thoughts, and I added that to the list of things I liked about the man. For more than twenty minutes, we cruised along and reveled in another spectacular Florida night, the waves breaking in plankton-lit foam in the background, the parade of tourists with their sunburned glow in the foreground. Louis launched into "La Vie en Rose." I was trying hard just to empty my mind, to let the cleansing breeze blow the events of the past couple of days away, but Collazo's words kept coming back to me. Why were so many people connected to me turning up dead?

"Would you like to stop and walk awhile?" he asked as we approached the most populated stretch of the strip.

"Sure, that would be nice," I said.

To my surprise, instead of heading for the beach, James turned up Las Olas Boulevard, away from the beach, and drove inland into the ritziest little shopping district in Fort Lauderdale. For a stretch of less than a mile, this quaint street was lined with old buildings—old by Fort Lauderdale's standards, anyway—that had been turned into galleries, cafes, and boutiques. Big old oaks grew up in the street's median, creating a canopy over the sidewalk eateries, and the homes just a block to the south were riverfront mansions. The area reeked of money, which is why it wasn't exactly high on my list of frequently visited shopping spots.

James parked in the lot behind the Riverside Hotel and walked around to my side of the car to open the door. I always feel like a complete incompetent sitting in a car waiting for a man to open my door, but I was trying hard to be socially correct. Why, I wasn't exactly sure. I had agreed to go out with this man in the belief that I would find out something about Harbor House that would provide some answers, and I found myself not doing a bit of interrogating, but rather wanting him to like me.

After a short stroll, James turned into an art gallery and walked over to a group of oils all clearly painted by the same artist. He didn't say a word and didn't look at me; in fact, he seemed to have forgotten I was there. He just stared at the paintings with a half smile.

From a distance, they looked like photographs. All five paintings were done in shades of black and white and gray, and they depicted very realistic objects against stark backgrounds: a single black enameled vase in an all-white room, a white sickle moon in the black sky, a black hand reaching for a silver knife on a white tablecloth. Two paintings hanging side by side were of matching eyes, huge eyeballs nearly a foot across, one in white skin, the other in black. Though you could not see the expression on the face in either painting, there was something disturbing about the eyes. I felt a chill looking into them. I knew the features outside the frame included raised brows, flared nostrils, and a mouth in an open scream. I had to look away.

"You did these, didn't you?" I said, turning to look at him, waiting for his answer, but he hadn't heard the question, apparently. He just stood there with that odd little smile.

WHEN WE PULLED INTO THE DRIVEWAY AT THE ESTATE, James was out of his door and opening mine before I'd collected my shoulder bag from the backseat. Oh, hell, I thought, I'm a big girl, and it's not all that late. Besides, I really hadn't learned anything from him yet.

But as I stepped from the car, I knew it was more than that. I could make all the excuses I wanted about how I was really inviting him in only to pump him for information, but in fact there was something very charming and exciting about the man, not to mention that his interest in me was doing great things for my recently bruised self-image. The fact that he might be dangerous as well only made him more interesting. Part of me hated myself for the attraction I felt, but it was not that part of me that spoke first.

"Would you like to come in for a drink? Actually, beer is about all I have. I haven't had a chance to do much shopping lately."

"That would be nice."

"I'd better go lock up my dog first. She can get a little weird sometimes."

I let myself in, took Abaco to the *Gorda*, and locked her into the wheelhouse. She stood up on her hind legs and rubbed her wet nose against the glass in the door. I felt sorry for her, but I pointed my finger. "Now, you be a good girl."

James was leaning against his Jag, his head back, staring up at the sliver of a moon, very similar to the moon in his painting. He looked just like something out of one of those perfume ads where all the gorgeous people appear faintly sad. The gate squeaked, and he turned to look at me.

"Are you okay?" I asked him.

"I was just thinking about Elysia. It was such a waste to lose her like that." His voice cracked, and his Adam's apple dipped as he swallowed. I walked over and leaned my butt against the warm car hood next to him. The stars visible through the the branches of the oaks were few and far between, as the lights of the city just across the river had washed most of them away.

"What do you think really happened to Ely?"

Over the sound of the insects humming in the underbrush, I again heard him swallow. He opened his mouth as though he were about to say something, but then he only looked down at me and rested a hand on my shoulder. "You said something about a beer?"

I led him back to the cottage and unlocked the door. Before swinging it open, I felt a little moment of panic. For all I knew, this man had played a part in Ely's death and could be plotting the same for me. After I'd switched the lamp on and the light filled the room, though, such fears seemed foolish. After all, he was the head honcho, the director of Harbor House. He probably dined at the mayor's house, for Pete's sake. And lots of people had seen us together this evening.

He went straight to the easel and paints.

"You paint?" he called out as I retrieved two beers from the fridge.

"Yeah, just as a hobby." I handed him the can, and from his look, I could tell he would have preferred his beer in a glass. He took a paper napkin from the holder on the bar and began to wipe the aluminum top of the can.

"Are you any good?" He settled on the couch and stretched his arm across the back. I wondered if I was expected to sit inside that arm.

"Hmmm . . . tough question. Technically, I'm decent, but I don't have the passion for painting—you know, the artistic temperament. My mother had it, so I know what it is." Standing in the center of the room with my back to him, I pointed to the dark canvas on the far wall. It depicted a bird-of-paradise flowering in an unruly garden in the midst of a threatening summer squall. "That's one of hers. My mother had all this emotion in her, all this thought and spirit and soul that she just couldn't express any other way."

"I know what you are talking about. That is why many people paint."

I turned to face him. "Of course. I saw that tonight in your paintings." I didn't go so far as to say that I found it very difficult to believe that such a warm, sociable person could make such cold paintings. "You said those canvases were several years old. Do you still paint?"

"No, I've found other outlets for my passion."

He said it matter-of-factly, without a wink or a leer. My mother had found another outlet, too.

I turned back to my mother's bird-of-paradise painting. "It tortured my mother when she couldn't paint, when what she managed to get on canvas didn't look like what was in her head. But when things were going well, she knew a real serenity. I just wish it had happened more often for her."

The sofa creaked when he stood, so I wasn't entirely surprised when he rested his hands on my shoulders.

"And your mother? Where is she today?"

I opened my mouth to speak, but nothing came out. As soon as the subject of her death came up, I was that little girl again, the one who couldn't speak for months.

James bent down and brushed his lips against the side of my neck, and I could barely hide the shiver I felt. "It's okay," he whispered.

No matter that I'd been insisting to myself that I really was only with him to try to get some information from him, when he slowly turned me around and kissed my mouth, I didn't push him away. My eyes closed, and I reached up and ran my hands lightly along his jawline. His skin was smooth and cool, not at all like B.J.'s.

B.J. I placed my hand in the center of his chest, applied gentle pressure, and our lips parted. "James, there's something I need to ask you . . ." I opened my eyes for just a second, and in that flash, I became aware of a movement just past his shoulder at the kitchen window. My eyes flew wide open, and I turned my head in time only to see the blur as a head ducked below the window. Through the closed window, I could hear the rustling of the vegetation as someone pushed through the bushes out there.

"What the hell—" I disentangled myself from James and ran for the front door.

My kitchen window, which is at the back of the cottage, is accessible only through the thicket of bushes that separates the Larsen estate from its neighbors. I pushed my way through the clipped ficus and bougainvillea, ignoring the thorns and branches that cut into my flesh. By the time I'd fought my way clear to the neighbor's large expanse of lawn, there was no one in sight.

"Damn!" I looked down at my thighs. Blood trickled down from numerous slashes. "Shit."

"Seychelle? Are you all right?" James's voice sounded distant, muffled as it was by the thick hedge. Then Abaco started barking inside the wheelhouse.

"Yeah," I shouted. "I'll be right there." I trotted down the hedge to the wooden gate that joined the two properties, where on the rare occasions when both sets of neighbors were in town at the same time, they could socialize without having to exit their enclaves. It was standing open.

James was in front of my cottage when I returned.

"Look at you," he said, the lines on his forehead clear above his arched brows.

I glanced down at my pareu. The cloth had ripped, and a piece hung to the ground. The blood on my legs was starting to coagulate.

"They're just scratches. No big deal."

The dog was still barking. "Abaco," I shouted. "Quiet!"

"What was that all about?"

"Didn't you see him, or at least hear him?"

James shook his head. "See what?"

"There was a man at my kitchen window. I didn't get a clear look at him. I just saw him out of the corner of my eye." I didn't tell James, but there had been something familiar about that fleeting glimpse.

Had it been a prowler, someone else come to rob me, or someone who was spying on me? Suddenly, I remembered B.J. watching me from backstage at the Mai Kai.

"I didn't know what was going on when you just ran out of there like that." James was looking at me as though I were something he had stepped in and he didn't know how to politely wipe me off his shoe.

Suddenly, I started laughing. "God, you must have thought I was nuts, huh?"

He stepped back, staring, as I bent over laughing. He nodded.

"Guess this whole thing kind of broke the romantic atmosphere, eh?" I tried to control myself, but the giggles just kept erupting every time I thought I was under control.

"Seychelle, are you sure you're all right?"

"Don't worry." I caught my breath and finally managed to pull off a straight face. "I'm fine. Whoever that was is long gone by now. Probably just a Peeping Tom," I said, although I didn't really think so. "I think we'd better call it a night, James."

"I agree," he said, smoothing out imaginary wrinkles in his shirt and tucking it tightly into his pants.

"Before you go, though, I've just got to ask one more thing. It's about this business with Ely and the sign-in sheet. I saw her go in the door and bend down to sign in, James. I could see there was a person sitting there behind the desk. Now you're saying no one saw her last night? I was just wondering if you *really* know everything that goes on at Harbor House. I mean, isn't it possible that those girls could be into something behind your back?"

"There is nothing that goes on there that I don't know about. I'm sure of that."

"Then how can you explain the fact that your story just doesn't mesh with what I know I saw?"

"I can't explain it, but I don't think I'll have to, either."

"What do you mean?"

"Seychelle, look at yourself." He spread his hands wide, smiling his little half smile. "Then look at me," he said. "Who would you believe?" It was his turn to laugh out loud.

The night felt very cold. The flesh on my arms was dotted with goose bumps.

Then he was flashing me that megawatt smile. "I'm just kidding you. There is a logical explanation for the discrepancy, and I trust that Collazo will find it. He seems very determined."

"Yeah, Collazo. I don't want just any answer, James. I want the truth."

"How sweet. Seychelle . . ." He started to say something, then paused and looked around. He jingled the keys in his pocket. "I really don't like leaving you alone if there is someone prowling around out here. I wouldn't want anything to happen to you. Are you sure you'll be safe?"

I wondered what he had been about to say. "I'll be all right. I can take care of myself, and I have the dog. You go on home. Hope you don't mind if I don't walk you out to your car."

After a curt good night and a peck on the cheek—he was careful not to touch me anywhere else—James let himself out through the gate. I heard his Jag start up when I let Abaco out of the boat. After she peed on the lawn, I called her inside and locked the door to the cottage. Sitting on the edge of my bed, I slipped out of my sarong and looked down at the scratches on my legs. I needed a shower, but I was afraid to stand alone and naked under that noisy stream of water. I switched off the bedside lamp, and in the dark, I sponged off my cuts, brushed my teeth, and climbed under the covers, pulling them up right under my chin.

I couldn't seem to get warm. The sheet was soon knotted around my legs, and the little voice in my head wouldn't shut up and let me sleep. There was no question in my mind that I had seen that figure at the window. Someone was watching me.

XII

WHEN *GORDA* MOTORED HER WAY OUT THE MOUTH of the New River on Sunday morning, it was still dark. I was astounded to see how many boats had turned up and were just circling around on the Intracoastal off the Lauderdale Yacht Club. There is a camaraderie of sorts among the folks who make their living on the waterfront, but I'd never realized before how many there were, and how much they had all liked Neal. When Neal and I broke up, for over a month I went around calling him an asshole to anyone who would listen, and most folks had agreed with me. But he was a likable asshole.

Nestor led the group with his boat, *My Way*. He blew once on his air horn and everyone fell in line behind him. I maneuvered *Gorda* up front, right behind the *My Way*. Jimmy St. Claire's old Chris Craft, *Rhumb Runner*, followed me. Then there were a couple of water taxis, some sport boats I didn't know, and Jack, the guy who had bought Neal's old sailboat, the *Wind Dancer*. I was surprised to see Hightower back toward the end of the line on the *Ruby Yacht*. He had planned to spend a week in the boatyard so he must have had some kind of problem with his haul-out. He was so bad at handling the old girl, he rarely took her out, although I noticed he did have Perry along as a deckhand.

As we went through the Seventeenth Street Bridge, I looked back at the *Rhumb Runner* and saw there were two people on the flybridge: Jimmy, and next to him stood B.J. Moana. My stomach did a couple of strange little flip-flops at the sight of him. He smiled and waved. It couldn't have been him last night outside my window, could it? The very idea seemed foolish in the light of the dawning day.

The *Top Ten* was still tied alongside the Coast Guard dock, and all heads turned to look at her as we passed. I shuffled my deck shoes across the nonskid when I saw *Gorda's* wheelhouse running lights reflected in the big yacht's hull windows. I was filled with the same restless discomfort that had plagued me all night.

As we filed out between the breakwaters, the clouds on the horizon were starting to glow around the edges. Overhead, Venus had yet to vanish, but otherwise, the night was nearly a memory. Along the beach to the south, where the Australian pines at John Lloyd Beach State Park obscured the hustle of the cargo port, the shallow turquoise water near shore appeared almost luminescent against the pale pink of the morning sky. A lone pelican flew a few feet above the smooth swells with a grace and precision no man-made machine could ever mimic.

The still air felt thick with humidity. Two little open boats anchored by the channel markers rolled uneasily in the small, glassy swells, and the Sunday fishermen watched our procession with little curiosity, their eyes still squinty with sleep, coffee mugs in their hands. A large white cruise ship passed us on her way into the port with surprisingly few people on deck. One man alone at the rail lifted a small child, who waved. I stepped out of the wheelhouse and waved back.

About three-quarters of a mile beyond the sea buoy, Nestor started his wide turn. He circled around until he was following the last boat. He blew his air horn again, idled his engine down, and we all followed his lead. Soon we were all stopped, gently rolling on the light sea in a circle formation.

Nestor spoke first, through his loud-hailer, telling a quick story about how Neal had once helped him out when a fat charter guest had fallen off the dock and Nestor hadn't been able to hoist him out of the water alone. Neal had figured out a way to use the dock fish hoist as a derrick. Everyone laughed at the comments Neal had supposedly made. They were funny, although not kind.

Then Jimmy told a story, with his loud-hailer in one hand, a can of Old Milwaukee in the other.

"Neal Garrett knew boats. He knew every goddam thing there was to know about the sea, divin', and boats." He belched into the hailer and the crowd cheered and applauded. "One time, down 'n the Tortugas, Neal was anchored next to me on his little *Wind Dancer* when a squall come through, an' it blew like stink. Most o' them boats dragged an' ended up on the beach that night, but not Neal's. She hung in there while he spent the whole night helping everybody else get theirs off. He worked his butt off, even though he was the only fucker smart enough not to drag." He held his beer can high. "To Neal." Everybody cheered.

Other people told their own stories after that, and I could feel eyes watching me, wondering what I would say or do, but I refused to be the star of this show. I could not eulogize a man I really did not believe was dead.

The boats were drifting farther apart and the tales had died when Nestor finally threw a flower wreath into the sea. I sprinkled the bougainvillea blooms I had picked that morning onto the surface of the calm water.

Nestor blew his air horn. On each and every boat, horns, whistles, bells, and sirens sounded, the cacophony as loud as the victory celebration after a championship game. They were celebrating Neal's life. He would like that, I thought. It was a hell of a racket.

The circle broke up, some of the boats heading out for a day of fishing, others heading back to the port. I was among the latter group.

As I motored through the group of sailboats waiting for the Seventeenth Street Bridge to open, I saw George Rice, a broker I knew who actually wore a blue blazer and an ascot. He was puttering toward me in his launch, a varnished clinker hull with a silly-looking white awning with scalloped edges.

"How's it going, George?" I asked as he pulled his launch up alongside *Gorda*.

"Fine, fine," he said, waving his manicured hand in the air. "I saw Madagascar yesterday at Gulf Stream. He told me *Gorda* is about to come on the market, and I took the liberty of filling out a listing notice for you." He looked around the aft deck, and flashed an expensive display of dental work my way.

"George, Maddy only owns one third of this vessel."

"Really . . . hmmmm . . ." He was eying the boat, looking her up and down like a convict on his first night out in a singles' bar.

"She really is very unique, isn't she? Is it too much to assume she'll pass survey?"

It was one thing for my brother to go behind my back and try to list *Gorda* with a broker, but when the broker started suggesting that she might not be sound, I couldn't take it anymore.

"George, *Gorda*'s not for sale. Take your listing agreement and cram it . . ." At that moment the bridge horn blew, and George Rice did not have the privilege of hearing my detailed description of what he could do with his contract.

After securing the boat and hosing her down, I marched into the cottage, yanked the phone off the cradle, and dialed Maddy's number.

Jane answered.

"Let me speak to my brother, Jane."

"He's sleeping right now, Seychelle, and I don't want to bother him. See—"

"Jane, go in there and wake him up. It's almost nine o'clock in the morning, for Pete's sake. That asshole is trying to sell my boat out from under me to pay his gambling debts. Did you know he's back at the track, Jane?"

"Yes. But listen, Seychelle, he—"

"I can't believe you're still making excuses for him. He's a bum. He's—"

"Sey, somebody beat him up yesterday."

"What?"

"Robbed him first. He was hurt pretty bad."

"Maddy?" I sat heavily on one of the barstools.

"Yeah, he'd had a good day. He was coming home with nearly three grand. They jumped him in the parking lot."

"What'd they do to him?"

"It's bad. His face is a mess, and they broke two fingers. But thank God they didn't kill him. They had a gun, he said. But he didn't want to hand over the money; we need it bad. He looks awful. They had to fix his retina. They said he'll never see right with that eye."

"Jane, I don't know what to say. I'm really sorry." I didn't know my sister-in-law well, and I couldn't find words that sounded right. "I . . . well, tell him I called. I guess I'll try to talk to him when he's feeling better."

"Sey, he said if you called, to tell you to take their offer and settle this."

"What?"

"I don't know what it means. He was all woozy from the pain pills and his mouth is all messed up, so he was really hard to understand. He made me repeat it. Take their offer and settle it, he said."

After I hung up the phone, I just sat there and stared for several minutes. When I finally began to comprehend the red light, it took me ages to pull my mind back to a conscious state. I blinked and hit the play button on the answering machine.

"Miss Sullivan. Hamilton Burns. I have been authorized to make a final settlement offer in regards to your efforts in towing the *Top Ten* to port. You will receive fifteen thousand dollars, after which you will sign a waiver agreeing to have no further interests in the affairs of the vessel and the members of her crew, including any court testimony. I will expect your phone call, and we can meet in my offices on Las Olas. Miss Sullivan, I must impress upon you that it is in your best interests to agree to this settlement. These are very powerful and influential people, and they will reward you for your cooperation. On the other hand, if you refuse, they won't hesitate to deal with you, Miss Sullivan." *Click.*

I turned the machine off and leaned on the counter, my forehead resting on the heels of my hands. Deal with me? And how on earth did Maddy know about these offers from Burns? Whoever the real owner of the *Top Ten* was, he seemed to have an incredibly long reach. Right into my brother's life.

It must be the debt again. Someone he'd borrowed from was pushing his buttons.

I pushed the speed-dial number for Jeannie. After four rings her answering machine picked up, and I hung up. She'd probably taken her boys to the beach. That sounded pretty good right about then. I used to try to go down to the beach almost every day, but it had been a while now since I'd taken the boat out for an ocean swim. Neal had been diving off the *Top Ten*; maybe it was time to have a look around the place where all this started.

I changed into my royal blue tank suit, then grabbed a beach towel and my keys. My scuba gear was gone, but I always kept an old mask in the dock box. I considered taking the Larsens' Jet Ski, but my thirteen-foot Boston Whaler was up in davits at the far end of the seawall. I hadn't run it in over a month, and I didn't want the fuel in the carburetor going bad from lack of use. I was glad when the twenty-five-horse Merc fired up at the first turn of the key. Abaco jumped down off the seawall, her tongue lolling and her tail wagging. She knew where I was headed. She loved to swim, too, and wasn't about to be left behind.

Once I got the Whaler outside the entrance channel, I opened her up. Abaco had always been a daredevil bow rider, and a trip in the Whaler, nose in the wind, was even better than going for a car ride. She stood all the way in the front of the boat, her ears blowing back, her legs bending to the boat's motion. There wasn't too much chop, but we pounded a little on the wind waves as we headed up the coast. I throttled down, searching about for approximately the same spot where the *Top Ten* had been drifting when I found her. There are very few reference points out on the ocean, and even with the coastline on one side, I knew I could be off by up to half a mile.

I started from the shallows where the yacht had wallowed and headed southeast, offshore, the direction from which the *Top Ten* would have drifted, allowing for the current and wind. When the water turned dark blue, I dropped the anchor over like a lead line to measure the depth. I had about twenty feet of line left when it touched. So, about eighty feet deep. I pulled the anchor back up. I didn't want to snag it on anything at that depth without my scuba gear. There was all kinds of junk on the ocean floor off the coast of Fort Lauderdale. South Florida has a very active artificial reef program. They take rusty old ships, barges, even a jet airplane, tow them to the spot where they want to create a reef, and then blow holes in them and sink them to make underwater habitats for fish— and anchor snares for unwary boaters.

I cut the engine on the Whaler and just let her drift. In the bow locker, I found the dive flag, stuck the pole in the flag holder on the stern, and flipped over the side the old piece of carpet that I had tied to a couple of cleats. That way Abaco could climb her way back into the boat by herself—her claws could get a grip on the carpet better than on the slick fiberglass. The dinghy painter on the Whaler was an extra-long length of nylon line I used whenever I towed the little boat behind the tug. I tied the rope around my waist, grabbed my mask, and slipped into the water. It was freezing, probably all the way down to seventy-two degrees. Abaco barked at me a couple of times, and then she dove in, too.

The visibility wasn't great, but I could make out some shadowy shapes. Several threads of silver bubbles wound their way to the surface. Scuba divers. I tried to pick them out in the blurry murk. Two of them. I lifted my head and looked around for their boat. There to the east, about a quarter mile off, was a twenty-foot Sea Ray. From the line angling off the bow, it was obvious she was anchored, but it looked like she was slowly dragging. Not surprising in this depth. It shouldn't be a problem for them, though. They could swim to it.

From the corner of my eye, I could see Abaco's legs underwater doing that mechanical even-stroked dog paddle of hers. She circled around me.

The divers were swimming across the sand and grass bottom, heading toward a big dark shadow just to the south of us. I wasn't sure whether it was natural coral or an artificial reef. I untied the line around my waist and began hyperventilating, fooling my brain into thinking that it had plenty of oxygen. Then I took an extra-large breath and dove.

I've always preferred free diving to scuba. There is no rasp and burble of air drawn in and out through a regulator. It's quiet except for the distant buzz of propellers far away, the pop and crackle of tiny oceanic shrimp, and the crinkling noise as I squeeze my nose, popping my ears during the descent. Since I'd started practicing, the length of time I could hold my breath had grown longer, and now I could stay down for over two minutes. My deepest free dive was to sixty-five feet. But not today, not without fins. I did get down deep enough, though, to see the scuba divers. The divers were about twenty feet off the bottom, swimming toward what looked like a small wrecked freighter. Judging from the number of holes in the thing, it was no accident that brought it to rest on the seabed. It definitely had been sunk intentionally, probably part of the artificial reef system.

It was also obvious that these divers were weekend warriors, not dive junkies. No expense had been spared in the gear they wore. I knew their type: more money than experience, and they bought everything the dive shop guys suggested. The smaller guy even had a bang stick strapped to his leg for shark protection. It was a pressure-sensitive device that when jammed into the side of an overly friendly shark would fire off a single shotgun shell. It worked, but you were more likely to hurt yourself diving with the equivalent of a gun strapped to your leg.

The bigger one noticed me, and I waved. I always felt superior to scuba divers. I felt free as a dolphin. He touched his partner's arm and pointed up.

There was something familiar about the smaller guy. I used my last reserves of air to swim a little deeper. Just as I began kicking for the surface, it hit me: his black hair floating upward around the top of his mask, the dark inkblot of a tattoo on his right hand, last night at the Mai Kai. Cesar Esposito.

By the time I hit the surface, the black was beginning to close in around the periphery of my vision. I had come too close to passing out. Abaco had climbed back into the Whaler already, and she was barking like crazy. She hated it when I dived. I rolled onto my back and floated for several seconds, my eyes closed, waiting for my breath and strength to return.

Cesar Esposito! I pictured him leaning over James Long's shoulder, and the feeling that I had seen him somewhere before last night returned. My eyes popped open, I rolled over, and I began swimming fast and furiously for the Whaler.

I pulled myself over the gunwale, threw my mask onto the floor of the boat, and scrambled for the varnished bench behind the wheel. The outboard sputtered and died at the first turn of the key. I glanced back at the engine, and in the distance, I saw the divers at their Sea Ray. Esposito was already in the boat, reaching over the transom and grabbing for his buddy's gear. The other diver climbed onto the swim step. He towered over Cesar. Even at this distance, I could tell he was huge; his chest and arm muscles were so big, his arms couldn't swing comfortably at his sides. He reminded me of a cormorant, the way they stand on rocks or buoys, their wings spread wide, trying to dry them.

I tried the key again. No go. Nothing but dying whines from my little starter battery.

Both men had dropped their scuba gear. I heard their big twin Johnsons roar to life. Shit.

Yanking the cover off the Merc with one hand, I reached into the stern locker with the other and pulled out my can of quick-start ether. I sprayed the carburetor, keeping my head turned upwind.

Cesar was on the bow of the Sea Ray, bent over, pulling in their anchor line.

The Merc coughed to life on the next try. The Whaler was pointing north, away from the inlet, but I jammed it in gear and shoved the throttle to the max.

I looked back over my shoulder. Now both men were on the bow of their boat, their butts up in the air, yanking on their anchor line. Whatever their anchor had snagged on, all that beef wasn't budging it. The bigger guy looked up when he heard my engine rev up. I turned back toward the inlet in a wide arc and waved to them as I passed.

Seeing them together had made me remember the night on the beach with Ely. I was looking at Big Guy and Shorty.

XIII

I T WAS NEARLY ONE O'CLOCK IN THE AFTERNOON WHEN I parked on the south side of Bimini Lane and fed the meter all three of my quarters before crossing over to Harbor House. I didn't see James's Jag anywhere on the street, but for all I knew there might be a fancy employees' garage behind the buildings somewhere. It was my fervent hope that he wouldn't be there on a Sunday afternoon and I'd get a chance to talk to Sonya alone.

Minerva was on the desk again, and she buzzed me into the building with a smile. I didn't smile back.

"May I speak to Mr. Long, please?"

"I'm sorry, he isn't in on Sunday. Would you like to make an appointment to see him on Monday?"

Excellent, I thought.

"Damn," I said.

Minerva looked at me with arched eyebrows.

I plastered an on-the-verge-of-tears look on my face.

"I guess I'll have to tell her parents that I just couldn't do it."

"Who?"

"The Daggetts. Elysia's parents asked me to stop by and pick up some of her things."

"Well, miss, I don't really have the authority . . ."

"They wanted me to speak to her friend Sonya, too, because . . . well, you know how parents are. They just have to find out everything she did on that last day. It's all they have left now."

Minerva scrunched her brows together and pursed her lips. The fine web of wrinkles deepened around her eyes and lips. "Well, I don't see any harm in that. Specially seeing as the two girls were roommates and all. You should have told me right off. You don't need Mr. Long's permission for that."

She picked up the phone and dialed an in-house extension. "Sonya? There's a lady here who'd like to talk to you about Elysia. You got a minute? . . . Uh-huh . . . Okay. I'll send her on back."

James hadn't mentioned Sonya was Ely's roommate.

Minerva pointed to the door opposite her desk. "Just go on through to room twelve. I'll open it for you. It'll be on your right. She's expecting you."

"Thanks." When I reached the door, a buzzer sounded and the lock released.

The bedroom door opened within seconds after I knocked. Neither one of us said a word at first, although we recognized each other. She was the blond girl who had run into James in the hallway yesterday. He'd called her Sunny. There was open distrust in her eyes.

"May I come in?"

I saw the gap in the door start to close, so I pushed my way in and just started talking. "Thank you so much for seeing me like this. I know it must be very hard on you, losing a friend like that." I crossed to the far side of the small room, noticing the open suitcase on the unmade bed. I pointed to the other bed. "Was this Elysia's bed?"

She nodded.

I sat down on the smooth navy bedspread. "Had you two been roommates long?"

She closed the hallway door and leaned against it, crossing her arms under her ample breasts. She was wearing a white tank top and green satin jogging shorts. With her long blond hair and shapely legs, she looked like the type of model who is usually photographed draped over an outboard engine or a motorcycle.

"I already talked to the cops, and I've got nothing else to say. Who are you?" she asked.

"My name is Seychelle Sullivan. Maybe Elysia mentioned me."

I saw in her eyes that she did recognize my name, but her defenses weren't down yet.

"Yeah," I went on, "we sure had some great times together. Did Ely ever tell you what we did on her seventeenth birthday?"

A hint of a smile sparkled in her eyes, and she nodded.

"She told you about the gorilla suit? She once told my friend B.J. that she loved gorillas. Well, I was complaining to him that I didn't know what to get her for her birthday, and he said, 'Let's rent her a gorilla suit!' And we did. We made her wear it all weekend— even to work. Only she's such a shrimp, it was the funniest-looking, shortest-legged gorilla you've ever seen." The room grew terribly quiet when I stopped laughing. "I mean *was*. She was such a shrimp. God, that's hard to get used to."

After another long, uncomfortable silence, Sonya stuck out her chin and said, "She called you her guardian angel. But I don't believe in angels."

"Yeah, she called me that because I was just trying to look out for her. I knew she didn't have parents who were going to care, but I cared. A lot. And Ely knew that."

She shrugged. "Yeah, I guess."

"And I still care about her now. I care about what they're saying about her, and I know it isn't true. I don't believe Ely's death was an accident or suicide. I don't believe she was willingly using drugs again, either. Someone killed her."

She walked over to the closet and began pulling clothes off the hangers, balling them up and throwing them into the suitcase. "I don't know anything about that."

I stayed quiet for a while, knowing the silence would work on her.

Finally she flopped down onto the bed and sat hunched over.

She stared at the carpet and rubbed her toes across the fibers. Finally she looked up. "What do you want? I don't know nothing. Leave me alone!"

"Were you working the door when Ely came home Friday night?"

Her blue eyes glanced up at me with a guilty look, the way Abaco used to look when she'd been left in all day and had peed on the floor in the cottage.

"I don't think I should be talking to you."

"Why not? I was a friend of Ely's. I'm just trying to find out what happened to her. Don't you want to know what happened to her?"

I almost didn't hear it, she spoke so softly. "No," she said, and she started to cry. She had looked so tough, so invulnerable at first, that I had nearly forgotten she was just a kid.

I pushed aside her suitcase and sat next to her. "What is it, Sonya?"

"Sunny, call me Sunny. Ely did. I hate Sonya." She wiped at her eyes trying to regain her composure, but the tears continued to spill down her cheeks. "Shit, I gotta get out of here."

"How old are you?"

"Fifteen."

Oh, man, at fifteen, I was still playing on a girls' softball team and hanging out on the river with my dad. I was tall and lanky then, dressed in cutoffs and T-shirts to hide what curves I had, and boys ignored me. I had no idea what it would be like to be a little girl in a woman's sex-kitten body like Sunny's.

"Where are you from?"

"Indiana."

"Don't you think your family misses you?"

She didn't answer right away. Then she said, "I don't have a family. My parents died when I was little."

"I'm sorry. I kinda know what that's like. My mother died when I was eleven."

She didn't say anything for a long while. The room was quiet aside from her occasional sniffles. Finally she looked up, her blue eyes now rimmed in red. "Do you still miss her?"

Decades can go by and you can think you are so over it, and then one little question can just rip it all open again and make the wound as fresh and raw as it was that hot day on the beach. "Yes. Every day of my life."

She nodded and didn't say anything more for a while as we sat there next to each other, each essentially alone with our memories.

She inhaled deeply. "I was raised by my sister and her husband."

"Where's your sister now? Maybe you could go back to live with her."

"I don't know where she is. Probably dead. She got on drugs, and then she tested positive. She just left."

There was more to the story, and though I felt pretty certain I knew what it would be, I had to let her tell it.

"That was when Ray started going after me. Then he threw me out because I wouldn't sleep with him anymore. Said I wasn't good for anything."

It was a different variation of the story told by most of the girls in this place.

"Is there anything I can do to help you?"

She turned and looked at me, as though calculating what harm or good I could do her. "You helped Ely a lot. She told me."

I took a deep breath to keep the quiver out of my voice. "She was my friend. I'm really going to miss her."

Sunny stood up and went into the tiny bathroom. I heard the water running. When she returned, the tears had stopped.

"I might know something that could help you a little. But see, I'm getting out of here. And I don't have all that much time or money."

I opened my shoulder bag and pulled a twenty out of my wallet. Her offer hadn't been well disguised, so I figured there wasn't any need to try to be tactful. I put the twenty on the bed. She snatched it up and stuffed it in a tiny satin handbag hanging on the doorknob.

"Okay. I came here about four months ago. That's when I first met Ely." Sunny went back to throwing things into the suitcase. "She didn't talk much at first; she was always busy with her work and all. But after a couple of months, she started giving me some hints about how to make it and all. She told me the real story about this place, trying to keep me out of trouble, but by that time, it was already kind of late."

"What do you mean, the real story about this place?"

She went on with the story, ignoring my question. "I thought I knew exactly what I was doing, and I wouldn't listen to her at first. But it turned out she was right after all. This place isn't what I thought it was."

"What do you mean?"

She didn't answer right away. When she did speak, the words came more slowly, more measured. "You asked me about if Ely was clean. Yeah, she wouldn't ever have used drugs again. Even if she wanted to kill herself, she wouldn't have done it like that."

Collazo now knew she hadn't killed herself, but I didn't see any reason to scare this girl with those kinds of details.

She picked up a small stuffed dog off the bed and hugged it to her chest. "Promise you won't tell anyone I told you this?"

I nodded solemnly. "Yeah. I promise."

"Okay." She took a deep breath. "I hope I'll be gone out of this town by tonight anyhow. See, I was working the door Friday night when she came in. She signed in and went back to the room. An hour or so later, she left. She went running out, real upset like, crying and screaming and all. Then yesterday morning, Minerva calls me into the office and tells me Ely's dead. She says the cops called and said they'd found Ely in the river and they were coming over here to talk to the people who knew her. She tells me I'm not supposed to tell anyone that Ely was here on Friday. She ripped the page out of the sign-in book where Ely signed in. She promised me something if I'd go along with them."

"What did she promise you?"

"I can't tell. It doesn't matter. Ely told me not to trust them, but I didn't believe her. I should have."

"What about James? Sunny, do you trust him?" At the mere mention of the name, she turned all teenage moony and love-struck. It was obvious she had a big-time crush on him.

"I can trust him all right. He's not like the others. He doesn't know everything that goes on here. He's gonna help me get a new start and all. I know he will."

The phone rang and she picked it up.

"Yeah? Oh, hi!" Her face stretched into a wide smile. "Uh-huh . . . okay." Her eyes flicked in my direction. "Yeah. Well, a little." The voice on the phone grew so loud, I could hear the angry tones across the room, and Sunny's smile slowly burned out. "Okay. I promise. Bye." She hung up the phone and turned to face me. "You gotta go."

"Who was that? On the phone, did somebody just tell you not to talk to me?"

She began scooping all the cosmetics on her bureau into a shopping bag, ignoring me.

"Sunny, what did you mean when you said Ely told you the true story about this place?"

She spun around to face me. "I can't talk to you no more. Go on. And please, don't tell anybody that I talked to you at all."

"Sunny, tell me what's going on here. I want to help."

"Well, you're not helping." Her voice sounded strained, frightened. "You're only getting me in trouble. Now go. Get out of here."

I set one of my business cards down on top of the clothes in the suitcase. "If you need help or a place to stay, or if there's anything you want to tell me, that's my phone number."

I found my own way out, and as I walked down the hall, I wondered why James had lied to me about Sunny. What had happened that night to make Ely so upset that she would flee—and then turn up dead?

Since Minerva was on the phone, I just waved to her as I passed through the lobby area. As I went out the door, I heard her saying into the telephone, "No, Mr. Burns, don't worry. I'll see to it."

Okay. So Burns is a fairly common name. But like Detective Collazo, I no longer believed in coincidences.

BY THE TIME I DROVE BACK OVER THE DRAWBRIDGE, IT WAS past three o'clock, and my stomach was protesting loudly. At a red light, I checked my wallet. Thanks to Sunny, I was down to my last twenty. A drive-through would be cheaper, but I was more likely to find work hanging out at the Downtowner. I headed for the restaurant and bar on the bank of the river.

Pete smiled when I came through the door, but then his expression turned serious, as though he had suddenly remembered something. He waved me over.

"Hang on a minute, Pete," I called out, and pointed to the back where the pay phone was. I wanted to talk to Jeannie first and find out how things were going on the legal front. I doubted she'd been able to do much over the weekend, but I hoped.

She picked up on the seventh ring, just as I was getting ready to give up. She sounded like she'd been trying to run a marathon.

"Jeannie, Seychelle here."

"Oh, hi," she said in between gasping breaths. "I was outside working in the yard when the phone rang."

I imagined Jeannie running up the stairs to her place, her muumuu flapping in the breeze.

"You catch your breath, and I'll tell you what I've found out so far. Then you can fill me in on your side of things."

"Okay."

Jeannie hadn't known Ely personally, but she had always had a good sympathetic ear. I found myself close to breaking down again as I told her about the events of the past twenty-four hours.

"I went back up to Harbor House and spoke to Ely's old

roommate. She was working the front desk the night Ely died. She said Ely did come in and then ran out upset and crying about an hour later. The folks at Harbor House tore out the page in the log where Ely signed in. Then they made this girl hush up about it and lie to the police."

"Do you think they had something to do with her death?" Jeannie asked.

"I don't know." I told her about my date with James and the face that I saw briefly at my kitchen window. "It was certainly not my imagination. Someone was spying in that window."

"Maybe it wasn't you they were spying on."

"James? I hadn't thought of that. Hmmm. To be honest, I can't figure James out. There's definitely something going on at Harbor House, but I'm not certain he knows about it."

"What do you mean?"

"I heard something strange when I was leaving Harbor House this afternoon. The lady at the front desk, Minerva, was on the phone, and she referred to the caller as Mr. Burns. I was wondering if it could be the same one. What have you found out about him?"

"Not much. He has an office off Las Olas, very high-rent district. The scoop from friends of mine is that in spite of his upper-crust veneer, he is a real scumbag. He likes to take criminal cases for the rich and famous, and he cleans up their messes. If some rich brat gets caught dealing dope in his prep school or a local commissioner is arrested for exposing himself up in Holiday Park, they call Burns. They like him because he's not a publicity hound like a lot of these guys. I can't get past his secretary, though, and he won't return my calls."

"Well, he called me." I told her then about the message on my answering machine. "Fifteen thousand is still chicken feed compared to what I could win if I took this to arbitration. They must know that or they wouldn't be threatening me."

"Fifteen thousand is better than nothing."

"Don't say that. You're my attorney, for crissakes."

"I know. But I'm worried about you, Seychelle. These are not nice people."

"Anything more on who's behind the Cayman Islands corporation?"

"Nothing concrete, but I have my suspicions. I suspect that slimeball Benjamin Crystal never really sold the boat. I could be wrong, but I've been doing a little research on him. Crystal is the owner of record of several Top Ten Clubs, all strictly legitimate. That's his public front. On the other hand, he is alleged to be involved with bookmaking, loan sharking, and prostitution through the clubs. They have been trying to gather enough evidence to close it down, but up until now, Crystal has been too smart. The only reason he's in jail right now is because of a coke bust that was a bit of a fluke. Normally, Crystal doesn't go near drugs—at least to import them. Not that he's above it, but he's making so much money on the sex business, why bother? But he did own this little interisland freighter, so the cops began to suspect he might be running drugs. They'd been over it many times with drug-sniffing dogs, but that boat was always clean. A man named Zeke Moss was captain—Crystal's cousin by marriage or something—and the cops now think he kept the freighter just to give this cousin a job. He was busted bringing a 'gift' to his cousin in the boatyard."

"Why would he want it to appear that he had sold the *Top Ten*?"

"He's been under surveillance for quite some time. He knew they were out to get him. He wanted to be sure they couldn't seize his toys. He's been doing the same thing with a couple of homes he owns."

"Jeannie, listen. I don't really care who owns the *Top Ten*; I just know I need *at least* twenty thousand—more like thirty, really—for this job. I know that sounds like a lot, but I risked a lot."

"If I'm right about this, it's not a lot to Benjamin Crystal. My question would be, then, how come he hasn't just paid the fee to get rid of you? That's what doesn't make sense. What does he really want from you?"

"I don't have a clue. Call Burns and make a counteroffer, say thirty, forty thousand. I need to settle this soon. Maddy is in real money trouble. I think I am going to have to buy him out of the boat somehow. If not, I'll have to sell her, and dammit, I don't want to do that."

A S SOON AS PETE SAW ME COMING BACK FROM THE PHONE, he waved me over.

"Seychelle, there's something you got to know. Something's going on and it stinks."

"What are you talking about, Pete?"

"I don't know who started it, but the word is that you're blackballed. Nobody's going to hire you anymore. They're saying you're late all the time, and you don't know what the hell you're doing. Guys you've worked for, who know better, they aren't even speaking up and saying it's a load of shit. I'm mad as hell about it, and every time I hear it start up, I go over and try to set things right, but it's no use. You know how it goes with gossip around here. People'll keep saying stuff they know ain't true just because other folks are saying it."

I patted him on the shoulder. "Thanks for letting me know, Pete."

"One more thing, Sey. That hairy cop dude? He's been in here twice looking for you, asking questions about you. People don't like it. You might not want to show your face in here again for a while."

If I couldn't work, couldn't even go to my old haunts to so-licit work, I'd lose the boat for sure. I suddenly lost my appetite.

XIV

WHEN I GOT BEHIND THE WHEEL OF LIGHTNIN', I wanted to slam the Jeep into gear and lay down some rubber to show the whole world just how pissed off I was. Luckily, I reconsidered. They, whoever they were, were the ones making all the moves, and I had just been running around re-acting. And the cops—I didn't know what they were doing, but it worried me that Collazo was investing so much time chasing after me. It was time to go on the offensive.

I stopped at the cottage and threw some old clothes and my in-line skates into the Jeep. I changed into some ratty old sneakers and put out fresh food and water for the dog.

As I drove down Andrews Avenue, I had a plan in the back of my mind, and I just wanted to drive for a while and let it brew. The next logical source of information seemed to me to be the *Top Ten* herself. Undoubtedly, the local cops had searched the boat, but they didn't necessarily know what to look for. Cesar and his buddy, Big Guy, had been looking for something offshore right around the same spot where I found the *Top Ten* drifting last Thursday. Maybe it was the wreck I saw them diving on, or maybe they were guess-ing, same as me. One thing I knew was that if Neal had been looking for something on the bottom, then the position of that something could be retrieved from the memory of the boat's GPS, Global Positioning System.

I turned east on State Road 84. These days everybody from lobster fishermen to sport divers use satellite navigation to pinpoint exact spots on the ocean. The longitude and latitude coordinates are stored as way points in the machine's memory. Whether or not Collazo and company knew about that, I wasn't sure, but I decided I would like to take a little look around the megayacht on my own.

When I turned right onto Federal Highway, I noticed the dark blue car with tinted windows behind me. It turned at the same time. It looked like it might be a Camaro or a Grand Prix or something that had been souped up and undoubtedly had speakers with a bass volume that could rattle the fillings right out of the driver's head. I slowed down and drove at the pace of an elderly French Canadian, letting most of the traffic pass me on my left. Normally, a car that looked like the one behind me would zoom around me in an irate huff. But this guy kept following and matched his speed to mine.

At the entrance to Fort Lauderdale International Airport, I veered to the right and drove down the off-ramp. The dark car followed. I drove slowly around the lower level, where arriving passengers collected their luggage and met their rides or boarded shuttles to the rental car lots. It was a busy Sunday, and the typically rude South Floridians tried to cut one another off, blew their horns, and double-parked, blocking traffic. Sheriff's deputies were directing traffic and trying to get the pedestrians across to the parking garage without their being run over. I pretended to be looking for an arriving guest, and I drove slowly, peering into the terminal and watching my rearview mirror. Whoever was back there behind those tinted windows didn't seem to care whether or not I knew I was being followed. He made no attempt at secrecy.

Just in front of the United terminal, I noticed a group of about twenty-five people, all looking very overfed and wearing flowered shirts, as if they'd just returned from a cruise. The officer was getting ready to stop traffic, but she was waiting for a particularly large lady wearing tight white polyester shorts that highlighted every bulge and dimple on her rear end. She had on those odd beige-colored knee-high support hose and fluorescent green sneakers that matched the tight T-shirt, and she was lugging an enormous cruise ship handbag. I slowed until the lady and her group had almost reached the crosswalk and the sheriff's deputy was starting out to stop traffic. The flowered-shirt people flowed into the right lane like ants out of a stirred-up nest. I hit the gas and yanked the wheel, squeaking around them on the left side. The officer blew her whistle at me and waved her arm, but I just kept going. The tourists flowed on across the street, blocking all traffic. In the rearview mirror, I could see the dark windows, and I imagined the furious face behind the glass.

I sped on to make sure I would be through the section where the highways forked north and south before he was clear of those pedestrians. I turned north, the way I had come, hoping that he would assume I continued south. Back on Federal Highway, I turned into Port Everglades, just to make sure he wouldn't find me again. Big tanker trucks rumbled out of the port loading docks. I wound my way in to my favorite spot.

A canal dead-ended by the roadside, and warm water from the electrical plant flowed into the canal at that point. A makeshift picnic area had once been set up around the perimeter of the water where a few scraggly pine trees survived in the shadow of a tank farm and the stacks of the power plant, but the authorities had removed the tables and attempted to cover the fence with blinds. What attracted people to this spot wasn't the trees but what was in the water: manatees. The big sea cows had started coming to the power plant's outflow during cold fronts. The warm water found there was a welcome relief from the cold winter temperatures.

Eventually, people started feeding them lettuce and bits of fruit, and now the manatees came as much in hopes of a free handout as for the warm water. They tried to keep the crowds away, but diehard manatee lovers had cut holes in the blinds.

I parked the Jeep as far off the road as I could get. There was a Latino family already there, with two little kids, about five and seven years old, all dressed up in their church finery. The littler was a girl, clutching lettuce leaves in her dainty hands, all pink ruffles and ribbons. Her daddy was holding her up so she could toss the leaves over the top of the chain-link fence down into the water.

"*Mira, mira,* Papa," she squealed, excitedly pointing into the water.

I walked to the fence and wrapped my fingers through the wire. At the bottom of the pit, a mother manatee lolled on the surface, slowly drifting toward any debris on the water, checking out its edible qualities. Her gray back was crisscrossed with white scars where boat propellers had slashed her. In her wake was a tiny calf: an adorable, chubby, unblemished miniature of his mom.

Mother and child. My mother's scars weren't visible, and I had been a kid. How could I have been expected to understand? I watched as the crisscrossed manatee mother nudged the calf over to the lettuce. She wore her motherhood so effortlessly.

After watching the manatees for fifteen minutes or so, I climbed back into Lightnin' and sat before turning the key in the ignition. I envied the little girl on her father's shoulders. I couldn't remember Red ever lifting me up like that; I was never Daddy's little girl. He was proud of me in a different way, because I was smart and knew boats and could pull *Gorda* in to kiss the dock from the time I was about eight years old. From a very early age Red talked to me like I was an adult, treating me sometimes as the woman of the house. When he'd leave to go on a job down in Miami, before he'd go out that door, he'd crouch down in front of me and say quietly, "You'll take care of your mother and your brothers, now, won't you?" Red knew that Mother sometimes was there to mother us and sometimes vanished behind her door and didn't come out for days. I would take over, feeding the boys hot dogs and pork and beans for dinner and shushing them, telling them not to bother her. Then Red would come home, and I could be a kid again. God, I missed my dad. I didn't know who I could trust anymore.

$\mathcal{XV}$

WHEN I HEARD THE BEEPING, I WAS AWARE OF WHERE I was, and I really had to pee. I'd slept a few hours at the Paradise Hotel just to get away from everyone. The room was spartan and what little was there was tasteless. I'd wolfed down a Whopper with cheese and large order of fries while balancing the food on my lap. Nothing in the room looked clean enough to eat off. In fact, I'd decided to turn the air down and nap on top of the covers. I didn't want to see what surprises might be on the sheets. The carbohydrate fix had made me even sleepier. I'd set the alarm on my watch for 1:00 A.M., and I was out the moment I was prone.

Now it took all the willpower I could muster to force my body up off that bed and into the bathroom. I sat on the john and wondered if I was a complete lunatic to try to break into a million-dollar yacht tied up to the docks of a United States Coast Guard base. My conclusion: probably. But I didn't know what else to do at that point. I was certain that everything that had happened during these last four days was connected. Ely and Patty both had been killed because of some secret, and Neal was hiding out because he knew something about it. Men like Hamilton Burns and his clients really valued only money. At the moment, I could use some of it myself, and that was just one reason I was determined to find out if the *Top Ten* held any of the answers I was looking for.

The motel was quiet and the streets were nearly empty when I pulled out onto the highway. I'd found an old navy blue zip-front hooded sweatshirt balled up in the back of my Jeep, and I pulled it on to cover my bright T-shirt. The dark jean shorts would be okay. I also had a collection of baseball caps under the seat for days when the wind in the Jeep got to be too much. With my hair pulled into a tight ponytail, I chose a dark cap with Sullivan Towing stitched in faded gold across the front. It had once belonged to Red.

It had been a long time since I had last been to John Lloyd Beach State Park. The park was on a long peninsula that formed the southern side of the mouth to the harbor at Port Everglades. This narrow strip of land was really a barrier island that stretched all the way down to South Beach and the Miami Harbor entrance. The ocean flowed on the outside, the Intracoastal on the inside. At the tip of the peninsula, the Coast Guard had their facilities, but you had to pass through the park to get down to their station. The State Parks people manned a security gate there round the clock.

I turned off into the parking lot at Dania Beach and parked in one of the metered spots. The best way to get past the gate would be on foot, going into the brush on either side of the guard station. But then it would be a good two-mile hike down to where the *Top Ten* was docked. I didn't think anybody would be on the road through the park at that hour. I grabbed the backpack containing my in-line skates. There was a flashlight under the driver's seat for emergencies, and I dropped it in the backpack as well.

I pulled my cap down low over my face as I crossed the Whiskey Creek bridge. I was in full view of the ranger station about fifteen hundred yards ahead, but I was guessing that the person on duty either had something to read or some music and he wouldn't pay much attention to my end of the road. At the bottom of the bridge, I turned off into the forest of tall Australian pines. The thick carpet of pine needles on the forest floor made it easy walking, although the trees didn't provide much cover. I passed the ranger post about a hundred feet away. I could see the headphones on the young man's head.

The road took a turn another couple of hundred yards past the guard post, and I sat on a chunk of dead coral on the side of the road and pulled on my skates.

The road through the park was dark and desolate. Pines lined the right side of the road, and on the left, short mangrove seedlings covered the bank before the dark water of the Intracoastal. I skated near the side of the road, ready to jump into the trees if a car approached. The asphalt was rough, and I tried to get into my steady rhythm of side-to-side sweeping strides.

Just across the Intracoastal, the mangroves began to thin out and the bright lights of the busy commercial port lit my way. On one side was the loamy smell of the dark pine woods, while across the water came the noises and machine smells of ships' engines and generators. Toward the end of the peninsula, the road curved, and through the trees, I could see the lights of the dormitories and buildings at the station.

There were several compounds out on the end of the peninsula that marked the southern half of the entrance to Port Everglades. After I replaced my skates with my sneakers, I checked the whole area over to make sure I was jumping the right fence. The entrance to the Coast Guard station had a closed chain-link gate that operated electronically, but no guard. Not even any barbed wire on top. Up until now, everything I'd been doing had been minor, but breaking into a U.S. military installation was a major offense. My pulse was throbbing in my neck as I hooked my fingers through the chain link. It took me several minutes to force myself to make the first step. Once over, I made my way around the perimeter of the compound to where I could see the *Top Ten* berthed behind a forty-foot cutter.

The gangway was down and no precautions had been taken to keep people from boarding. The Coasties probably didn't expect anybody to get this far without being challenged.

Stepping onto the deck, my memory flashed back to when I

had jumped aboard last Thursday. The same eerie feeling came over me as soon as I stepped aboard. Lots of sailors and fishermen get to thinking their boats have personalities and wills of their own. I've always been a skeptic about this, but this ship did feel as though she had lost her soul.

I started at the bow on the lower deck and worked my way aft, jiggling all the doors and windows, trying to find my way in. The police had placed yellow crime scene tape across the doorways, but at this point it was the locks that were most effective at keeping me out. On the stern, I made out a dark shape on the side deck that I hadn't noticed the last time I was aboard. A black oilcloth tarp covered what looked like some kind of machinery. Yachts of this size and caliber didn't normally need to have machinery stored out on deck. I pulled off the cover and found what looked like a small engine mounted on top of a pair of tanks. Squatting down below the level of the bulwarks, I clicked on my flashlight and examined the aluminum plate on the side of the red steel tank: Powermate Contractor, 5.5 HP, 120 PSI Max. Pressure. It was apparently some kind of gas engine–driven air compressor. Red had installed a small compressor on *Gorda* that we sometimes used for filling tanks. What was this one for? For filling dive tanks? That didn't make sense. The *Top Ten* already had an electric compressor in her engine room below deck. I wondered why on earth Neal had brought it aboard.

I heard a loud scraping noise aft, and I clicked off my flashlight. At first I heard nothing but my own heart pounding and the whistle of the air in my nostrils as I tried to slow down and breathe normally. Then I heard the noises of the port across the turning basin, the beeping of forklifts loading containers onto ships, trucks and tugs moving and working. A pilot boat passed on the channel side, and the *Top Ten* strained at her dock lines. The aluminum companionway creaked as it rolled on the seawall. When my heart finally slowed to a mere gallop, I stood and peered around the cabin on both sides of the yacht. There was no one there.

On the seaward side, I found a window left open a crack for

ventilation. I slid it open wider and managed to squeeze through, although I had to leave my pack outside on the deck. I was in the main salon, close to Neal's cabin.

In the beam of my flashlight, I could see that the police had left the place a mess. They had probably already found everything that was worth finding, but I had to try.

The crew's quarters were up forward in the bow. I had visited Neal's cabin several times before we finally broke it off for good. The door stood ajar. Most of the personal possessions in the cabin were the same ones I had picked up and put away over the months that Neal had lived with me in my cottage: his clothing, a machete he'd picked up in Panama for opening coconuts, a scrimshawed whale's tooth. Nothing there told me anything new about the life he had been leading. I closed the door to his cabin and headed up to the bridge.

Somebody had cleaned up the blood. I began to search through the paraphernalia. Various letters, bills for boat maintenance, marina charges, fuel receipts. Neal never had been very good at bookkeeping. Finally, I picked my copy of Bowditch's *The Practical Navigator*. Inside the cover there were some personal letters and some photographs, including several of me.

I leaned against the helmsman's seat and examined a picture of the two of us taken down at Fort Jefferson in the Dry Tortugas. We were up on top of the fort, sitting on the ramparts with the various blues and greens of the anchorage in the background. From that picture, you would think those two would never be apart the rest of their lives.

Tucked between the pages of Bowditch, I found some odd sketches. I had no idea what they were. Obviously the police hadn't thought they were important, if they'd looked at the book at all. Near as I could tell, the drawings delineated some compartment or container. The measurements were sketched in as well as the rough calculations of the square footage of the space. I slid the sketches and the photo back into the book. I felt fairly safe taking it now. I doubted the cops would even notice it was gone.

It wasn't difficult to find the GPS, but I had never used this model before, so it took me several minutes to figure out how to recall the way points that were stored in memory. Neal had way points for Miami Harbor entrance, Bimini, Marathon, West End, you name it. Each way point was named with a three-letter code name like MIA, MAR, or WND. The last position entered was located just north of the entrance to Port Everglades. I lifted up the chart tabletop and rummaged around inside for a slip of paper and a pencil. I wrote down the coordinates, latitude 26°09.52'N, longitude 80°04.75'W, as well as the name, BAB. What the hell did that mean?

I slipped the papers and photos back into the book, let myself out the side door, and made my way to the aft lower deck, where I'd left my backpack. I slid the copy of Bowditch in between the skates and zipped the pack closed.

I heard a noise behind me. I whirled around, twisting in a crouched position. The next thing I knew was blinding, searing pain as a blunt object slammed down on my left shoulder. A figure dressed in black grunted and pulled a fire extinguisher back into the air, preparing to hit me again.

My attacker looked like a giant Pillsbury Doughboy in blackface. He growled a deep animal-like noise and came at me again. This time I rose up swinging the pack with every bit of pain and fury I had in me. The pack smashed into the black ski mask. I heard him groan, then gag and spit. I raced for the aft deck, looking frantically for another weapon, anything.

He hadn't stayed down more than a couple of seconds. I tried to turn around at the end of the main cabin area, but my feet slipped on the sharp right turn. I heard him before I felt his hands grab hold of the cap hanging from my ponytail. He threw it to the deck and grabbed my ponytail. He yanked my hair so hard, I could hear some of my hair being pulled out at the roots, and then he slowly pulled my head farther back. I thought he'd break my neck. I couldn't breathe. Every time I struggled, he pulled harder.

"Bitch," he breathed in his deep voice.

He forced me to the back corner of the deck opposite the covered compressor. Just as I thought I was about to black out, I felt his other hand reach between my legs and grab me by the crotch.

He yanked my hair back harder, and when I tried to scream, nothing but a pain-scrambled gurgle came out. Then I was rising, being lifted by my hair, the hand between my legs. I saw the turbulent black water of the inlet beneath me.

"*Adiós,* bitch."

He heaved me into space.

Grabbing the swim step would be my only chance to stay with the boat, a lesson my father had taught me since childhood. As I fell, I swung my right arm in the direction of the teak platform. I heard the skates crash onto the wood, and my wrist slammed down onto the steel strip at the edge of the step. My right hand went limp, releasing the strap, unable to grab hold of the swim step, as a new, mightier pain tore up my right arm.

The water was shockingly cold. I let my body go limp, my heavy wet clothes pulling me down. When I didn't move, the pain was less—maybe, I thought hazily, I should just stay down there in the cold agreeable depths and sleep.

Then my lungs started to burn. My arms were nearly useless. The blackness was closing in, the world was a tunnel. It hurt like hell, but I kicked and flailed my ineffectual arms to struggle to the surface.

Pulling air into my lungs hurt, yet it tasted so sweet.

The *Top Ten* was about fifty feet away, and the gap was widening. I was thankful for the ebb tide that was sucking me out to sea, away from that fire extinguisher and madman. The fight in me was gone. I just wanted to drift away. The bulky figure on deck pulled the ski mask off, and I didn't need to see the spiky hair to know who it was. Esposito. He spun around and ran for the gangway.

Because of my sore left shoulder and bruised or maybe broken right wrist, my legs were having to do all the work of treading water to keep my head up. My sodden sneakers were weighing my legs down. I kicked them off and let my legs float. I knew the tide was carrying me alongside the jetty, but I had to rest before I could swim.

Then I heard the high-pitched whine that an outboard makes underwater. Thank God. Some crazy guys are fishing at this hour of the morning. I saw the boat headed out in the middle of the inlet, and I began to raise my arm to wave at them, when I realized the boat looked very much like a certain white Sea Ray I had seen before, only then there had been two divers aboard. Now, a lone man stood at the center console, and he seemed to be slowly searching the surface of the water on either side of him.

Damn.

I ducked my head underwater and pushed my hair forward over my face to cut down on the reflection of the shoreside lights on my white skin. I raised my head just enough to breathe through my nose. And I watched.

He didn't appear to have seen me, but nonetheless, he was coming straight for me. I waited as long as I thought was safe, slowly hyperventilating. Then I dove.

I don't usually open my eyes underwater, but I wanted to try to see when it would be safe for me to resurface. But it was just all blackness, everywhere. It made me feel disoriented, as though I didn't know which way was up, and which was down. Like most women, if my lungs are full of air, I float, so I had to struggle to stay under. Even moving slowly as he was, it should have taken him only a few seconds to pass over me, but the whine of his outboard surrounded me in the water. I had no idea which direction it was coming from. My chest was already starting to constrict. There hadn't been time to get a proper breath before diving. I swam in the direction that I thought would take me away from the boat, but the outboard whine only grew louder, then overpowering. I thought I was going to get hit by the prop. In my imagination, I could see the whirling, slicing blades all around me in the water. Going against every fiber in my body that was screaming out for air, I tried to swim deeper, or at least in the direction that I thought was down. In a flash, I imagined this was how my mother had done it, walking into ever-deeper water until it closed over her head, the sheer force of her will refusing to answer all the cues and calls and demands of her body. But deep in the cerebral cortex, at the simplest levels, before thought, perhaps even before instinct, resides the species' imperative to survive. My self-preservation autopilot took over and reversed my direction. The hell with the props. I needed air. Desperately. Now.

I broke through the surface of the water no more than fifteen feet behind his churning outboard. The engine noise was much louder at the surface, thankfully, because I was making a hell of a lot of noise gulping down air in rasping breaths. He seemed to be moving faster; the gulf between us was broadening rapidly. I turned around to swim away from him, thinking I would be swimming back into the inlet, but I saw nothing but dark black sea and sky. The reason he had seemed to be coming from every direction at once above me was because he had been turning his boat around right over my head. Esposito was motoring back into Port Everglades. I was drifting out to sea.

XVI

I COULD SEE THE LIGHTS OF HOLLYWOOD BEACH APPEARING
as I drifted past the end of the breakwater. I estimated the current was running at least two knots. The water grew rougher as
the outgoing tide ran into the incoming wind chop. Several waves
broke over my head, and I swallowed a mouthful of seawater. My
eyes and nose burned, and I still didn't have much movement in either my left arm or my right hand. There was no way I could swim
against that tide.

Lifeguards teach swimmers that if they are ever caught in a
riptide to simply relax, let the current carry you out, then swim
parallel to the beach and go ashore where there is no outbound
current. That would not have been a problem if I had been fresh,
but in the exhausted and injured state I was in, I doubted that I
would make it back in to the beach. I was having enough trouble
just treading water and trying to keep my head above the waves.

On the south side of the channel, I suddenly heard an explo-
sive puff of air, followed by a deep groan. Squinting to clear the
water out of my eyes, I made out the green light on a channel buoy.
It was farther away than I expected; clearly, the Gulf Stream was already carrying me north. The buoy's air horn moaned again as it
rose and fell on the waves.

I turned my eyes seaward. There should be another marker, the harbor entrance buoy. The light on that one would be red and brighter, and the buoy itself would be bigger. Maybe, big enough to crawl onto.

On the crest of a swell, I spotted the red light, but it disappeared when I dipped down into a trough between swells. On the next peak, I found the light again, and was alarmed to see how fast I was drifting. I might pass the buoy before the tide carried me out there.

I turned south and started kicking, trying to fight the Gulf Stream, that mighty current that flows with the strength of all those trade-wind seas that pile up in the Gulf of Mexico, only to spill out toward the north. The ebb tide was carrying me out to the buoy, but I had to fight the current from carrying me up the coast before I made it out there.

Trying to ignore the pain, I began to stroke with my left arm, a sidestroke and a scissors kick, trying to hold my hand steady on the wobbly wrist. Half the time I wasn't even sure I was going in the right direction when for several waves I wouldn't see the red eye glowing in the darkness. Then it would appear again, I'd adjust my course slightly, and kick with renewed vigor.

The cold water was numbing the pain in my shoulder, and I drank in the brilliant night sky awash in stars, the glistening lights of the coastal condos, the luminous green bursts of the phosphorescent plankton as I stroked through the sea. There was nothing frightening about this night. Some people probably believe right up to the last minute before they drown that they can save themselves, that their efforts will be enough to snatch them back from the precipice. Perhaps they never become aware that it isn't enough; they fight to the end, and then there is nothing. And then again, there are those, like my mother, who never even try to save themselves.

The next time I saw the light I was startled to see how close it was, and I heard the bell clanging for the first time. I wondered if I had blacked out for a minute or just gone into some kind of dream state. But the buoy was right there. I was slightly to the north of it, though, the stream having pushed me even farther off course than I thought.

My arms and legs felt leaden. The water was so much warmer than the chill wind on my face. The water wrapped me, blanket-like, comfortable, appealing. I wanted to stop swimming, to rest, to sleep. Forget the damn buoy.

A wave slapped my face and drove salt water up my nostrils. The pain seemed to explode white hot and searing in my brain. No, dammit. Swim, stroke, go, go. I'm better than this, I can do it. In an all-out frenzy of flailing limbs and thrashing water, I covered the last hundred feet straight up into the current.

The bell was clanging, deafening. Red flash, one-two-three, red flash. I reached up and grabbed one of the bars that supported the light and the battery pack. The buoy was rocking and rolling in the swell; on each rise, my body was lifted out of the water to the waist, and my injured hand nearly let go. It was several minutes before I had the strength to pull myself out of the water. I was dimly aware that my forearms and belly were getting sliced up by the barnacles as I dragged my body out of the water. The wind numbed my face as I curled my body into a tight ball on the narrow platform beneath the flashing red light and clanging bell. I wrapped my arms around the bars so as not to fall off as the buoy rocked in the swells and closed my eyes. I was still alive.

FAR, FAR OFF IN THE DISTANCE, AS THOUGH DOWN AT THE end of a long tunnel, I heard an outboard running at a good pace and then idling down. I had no idea how long I had been curled up on the buoy, shivering in the wind, trying to conserve body heat. I knew I should open my eyes, but I felt like the little kid who closes his eyes and thinks he is hiding. If it was Esposito, I didn't want to know about it. There was no place I could go to escape, and back in the water meant hypothermia, death for sure.

Even with my eyes closed, the whole world suddenly seemed

to turn red as a spotlight lit up the buoy and shone through my eyelids. I lifted my head and squinted toward the light.

"Hey!" a voice called. A deep voice, a male voice. "Hey, lady, are you okay?"

Stupid as it may sound, I started to laugh. What was I supposed to say? No, go on, I'm fine, thank you?

"Hey, lady?" he called again. "Jason," he said more softly, "move in a little closer, okay?"

"Dad, are you sure we oughta? She looks kinda scary. Like, do you think she might be crazy or something?"

I lifted up my head and tried to shield my eyes with my forearm. "The light," I called out, waving my arms and pointed at their spot. The bell drowned out what I said, but apparently they understood the pantomime. The spotlight went out, leaving the world dark, but my eyes were still blinded by bright red spots.

I followed the sound of their idling engine as they drew closer. Then I heard the crunch of crushed barnacles as their boat eased alongside. Out of the darkness, a hand touched my arm and pulled me to the edge of the buoy. I went willingly, still blind.

"Thanks," I said as someone wrapped a thick, warm beach towel around my shoulders. I began to be able to make out their faces. I didn't think I'd ever stop shivering.

"Jason, we'd better head back in with her." The driver turned the boat around, and we headed for the inlet. My vision was clearing rapidly now. The man who handed me a Styrofoam cup of coffee had gray hair and a beard and looked about fifty years old.

"Are you gonna be okay?"

Nodding, I answered, "Yeah, now I am. Thanks to you. I don't know how much longer I would have lasted out there."

"What happened to you?" he asked.

Even with only half my wits about me, I knew better than to try to explain the whole story. This guy's son would really think I was crazy if I tried that.

"I fell overboard," I said.

"Where's your boat?"

I pointed out to sea. "I think she went down. She was taking on water, and when I went up forward to get an extra pump, I fell overboard. I guess I kinda panicked."

"Well, you're mighty lucky we came along."

"I sure am." I smiled at him. I meant it.

Then we were approaching the *Top Ten*, and I craned my neck to see over his shoulder. The interior lights were all on, and I saw several uniformed police officers in the main salon.

"That sure is a pretty vessel, isn't it?" the man said, turning to look at what was distracting me.

On the swim step I saw a black shadow against the glistening white hull.

"Hold up," I said. "Could you swing by there so I could pick up that bag?"

The kid driving looked where I was pointing, then to his dad for permission. The man nodded.

"Sure," the kid said, and spun the wheel.

The father reached down and picked up my backpack. "Oof, this thing is heavy. Better not be cocaine or some damn thing in here."

I smiled at him and unzipped the top of the pack, revealing the contents. "No, just my roller skates."

Father and son exchanged a look that seemed to say, Son, you're right—she is nuts.

XVII

COMMUTER TRAFFIC WAS THICK ON FEDERAL HIGHWAY.
Driving with my sore shoulder and wrist was difficult, but
I was relieved to see that I was starting to get some mo-
bility back in both—that apparently nothing was broken or perma-
nently damaged.

By the time I got back to the Paradise Hotel, the sun was well
up. Checkout time wasn't until eleven, though, so I closed the
drapes and slept for three hours.

When I woke up, even blinking hurt. Every muscle and tissue
in my body screamed for me to stop when I tried to roll off the bed.
Getting up into a sitting position felt like a major accomplishment.

I looked up and saw my reflection in the mirror over the
dresser. God, what a sight. No wonder that fisherman and his son
thought I was a crazy lady. Most of my hair had come loose from
the rubber band, and it stood out around my head in sticky, salty
clumps. There was a nice purple bruise around the hairline on the
right side of my face where that fire extinguisher had managed a
glancing blow on my head, and my T-shirt was now stiff with salt
and blood. My forearms were laced with bloody scratches, and the
dark circles under my eyes may have been from the bang on the
head or just pure exhaustion, I wasn't sure which. One thing I

knew: I needed a nice long clean shower. The hell with it all. I was going home.

I DIDN'T SEE ANY SUSPICIOUS DARK-WINDOWED CARS PARKED along the road anywhere in my Rio Vista neighborhood. Nobody was following me, either. I drove around the block a few more times just to be sure. It felt a little odd driving barefoot, but I'd left my sneakers somewhere on the bottom of the Port Everglades inlet.

Abaco was beside herself when I came through the gate. She jumped and whirled and yelped. I sat down on the grass and held her, scratching her ears while she moaned and rolled her eyes back in pure canine bliss.

I kept the dog inside the cottage with me when I got into the shower. It's bad enough feeling like somebody's out there gunning for you, but to have to climb into the shower after growing up watching *Psycho* on the late show was really nerve-wracking.

Even the lousy pressure in my shower hurt as the jets of water hit my aching body. The barnacle scratches on my arms and belly stung as the salt washed off, and I could barely lift my left arm to lather my hair.

I was wearing nothing but a towel wrapped around my head, and had just finished drying off my legs, when I remembered the book with the drawings in my backpack. I went out in the front room, pulled the stuff out of my slightly soggy backpack, and set the papers and photos out to dry on the bar. I was studying the photo of Neal and me in the Tortugas when I heard the knock at the front door. In an instant, my heart rate doubled. Abaco barked once, and then started whining. My great protector.

I felt naked. I *was* naked. I wrapped my hair towel around me, sarong style, and looked around the living room. There was nothing remotely like a weapon anywhere in sight.

Another knock. The dog should have been barking her head off, but she just sat there looking at the front door, smiling and panting. I picked up the cordless phone, ready to bean somebody over the head with it if necessary, and went to the door.

"Who is it?" I asked, face to the crack in the door.

"It's B.J."

"Shit." I twisted the dead bolt and swung open the door. "Sorry. I thought you were one of them."

He looked at my face, then at the phone gripped in my white knuckles, and then back at my face. "What were you going to do? Talk me to death?"

"It's not funny," I said, motioning for him to follow me inside. "You don't know what I've been through in the last few days."

"How'd you get that bruise?" He pointed to his own forehead.

I fingered the spot I knew was purple. "This . . . ow. Got hit with a fire extinguisher. That was before I was thrown overboard and nearly drowned."

"Seriously?"

"What do you think, I'm doing a stand-up routine here?"

"You sure don't look good."

"Thanks. Just what a girl wants to hear. You have such a way with words, Mr. Moana."

As I was speaking, he went into my bedroom, pulled the quilt off the bed, and with a big flourish, spread it out on the living room floor.

"Lie down."

"What?" I said clutching at my towel. "B.J., last night somebody tried to kill me. And they came damn close."

"Facedown." He picked up a pillow off the couch and set it on the floor. "Put this under your neck and let your head hang off the other side."

"I don't have time for this . . ."

He put his hands on my shoulders and pressed down. I resisted at first, but the weight of his hands suddenly felt overpowering, and I bent my knees and spread out on the quilt.

"Take off the towel."

"Why?" I lifted my head and looked over my shoulder at him.

A faint smile lit his eyes. "Just do it, Seychelle. Trust me."

I hesitated only a fraction of a second after looking at the familiar planes and angles that made up his face. "Oh, B.J. I'm just so tired." I unwrapped the towel, and he slid it down so that it was draped across my butt.

"Shh. I know. Just try to empty your mind." He knelt on top of my back with a knee on either side of my rib cage and began to knead the muscles in my shoulders. His hands dug deep into the fibers of that damaged left muscle, and it felt as though electricity coursed through his fingers. A very real and palpable heat penetrated from his skin deep into the pain-wracked tissue. It hurt, but there was an exquisite pleasure in the pain.

I closed my eyes and surrendered my consciousness to the world of sensation. Explosions of color lit up my inner eyelids. But before long, my memory kicked in and a montage of memories played in my mind without plot or destination, the way dreams sometimes jump from image to image with no discernible connection.

Pit and I played dress-up next to the family's Dodge Valiant, getting into Red's navy footlocker, trying on his uniforms, the big brass latches on the locker gleaming in the late afternoon light, the garage filled with the odor of old motor oil and mothballs. . . .

Standing in front of an easel, my mother's arms wrapped around me from behind, her warm bosom pressed against my back. She was steadying my right hand and the brush it held, whispering in my ear, "Light strokes, yes, that's it, lovely," as I washed in the blue sky around the white clouds. . . .

All five of us were on board *Gorda*, probably the one and only time it ever happened. It was the Fourth of July and we were offshore waiting for the fireworks on the city barge. It was a night so dark and still, the sea looked like star-splattered black glass. Meanwhile, Maddy, the only one allowed to use the lighter, lit Pit's and my sparklers ever so slowly, and we were screaming at him to hurry up, to stop trying to be such a big shot. Red told us all to shut up. Mother went up to stand alone on the bow. He didn't go after her. . . .

We were in the living room and Red was crying. I'd never seen my father cry. I hadn't said a word to anybody all day. Not to the lifeguards. Not to the police officers. Not to my brothers. Not to my father. "Didn't she say anything?" he kept asking. "I don't understand. Why? Why did she do this? She must have said something." I didn't think I would ever talk again. . . .

The summer burned up through my towel, sandwiching me between rays of the sun and the dry oven heat of the sand. On a radio, several blankets over, Carole King was singing "Up on the Roof." I was pretending to read the words of my book.

"Seychelle," my mother said.

I didn't answer her. I kept my eyes moving over the print on the page.

"Honey." I was still mad. I wanted to be back with Pit and Molly. "Try to understand. Sometimes it's just *too hard* to do what we know is right.

"Seychelle, will you ever forgive me?"

I answered her.

She stood up and walked down to the water. . . .

"**D**ID YOU FALL ASLEEP?"

B.J.'s voice brought me back. The pain was nearly gone. I felt rested and renewed.

I sat up, shifting the towel around me, and rotated my arm and shoulder. There was a little remnant, sort of a phantom pain, but I had regained 90 percent of the movement in my wrist and shoulder.

"That's amazing, B.J. What did you do?"

"Just a little shiatsu. It's like acupuncture, only using massage instead of needles."

"That's amazing," I said, trying to stand gracefully without losing the towel. "Thanks."

He shrugged. "What are friends for?"

I walked closer to him and watched his eyes. "You are my

friend, aren't you? I mean, after what happened the other night at your house . . . I don't know, I was kinda crazy."

"Always, Seychelle."

He was right. I could see it in there.

"You wouldn't believe what I had started thinking about you. People have been following me, spying on me, trying to hurt me, and I haven't known who to trust."

"Trust your own instincts," he said, and wrapped his arms around me.

My own arms were crossed in front of my chest, clutching the towel, and I folded into his embrace feeling slight and fragile in the circle of his arms. It was rare and remarkably pleasant for me to feel almost petite. I nuzzled my face into his chest, smelling him and feeling the thudding of my pulse deep in my tight throat. I wanted to say something, to explain that I'd never felt anything like his touch, but the words wouldn't come. I pressed my body to his and was about to toss my towel and reach around those shoulders when he placed his hands on my arms and gently pushed me away.

Our eyes locked. He brushed the backs of his fingers across my cheek. Smiling, I playfully bit his pinky.

B.J. pushed out his lower lip in a playful pout and shook his head. "Seychelle."

I loved the sound of his voice speaking my name. "How do you do that? I was in so much pain, and you just made it all go away."

"No." He sighed. "Not all of it." He pressed his fingers against the tendons on the side of my neck, and I winced. "See that tightness? You are still holding on to something, something I can't massage away. I don't know what it is . . . maybe you don't even know what it is. But until then"—he turned me around—"this is not the time," and he pushed me through the bedroom door. He didn't follow.

After kicking the door closed, I flopped facedown on my bed, grabbed a pillow, pulled it tight over the back of my head, and screamed into the mattress. Pain? Yeah, I knew pain—the pain of rejection. The fabric around my face grew wet with spit. I didn't care.

When I finally got up, I took a few deep breaths and looked around my room. It was a mess, like my life. Why, oh why was I coming on to B.J. like this? I was behaving like an idiot. I sorted through several piles of wrinkled clothing before finally settling on a pair of jeans and a plain green T-shirt. When I walked out into the living room, still combing the snarls out of my hair, B.J. was sitting on the couch drinking a glass of orange juice.

His smiling eyes watched me cross the room. "Jeannie called me," he said. "She was worried about you—sent me over here to find you. I guess she's been leaving messages on your machine and trying to reach you for almost twenty-four hours."

I glanced at the machine. The red light was blinking.

"Did she say what she wanted?"

"Just that she's pinned down the owner of the *Top Ten*. She said she needs to talk to you about it."

I dialed Jeannie's number but just got her answering machine again. I left a brief message so she'd know I was alive, and told her I'd call back later.

"Do you want to talk about what's going on?" B.J. asked.

I opened the fridge and searched fruitlessly for something edible. I reached for the orange juice and got a glass for company's sake.

Flopping down into my mamasan chair and tucking my feet under me, I considered how much to tell him. Not that I didn't trust B.J., but I didn't want to get him worried—or more worried.

"As near as I can tell, Neal was after something when he went out there on the *Top Ten*. He was diving for something on the bottom. Remember those two guys I told you had hassled me and Elysia?"

"Yeah."

"Yesterday, after I got back from the memorial service, I took the Whaler and went back out to try to find the same spot where I found the *Top Ten*, and those two guys were diving out there. They were checking out some artificial reef wrecks. Neal knew where it was—whatever it is—so that's why they were trying to find Neal the night they jumped us. I have no idea what Elysia had to do with it, but I'm sure her death is connected.

"So, anyway, last night I went aboard the *Top Ten* and got the last position out of the GPS. And it seems at least one of those guys had the same idea. While I was poking around the boat, I noticed something weird on the afterdeck. It was this big compressor. Maybe Neal was planning on using it as a hookah rig so he could stay down longer than he could on a tank. But I don't know how deep you can go on a rig like that."

"Me neither."

"I thought maybe I would go over to Pier 66 and ask some questions, see if Neal had talked to anybody about it when he brought it aboard."

"I think you need to leave things alone, Seychelle. Let the police deal with this."

"Yeah, right. They wouldn't even know the right questions to ask—that is, if they were even interested in asking them." I punched the button on my answering machine to see if anyone had left messages besides Jeannie. As the third message started to play, I recognized Detective Collazo's voice.

"Miss Sullivan, I need to speak to you. It concerns the Daggett girl. Please call me or beep me immediately."

The robot voice on the machine told me that his message had been recorded at eight-thirty in the morning. Neither B.J. nor I said anything for several long seconds. I just sat on my stool rubbing my hand across my lips and chin, staring at the machine.

B.J. was the first to break the silence. "Are you going to call him?"

"I don't trust him, B.J. I think he's just using Ely's name to make me call. There were cops on the *Top Ten* when I came back by it this morning."

"The police are not the bad guys, Seychelle."

"They think I killed Neal and Patty. Pete says Collazo's been poking around the Downtowner, asking about me. He's not even looking for other suspects. What's he going to think when they figure out it was me on the *Top Ten* last night?"

"You want me to drive you over to Jeannie's? She'll know what to do."

"Yeah, but she's not home, remember?"

"We'll wait for her."

"B.J., these guys scare me, but jail scares me even more. This guy Collazo, he's just too focused on me. I didn't do anything, but I've watched enough segments of *60 Minutes* to know that innocent people do go to jail for crimes they didn't commit—and it's usually because of some pit bull type of cop who just won't let go and makes the evidence fit the perp he wants it to fit. Naw, I've got to do this other thing first. I need to find out what the story is on that compressor on the boat. If I can figure out what Neal was doing out there that morning, then okay, I'll feel a lot more comfortable talking to the cops. But not till then."

He shook his head but smiled. "You are one stubborn, hardheaded woman."

I grabbed my shoulder bag off the bar and rummaged around for the keys to Lightnin'. "I'll be fine." I lifted my arm and rotated my wrist. The pain was barely noticeable. "Thanks for everything, B.J."

"Okay. But I'm going to be working around here the rest of the day. I'll be inside the big house. If you need me, I'll be here."

XVIII

T HE *TOP TEN* USED TO BERTH ON B PIER, IN SLIP B37. IT was third in from the end, so I walked out the length of the pier. Most of the bigger boats had changed since the days I used to visit Neal there. These megayachts usually stayed on the move in order to remain one step ahead of the tax man. Their transoms bore hailing ports such as George Town, Cayman Islands; Road Harbor, B.V.I.; or Hamilton, Bermuda—all exotic ports with little in the way of industry for their people, so providing tax-dodge hailing ports kept the millionaires in town for a few days out of the year.

My Way was in her slip, but the boat was all locked up. I didn't see Nestor around. The docks looked deserted. I thought I would at least find Raymond out here working on the deck of one of the big yachts. Raymond was from down island. He had come up to the states from the Caribbean as a crewman on board a big classic wood charter yacht and then had some kind of falling-out with the skipper in Lauderdale. That was about four years ago, and he had supposedly been working to make his fare home to Bequia ever since. He worked illegally, on a cash-only basis, but he could lay down a coat of varnish that looked like glass. His skin was nearly as black as the Ray-Ban shades he always wore, and his dreads were shoulder length. He always looked like he was just loafing around, but he got more work done than three average men, and the skippers fought to hire him. He rarely spoke, but he was always listening.

"Seychelle, ova hea." The voice came from the foredeck of a hundred-foot-plus British flagged schooner.

I walked a bit out the finger pier. Under the low blue foredeck awning, Nestor and Raymond sat grinning and passing a joint back and forth.

"Come join the party, Seychelle," Nestor said.

I grabbed the wire lifelines and climbed onto the high deck of the schooner. She was an old-timer, dating back to the twenties, but she was in immaculate condition. I remembered her from a few years back when Red towed her up the New River. The captain was a British gentleman who had invited me below for a tour. She looked like she had been under Raymond's care for several weeks. Her brightwork shone like blown glass.

Up on the foredeck, I ducked under the awning and joined the two guys. Nestor was wearing the usual hired captain's uniform—blue cargo shorts, Top-Siders, and a white polo shirt with the name of his boat, *My Way,* embroidered over the breast pocket.

I perched on the edge of a skylight hatch. "I wanted to ask you guys a couple of questions."

"You okay?" Raymond asked when he saw my cuts and bruises up close.

"Yeah, it was nothing. A long story."

"You like some ganja, mon?" Nestor offered me the joint. His fake accent was pathetic, and he looked pretty stoned. As a third-generation Cuban American, there was very little Caribbean left in him.

"No, thanks."

"What can we do for you, lady?" Raymond smiled his shy, uneven grin. The man could smoke dope all day and never get the least messed up; I'd seen him do it on the *Top Ten.*

"I'm trying to figure out what Neal was doing out there last Thursday. Did he say anything to anybody about what he was taking the boat out for?"

"Naw," Nestor said. Raymond shook his head.

"Okay. Did you ever notice Neal loading a compressor onto the afterdeck of the boat?"

"Yeah." Raymond nodded, his dreads bouncing. "He axed me to help him wit it."

"Oh, yeah," Nestor said, "I remember that day."

"Did he say what he wanted to use it for?"

"Yeah," Nestor said, taking a deep drag and holding the smoke in his lungs. I waited for him to finish. And waited.

He exhaled with a whoosh. "He said he was going to do a little diving out on a reef offshore, shoot some grouper, maybe some summer crab." Neal had always been guilty of taking lobster out of season. I could almost hear him bragging about it to Nestor.

"But why would he need another compressor? The *Top Ten*'s already got one below for filling tanks. Neal was always a tank diver."

Nestor shrugged. He wasn't looking at me. His eyes stayed on the joint. "He just said he wanted to try diving with a hookah rig once. It was the boss's money, he said. You know, he might as well experiment."

A hookah rig was one where the diver was connected by a long hose to a compressor on the surface. Usually, though, they used small compressors that had been fitted inside a flotation device so that the compressor followed them around on the surface. I couldn't imagine any reason why Neal would try out a hookah rig.

"Why, looky who's here," Perry Greene called out as he walked down the finger pier and prepared to climb aboard the schooner. "If it ain't Miss Sullivan herself. Whooee, sure looks like somebody beat the crap outta you."

"Hey, Perry, leave her alone," Nestor said. "What's up?"

Perry's white-blond hair hung in his eyes as he ducked under the awning and dropped his butt onto the teak decks. The hair did not conceal the open greed in his eyes as he watched the two men smoke, nor did his cutoffs conceal much of anything, the way he was sitting on the deck. I turned my head aside in disgust.

"Hey, you guys wanna pass me a little of that?" He reached for the joint and sucked in smoke hungrily.

Raymond looked at me for several seconds before turning to Perry. "The captain is not hea."

Perry exhaled loudly. "Shit, and here I thought we'd get some business done. Got some paperwork to take care of." He grinned at me, waiting for me to ask.

I couldn't believe it. He had to be talking about a job. They were headed upriver with the schooner for a haul-out, and they were going to be hiring Perry to help them make the trip? I caught Raymond's eye, and he nodded at me, confirming it.

"So the Brit's hiring you, is he?"

"Yes sirree, boy. What, they didn't ask you, Seychelle? Now, what the hell do you make of that, huh?" He sniffed and wiped his nose with the back of his hand. "Looks like nobody wants to hire a bitch to do a man's job."

"Perry," Nestor said, "why don't you just shut up? Even if having balls was all it took to be a good captain, you'd still have trouble meeting the criteria."

"What're you trying to say?"

"I tink he say it already, mon," Raymond said, laughing. "Da captain be back later. You come back."

Perry stood. "Don't matter what you say, the word is out on Sullivan Towing." He climbed down to the dock. "Seychelle, honey, you're gonna be able to sit home and eat bonbons and watch the soaps every day." He laughed his high-pitched hillbilly cackle, turned, and walked up the dock.

Nobody said anything for several minutes as the two men quietly smoked. Finally Nestor tossed the last of the joint overboard, and it sizzled as it hit the water. Neither man would look at me.

"It must be pretty bad, what they're saying about me," I finally ventured.

"Seychelle, I haven't believed it, especially not now that I see you and talk to you. People are saying you've had some kind of a nervous breakdown, that you're acting erratic, that you can't be trusted. It'll pass. You know how rumors fly around the docks."

"But you also know what it's like to have boat payments to make. Nestor, I can't sit around and wait for my reputation to clear. It's all tied to this *Top Ten* business, I know it is. Is there anything else you guys can think of that was weird about Neal or the boat that day?"

"Well, there is one thing. The only other guy living on board the *Top Ten* was the engineer, Matt. You knew him, didn't you, Sey?"

"Yeah, he came on board just before Neal and I split up."

"Well, he told the cops that Neal had given him the day off, but he told me that morning, right after the *Top Ten* left the dock, that Neal had just fired him. Said he wouldn't be needing him anymore. You know as well as I do that you couldn't find a better engineer."

"Where is Matt? I need to talk to him."

"That's the other thing. He's gone. Left town awful fast. Said he was headed up to Newport to find a job up there."

"Man . . . that is strange. Neal was a pretty decent mechanic, but he wasn't good enough to keep the engine and generator running on the *Top Ten*. And owners of a boat like that surely wouldn't cheap out on keeping an engineer."

I turned to Raymond to see if he had anything else to offer. "Lady, I don' like da people Neal was workin' for."

"Do you know anything about them? Who they are?"

"I don' know dey names." He pushed his shades down his nose and looked at me over the top of the dark glass. "But I see dey bad men. Be careful wit dem, lady."

O N MY WAY BACK HOME, AS I CROSSED OVER THE SEVENTEENTH Street Causeway, I noticed the soot-colored clouds building up out over the Everglades. It was still sunny here along the coast, but it wouldn't be for much longer, not once the dropping sun slid behind that dark wall. It was early in the year for that summer weather pattern.

My last stop was at Lauderdale Divers. When I pulled the Jeep into the parking space in front of their display window, I saw an example of a typical hookah rig in their window. It was a small compressor mounted inside an inner tube. It was similar to the compressor Red had on the *Gorda,* although ours was not portable or floatable. These little compressors didn't have big accumulator tanks like the one on the *Top Ten.*

A couple of cruise-ship–type tourists were browsing through the T-shirt display, but otherwise, the fellow at the back of the store was alone, immersed in an issue of *Scuba Diver* magazine.

"Hello?"

He dropped the magazine. "Hi, what can I do for you?" He was about fifty, with graying hair, and he had that grizzled, squinty-eyed, old-time diver look.

"I just want to ask you some questions about compressors."

"Do you want to use it for tank fills or for hookah diving?"

"I don't want to buy one. But I saw a compressor on a boat, and I'm trying to figure out what it might have been used for." I reached into my shoulder bag and pulled out the info I had copied off the side of the compressor. I showed it to him.

"That's not a dive compressor. See, right here it says 'contractor.' That unit would be used for running air tools. On a boat, you don't need to keep the air like they do. We put it right into the scuba tanks, so we don't use the big accumulators."

"What kind of air tools?"

"Could be anything: air hammers, nailers, impact drivers. Mechanics use them a lot. You know, like the tools you've seen when they change your tires in a garage."

I nodded. The older woman from the front of the store walked back carrying a Divers Do It Deeper T-shirt and asked if she could try it on. He pointed to the back of the store, then went back to his magazine.

"Do you have any idea what someone would use that com-pressor for on board a ninety-two-foot Broward?"

He raised his eyebrows and looked out the window across the parking lot. "Not a clue," he said. "But he sure as hell wasn't using it to breathe." He went back to his magazine.

Neal had done enough work in boatyards over the years to know his way around tools. What was he planning? Was he going to build something? I wished I'd had more time to look around on the boat. Maybe the tools themselves would have told me what it was he had in mind.

I wandered over to the glass case the diver guy was leaning on and examined the books and charts on display there. One book, *Diving Locations,* particularly caught my eye.

"Could I see a copy of this?" I asked him.

He sighed, moved behind the counter, and handed me the book. I flipped through the pages. It was a collection of all the coordinates of the major wrecks and reefs off the South Florida coast.

"They're not all in there. That's over a year old now. Been some sunk since then."

"Some what?"

"Ships, barges, whatever. You know, artificial reefs." His voice took on a different quality as he launched into this well-rehearsed explanation. "We have some coral off our coast here, but mostly it's just a sand bottom. In order to have fish, there have to be places for the fish to hide. You take an old abandoned shipwreck, and after it's been on the bottom awhile, it will be full of little fish—and where there are little fish, there will soon be big fish trying to eat them. Divers love to dive on shipwrecks, and since these days ships just don't sink often enough, we make our own. They're sinking new shit out there nearly every other month. Keeps me happy—more places to dive, more people will go diving. It's good for business. You interested in going out for a dive?"

"No, just curious, that's all."

He tapped a newspaper clipping pinned to a bulletin board on the wall behind the counter. "You'd like this one here—she's new, the *Bahama Belle*, a nice little freighter. She's going to be real rich when she gets a little more growth on her. It takes a while, you know. They sink this stuff so the fish will have hiding places, but they also need the food source. Right now, there's not enough coral or algae growth there to support much of a fish population."

I squinted at the blurry black-and-white photo of a vessel surrounded by puffs of white smoke.

"So that's all people are interested in, huh, fish? Do you think somebody could find anything of value of any of these wrecks?"

He laughed. "Are you kidding? First of all, the Coasties have guys strip these ships clean of everything before they sink 'em. Then they blow holes in every single compartment to make sure that divers can't get caught in any little holes. Then there's hundreds of divers a week exploring all over these things. Honey, you couldn't find diddly-squat on one of these wrecks."

I handed him back his book. "Hmmm. Okay, well, thanks for all your help. See ya."

I paused on the sidewalk outside the store and took a last look at the hookah equipment in the dive store window. The hand on my arm was totally unexpected because I had not heard the slightest sound of his approach.

"Hey, lady," he said, and I jumped, yanked my arm from his grasp, and backed off, ready to run. James Long was staring at me, equally startled by my reaction. "I didn't mean to scare you." He held his hands up in the air, and I noticed he was wearing a white martial-arts getup, and even that outfit was ironed, with sharp creases on the sleeves. "It seems every time I touch you, you bolt like a startled deer."

I laughed. "Geez, James, I was a million miles away. I didn't even hear you come up on me." I didn't go into the fact that somebody had tried to kill me last night, and that does tend to make one a little jumpy.

He looked at the name of the store written across the top of the window and raised one eyebrow. "So the lady captain is a diver, too?"

I tried, unsuccessfully, to raise one eyebrow as well. "And the gentleman executive is a kung fu artist?"

He flashed those incredibly white teeth of his at me again, and I felt like an idiot grinning back at him. "Tai chi, actually. I like the study of the Taoist philosophy, and it keeps me in shape, teaches me things about the body. I try to come for classes here several times a week." He pointed a few doors down to a storefront with Chinese characters across the front window and the words Florida Kung Fu and Tai Chi Chuan. "Don't suppose you'd be willing to join me for a late lunch?"

Truth be told, I was starving. My eating habits these last few days would have had Red steaming mad. He was always trying to get me to eat more regularly. He claimed I preferred to graze, eating only when I was hungry. The thing was, though, I needed to get back to the cottage and call Jeannie. I'd promised B.J.

"James, I'm tempted, but I've really got to get back. If you've got a second, though, there is something I'd like to talk to you about."

"Certainly, Seychelle. How can I help you?"

"I went by Harbor House yesterday." I decided not to get into his little deception about Sunny/Sonya when I'd first met him on Saturday. "When I was leaving, I heard Minerva on the phone with somebody named Burns. Do you know Hamilton Burns, an attorney?"

"Of course. We've been involved in legal matters with Mr. Burns on several occasions. He is very well known in this town."

"What kind of legal matters?"

"I'm sorry, Seychelle, I really can't discuss that with you. You realize, of course, that there is a very sensitive side to what I do. Sometimes these runaways come from families that would rather not let it be known that their little darlings ended up on the streets. They want to make any criminal charges go away and whisk them back to their former lives. Burns helps them with that."

"That's not right."

"It's not a bad thing. What about the ones no one ever misses?

"Look, are you sure you won't join me?" he went on. "We could continue this conversation over margaritas over at Carlos and Pepe's?" He pointed to the restaurant across the parking lot.

I sighed and looked at him and came real close to giving in and going. James Long was damned likable. Some other day, when all this is over, I thought, if we are both left standing when the dust clears, I would really like to get to know him better.

XIX

I WAS ABOUT TO TURN ONTO MY STREET WHEN I NOTICED the white unmarked car parked across and a few doors up from the Larsen place. The thunderheads had cast an early dusk over the street, but I could still make out two shadowy figures sitting in the front seat. I just kept driving right into the cul-de-sac, where the street dead-ended at the New River. I parked the Jeep and climbed over the wood fence around the Martinez place. The fences on these riverfront properties, when there were any, ran only to the seawall.

The Larsens' yard was clear. I didn't even see B.J. around. I had hoped he might be on the *Gorda* piecing that head back together, but no such luck. Once inside my cottage, I knew I had to do something about food. It was already past four, and I hadn't eaten a thing since the quick meal I'd grabbed from Burger King the night before. I rummaged through my cupboards, finally coming up with the last dented can of Campbell's bean-with-bacon soup. While it cooked in the microwave, I tried Jeannie's number again, and amazingly, she picked up on the second ring.

"Jeannie, it's Seychelle."

"Oh, thank God. I was just about ready to call the police and report you as a missing person. Honey, you've got to stop worrying me like this. You've got to check in more often. These are not nice people you're playing around with."

"This is not something you need to tell me, trust me, Jeannie. I'll tell you all about that in a bit, but first, have you found out anything sure about the owners yet?"

"Okay, well, here's the deal. Everywhere I turned, I kept getting the door slammed in my face. Finally, I decided the only way I was going to get through was to use a little deceit. I won't go into details, but suffice it to say I could get disbarred over this one. Anyway, I was right, it's Benjamin Crystal still . . . he never really sold the boat. Well, I mean, he sold it, but he sold it to himself. The company that owns the boat is located in the Caymans and it goes through subsidiaries of larger corporations, but it all comes back to Mr. Benjamin Crystal."

"That son of a bitch."

"He is that."

"That's not exactly what I meant." Neal had known all along. He had to have known, he was captain of the boat. All that bullshit he'd given me about how it would be different once the boat was sold. Lies. All lies. "What does this mean to us, Jeannie? To my salvage claim?"

"Well, it's not going to be easy. I couldn't exactly explain to a court of law the way I found out. I think we should continue dealing with Burns. I'll fire him another counteroffer, and let's keep our knowledge of the real owner as our trump card."

"Okay, that sounds good."

Suddenly someone started pounding on the front door. My heart felt like it was trying to leap out of my chest. Abaco began to bark.

"Seychelle, open the goddamn door."

Abaco stopped barking, and she was wagging her tail. We both recognized that voice. "Honey," Jeannie said, "what is going on over there?"

"I thought for a second it was the cops, but it's my brother, Maddy. I've got to go, Jeannie. Call Burns and then call me back. Talk to you later."

Maddy strode in with his face looking like a bruised, overripe peach. One eye was covered with gauze and bandages, his lip was swollen and split with black knotted thread holding the two halves together, and the swellings on his cheek and forehead were that greenish purple color of day-old bruises and bottle flies. Metal splints like birdcages surrounded the index and middle fingers of his right hand. He headed straight for the fridge, opened the door, and helped himself to a beer. Popping the top one-handedly, he settled on the low couch with a loud exhale.

"We gotta talk." He gulped the beer.

"You really look awful. What are you doing out of bed?"

"I've got a business to run. Family to support. You don't look so good yourself."

I rubbed the bruise on my temple. "Yeah, well, long story."

"I need the money. Now, Seychelle."

"Maddy, I've got the cops sitting out front watching for me—they're probably on their way back here right now. I don't have time for this. You've got to get out of here." Standing over him, I tried to pull him up off the couch.

"I came here to say something and I'm gonna say it. Settle this salvage business and sell the boat. That's it."

"Maddy, what the hell is happening with you? You know I'll fight you any way I can on this—that boat's my life."

He lowered his face into his hands. He was still for the longest time.

I sat down next to him and put my arm around him. He shook me off, irritated.

Sinking back into the far corner of the couch, I tried breathing slowly. Stop reacting like a twelve-year-old, I told myself. Calm down, relax. "Maddy," I said in a soft voice, "can you tell me what this is really all about? What have you got yourself into?"

At first he didn't say anything. I was tense, poised for flight, not sure what my volatile big brother might burst out with.

"They sent me over here, Sey." He spoke quietly, his hands on his knees, and then he stuck out his chin, letting me get a good look. "See my face? The people who did this to me—they sent me over here to talk to you. I owe 'em . . . shit, I don't even want to tell you how much. I know it was stupid, but like every other god-damn sucker out there, I thought I would win." He shook his head and sighed. "Anyways, they're threatening to take *my* boat. I got a family, Seychelle. There ain't squat I can do besides take assholes out fishing. I know you can always go back to lifeguarding or something. Hell, you're really smart, you could go back to college and get out of boats for good. You and Pit, you were always the smart ones—you could do anything. Not me. I can't lose that boat. They told me to make you settle with them—to call in the debt on the *Gorda*, to put the screws on you so you'd see things their way. They said if you don't help them out, they're gonna hurt you, bad."

"What are you talking about, Maddy? Who are these people you keep referring to as 'they'?"

"See, that's just it, Seychelle. You ask too many questions. I'm at the track and I'm losing, and some guy tells me that if I call this other guy, he can loan me some money. I don't ask for no refer-ences. I don't really want to know who the guy is. The point is, I owe these guys a lot of money. And now they're sending some dude about as wide as he is tall to play basketball with my head in the track parking lot. He's saying, 'Shut your sister up, we want her out of the salvage business for good.' They beat the crap out of me because I can't make you cooperate, and they're going after you next. Only next time it won't just be a beating."

"It doesn't make sense, Maddy. What do loan sharks at the track have to do with what happened on the *Top Ten*?"

"Like I said, Sey, you ask too many questions. If you want to save both our boats, and butts, then just shut the fuck up, take their money, tell them whatever they want to know, and count yourself lucky."

Maddy stood and crushed the beer can in his good fist as though to punctuate his sentiments. He walked over to the counter and lifted the photo of me and Neal I had found on the *Top Ten*.

He squinted as though trying to recognize the people in the picture. "What do you reckon happened to Neal?"

"I don't have any idea, Maddy." I snatched the photo from his hands and slid it out of sight into the zippered side pocket of my shoulder bag along with the photo of my mother and us kids I'd rescued from my trashed cottage.

"If he was still alive," he said, "I suppose he'd probably contact you—if he contacted anybody. These guys I've been talking about, they'd pay a lot of money to know where Neal is—enough money to get me out of debt for good."

"I don't know any more about it than you do."

"Seems Neal was mixed up with these people pretty deep. Wouldn't make sense for you to protect him, after the way he treated you and all."

He never was very subtle, my brother, but I had always at least thought he would honor family loyalty. It appeared he had sold out loyalty to anybody but himself a long time ago.

"That's it. Just shut up and get out of here, Maddy. I'm going to take care of it. If they ask again, you tell your 'friends' that I don't know anything about Neal. In the meantime, I am going to come up with some way to get us all out of this. I can't get you out of debt—that's your problem—but I am not going to let anybody else get beat up or killed." With that I shoved him out the door and shut it in his face.

I wished I could believe what I'd just said.

Through the closed door I heard him say, "Leave it be, Seychelle. Listen to me. Don't fuck with them."

It occurred to me I had heard almost those exact words from someone else. Burns. He, too, had told me that these were not people to anger.

I took my lukewarm soup out of the microwave and turned on the TV to catch the news. Suddenly, I was aware of the overpowering sensation of being watched. I glanced around at all three windows, thinking I might see the same glimpse of a head as I had that night with James.

I stood upright, opened the front door, and scanned the grounds. Stepping outside into the sunshine, I listened. Mocking-birds singing, insects humming, no noises to trigger this sense that someone was out there.

The cops had seen Maddy come in here. They might even have been able to hear him shouting my name.

The back door to the Larsens' swung open. I started to jump back inside when I recognized B.J. He waved at me.

"Hey, you fugitive, you."

"What?" I crossed the yard to speak to him.

"You're a wanted woman. A couple of police officers just came to the front door. I hadn't worked on the library here in over a week, and I'd just started back to work when they began beat-ing on the door. They've got a warrant for your arrest on burglary and evidence-tampering, and the only good thing is, they think you live in the big house—evidently these guys don't know about the cottage."

"Thank goodness for that."

"But they did say they saw a man come back here."

"That was Maddy. He just left."

B.J. nodded. "Okay, I told them you weren't home. I didn't think you were until I saw you out the window just now."

"I saw their car out there when I started to turn down the street, so I parked Lightnin' on the cul-de-sac and walked down the seawall."

He nodded. "Well, they're still out there sitting in their car. You need to call Jeannie and deal with this, Seychelle, or you're go-ing to jail."

"I've already talked to her, and I'm not going to jail, B.J. I didn't do anything wrong—well, except a little breaking and enter-ing, maybe." I shrugged.

He shook his head and turned back into the main house.

The soup worked its magic as comfort food, and I felt my-self growing drowsy. More than anything, I wanted to crawl under the covers and just sleep—probably not a good idea with the cops parked out front. As I washed my bowl in the sink, I figured I'd better call Jeannie back to let her know about the actual warrant and ask her what to do next.

Suddenly, the face on the TV screen looked familiar. I hadn't been listening, so I didn't really know what the story was about. The reporter was interviewing a man leaving a building, and I had seen that face somewhere just recently.

The reporter, holding one finger to her ear, turned to face the camera. "Rick, Benjamin Crystal is refusing to answer any reporters' questions about his arrest or release here at the Dade County Courthouse this evening. The prosecutor's office has planned a press conference for later this evening, and we will be here to bring it to you live." The camera panned back to the man climbing into the back-seat of a large, dark-windowed car.

I snapped off the TV when the news anchor started in on a human-interest story about kittens. I remembered where I had seen that face. Harbor House. The photo on the wall with the three couples—Benjamin Crystal was the Hispanic man in that photo, standing next to James Long. Some things were starting to make sense.

I SCOOPED UP THE PAPERS I HAD FOUND INSIDE MY COPY OF Bowditch, along with the coordinates from the *Top Ten*'s GPS, and walked out to *Gorda*. The alarm beeped when I punched in the code, and I slid the door to the wheelhouse open. The offshore chart for the coast from Palm Beach to lower Biscayne Bay was the best scale I could find in the chart table. My only large-scale charts were of the Intracoastal Waterway. Still, I'd be able to get an idea if I was right. I located the Hillsboro inlet on the chart. The *Top Ten* had been anchored south of there. Finally, I broke out the dividers and the parallel rulers and plotted the position of BAB. Latitude 26°09.52'N. I drew a pencil line. Longitude 80°04.75'W. Another line. I drew a dot on the chart where the two pencil lines inter-sected and chewed on the pencil eraser as I stared at it. I eyeballed the distance north of Port Everglades, and it looked just about right. I'd seen Esposito and Big Guy out there diving on what must be the *Bahama Belle*. The coordinates of the location of the sunken freighter were public knowledge. They knew where the boat was, so what was it that they still thought Neal could tell them?

I reached for Neal's drawings. They reminded me a little of the reams of drawings I'd inherited from when Red built the *Gorda*. He'd had her designed by a professional naval architect, but Red sat in on every step of the process, bringing his twenty years of experience on navy ships to the task. He had saved all the drawings, which actually made things easier for me now when I needed to make repairs.

Neal's drawing appeared to be of a compartment of some kind. Actually, there were two views, one overhead and one from the side. It could be a compartment in the bow of a ship. I could make out the bulkheads, the backbone that ran right up to the bow. In most ships, this part of the bow was where they stowed the anchor chain. But why hadn't they found whatever it was they were looking for when they sank the the old rust bucket? It's not like an anchor chain locker is a great hiding place.

I reached up and switched on the VHF radio hanging above the steering station. Taking the microphone, I waited for a break in the constant traffic and then called, "*Outta the Blue, Outta the Blue,* this is *Gorda.*"

Only a few seconds passed before he replied, "*Gorda,* this is *Outta the Blue.* Wanna switch to zero six?"

Once we were on the working channel, I asked Mike where he was. I could hear voices in the background.

"I'm just off Pompano headed south on a broad reach. I've got a charter of six legal secretaries celebrating one gal's birthday. They wanted to know if it was okay with me if they sunbathed topless." He held the transmit button long enough for me to hear his laugh.

"It's a tough life you got, Mike. Listen, I hate to get serious on you, but I need to talk to you—but not on this open channel. Have you got a cell phone on board?"

215

"That's a roger, Captain Sullivan."

"Could you call me at my place in about ten minutes?"

"Will do. This is *Outta the Blue,* clear and going back to channel sixteen."

When I finally left the tug and started across the yard toward the cottage, the sound of the phone ringing caused me to trot. Just as I was about to pick it up, I thought that it could just as well be the cops calling from a phone out front. My hand froze for a moment, suspended over the phone. But I really needed to talk to Mike.

The machine clicked on and my recorded message told the caller to call back or leave a message. The machine beeped, and a young girl's voice came on.

"Seychelle? Are you there? Please pick up if you are." I recognized the voice, and she sounded nervous.

I snatched up the phone. "Sunny, it's me. I'm here."

"Like, you told me I could call you if I needed something, right? Well, I'm at the Top Ten Club, and . . . I'm kinda scared. Could you come over here?"

"Sure, but what's going on? What are you afraid of?"

"I just really want to leave. I need a ride. Please?" Her voice dropped to a whisper. "I can't tell you right now. Uh, shit, he's coming back. . . ."

"Hey, listen up." There was no question about whose deep voice was speaking. "I like this girl. Mmm . . ." He laughed with that deep, throaty chuckle that made me want to reach through the phone lines and strangle him. "You want to see her? Hey, maybe you the kind likes to watch." He laughed again. He seemed to be enjoying himself. "You don't want me to hurt Blondie here, now, do you? Then come to the club. Alone. No friends. No cops." The phone clicked and went dead.

Cesar sounded like he had been watching too many movies. In my mind, I went over all the reasons why it would be really stupid for me to dash off and go over there alone.

The phone rang again, startling me, and I grabbed it without thinking this time.

"Hello, this is your local mid–Gulf Stream substation of the retired Fort Lauderdale Police Department. What can I do for you, ma'am?"

"Can you talk?"

"These ladies have had enough *Outta the Blue* special Pusser's Rum punch; they won't remember much of anything tomorrow. I'm countin' on it. What's up, Seychelle?"

"It's not looking real good about now. The cops are looking for me. They've got a warrant out for my arrest."

"Shit, Seychelle. How can I help?"

"What do you know about Benjamin Crystal?"

"His name does seem to keep popping up today."

"You heard the news, huh?"

"Yep, on the radio at lunchtime. How're you mixed up with that scumbag?"

I thought about my mother and Neal and Elysia, and how in the end I hadn't been able to save a one. And now there was Sunny.

"I can't tell you all about it right now, Mike. I'm not really in trouble yet, but I could be later. Listen, keep your VHF and your phone open for me all night. If you haven't heard from me by day-break, break out the calvary and come looking, okay?"

"Sey, you can't be messing around with these guys—"

I slowly lowered the receiver into its cradle.

Maybe this would be my one chance to get it right, I thought as I gathered up my Jeep keys and shoulder bag and headed out the door.

XX

MY KNUCKLES WERE WHITE WHERE I CLUTCHED Lightnin's steering wheel at ten and two o'clock, charging down Federal Highway to Seventeenth. The rain started just about the time I pulled into the Top Ten Club parking lot. My stomach felt twisted and gurgling, like I might vomit at any minute. I'd considered telling B.J. where I was going, but I knew he would try to talk me out of it.

The early-bird dinner hour on a Monday night was obviously a slow time at the Top Ten Club. The valet parking attendant was sitting on his stool under the front door awning with his Walkman headset on, eyes closed, head jerking in rhythm to the music. He didn't even notice me as I slipped into my spot back by the Dumpsters. I tucked my shoulder bag under the front seat and slipped my wallet and keys into my pocket. I wanted to be ready to run.

The same short, muscled Hispanic guy was on the door, and even before he turned to greet me, I wondered why I hadn't realized who he was, why I hadn't put that part together yet. I saw the instant recognition in his eyes. He smiled, and I felt some small satisfaction at the gap in his teeth caused undoubtedly by my skates, but the sickness in those eyes made me look away. I didn't want Cesar to see my fear.

I heard his deep laughter as I headed straight for the back, where Teenie stood behind the bar. I shook the rainwater off my arms and slicked my hair back as I slid onto a stool.

"Hi, Teenie." Out of the corner of my eye I saw Cesar disappear down a hall into the back of the restaurant.

"Hey, girl, what're you doing here? I don't think that's such a smart move on your part, honey. Our doorman really doesn't like you. He had a fit after you left last time."

"The feeling's mutual."

She laughed. "He's not exactly Mr. Charming, is he?"

"No," I said, and smiled when she placed an iced Corona in front of me. "Do you know a young girl named either Sunny or Sonya? She's been staying at Harbor House." My voice sounded higher-pitched than normal, and I was having trouble breathing. This whole thing was beginning to feel like a terrible mistake.

"Nope, never heard of her."

"Maybe you've seen her around here—a gorgeous blonde?"

"Now isn't that special," she said with a grin. "Sure don't see many of those in here." She looked up at the music video on the TV set suspended over the bar.

"Look, she left a message on my machine less than an hour ago. Said she was here."

Teenie looked straight at me, all traces of her smile now gone. "I don't know nothing about nothing. Got it?"

It was pretty clear she'd been warned not to talk to me. "Right, and thanks for all that nothing," I said. I'd started to turn away from the bar when Cesar appeared at my side.

"Follow me," he said in that sickening voice.

"Where's Sunny?" I asked his back as he headed across the club to a hallway. I shrugged, raised my hand in a goodbye to Teenie, and took off after him. I saw fear in Teenie's face.

Cesar led me down a long hallway past several open doors where girls were entertaining men in private rooms. To me the only difference between lap dancing and prostitution was whether a zipper was up or down.

"Where's Sunny?" I said again to Cesar's back.

Cesar stopped at the end of the hall and grinned at me. His wide-set Indian eyes didn't look quite right. It was no wonder he nearly always wore sunglasses. He then grasped my forearm and opened the door at the end of the hall. The warm, moist night air blew in from the parking lot beyond. A light rain had started to fall. Behind the club, a small white limousine was parked with the engine running.

"Whoa. Hold it. I'm looking for Sunny, and she said she was here."

Cesar looked around as though to see whether or not anyone was watching.

"Hey, shut up. You're going to see Sunny. You're gonna see a lot of her," he said, and laughed that guttural laugh of his.

I struggled against his grip. "Let go of me!"

He opened the door to the backseat and, squeezing my arm in his ironlike fist, forced me into the car and slammed the door.

XXI

THERE WERE NO DOOR OR WINDOW HANDLES ON THE inside of the backseat doors, and a Plexiglas partition separated the driver's and passenger's seats. Cesar climbed up front and flashed me that smile that made me want to bust his teeth.

I kept track of where we were going. The car executed a number of turns. At first, we headed north up U.S. 1, but soon we turned west on Davie and back into the Riverside neighborhood on the north bank of the river. There were parts of this neighborhood I wouldn't venture into after dark. Though there were some waterfront homes, most behind locked gates, much of the area was made up of poorly tended cinder-block homes and federally funded apartment buildings. Heaps of trash lined the streets, and little kids in dirty underpants turned to stare at the big car as we passed.

It scared me that Cesar didn't seem to care about my seeing where we were going. I'd read enough thrillers to know that this was definitely a bad sign. He wasn't worried about my being around long enough to point fingers. I started exploring the interior of the car, trying to find something I could maybe break off and use as a weapon. I slid my fingers down in the crack behind the seat, and something sharp pierced my skin.

"Ouch!" I pulled my finger out; it was bleeding a little. More carefully this time, I felt around for the sharp object. I touched something finally, and pulled out a thin chain with a tiny golden angel. Ely's angel. She'd had it on the day we walked on the beach, so she certainly must have ridden in this car. I closed my eyes and pressed the angel to my cheek, wondering if she had left it there intentionally as evidence. I suspected she had. I slid the necklace into my pocket and watched the big dark eyes of the neighborhood children staring at the tinted windows of the limo.

We pulled up finally in front of a large ranch-style house, all ambling stucco, dark-tinted windows, and overgrown, unimaginative landscaping. Dense areca palms shielded the house from both the street and the neighbors. Cesar got out, opened the backseat door, and stood there glaring at me, waiting for me to crawl out. I hadn't even stood up straight when he grabbed my upper arm again and nearly yanked me off my feet.

"Hey!" I started to complain, but suddenly my face stung and my head flew to the side from the force of the open-handed slap.

"Shut up," he said. And I did.

Cesar pulled me to the front door, opened it, and pushed me inside. From the entryway, I could see through the living room, decorated apparently by the designers from Motel 6, and out the sliding glass doors to the pool. The rain had stopped and the last rays of the sun angled in under the dark clouds bathing the scene in an orange sunlight. A white powerboat was tied to the dock outside, *Hard Bottom* written in script across the bow. A smaller runabout was tied up behind it. It looked like the Sea Ray.

Two men stood on the wood deck by the Jacuzzi talking. One was the tall body builder, Big Guy. He had two bags of diving gear in his arms. The other was a rail-thin man with a long blond ponytail. I could tell from the way they were gesturing that an argument was under way.

Big Guy saw me through the glass door and nodded in our direction. The ponytailed man glanced at me briefly, then walked off to the far side of the pool.

Big Guy opened the sliding glass door and stepped soundlessly onto the thick carpet. He was wearing swim trunks, and blue veins stood up like a relief map on his forearms as he slid the door closed with his one free hand. He walked over to the hallway and whistled once. A huge black-and-white pit bull bounded into the room. The dog turned his massive head briefly to inspect me, and a deep low growl vibrated across the room. Then he returned his gaze to the big man.

"Zeke, look who's here," said Cesar, tilting his head in my direction.

Zeke. I'd heard the name. Then I remembered he was Crystal's cousin, the one Jeannie had told me about, the freighter captain Crystal had been bringing drugs to when he got busted.

"Heel," Zeke said to the dog, then walked over to join us. "Hey, Cesar. This the girl? Funny, she doesn't look so tough." I recognized his high-pitched, almost effeminate voice from that night on the beach. The dog stayed at his side but reached his muzzle out and licked Cesar's hand.

"Ugh, get your fuckin' dog away from me, Moss. Christ, that dog slobbers all over everything."

"Chewy, sit." The dog obeyed like a well-trained soldier. Zeke walked over to a milk crate full of dive tanks and dumped his bags of masks and fins. "Hey, Cesar, take this crap out to your car." He kicked the dive gear toward Cesar. "The boss isn't here yet. He wants the boat all cleaned up, and you know how he gets." The new, shining gear was encrusted with salt. The jerks hadn't even bothered to rinse it off when they got back from their dive yesterday. "He said he didn't want us trying to talk to her"—he jutted his chin in my direction—"till he gets here."

Cesar pointed to the couch. "Sit," he said to me. I complied. "Hey, Zeke, this bitch obeys as good as Chewy." He laughed and went out through the front door carrying all the fins and tanks in one load.

Zeke got a beer from the fridge, sat on a high stool at the bar, and ignored me.

"So who's workin' tonight?" Zeke asked as Cesar came back in the door.

"He brought this new chick. Boss is really gonna like her."

"They doin' a threesome thing again with Lex and the ponytail?" Zeke nodded his head in the direction of the third man on the patio.

Cesar helped himself to a beer, and the two men were laughing. "Yeah," Cesar said. "I mean, you should see the tits on this chick." He cupped his hands in the air.

"Yeah?"

"Oh, yeah." Cesar's deep voice made it sound like the word crawled up out of his belly. He curled his upper lip into his snarl-like smile and reached into the kitchen, grabbing an open bag of chips. He stuffed a handful in his mouth. *"Muy guapa."* Small flecks of bright orange spittle flew out of his mouth. "And young, whoo, not more than fifteen goddamn years old."

Zeke grabbed the bag from the other man and reached in. He chewed with his mouth open and licked the salt from his lips.

"We're talking *fresh* pussy—natural blonde, too."

I clenched my fists and literally bit my tongue, hoping the pain in my mouth would be something to concentrate on so I wouldn't hear what they were saying and do something really stupid. I had to be smart to find a way out of this, and I intended to take Sunny with me.

Other than the living room, there was a hall to the right of the front door that led into what looked like a dining room. The kitchen was opposite that, and a pass-through bar made part of the kitchen visible from where I sat. I slid over on the couch to try to see what was down the other hall, to the left of the front door. The dog, Chewy, made a rumbling noise low in his throat when I moved.

"You better not try nothin'. Chewy'll kill ya' if I tell him to," Zeke said. "Chewy, ready?" The dog rose to his feet, the fur around his neck bristling. The big man laughed, and his suntanned pectoral muscles bounced. "Down, boy." The dog lay back down. "Good boy."

The glass door slid open again, and the skinny ponytailed man walked in on a gust of warm, humid air. He, too, wore swim trunks that rode so low on his imperceptible hips that I wondered how they stayed up. After a quick glance at the two beer drinkers, the corners of his mouth turned down and he ignored them.

Cesar spoke to the ponytailed guy. "Eddie, you seen her yet? The new girl?"

"Shut up, asshole."

"You fuck . . ." Cesar started up off his barstool, but Zeke's straight arm prevented him from going after the skinnier man. "I'm so fuckin' tired of his attitude. Think I need to teach him to show a little respect."

"Respect for what?" Eddie sneered. "Some muscle-bound goon dumb as a rock?"

"Hey," Zeke said. "I promised the boss I'd keep him from killing you, but you gotta stop saying shit like that, Eddie, or I'm gonna let him go. I swear. For a smart guy you sure do act stupid sometimes."

Eddie sniffed, hitched at his swim trunks, and turned into the hall. He disappeared into the first bedroom.

Cesar looked at me. "What are you looking at, bitch?"

"Come on, man," Zeke said. "We're not supposed to talk to her. Wait till the boss gets here."

Cesar swung around on his stool to face me. "Bet you're wondering why you're here."

"Yeah, I wonder what is worth kidnapping me for." I tried my hardest to sound tough, sure of myself.

"Well, Crystal thinks you know where that asshole Garrett is, and Garrett knows where something of Crystal's is, see, so Crystal's gonna get you to tell him where the asshole's hiding out."

"Neal is dead."

Cesar opened his eyes wide and made an O with his mouth. Then he dropped the feigned look of surprise and stared at me with a challenge in his eyes. Softly, in that voice that sounded like a deep belch, he said, "Bullshit."

From outside we heard car doors slamming, but the noise didn't distract Cesar from his little stare-down game. He pointed at me and mouthed the words, "You're mine." I looked away.

Zeke jumped up and hurried to the front door. Before he could reach the knob, the door swung open and Benjamin Crystal strode into the room, shouting, "The man can't drive. Find me a lawyer who can drive next time."

Hamilton Burns, looking red-faced and shaken, entered the room behind Crystal. When he saw me, the color left his face. Crystal didn't look at Zeke. He was so much shorter, he would have had to bend his neck back to look Zeke in the eye. Then there was his skin. In the photos, it had looked pockmarked from childhood acne, but in person, it was much worse, so scarred and bumpy and discolored as to look grotesque.

Before anyone could answer, Crystal's eyes met mine. "Good. You're here. We've got to talk." He called back over his shoulder to Zeke, "Fix me a drink, *conjo.*"

He settled into the armchair opposite the couch. Zeke brought him what looked like a rum and Coke with lime. His guayabera did not look as crisp and clean as it had on the TV at noon. His carefully pomaded hair now looked tousled, and his big eyes protruded red-streaked from his head. Crystal drank down half the glass, then smacked his lips. "So, you're going to tell me where that asshole is, right?"

I was taken aback by the man's appearance. His skin was so disfigured, I felt awkward looking at him, almost as though I were staring at a burn victim.

He looked at me expectantly, waiting. "So?"

"So what? As far as I know Neal is dead."

He threw the glass at the bar, and it shattered, spraying glass fragments and splatters of brown sticky liquid across the white tile. "What do you think I look like? An idiot?"

I decided he really didn't want me to answer that question.

Crystal reached into his breast pocket for a pack of cigarettes, and Zeke stepped forward with a lighter from the bar. Crystal began speaking softly. "Your boyfriend—"

"He's not my boyfriend." My voice sounded loud after Crystal's hushed tones.

"You're a fucking idiot," he said.

Zeke brought him another drink, and he nearly drained the glass in one long gulp. "God, I missed that," he said, then slurped at the last of the drink's ice cubes. Brown liquid dribbled down his chin. "So, Miss Sullivan, you've become a pain in the ass—and stupid as well, to turn down thirty thousand dollars on that salvage business."

"Thirty? The most Burns offered me was fifteen."

Crystal opened his mouth, then closed it, then opened it again as it dawned on him. "Fucking Burns. Where is he?"

Zeke trotted to the foyer, then looked out the front door. "He's gone."

"Nobody steals from me. Cesar, deal with him."

"My pleasure, boss." Cesar picked up the cell phone from the bar and headed into the dining room to make a call.

"So maybe you aren't as stupid as I thought. That's a pity. Well, it's never really been about the salvage money, anyway. I figured you'd get to the point where you'd be willing to trade—Neal's whereabouts to get your life back." He took long deep drags on his cigarette and squinted his eyes at me, looking me up and down. "Neal never stopped talking about you. Even Patty said so. So where the fuck is he?"

"I really don't know. But what would you want with Neal—assuming he were alive?"

"Oh, he's alive, all right. He called me in jail."

The room suddenly felt off kilter, like one of those haunted houses where everything is on a slant and water appears to flow uphill. "You talked to him?"

"No, but he left a message. It could only have been him. He told me he'd be the first to ring the bell."

"Ring what bell?"

He smiled, a distant look in his eyes. "I have to admire him in a way. I'd do the same thing myself in his place."

"What did he do?" I couldn't follow what he was talking about.

Crystal took a deep drag on his cigarette, crushed the butt out in the ashtray on the table in front of him, then waved his hand in the air as though dismissing my question.

"I have you now, and he'll come for you." He slid forward on his seat and looked me up and down. "Yes. That will be his downfall. He's a fucking romantic." He rocked his head back and laughed.

Neal had robbed me and given me no hints as to his whereabouts. I didn't want to tell Crystal, but I felt certain I was useless to him as bait. Neal Garrett was not the man I thought he was.

He glanced at the watch on his wrist. "Zeke! Are they ready?"

The big man hurried into the bedroom where Eddie had disappeared earlier. His head appeared back out the door. "Just about ready, Mr. Crystal."

"Good. Put her away. We'll use her later."

Cesar came into the living room and motioned for me to stand. I was trying to be cooperative, biding my time, looking for my opportunity. It hadn't come yet. But I knew I'd better figure it out before they decided to "use" me later.

Cesar grabbed my upper arm, and we started down the hall. Crystal called out, "Cesar, if Garrett doesn't show up, you'll take care of it for me?"

"Sure thing, boss." He tightened his grip on my arm and pulled me closer to him. He spoke right into my ear. "I'll make her sweat." He stopped at the first bedroom door. It stood ajar. I could feel a soft heat flowing out the door.

Inside the room was a massive array of electronic equipment. Zeke was sitting in a swivel chair and watching a video on one of three monitors above a computer keyboard. The ponytailed guy, Eddie, sat at another computer working his fingers swiftly across the keyboard, intent on a large screen filled with images on a graphics grid. It looked like a Web page with buttons down the left side of the screen. He typed in text, then moved the text box to another location on the page.

Cesar pushed me through the door. "Mr. Crystal wants her to sit for a while," he said, gesturing with his head toward the end of the hall.

Cesar walked around me and sat on a couch. There was nothing between me and the door. If I could just get outside the house, I'd be able to outrun these muscle-bound weight-lifter freaks. I inched closer to the door.

"Come on in and catch the show. Recognize anybody?" Cesar asked, leering and pointing to the monitor.

On the screen was a video showing a young girl standing, naked but for the leather thongs that bound her wrists, suspending her arms high over her head, and the gag that covered her mouth. Her terrified eyes were looking back over her shoulder at the man behind her, the same ponytailed man who was sitting right there. Her auburn curls fell forward to cover her eyes when he pushed her.

It was as though suddenly all the fight and grit and nerve had just been sucked out of me. I looked away and bit my tongue.

"We all enjoyed that one," Cesar said.

My mind was a blur of images. Ely in my lifeguard tower, at work, laughing in the back of B.J.'s truck.

"Eddie was just warming her up. We all got a chance at her. Zeke was just gonna get his kicks and get her to talk to him, tell us what you two knew about Garrett. But she didn't scream or nothing, so I took over. Ain't fun unless they got some fight in 'em. Bitch just kept staring at me."

Eddie walked over and stood behind Zeke, smiling as he watched the monitor. "This shit's priceless, man."

Cesar stood and joined the other men around the video monitor. "The look in her eyes. Look." Cesar pointed to the screen as the camera zoomed in on her face. His fat fingers clawed at the glass over her eyes. "Fuckin' terrified. I'm gettin' hard again just watchin' her."

I squeezed my eyes shut, refusing to look.

"Want 'em to fast-forward to the snuff?" His guttural voice made the question hurt more. "This time it's real, and we got it on tape—tell me that ain't gonna stiffen a few peckers."

I heard the sound of the machine speeding up and then a downward whine as it resumed the normal speed.

"There he is," Zeke said. "Man just kind of lost it, and there we were, cameras rolling. Now Eddie here's just gonna change the face and . . ."

Cesar grabbed my arm in one hand, my chin in the other, and forced my face to within inches of the monitor. I hadn't wanted to look, but when he'd grabbed me, I couldn't help it, I'd opened my eyes.

"Man doesn't know his own strength," Zeke said.

"Shut up. You talk too much, man," Eddie said.

I pressed my eyes shut, but not before I saw the close-up on Ely's face, her eyes bulging out of the tearstained skin, a brown hand wrapped around her throat.

"Fuck you. It's not like she's gonna tell anybody." Cesar laughed. "Lady Captain here just might get her own chance to be a porn star tonight."

"Hey, asshole, I don't give a rat's ass what you do with her," Eddie said. "You morons don't understand, I got real work to do here. I got to get this shit back up. Boss isn't making money when the page is down."

It was as though it wasn't really happening, like I had left my own body somehow and I was hovering above this scene, seeing it from a distance, and we were all mannequins dancing around a little stage.

"Look at her," he said, forcing me back to the present, squeezing my face harder, his fingernails digging into my skin. "Your turn's coming," the deep voice whispered, spraying my ear with his spit.

I struggled, trying to break free from his grasp, trying to get away from those images on that screen. One arm pulled free, and I squirmed my head out of his grasp. He grabbed my ponytail before I could get out the door and yanked back so hard I fell to the floor.

"You're a strong bitch. We're gonna have some fun."

Eddie spun around in his computer chair. "Would you get the fuck outta here? How the hell am I supposed to work?"

Zeke stood, saying, "Let's put her away. Chewy'll keep an eye on her till we're ready for her. Come on, boy."

Cesar hauled me to my feet by my hair and then dragged me down past another bedroom, empty, but lit with huge bright lights, to the last door at the end of the hall. He shoved me into the room and opened the door to a walk-in closet. He pulled me close to him and put his face less than an inch from mine. He smelled of Doritos and beer, and when he spoke, I could feel the moist heat of his breath on my skin.

"You'd really get off on it, wouldn't you, bitch?" He wrapped his free hand around my throat and began to squeeze. "You like this shit, admit it to yourself. I could make you scream good. You just think of every bad thing you ever done—I'll make you hurt for every one." His fingers constricted, and all air stopped. Blackness started closing in like when I'd stayed down on a dive too long. "Your friend, she was a bad little piece. She got me in the balls on the beach that night." He sounded far away when he laughed. "Had to make her pay for that." His hand released its grip, and I sucked in air.

"That makes you a man, Cesar? Having sex with a child?"

"Shut up, cunt."

"You're a freak. You're nothing but garbage."

"You think I give a fuck about you or that other piece of pussy, Sunshine, or whatever the hell her name is? There's always gonna be more where she came from. They *want* me to fuck 'em." He grabbed at his crotch. "They want a piece of this."

I turned my head to the side. My face was contorted in a painful grimace, my lips pressed together, my eyes squeezed shut. I wasn't about to let him see me cry. The bastard.

Suddenly he pushed me away so hard I fell to the ground and hit my head against something metal on the floor behind the hanging clothes.

"Ugh, you fuckin' dog. Get the hell offa me," he said. The door slammed, and I found myself in total darkness, feeling the warm, sticky liquid flowing from the growing bump on my forehead. "Chewy, stay."

I heard the outer bedroom door close.

XXII

A T FIRST, I LAY MY HEAD ON THE MUSTY CARPET, CATCHING my breath, massaging my throat. Then I sobbed, wetting the fibers with my spit and tears. I felt vomit trying to crawl up my throat, and I swallowed it down, sick with the vision of terror in Ely's eyes. I wasn't certain I ever wanted to move again. Who would want to live in a world with men like Crystal, Zeke, Eddie, and Cesar? I saw that hand again, those fingers wringing her life away, and heard their laughter as they watched the video again. My mind eventually went numb as I just sobbed quietly, curled up on the floor.

When the tears stopped, I felt nothing. I slipped into a half-awake, half-asleep state, only vaguely aware of what was going on around me. Every once in a while I heard voices in the distance, but I couldn't make out what they were saying. The crack of light under the door slowly grew dimmer. That was the only way I knew that time was passing. Once the light was completely gone, and no one came to see if I was alive, I began to sense a weird disorientation. What if they were just going to leave me in here to die? No food, no water, and with the way my bladder felt, I'd soon be lying in my own waste. After a while, the walls of the closet seemed as though they were closing in, then tilting. In the blackness, I lost the sense of which way was up as the room began to spin.

I forced myself to stand and spread my arms out in front of me, touching the sides of the door. Not all men are like them, I told myself. I thought about B.J., my father, my brother Pit, even Maddy. There were good, decent men out there.

I began to explore the inside of the closet. All the clothes appeared to be men's clothes—slacks, shirts, jackets, shoes, nothing unusual or distinctive. The jackets smelled sharply of a musky cologne and faintly of cigarette smoke, as though they had been worn only to parties or clubs. Clothes filled only half the closet. The other side was piled high with sealed cardboard boxes. I tried lifting one—it felt very heavy, like it might be filled with paper or books.

There was a safe in there, too, about three feet high. I had bumped my head on the corner, and I pulled a shirt off a hanger to wipe the encrusted blood off my head.

The closet's doorknob was a round ball, the old-fashioned sort of lockset found in the fifties houses in Lauderdale. These old doorknob locks were laughable. In the center was a depression, a hole, and if I had a bobby pin or a screwdriver, I could stick it in there and turn the lock. I needed something about an inch long, maybe a little more—assuming this was the only lock on the door. I tried jiggling and rattling the knob. Sometimes in these old houses, things were loose enough you could just jiggle the lock free. It didn't work this time, though, and from the sound of the throaty growl on the far side of the door, I suddenly understood why they weren't worried about the stupid little lock.

"Hey, Chewy, good dog, good dog," I said aloud, and my voice sounded funny in the darkness. He growled, and I heard him snuffling along the base of the door.

"Good dog, nice dog. You don't want to eat me now, do you?" I continued the soft friendly tone, saying lots of nonsense but giving him time to get used to my voice. I put my fingertips at the base of the door and let him smell me while I sweet-talked him.

I stood and began going through the pockets of the clothing hanging in the closet, all the while continuing to talk softly to the dog. It was possible I'd get lucky and find a pocketknife, a nail clipper, something I could use to unlock that door. He (whoever he was) had shirts, jackets, parkas, robes, and racks of ties, belts, and shoes. He favored the molded plastic hangers—there was not a wire coat hanger in the place. I found lint balls, packs of gum and cruddy old wrappers, crumpled receipts, broken cigarettes, and lots of change, but nothing to help me open the door.

I slid to the floor and leaned my back against the door. Chewy whined, this time for more attention.

I got up and felt my way to the safe, shoved the hanging clothes aside, and climbed on top of the smooth metal box. When I stood, I whacked the back of my head against the edge of a wire rack, but by holding on to the bar I was able to lean back and feel what was on the shelf. Nothing on this side. I grabbed the wire shelf and tested it for sturdiness, then leaned across to feel the other side. Much of the shelf was empty, but shoved all the way to the back was another cardboard box. I could just get my fingernails into the crevice on the bottom of the box. Swinging my leg out, I searched for some of the boxes on the other side to prop my leg on. I found one and had just started to pull the box off the shelf when I lost my balance and fell, pulling the box down on top of me. My head avoided a blow for the first time in a while, and thankfully, the contents of the thing were not heavy. As I reached around the floor, feeling for what had fallen, I found only scattered papers and a three-ring binder—nothing to work on the lock on that door.

Damn. He's got belts in here, I thought in frustration. I could always hang myself.

Belts. I stood up and began feeling my way down the row of clothing until I came across the hanger containing the collection of belts. I felt my way to the buckles and began searching for one with a flat metal prong. The first one I tried wasn't long enough to reach inside the locked knob, and the second was too big around to fit in the hole. The third slid right in, and after I jostled it around a bit, it slid into the slot, and I felt the lock turn.

So far so good. Now I just had to keep from getting eaten alive by the friggin' pit bull. Then I remembered . . . the gum! I searched through several jackets before I found the first pack. I slid it into my pants pocket and kept on searching. I wound up with five partial packs of gum.

I crouched by the door and called softly to Chewy while un-wrapping a stick. I folded and stretched the gum, releasing more scent. The dog's nose was snuffling, working overtime along the crack at the door base. I slid the gum through and heard the slob-bering sound as he devoured the first piece.

I had this dog eating out of the palm of my hand, literally. I slid another piece under the door. My heart was coming up my throat as I turned the knob and slowly swung the door open. The dog's dark shape slowly advanced on me. I held a stick of gum at arm's length and watched the huge muzzle closing in on my hand. Chewy opened his mouth and licked my fingers before taking the last stick of Cinnamint. The lump that should have been his tail waggled back and forth on his rump.

The dark bedroom appeared bright to me after what had seemed like hours in the closet. The drapes were drawn, and the door to the hall was closed, but I could see a sliver of light under the door. I scratched Chewy's ears and checked my gum supply. Nothing but Juicy Fruit left. I gave him another piece, thinking he was going to be sorry in the morning.

I listened for noises out in the hall. The house seemed eerily quiet. Judging from the size of the waterbed that dominated the cen-ter of the room, I was in the master bedroom. I checked the desk and both nightstands, but there was no telephone. Most of the desk draw-ers were empty, with not even a letter opener to use as a weapon.

Across the hall, I heard voices, and I darted back into the closet and closed the door. I picked up the three-ring binder, disap-pointed that there was not more weight to it, and held it high, ready to bean the first person who walked through the door. But the low murmur of voices stayed at a distance, just conversation, men's laughter. I opened the door a crack, and Chewy pushed his nose inside, demanding to be petted.

"Okay, okay," I whispered, scratching him behind his ears. I was still carrying the three-ring binder, and when I turned to return it to the closet, I noticed the name written on the cover in black Magic Marker. *Bahama Belle.*

At the window, in the silver moonlight, I read the log of the *Bahama Belle* as captained by one Zeke Moss. Four seemingly uneventful trips to the Cayman Islands were chronicled. They were hauling American consumer goods, washers and dryers mostly, on the way down, and then bringing back a much smaller load of craft items and cases of Tortuga rum. Each time they came back into the port of Miami, U.S. Customs thoroughly searched the boat and her cargo, and each time they found nothing. Captain Moss seemed very smug in the entries where he noted that nothing illegal had been found aboard.

Then my eye was drawn to the last few entries. Moss noted that the vessel had gone into dry dock and was undergoing the usual assortment of repairs. He wrote that Neal Garrett had come aboard and was doing some kind of work for Crystal. Neal wouldn't explain to the captain just what he was doing, and that really irked Moss. Finally, Moss was ordered by Crystal to take three days off, leaving Garrett in charge. When Zeke returned, Neal had vanished and the boat was unmanned in the Miami River yard. Moss noted that they were very fortunate nothing was stolen.

The log stopped on the date of Crystal's arrest. Zeke must have called Crystal and complained about Neal's irresponsibility, and that's when Crystal came over with a gift of a little dope to appease the angry captain. He didn't tell him what Neal had been up to.

Thinking about the drawings I had found inside my copy of Bowditch, it was becoming clear that Neal had created some kind of hidden compartment aboard the *Bahama Belle*, and had done so on orders from Crystal. But whatever was there, neither Crystal nor the Coasties nor the demolition crew had been able to find it.

The voices from down the hall grew louder. It was clearly an argument.

I hurried back into the closet and returned the ship's log to the box. I grabbed some other papers out of the box and carried them to the window. Chewy followed me across the room, and I reached down to scratch his ears as I read. There were pages and pages of financial records. I could easily see that the transactions amounted to hundreds of thousands of dollars. Given the number of cardboard boxes in there, the totals must be in the millions. Maybe Crystal wasn't trying to smuggle anything into the country, but was smuggling something out: cash.

I certainly knew enough now to interest Collazo. I just had to get out of this place.

I drew one corner of the drape back slowly and found that the window opened onto a tiny courtyard on the side of the house. A small, dried-up fountain stood at the center of the brick patio, lit only by the moonlight. I unlatched the window and slid up the wood-framed glass. Warm, humid night air flowed into the air-conditioned room, along with the night noises of crickets, frogs, and cicadas. I looked back over my shoulder at the door and down at Chewy. The dog's dark eyes followed my every move.

I pushed the bottom of the screen outward and slid it to the grass, then ducked through and dropped to the ground. Chewy stood on his hind legs, poking his massive head out the window.

"Chewy, sit." He immediately dropped to the floor and obeyed. Abaco had never listened to me the way this dog did. "Stay." I slid the window far enough closed to prevent his escape.

From the patio, a brick path led toward the street along the side of the house past the other bedroom windows. The overgrown areca palms grew like a massive hedge to ensure total privacy in the compound. I had to dodge the overhanging fronds to make my way down the walk, and I stepped carefully around the fanlike branches on the ground lest they crunch underfoot and call the attention of someone inside. This side of the house had not seen a gardener's care in months, and after the rain, the night air was thick with the sweet smell of layers of rotting vegetation.

The middle bedroom's miniblinds were drawn, but one of the bottom slats was twisted, and I could see a tiny sliver of the bedroom. The bright lights were on, and a couple of video cameras were focused on the far side of the room. I inhaled sharply when I moved my head to the right and recognized the people in the brightly lit bed. All three were nude. The ponytailed man was sitting on the edge of the bed; Sunny lay on her back spread-eagled, her hands bound at the head of the bed, her eyes wide; and Alexis, the dancer from the Top Ten Club, was kneeling between her legs. All three were listening to Crystal, who was standing beside the bed, giving directions, waving his hands around, evidently shouting, though I couldn't hear him over the noise of the air conditioner a few feet away from me. Sunny's eyes held the same look of terror I had seen on Ely's on the video screen. Crystal went over to Alexis as though to demonstrate something and suddenly backhanded her, knocking her off the bed. Sunny struggled, but the ponytailed man held her legs, laughing. Crystal turned to yell something at one of the cameramen; as the lights lit his eyes, I saw the raw sexual excitement there, and I felt my throat constrict. He advanced toward Sunny, opened his mouth wide, and stuck out his tongue, running it around his lips in what he must have thought was a sexy gesture, but instead only made him look more hideous. His bug eyes stared at her as he began to unbuckle his pants. I moved away from the window. Running for help now was out of the question.

XXIII

CHEWY WAS STILL SITTING BENEATH THE WINDOW LIKE an obedient sentry when I slid the glass open again and reentered the room. His rump twitched and he dog-smiled at me, his tongue falling out the side of his mouth.

I had to get the men to leave that room, leaving the girls behind. I stood in the middle of the room and stared at the closet door, thinking that my idea just might work.

Walking over to the window, I tried to imagine what they would think when they ran into the room and saw the open window. I kicked off one of my worn old deck shoes and dropped it on the carpet in front of the window. I thought about whom I was dealing with and kicked off the other shoe as well, dropping it on the lawn outside the window. Stepping into the closet, I made sure that I could fit behind the clothes with my legs hidden by the safe. Yes, it just might work.

I opened the door to the hall and peered out. All was quiet. The next bedroom door was closed. I felt in my pocket for the last piece of gum.

I stepped into the hall and held the gum out for Chewy. "Here, boy." He ambled into the hall and I eased around him, then backed into the doorway.

"Chewy," I whispered. "Go get Zeke! Where's Zeke?" The dog's ears pricked up, and he trotted to the next door. I closed my door, dashed into the closet, and hid. I heard Chewy whining and scratching at the door down the hall, then I heard the door open. "What the fuck? Hey, Cesar, come here, quick. We left the dog in there with her."

The door to my room flew open, and the two of them raced in and went straight to the window. "Shit, son of a bitch! She got out." They pounded out of the bedroom and back next door.

Soon more footsteps headed down the hall. Crystal was shouting incomprehensibly in a mixture of Spanish and English. The dog was barking, excited by the men's agitation. I heard the front door open and slam several times, as well as the sound of cars starting up.

I tiptoed to the closet door and peered out. So far so good. The hall was empty. I padded barefoot to the studio room, and as I had hoped, the two girls were there. Sunny was curled up in a fetal position crying, while Lex sat smoking a cigarette. Lex saw me first.

"You're shittin' me," she said.

I held my fingers to my lips. "Shh." The knots in the leather thongs that bound Sunny's hands were tight, but after several seconds, I had loosened them and set her free. I smiled at her, then jerked my head to indicate they should follow me.

"You coming with us?" I whispered to Lex.

"Yeah," she said, grinding her cigarette out on the wood nightstand. "They ain't paying me enough to do Crystal. What a freak."

Neither of them had a stitch on, but that was the least of our worries. I led them back to the end bedroom, and we climbed out the window. This time we turned toward the river side. The brick patio led around the corner of the house and joined the pool and boat dock area. I turned to the girls.

"We're going to run for the river and swim for it. I can't see anybody, but that doesn't mean they won't see us. We're going to be really exposed running across that lawn."

"You can say that again," Lex said, and smiled at me.

"Yeah, right. Look, don't stop for anything. The tide is flowing downriver right now. If somebody sees us, swim to the middle of the river and try to keep your head underwater as long as you can. If we get separated, we'll meet up again on the far side of the river by the next bridge. Okay?"

Sunny looked so scared.

"You can swim, can't you?"

They nodded.

"Then let's do it."

We took off running across the lawn, jumped onto the wood deck around the pool, and leaped down the three steps to the dock. Right as I passed the Jacuzzi, I heard Crystal's scream.

"It's them! Cesar, Zeke, they're back here!"

I jumped, stretched out, and flew through the air in one of the finest racing dives I have ever executed. I heard and felt the impact of the other two behind me. I was probably a much stronger swimmer than they were, but then, I was weighted down by my clothes. They didn't have that problem.

The first time I came up for air, I saw Sunny struggling far behind me. She really wasn't much of a swimmer. She was dog-paddling and looking like she was trying to climb up out of the water.

"Sunny, hold on. I'm coming."

Back at the dock, I could see three figures on the *Hard Bottom*, their muffled voices unintelligible across the water except for a few words: "Keys . . . assholes . . ."

When I was about three strokes away from Sunny, I heard her take one of those desperate inhales, as she sucked water and went down.

I filled my lungs as full as I could and dove. It was so black that there was no point in even trying to open my eyes. She had to be right here. I had lost too many lately, and I wasn't about to lose this one. She was already deep when my fingers finally brushed through her hair. I twined my fingers in the strands and reached for her as my lungs started to ache. I pulled her to the surface, but mine was the only gasp for air.

I heard the boat rumble to life about the same time the spotlight clicked on. I was almost to the far bank of the river with Sunny. She still wasn't breathing, but I saw a sportfisherman with an aft swim step and folding boarding ladder. I had a heck of a time when I tried to pull her up onto the swim step. I stretched her out, cleared the airway, and started mouth-to-mouth. Before long she gagged, puking up river water, and I dragged her to the side deck, out of sight of that damn spotlight. She was groggy and confused, and I hushed her and lay down on the deck next to her, exhausted, looking up at the stars, watching the spotlight glide along the riverbank and listening to the music of her breathing.

After several minutes, she coughed a little and started to sit up.

"Shh. Lie down. They're looking for us," I whispered.

The spotlight lit up the superstructure of the boat and shone beyond into the bushes and pathways of the homes on the riverbank. Sunny lay quiet as we heard the burbling of Crystal's boat passing just alongside ours. I could tell from the voices that Cesar was up on the bridge, Zeke down on deck level. Although I couldn't understand most of the words, I knew they were arguing, shouting at one another.

Suddenly, Cesar shouted, "Look! Over there! In the water!" The boat's RPMs increased, and we heard the *swoosh* of the prop wash, followed by the creaking dock lines as our boat pulled against her moorings in the turbulent water. I crawled forward and watched over the bulwark as their white boat tied up to an empty dock and Cesar took off running across a lawn. I assumed it was Lex they'd seen or heard. I hoped she wouldn't get caught.

I turned around, leaned my back against the inside of the bulwark, and tried to think. Sunny was sitting on the deck, hugging her knees to her chest, shivering, and looking up at me like she thought I knew what we were going to do next. Naked and wet, she looked miserable. How the hell was I supposed to get all the way across downtown Fort Lauderdale with a gorgeous, naked fifteen-year-old girl?

I crawled aft on my hands and knees, keeping my head below the level of the bulwark. There was a big white fiberglass deck box on the afterdeck. Under the dock lines, swim fins, tackle box, and snorkels, I found a man's shortie wet suit. At least this would keep her afloat.

"Put this on," I whispered, handing it to her.

I peeked around the edge of the bulwark. Crystal's boat was still tied up at that house downriver from us, her engines idling. I couldn't make out who was aboard, but my guess was that both Zeke and Cesar had jumped ashore to search. I couldn't be sure though.

"We're going to have to go back in the water," I told Sunny, and her eyes opened wider in fear. "I was a lifeguard. I won't let you drown. Besides, this wet suit is made of material that floats. It'll keep you up—you couldn't sink in this. Okay?"

She nodded, her mouth set in a tight line. She was showing more guts than I'd expected.

"Come on." I led her aft, and we slipped back into the river off the swim step. "Keep your face turned away from their boat. The light reflects off your face, and they might spot us. Just float. Take my hand."

We pushed our way around the stern and into the current. The river was only about fifty yards wide here, so we would be passing fairly close to the boat, even if we stayed to the far bank. The hardest part was not looking in that direction. I wanted to see who was on the boat and if they had Lex with them, but I knew it would be foolish to turn my face in their direction. As we drifted past an empty dock on our side of the river, a dog started barking up in the yard. We could hear him running, claws scratching against a wood deck.

"Shut up, you fucking dog," Cesar called across the river.

I felt Sunny squeeze my hand tighter. Neither of us breathed for several long seconds as we floated just opposite their boat. The

barking dog raced to the end of the dock. He had finally noticed
our dark shadows in the water.

"Come on, Cesar, we lost them. Crystal's gonna be pissed,"
Moss said just before the idling engine revved and we heard the
thump of dock lines being thrown on deck. The noise of the boat
began to move upriver, away from us.

Sunny was shivering, and I could feel the trembling in her
hand. I had to get her out of the water. I began scanning the docks
and banks of the river for a small boat. Nearly everything we passed
was chained up and locked. The river residents knew better than to
leave boats loose in this town. We finally came by a little trawler
with a punt tied alongside. The punt was no more than eight feet
long, and it was so beat-up and ugly, its owners must not have worried about thieves. There were two oars tucked under the center
seat. It would do. I held down the bow as Sunny climbed in over
the stern, and I soon followed her. After untying the lines and fitting the oars in the locks, we were off, my back and arms straining
to pull those oars as hard and fast as I could.

At the Fourth Avenue Bridge, I pulled off to the side and
grabbed hold of a piling. The noise of the cars passing on the steel
grate overhead sounded like the rumbling of a jackhammer. This
was where I had told Lex we would meet up with her. I waited five
minutes before moving on.

The city was dead quiet as we passed under the downtown
bridges. A few cars passed on streets parallel to the river. Each time
I held my breath, terrified that it might be them. But even along
Riverwalk, there were only a few solitary couples far too wrapped
up in themselves to pay us any mind as our creaky oars pulled us
downriver.

Lex would be fine. She was a survivor, I told myself. Then I
remembered the last time I had heard that.

XXIV

WE DIDN'T SAY A WORD TO EACH OTHER. I DIDN'T know what Sunny was thinking, but I was wondering what I would find at my place. Nervous as I was about what I would find, my hands were grateful as the *Gorda* came into view on the river. The red ovals on my palms would surely puff up into nasty blisters soon.

Sunny had nodded off, slumped over in the stern of the dinghy. The wet suit rode up so that the shoulders were at the level of her ears, but the arm holes still gaped at her waist. She'd tucked herself inside, turtlelike, crossing her arms over her breasts. I tapped her on the knee to wake her and lifted my finger to my lips, motioning her not to speak.

After tying the punt's bowline off to a piling, I climbed on the dock and gestured for Sunny to stay in the boat. I whistled very softly, not wanting to scare Abaco. I heard her get up from her spot in the bushes, a low growl beginning in her throat, but then she saw me and trotted over, jumping up on me to be petted. I motioned for Sunny to reach up and let the dog sniff her hand.

Peering through the crack in the gate, I saw the dark shadow of a vehicle parked out in the Larsens' driveway. I slipped through the gate and, crawling on my hands and knees, made my way to the drive. When I lifted my head to have a look, I saw a black El Camino, B.J. slumped over in the front seat.

I made my way around to the driver's side of the car. The window was rolled down. I didn't know if he was asleep or unconscious or worse. I reached in and shook his shoulder.

He started awake, wide-eyed and alert. "Uh . . . what?"

I held my fingers to my lips. "Shh."

"You okay?" he whispered.

"Yeah." At that moment I heard a car start down the street. "B.J., duck, hide."

I made my way to the front of B.J.'s truck, where I couldn't be seen from the street. The car, the same dark blue Camaro with tinted windows, slowed to a stop at the Larsens' drive. I could hear the radio tuned to a rap music station, and then Cesar's deep voice. "See anything?"

"Nah, it's too soon, man."

The car moved on, making a U-turn and then coming back past the house once more before leaving the neighborhood.

I slid back around to the window. "Come on. Let's go out back." He sat up and opened the door. The noise it made when he closed it made me cringe. I hoped they were well down the street. We hurried back through the gate, and I led him down to the dock, where Sunny still waited in the boat.

"Help her up, will you?"

Sunny reached up one arm, and he lifted her out of the boat.

"I don't think we ought to go into my house. Let's go into the Larsens'."

"Good idea," B.J. said, and went for the key hidden by the back kitchen door.

Food smells lingered in the kitchen when B.J. opened the door.

B.J. reached for the wall plate, and I grabbed his hand. "No lights."

Sunny leaned against the wall, her arms wrapped around her midriff, her glazed eyes staring into space.

"We need to get her into a warm shower. She's been too cold too long."

"You, too," B.J. said. "You need to get out of those wet clothes. You're shaking."

I hadn't even noticed it, but he was right. Taking her by the hand, I led her through the dining room to the downstairs guest bedroom and bath. At first she didn't want to take a shower in the dark, but once I explained the situation to her, she agreed. I found huge, thick towels folded in the closet, and I set one out for her and another for myself, then turned down the covers of the queen-size guest bed. She didn't speak to me when she got out, just toweled off and crawled under the covers.

The clothes I peeled off stank of the river: rotting vegetation, oily street runoff, and sewage. The clean hot water felt good, but it restored feeling to my limbs and body, which had been pleasantly numb. Now the many aches returned. In the dark I ran my fingers over the little barnacle cuts on my belly and thighs, the bumps on my head, the deep bruise in my shoulder, the raw blisters on my hands.

After toweling off my wet hair and combing it out, I wrapped myself in a huge white bath sheet and went in search of B.J. I found him standing to one side of the unshuttered entry window, keeping watch over the front of the house.

"Any sign of them?"

"They've driven by twice so far. Now they've parked. See, down there by the stop sign."

"What happened to the cops who were out there?"

"They left around seven o'clock. I guess they gave up."

B.J. continued to stare at the vehicle down the street. "I bet they're talking right now, saying you've probably gone somewhere else tonight, but they know you'll eventually be back. They'll just wait. And they're right." He turned to face me. "You can't hide in here forever."

"No, I know that." I looked around the front room. "Any idea what time it is?"

"It's just after two. I saw a clock in the kitchen."

"So we have some time before daybreak. The Larsens shut off the phone when they're out of town. So I have to sneak over to my cottage and call Mike Beesting in a bit. I know why Neal was out there that day on the *Top Ten*. We'll take *Gorda* out in the morning."

"What are you talking about?"

"I know what Neal was diving for out there, and I know why people are getting killed."

He reached out and ran his hand over my slick wet hair. He felt the old bump from the fire extinguisher and then the new one from when they pushed me into the closet.

"Come, tell me the story in here." He led me into the family room, where a big-screen TV sat opposite a soft, deep nine-foot couch, the kind of couch you sink into and have a hard time getting out of. When we fell into the soft pillows, I made sure we were a safe distance apart and that my towel remained discreetly wrapped.

I puffed out my cheeks and exhaled loudly. "B.J., you can't imagine what I saw tonight." My throat tightened. "We've got to stop them."

He chuckled. "Like I said, out to save the world."

"No, not the world . . . just some girls, like Sunny in there. I didn't save Elysia; in fact, I probably even contributed to her death. I mean, if I hadn't gone to talk to her that night . . . I think she'd still be alive."

B.J. reached over and took my hand in his. There was more compassion than romance in the gesture, yet my body reacted to his touch as though an inner fault line were shifting.

I looked into his almond-shaped brown eyes. B.J. was a man, like Neal, like Cesar. Could I trust this man? I'd made so many bad choices recently, I didn't trust my own judgment anymore. Was this man any different?

He stared back at me, unflinching. "It's okay to ask questions," he said.

I slid over the cushions, wrapped my arms around his waist, and rested my head against his chest. "And that's why you *are* different," I whispered.

We sat like that for a while just holding each other. And then, with those miracle-worker fingers of his, he began massaging my head, easing the pain in the bumps and taking the tension out of my temples. I twisted around until I was leaning against him like a backrest and started to tell him the whole story.

"See, B.J., people don't normally build compartments into ships to smuggle stuff out of this country. That didn't make sense to me at first."

"Mmm-hmmm."

"But then I thought about where they were going, the Cayman Islands, and then it all made sense." From my head to my neck to my shoulders, his fingers worked, bringing life and warmth and tingling and pleasure.

"What made sense?" he asked.

"What are the Caymans known for?"

"Diving and banks," he said, and began kissing me on the side of my neck.

"Right. So if you've got lots of illegally obtained cash . . ."

I started to ask him where he thought Neal might have hidden the money on the freighter, but just then his hands reached over the tops of my shoulders.

I needed to check on Sunny, I needed to call Mike, but all that faded with this other need. Leaning back into B.J.'s chest, forcing his hands to slide lower, I pulled loose the bath sheet so that his hands were free to slide over my breasts and down my belly. From deep in his chest I heard a murmur, maybe a groan, and I knew, as surely as he had known the time was wrong before, that this time was just right.

XXV

W E LAY NAKED ON THE COUCH, OUR BODIES ENTWINED, and I tried to join B.J. in that much-needed world of sleep. I'd had almost no sleep in the last forty-eight hours, and the fatigue I felt was bone deep. But I was too tired to sleep. I wanted and needed the rest so badly, I was trying too hard. My eyes simply would not close, so I lay there staring wide-eyed at the ceiling, willing myself to get some rest.

Once again I had a feeling that we were being watched. All the windows except that one by the front door were covered on the outside with aluminum hurricane shutters. No one could be looking in. I glanced toward the entry, wondering if I was sensing someone coming to the front door. Or was it just paranoia, a reaction to the days of dealing with these wackos?

My heart rate had quickened, along with my breathing. Thoughts went around inside my brain like clothes in an electric dryer. I felt trapped under B.J.'s arm, so I slowly rolled off the couch, out from under his embrace. He moaned and rearranged himself but didn't wake.

I had to get to a phone, call Mike, then get out to the wreck site. There would be clothes upstairs. Mrs. Larsen was shorter and heavier, but I wasn't up to crossing the yard in the buff.

Their bedroom was at the top of the stairs, and in the dresser I found some navy shorts and a black T-shirt. With a belt from the closet, I was able to keep the shorts up. The shoes were all too small for my size nines. Padding down to the toilet at the end of the hall, I thought I heard a noise from behind a closed door. I stopped for a moment and listened, but I didn't hear it again. In the bathroom, I heard it again. It was a creaking metallic sound.

As I pulled up my shorts, I thought about the closed door out there in the hall. I knew the house fairly well; the door led to another guest bedroom. I couldn't imagine why this door was closed, unless B.J. had closed it for some reason. Reaching for the doorknob, I heard the sound again, much louder, more distinct this time. I froze. I knew that sound. It was the sound of the aluminum hurricane shutters rolling up.

The hallway seemed wide open and very exposed. I pulled my hand back from the doorknob, my pulse now pounding in my throat. Cesar must have figured out we were in here. But how did he get up onto the second story?

Unless . . . The idea forming in my mind seemed far-fetched at first, but then all my tumbled thoughts fit together. Maybe someone trying to get *out*, not in.

I crept down the hall to the spare bedroom and put my ear to the door. It was quiet, almost too quiet for anyone to be in there. Then, far off, I heard the sound of an outboard cranking over. My outboard.

I opened the door and the light from the open window lit the interior almost like daylight to my unaccustomed eyes. Stopping short in the middle of the room, I stared at the mess around me. There were food wrappers, dirty dishes, and soda and beer cans all over the carpeted floor. Some tools and hoses were set out on blankets on the floor, and several torn-open FedEx boxes were stacked by the closet. The linens on the bed were twisted into a crumpled, dirty jumble. A rope tied around a large armoire led over to and out the window. Rags and towels with dark stains were strewn about everywhere. I picked one up and held it up to the light. Bloodstains.

The outboard engine caught and roared to life. I made it to the window just in time to see a familiar silhouette throw off the lines from the davits and take off upriver in my Boston Whaler.

XXVI

M Y FEET BARELY TOUCHED THE CARPET AS I FLEW down the stairs. Damn him! First my money, now my boat! That son of a bitch! I didn't bother closing the kitchen door behind me. Abaco yipped at my heels as I ran down the path to the dock. She liked this game—first she got to chase her old buddy Neal, and now I was playing, too. Only this was no game.

I yanked the door to the Jet Ski's boathouse. Locked. Keys . . . keys . . . where were the keys? That's right, *Gorda*. I ran over, punched the code into the tug's alarm panel, and yanked open the wheelhouse. Chart table drawer. It was a mess, jam-packed with pencils, old fuel dock receipts, brass dividers, a small hand-bearing compass, and down in the bottom of the mess, the boathouse keys.

The key turned easily in the lock. With a single tug, the Jet Ski slid out and down the carpeted ramp, splashing into the water. I jumped on and hit the button with my thumb. Nothing happened.

"Damn!"

I glanced upriver in the direction Neal had gone. Just as I was about to give up, I remembered the emergency kill switch—a tab that had to be in place for the bike to start. I threw an extra dock line over the water bike and crawled into the little boathouse on my hands and knees. I felt the coiled plastic-coated wire, grabbed it, and hopped back on the boat. I slipped my hand through the Velcro wristband and slid the tab into place. I prayed the gas in the water bike wasn't too old. She started right up. I hunkered my body down tight to the machine and cranked that baby up full bore.

Only a few hours earlier, Sunny and I had rowed quietly down this waterway. Now the Jet Ski screamed back upriver, her engine's whine echoing back off the houses lining the riverbanks, the wind making my eyes water and tying my loose hair into knots. I'd ridden this thing only once before, and I found myself oversteering, zigging and zagging, nearly slamming into one seawall, then the other.

The startled bridge tender's moonlike face appeared behind the glass as I roared under the Andrews Avenue Bridge. He must have wondered what the hell we were doing tearing upriver at that hour, first Neal in my Whaler and now me, maybe two to three minutes behind him.

After I passed under the I-95 bridge and the river widened, I could see the remains of the Whaler's wake ahead of me. I knew I was closing on him.

A S I APPROACHED THE FORK IN THE RIVER, I WONDERED which direction he would take—west toward the Everglades or south to the Dania Cutoff Canal and a big circle back to the entrance to Port Everglades. I bet on the Dania direction, and that choice was confirmed when I saw that his wake still ruffled the water in that direction.

I was entering Pond Apple Slough, one of the few remaining freshwater swamps in South Florida. Though developers had built a trash incinerator, a superhighway, and industrial parks all around the swamp, the environmentalists had managed to save these last few acres. It was totally undeveloped and dark as hell. The amber light of the highway did little to penetrate the tangle of grass, mangrove, and dead cypress. Tearing upriver, I feared hitting some obstruction. I eased off the gas a little just before I heard the gunshot.

I swerved violently, then overcorrected in the other direction. The shot had come from somewhere along the left bank, and I had to get control of the bike to put some distance between us. I was trying to remain upright when another shot hit a tree just behind me.

"Shit," I said aloud, my lips nearly touching the handlebars. I couldn't see him, but obviously he had stopped somewhere deep in the brush along the eastern bank. If he could hide in the brush, so could I. There was an opening ahead, like a little tributary stream, and I turned into it, cutting the engine. The Jet Ski barely fit into the slot between the mangroves, and I used the overhanging branches to pull myself forward.

My skin was soon covered in a thin sheen of sweat. I continuously wiped my palms on the shorts I'd borrowed. My smell seemed to be attracting every bug in the swamp. Several tones of offkey buzzing assaulted both ears, and the stinging started about my calves. When I dipped my bare feet into the water to discourage the biting, they sank into the muck on the bottom.

The Whaler's outboard started up, and the sound of Neal searching for me filled the night.

He stopped at the break in the brush where I had entered. I winced when I heard branches and roots scraping the sides of the Whaler's hull. Then the prop hit the mud and the engine started to sputter. There was no mistaking the voice doing all the cursing: Neal.

The night suddenly grew quiet in the void left after the engine's roar quit. I froze holding on to two different mangrove branches, my arms spread wide, imagining a bullet striking between my shoulder blades at any moment. The mosquitoes buzzed more insistently, and one even flitted into my ear canal. It took every ounce of willpower not to flinch.

"Seychelle, is that you in there?" His voice sounded strong, confident, and much too close. "Because if that's you, I'll put this gun away right now. You know I wouldn't ever do anything to hurt you, Sey."

I kept quiet, listening.

"Shit, I know you must really be pissed at me, but I can explain it all to you."

Water sloshed around the Whaler as he shifted position in the boat. I wanted to turn around to see if I could see him back there. Though the moon had set, the glow from the city grew brighter as my eyes adjusted to the night.

"Your money. Okay. I had to take that. There were some tools, things I needed to buy. But I'll be able to pay it all back soon, baby. With interest. You'd better believe that."

I felt a mosquito land on my face next to my eye, and then the tiny sharp pain as it pierced my skin.

"I don't know what they've been telling you, but I'm the victim here, Sey. These guys, they want to kill me. They sent that girl, Patty, to kill me. You believe me, don't you, Sey?"

Part of me wanted to believe him, to believe that all this had just been a colossal mistake, to believe that there was an explanation, that I just needed to listen to Neal's side of this and it would all suddenly make sense.

"Come on, I know you're there, but I feel stupid talking to the mangroves. Just come out and I'll explain it to you."

My face, my legs. I tried to concentrate on not scratching, not moving, not believing what he was saying.

"Okay. Look, here's what happened. I surfaced when I heard the engines shut down and found her there talking to them on the VHF, telling them where we were. I had to stop her. *She* shot *me*. A little lower and I'd be dead. What the hell was I supposed to do? Talk to me, Sey. Come on out of there. You know me."

About fifteen, twenty feet away, a little to the south of where Neal waited, I heard something move, causing branches to quiver and a *shhhhh* sort of noise as the thing moved through the water.

"You don't know what it's like, Sey, working for a man with all that money, a complete asshole."

The little ripples on the surface of the water caused other branches to shift, turning leaves in the half light, making the trees creak slightly as wood rubbed on wood. I squinted as I looked over my shoulder.

"Guys like that don't deserve it." When Neal spoke, I could hear the direction of his voice change as he swung his head around, listening to the swamp. "I'm not leaving till you come out of there, Sey. I know you want to believe me."

I struggled to see what was moving through the water. My mind whirled with visions of reptilian jaws opening as they neared my ankles. Ever so slowly I lifted my toes out of the muck. Placing my feet on the footrests, I slowly reached for another branch, but the stick broke off in my hand with a loud snap.

Shots boomed out and bullets flew into the brush around me. I hunkered down against the water bike, my eyes squeezed shut. A startled large bird flew out of the scrub, letting loose with an eerily childlike cry, the sound of its wings audible as it circled and turned west. I leaned back down and pressed my cheek against the warm metal of the water bike. My heart felt like it was battering at the inside of my rib cage. Neal cursed the bird and fired off another three or four shots. I heard one bullet shatter a tree branch less than a foot above my head.

He had not been shooting just to scare me.

I waited, but he didn't say anything more. There wasn't much more to say.

I hoped he would think it had been the bird that had snapped the branch. More carefully now, I reached out for another branch, gently pulling on it to test the strength of the wood before I put any strain on it. I continued to pull myself deeper into the swamp, following the snaking turns of the narrow open space, just fitting through whatever holes in the vegetation I could find.

My eyes had grown quite accustomed to the darkness, and I began to see freshwater shrimp and other fish moving in the dark water, breaking the surface with fins and feelers. In the branches of a dead cyprus, high over the pond apple trees, I saw a raccoon rouse himself from his sleeping position and climb down the dark trunk. Big fronds of ferns and palmetto directly over my head made dark silhouettes against the starlit sky. There was a Jurassic feel to the place, as though a T. rex could come charging through the brush at any moment. My mother used to tell us a story about venturing into the Pond Apple Slough with friends back in the fifties. She insisted there was still a hunting shack back in the swamp, a place built by the Rivers brothers, trappers of local legend. She and her friends would canoe back in there and get drunk on weekends, or so Red told me later. If that shack still existed, I'd love to find it now.

When the Whaler's outboard started up again, I was surprised by the faintness and the direction of the sound. Already I'd become disoriented in the dark swamp, with no landmarks. The outboard noise grew fainter until finally it vanished. I tried to get my bearings, but it was difficult to be certain, the way noises surrounded you in there.

I had to climb off and step down into the muck to turn the water bike around. My bare feet are pretty tough, but the rocks and roots protruding from the mud hurt like hell. Not only that, I could have sworn things were moving in the water, brushing against my calves and ankles. The opening in the brush had narrowed so that I had to push the bike into the vegetation in order to horse it around, and the handlebars kept getting caught on a creeper hanging down from a dead cypress tree.

"Shit!" A branch I hadn't seen ripped a gash across the back of my hand. The blood oozing out appeared black against my pale-looking skin. Drops were falling in the water, and I wasn't quite sure what they might attract. I licked the blood off and held my hand straight up in the air to try to stop the bleeding.

Damned deadwood. The swamp was choked with it. I'd heard that saltwater intrusion was killing off Pond Apple Slough. I just didn't want the swamp killing me.

After about a minute, the bleeding had pretty well let up, and I climbed on the bike, happy to get my bare legs out of that water.

The entire insect population of the swamp seemed to zero in on my ankles at that point, but I was less worried about their bites than those of whatever might live in that water.

The bike hadn't gone five yards when I came to a fork in the watery trail. Of course, I couldn't remember which one I'd come through on, probably hadn't even been aware there was a fork at the time.

When I heard the low rumble of an engine, I was sure it was Neal, coming back to finish me. I strained my ears trying to figure out where the sound was coming from, swiveling my head around, using my ears like radar antennae, when I suddenly realized the noise was coming from overhead. The red, green, and white lights of a small plane twinkled almost directly above me. The wind was out of the east, and he was surely going to land on the east-west runway at Fort Lauderdale Airport. Therefore he was headed due east. I took the right fork.

By the time I got back out into the New River, I wasn't worried about gators or murderous ex-boyfriends. I'd been hit, scratched, bitten, and attacked quite enough for one night. I fired up the Jet Ski and headed home at full throttle, my jaw set so tight my teeth ground hard with every bounce of the water bike. I didn't wave to any bridge tenders, I didn't worry about Crystal's boat, and I didn't even see the buildings of downtown. I just wanted to get home.

An empty dock was all I saw when I came around the bend upriver of the Larsen place. I didn't notice anything else about that stretch of the New River except for that long stretch of gray, vacant seawall. *Gorda* was gone.

XXVII

 I TURNED THE THROTTLE WAY DOWN AND CIRCLED AROUND so I could pull into the dock against the current. As I turned, I noticed my Boston Whaler downriver, lodged between a big Hatteras and the seawall. Neal hadn't even bothered to tie it up. The bastard had just set it adrift.

"Sey!" Sunny appeared out of the bushes, running toward the empty dock. She was wearing a man's T-shirt, and it looked like a billowing white dress on her. Her legs and feet were bare, and with her tousled blond hair, she looked like a little girl. Heck, she really was a little girl. "Come on! Quick!" she said, waving her arms, signaling me to hurry. Her voice was like a loud stage whisper, and it was difficult to hear her over the idling water bike. I cut the engine.

"You've got to help him!" she said.

I grabbed a spare dock line and tied up the Jet Ski. "Who? What are you talking about?"

"It's B.J. He's hurt!"

I brushed her aside and ran up the walkway leading to the back door of the Larsens' house. Sunny ran behind me, panting and trying to spit out the story.

"When I woke up, I heard voices. I started to get up, but I could hear them fighting. I hid. I was too scared to come out."

I ran into the living room and saw B.J. on the floor. There was blood in his hair, just above his temple, blood staining the rug under him.

"Oh, man . . ." I dropped to my knees and slid one hand beneath his head while the other caressed his cheek. His skin felt warm.

Sunny was still talking. "The other man, the one with the gun, ran away. He got a bunch of stuff from upstairs and left on that boat that was out there. I tried to call nine-one-one, but the phones don't work. I wanted to help your friend, really, but I went to the front door, and those men were out there in their car, parked right in front of the house, and I was so scared. I didn't know what to do. Is he dead?"

My fingers probed his neck under the jawbone and felt an even, rhythmic pulse. Thank God. I leaned down and pressed my lips to his forehead. He moaned softly.

"B.J. Are you okay?"

His eyes flicked open, then shut, then open again, swimming in their sockets. He reached up to touch his head and winced in pain.

"What happened?"

"I'm not sure. Sunny said . . ."

"Neal," he said.

"Yeah, I know. He did this?"

"I'm gonna . . ." He went to heave himself into a sitting position, but collapsed back onto the floor. "Oh, man. What the . . ."

"He shot you. I think it's just a flesh wound, but you've lost a fair amount of blood. Here, let's get you onto the couch."

With Sunny's help I got him onto the same deep sofa we'd used for lovemaking only a few short hours ago. I told Sunny where to find the key to my cottage and what to tell the police dispatcher.

"Be careful. Those guys are still cruising this neighborhood.

I doubt they've come into the yard or Abaco would have alerted us. All the same, go slow, stay hidden, and try not to make any noise."

"I'll be okay." She smiled at me and took off to go call 911.

"How're you feeling?" I asked B.J.

"Gonna have one hell of a headache."

"He took *Gorda.*"

"What?" He tried again to get up, but I eased him back.

"I'll deal with it, B.J. I know where he's going, but I don't have time to explain. I've got to get my boat back."

"I can help. . . ."

"Forget it. Look, I know what Neal's up to. He took my dive gear." I kissed him on the forehead again. "I'll be right back."

The "bunch of stuff" Sunny was talking about must have been my tank and the regulator that he had stolen out of the cottage. Judging from the FedEx boxes upstairs, he had also been buying gear with my money and having it delivered to the house when he knew nobody would be around. I wondered how he got from the beach to my place on the day I'd towed in the *Top Ten.* He swam ashore, but then he made it across town in swim trunks with a bullet in him. He certainly was resourceful, but then again, this was South Florida. I figured that once here, he broke into my cottage and took my money and scuba gear. He'd spent the last few days up there healing and planning how to get at Crystal's money without the use of the *Top Ten.*

I trotted outside to the large shed where the Larsens stored some more gear. There was a small padlock on a thin metal hasp, and I picked up a geranium-filled urn and bashed the lock. It let go on the third bash. In amongst the bikes and water skis and windsurfers, sure enough, I found tanks, regulators, masks, and fins. The fins were huge, even for me, but they'd work. I took what I needed and walked down to the dock. I was surprised Abaco didn't join me, but I decided she must be nosing around with Sunny. With the boat hook, I retrieved the Whaler and tied it up to the dock. After dropping the dive gear in the dinghy, I jogged back up to the house.

"How're you doing?"

B.J. shrugged.

"Where's Sunny?" I asked.

"She hasn't come back."

B.J. didn't look so great. He needed to see a doctor, soon. "I'm going to go see what's taking her so long."

As I slipped out the back door of the Larsens' place, I stepped into the bushes that ran along the base of the house and surveyed the yard. Sunny should have been back by now. How long could it take to call 911 at four in the morning? Something was wrong. Keeping my body low to the ground, I trotted across the grass to my cottage and peeked around the corner of the door.

"Sunny?" I whispered. "You there?"

Nothing.

It took no more than fifteen seconds to glance into the bedroom, into the bathroom, and behind the bar in the kitchen. I picked up the phone on the bar to dial the police myself. It was dead.

Maybe she had gone next door to the neighbors'. Maybe the phones were out all over the neighborhood. Or maybe the crew out in front of the house had cut the phones to this property. I was still standing there staring at the dead receiver when I heard a soft whine.

"Abaco?" I said aloud, and the whine grew louder.

I followed the sound to the walk-in closet in my bedroom. Even without the lights, I could see the outline of a girl, her hands and feet tied with rope, her mouth gagged with a scarf of my mother's I'd saved for years but never worn. Next to her, a huge pile of my clothing had been dumped off the hangers and then covered with my spare anchor chain. It was from inside the pile I heard the weak whine. I shoved the clothing aside until Abaco's head came clear. She licked my hand, then squirmed out, groggy from lack of oxygen but alive. Sunny's eyes held that too-familiar terror.

The girl's arms and legs were bound with some light polypropylene line I'd had stored in my closet, and the knots were so tight I couldn't budge them. "Just a minute. I'm going to get you out of here." I went to the kitchen and was about to open a drawer to grab a knife when Abaco started barking like mad.

"Shh." I grabbed the dog in the middle of the living room just as James Long poked his head around the open front door.

"Hello? Seychelle?"

I held the squirming dog tight as James walked in, cool and immaculate in his violet silk shirt, open at the neck, and his long, crisply pleated wheat-colored slacks. Abaco wouldn't stop barking.

"Abaco, no! Shh!" I stroked her head and grabbed her muzzle while keeping her in a headlock.

"Seychelle, are you okay?" He sounded genuinely concerned.

"What are you doing here?"

"I got this call from Sunny on my cell. She told me to come over here fast, that you were in trouble." He reached into his pocket and pulled out his phone, offering it as though it proved his story was true.

Abaco was still growling deep in her throat. I didn't dare let her go.

"What's going on here, Seychelle? What did she mean by trouble?" He held his hands wide, his palms lifted. "What can I do to help?"

"Sunny called you?"

"Yes. Where is she?" He looked around the combined living room/kitchen and then headed into the bedroom. Abaco tried to lunge at him as he walked past us, and it took all my strength to hold the dog back.

From the bedroom I heard him say, "Sunny, it's okay. I'm here now." There was something not quite right about how he said it. It was too calm.

I got my fingers firmly around the dog's collar and dragged her to the bathroom, and locked the door.

When I turned around, James was kneeling in the closet opening, and he had freed the rope around Sunny's legs with a small keychain knife. He helped her to her feet. He'd removed her gag, and she shouted, "Sey!" before her voice was cut short so suddenly, the silence that followed sounded louder than her cry.

In my dark bedroom, the scene lacked color of any sort. The walls, the closet with the swaying empty hangers, the back of James's head, all were colored only in black and white and muted shades of gray. In that quick glimpse I'd caught of her face, Sunny's wide white eyes and pale skin made me remember James's paintings hanging in the gallery down on Las Olas.

"James, what . . . ," I started to say, but then I saw that same little half smile on his face, his head cocked to one side. His hand was wrapped around her throat, his brown skin contrasting with hers, the position grotesque yet familiar.

"James, let go of her!" I grabbed his arm and tried to wrench it free. A burst of lights went off in my head, and I found myself on the floor, the side of my head feeling like a firecracker had exploded in my ear.

"Man, that feels good." Cesar was standing just inside the door to my room, smiling and rubbing his fist. Zeke pushed past him and took James by the arm.

"Mr. Long, not yet. We can still use her." He peeled James's fingers from Sunny's neck. She began coughing and gasping for air. Zeke shook his head and said to Cesar, "The man just doesn't know his own strength."

James adjusted his shirt and cleared his throat, blinking at Zeke for a moment as though struggling to remember who he was. "That's enough, Zeke."

"No disrespect, but the boss would be pissed if you did this one before he got a shot at her."

In the video. The arm.

I launched myself at James before I'd had time to think it

through. A high-pitched wail filled the room, and even I was startled at some deep level to realize the sound had come from me.

Finally, Zeke grabbed me about my midsection and pulled me off him. James had never stopped smiling.

B. J. WAS HALF ASLEEP OR UNCONSCIOUS WHEN WE ALL CAME into the house through the kitchen, but the noise woke him, and he started to heave himself up off the couch before he saw the gun in Zeke's hand.

"What . . ."

"Relax, lie back down," James said. He turned on a small lamp. "See, everyone here is fine."

"Sey . . ."

I didn't answer him. There was nothing left in me. Zeke pushed me toward the love seat, and I fell back into the cushions and covered my face with my hands.

I had kissed those lips. I had touched him, laughed with him. If we hadn't been interrupted that night by someone, probably Neal, looking in the window, I might have slept with him. First Neal, then James. What was wrong with me? I rubbed at my lips and felt dampness, and realized I had been crying.

Cesar dragged Sunny into the room with his big hand clamped over her mouth. "I think she likes me." He stuck out his thick tongue and ran it over the side of her face.

"Hey, let her go," B.J. said, pushing up into a sitting position and then finding Zeke's gun again pointed at his face.

Sunny's eyes met mine, looking not so much afraid as resigned. Cesar's hand held her head tight against his upper abdomen.

I forced myself to sit up on the couch. "Dammit, James." Even my voice sounded soft. "Make him leave her alone."

"Seychelle, you're so predictable. It's certainly made it easy to follow you. We would have been here sooner except for the fact that this idiot"—he motioned toward Cesar—"couldn't put two and two together when he heard the boat engines start up earlier."

Cesar looked at James through his wide-set eyes and his upper lip curled.

"I'm surrounded by idiots." He waved his hand at Zeke and Cesar.

Cesar's grip on Sunny's head grew so tight, the blood drained from his fingers. He and James were locked in some sort of staring match.

"She's just a kid, James," I said. When I got no response, I added, "I don't know why I'm even bothering. You're no different from either of them." I jerked my head toward Cesar and Zeke.

"Actually, I'm quite different." James turned to face me, and his smile turned into a self-satisfied smirk. "I see her as a commodity. I understand the business potential. Men have an appetite for young girls like Sunny." He spread his hands apart, palms up. "It's the law of supply and demand."

"You sick, twisted jerk."

"No, Seychelle, it's not that much different from selling cars or shoes. I'm just a good businessman. It takes a certain kind of talent—insight, if you will—to recognize opportunities."

"Talent? Who are you kidding?"

"I'm serious. I first met Crystal at a Harbor House fund-raiser, and I recognized the opportunity immediately. I could see he was fascinated with what I did, working with young girls every day. He told me he was interested in meeting privately with young girls, and I had an endless supply of runaways. We never had enough beds for all of them at Harbor House, anyway."

"Stop it. Why are you telling me this?"

He reached over, took my hand, and pressed it between his. I yanked my hand back as though I'd been burned. "I'm just a good businessman, that's all. Crystal's the one with the need, always wanting someone fresh, unsuspecting, someone who will fight hard. Who am I to judge? Live and let live." He laughed out loud then, as though at some private joke.

"When it was just the beatings, I paid the girls well, and they left happy. He got jobs for some of them in the club, and they could make lots of money there.

"Then he started with the video camera. The timing was perfect. I got us onto the Internet, contracted with servers around the world."

"That's right, Long," Cesar said, his guttural voice lower than usual. "You're the man." He turned to me. "Dude never wanted to get his hands dirty, always acting like he's better than us, till one day he found out he likes squeezing off chicks."

James moved so fast, Cesar never saw it coming. Sunny fell to the floor, and James held Cesar's wrist twisted high behind his back. "No one asked your opinion, now, did we, Mr. Esposito?"

When Cesar didn't answer, James applied more pressure to the bent wrist. Cesar grunted.

"I didn't hear you."

"I said I'm fucking sorry," Cesar said, his voice strained.

The room seemed unnaturally quiet just before we heard the crack of breaking bone, followed by Cesar's scream.

James smiled as he looked down at the man now crumpled on the floor cradling his wrist and whimpering. Then he smoothed out imaginary creases in his clothing, reached into the pocket of his slacks, and pulled out a cell phone. "You look a mess, Seychelle, you know that? That's a shame, beautiful girl like you."

"James, Neal's outsmarted us all. He's out there collecting Crystal's money," I said.

He flipped open the phone and began to dial.

"He took *Gorda* and went out there over an hour ago. I was going to go out in my Whaler and stop him, but since you've been playing games and telling us your life story, he's probably had time to grab it all and take off."

"Crystal," he said, "yes." He turned his back to us and spoke into the phone. "Yes, sir, we're here at the girl's place." He stared straight at me. "All right," he said, "then you'll bring the *Hard Bottom* down here, pick them up, and meet us out there." He laughed. "You're right."

He snapped the phone shut and slid it into his pants pocket. "Zeke, the dive gear, in the car." He jerked his head, and Zeke Moss hurried toward the front door. "Crystal says you and I are to go ahead without them. You find the wreck site, and I'll take care of Garrett. Our friends will be along to join us later."

As we rode the tide downriver, I could see the sky lightening behind the houses and trees. The stars were slowly winking out as a watery blue tinged with pink washed in from the east. James sat next to me on the varnished wood midships seat. His thighs showed a tan line—the trunks he had borrowed from Mr. Larsen's bedroom were too short for his long legs. Between his feet lay the mesh dive bag Zeke had brought in from their car with all the shiny new equipment: mask, fins, and Cesar's ever-present bang stick. I was more nervous about the firepower of the pressure-sensitive bang stick bouncing around on the floor of the dinghy than I was about the gun that he held low, tucked under his arm, barely visible.

By the time we reached the Intracoastal, dozens of sportfishing boats were headed to the harbor entrance, deckhands readying the baits and outriggers in the growing light. Those big charter boats usually passed me when I was running my tug, but this morning in the Whaler, I jockeyed my way between and around them and pounded my way out through the swells in the harbor channel.

At the sea buoy, the charter boats fanned out in all directions, their white wakes etched in the water like the spokes of a wheel. The rim of the sun peeked over the horizon, and within seconds, the whole orb popped into the sky. The sea was flat, and the tiny wavelets reflected back the horizontal rays, making the sea look covered in jewels. The day was shaping up to be hot and almost windless, with no sign of yesterday's squalls. Summer was nearly upon us. I knew exactly where to head—north, off the condos of Galt Ocean Mile. The coordinates were etched in my memory, the picture of the chart clear in my mind. As we flew up the coast, I tried to come up with a plan, to figure out just what I would do once we got there. When I could make out the *Gorda* rolling slightly in the little waves, anchored in the same spot I'd found the *Top Ten* just a few days ago, I still didn't have a clue.

XXVIII

WE WERE ABOUT A HUNDRED YARDS OFF THE *GORDA* when James waved his hand, palm down, motioning me to slow down. Faintly, across the water and over the sound of our own outboard, we could hear the higher-pitched roar of an engine running. I knew that sound.

"What's that noise?"

I couldn't see any reason not to tell him. "It's a compressor. I use it for filling scuba tanks, hookah diving sometimes."

He nodded. "I guess we'll just watch from here. He'll have to come up sooner or later."

It was only a few minutes after sunrise, and the heat was already building. I let him sweat for a while before I spoke.

"How far do you think it is to shore from here?" I asked.

"Who cares?"

"I guess that's the way Neal got off the *Top Ten* before—you know, after he killed Patty. I guess he used his scuba gear and just swam under the water and came out on the beach."

James squinted toward the shore.

"He could do the same thing right now, you know. He doesn't care about the *Gorda*. Maybe he's already got the money and he's swimming for shore as we speak. You may not believe it, but I don't want to see that son of a bitch get away with that money."

He raised one eyebrow and swung his head back and forth a couple of times, trying to gauge the distance, to decide if what I was describing was really possible.

"Okay, let's go over there. Tie up to your boat."

We tied the dinghy off to the midships cleat and climbed over the bulwark. The compressor was chugging on the afterdeck, making too much noise to permit speaking. The air hose led over the side toward the bow. James stayed behind me, the gun still pointed at the small of my back. I leaned over the bulwark and pointed off the starboard bow to a spot where lots of bubbles were breaking the surface.

"He's still down there," I shouted over the roar of the compressor. "Right there."

James nodded, then searched the horizon to the south, probably hoping to see the *Hard Bottom* coming out of the harbor entrance.

"One of us could go down, check it out, see what he's doing," I said.

He rubbed his chin, staring at the small patch of bubbles off *Gorda's* bow.

He motioned with his head. "Rope—where do you keep it?"

"This way," I said, and passed through the companionway into the wheelhouse. In the passageway heading to the engine room door, I saw that the toolbox was still open on the floor. James was right behind me with the gun, but I reached down and grabbed a big piece of angle iron out of the tin box. I brought the iron up under the gun and tried to carry it through right under his chin.

He was caught by surprise, and as the gun flew up, the noise exploded in the wheelhouse compartment. The starboard wheelhouse window shattered, the safety glass flying in pebble-sized bits and clattering onto the aluminum decks. The gun tumbled to the deck in the wheelhouse, and when I tried to duck under his arms and push past him to get at the weapon, his hands twisted me onto my belly, pressing my face to the deck. I was unable to breathe, and he had my left arm behind me, my wrist in his hands. He stepped over me, reaching for the gun. My right hand was free and my fingers could barely touch it, so I pushed it as hard as I could. It skittered across the aluminum deck and slid out the scupper and over the side of the boat. I heard the clunk as it fell into the Whaler tied alongside.

The pressure on my wrist increased, and I waited for the bone to pop.

"I think not." He pulled me to my feet. "I have something much more interesting in mind for you later. And I want to see your eyes when I do it."

He used a length of half-inch nylon dock line to tie my hands to the top of *Gorda's* wheel. When he was sure the rope was tight enough to cut off my circulation, he said, "The *Hard Bottom* will be here soon. The more you struggle," he told me, pointing to my hands, "the more damage those ropes will do."

As soon as he left to go back to the dinghy, I reached my foot out toward the bottom drawer under the navigation station. After several tries, I got my big toe through the latch ring that locked the drawers, and pulled. It made a loud clatter when the drawer hit the deck, but the compressor noise covered everything. Each movement seemed to draw the ropes tighter about my wrists. Pain wasn't about to stop me, though.

I pulled the drawer closer and riffled through the junk with my toes: bolts, shackles, old teak plugs, bits of line, and down in the bottom, the stainless-steel rigging knife Pit had given me years before. I pushed the drawer over with my foot, spilling the contents across the cabin sole, and I pulled the knife closer to me, sliding it across the aluminum deck. It took several tries before I was able to grasp the thick knife with my toes and pick it up. Leaning my butt back, I lifted my foot toward the hands tied to the locked wheel. My toes reached to within about four inches of my hands with the muscles in my back and legs stretching and straining. When I was almost there, the toes let go, and the knife clattered to the floor.

"Damn!"

Finally, on the third try, I got the knife lodged between my toes in a very firm grip. My fingers plucked it right out of my toes, and though I was losing all feeling in my hands and my fingers felt like fat sausages, I eventually pulled the knife out of the handle. The blade cut through the rope in seconds.

I saw that James had taken the Larsens' tank but used his own mask and fins. His mesh dive bag, shirt, wallet, gun, and keys were neatly stacked in the stern. I could have sat in the dinghy and waited, but even though Neal was a former Seal, James had the element of surprise on his side, and I figured it was about even odds who would be most likely to surface alive. I wasn't willing to wait and give either of them that element of surprise over me.

The shorts and big T-shirt I'd borrowed back at the house billowed up around me in the water, even as I tried to squeeze the air out of the fabric. I wished I could take them off, but I had nothing on underneath.

The water was exceptionally clear. *Gorda's* anchor was in the sand off the port side of the wreck, so the tug was floating just over the stern of the freighter. I could make out the superstructure of the *Bahama Belle* and see the bubbles rising out of her bow. The top of her mast was only about thirty feet down, but her deck level was a good fifty feet below the surface. I swam slowly toward the bow.

In only a few short months, the sea had already started reclaiming the lump of iron that had once been a working interisland freighter. Dark spots that would become the bases for soft corals were starting to grow around and on top of the pilothouse. Parrot fish, grunts, and trigger fish cruised in and out of the holes that had been blown in the aft cabin areas and around the bridge area. A lone barracuda hovered halfway to the surface, up over the bow.

I heard Neal before I saw him. It was a noise that sounded like a monstrous underwater woodpecker. He was down below the main deck level, visible through a hole that the dynamite had blown in her decks when they sank the ship. The air hose fed into the hole where a yellow dive light illuminated the whole compartment. Debris from his work floated in the water around the light, giving everything a fuzzy appearance. Using some kind of an air hammer, Neal was chipping away at the ballast cement in the anchor chain hold. As he worked, bursts of bubbles emerged from the compartment, and he tossed aside large chunks of cement.

I smiled so wide, water leaked in around the edges of my snorkel. Of course—very clever, Neal. It wasn't unusual for ships to add some cement ballast to make the ship float properly on her lines. Neal had probably chipped out the old cement while in the shipyard, stowed the money, and then cemented over it. Add the anchor chain resting on top of the cement, and who would ever know? Obviously not Customs, the cops, or Crystal and his men.

The noise of the air hammer stopped. The yellow light was momentarily covered by Neal's body as he maneuvered himself around in the cramped space. He seemed to be straining, trying to pull something out of the hole he was creating.

The barracuda cruised down for a closer look, attracted by the sudden movement in the water.

Down in the murky water, Neal was slowly surrounded by floating shapes. For a moment, I thought it was a school of fish swimming out the forward hold, like the blue tangs that travel in schools so thick they can cast a single dark shadow on the bottom. But these shadows moved too slowly for fish. And there were hundreds, thousands of them, waving in the current like gentle sea fans. Neal swam out and grabbed one, then another, and another. He stuffed them into his trunks. They were bills.

At that moment, I noticed a string of bubbles rising off the port side of the ship, headed toward the bow. James. His dark head appeared over the bulwark, and he paused to watch for a moment as Neal worked both hands down in the forward hold. Neal was so intent on his work, plucking the bills like fruit from the sea, that he didn't spot James rising over the ship's gunwale behind him.

I'd already thought Neal was dead once. I'd loved him, mourned him, and almost been killed by him, but I couldn't sit back and watch him be murdered.

I started hyperventilating, puffing, blowing, in, out, super-oxygenating my system for a long free dive. Neither man had seen me yet. Divers often don't look up. I sucked in air until my lungs ached and I was so dizzy I nearly passed out. Then I dove.

They were below me, moving in slow motion, one man gliding up behind the other with a fluid, graceful movement, wrapping his arms around the other like a ballet dancer hoisting his partner into the air. James held Neal from behind, sliding his arm around Neal's neck. Neal's legs splayed, his fists beating on James's arm and head and body, but the bicep crushing his air supply held firm. James's head was cocked to one side, and even though I could not see his face, I knew the smile that danced around his eyes.

Ely. God knew how many others. Not Neal.

The borrowed fins flapped loosely on my feet as I kicked and stroked and pulled deeper, faster. As I approached the two struggling men, I swam through the school of money, surprised at the coolness of the paper as I pushed aside the bills with each stroke. Swimming up behind James, I grabbed his air hose, braced my shoulder against his tank, and yanked with all my strength. The regulator pulled free, waving through the water like a dancing serpent, spewing silvery bubbles. His head jerked around as I kicked to distance myself from him. Neal swam off as James grabbed my leg with one hand and with the other reached around for the life-giving hose. I kicked and struggled, but his grip only tightened around my ankle. I had to get to the surface. James pulled me toward him by the leg, grabbing my knee, then my thigh, reeling me in. He clamped his arm around my waist like a metal bar, the strength of his embrace so unyielding that my body went limp with fear. His fingers clamped around my throat.

Neither of us had a regulator; neither would last much longer without one.

This was where I would die, drowning, like my mother, I

thought. After all these years of being so angry, angry at her, angry at myself, I now saw it differently. I felt sleepy. It would be nice to sleep for a long time. I even thought for a moment that I saw my mother, a shadowy presence swimming out of the darkness to welcome me. My body relaxed, and James let go of my throat to reach back for the regulator. Let him have it, I thought, let me sleep.

Suddenly James jerked and arched his back, squeezing my abdomen. I tried to hold on to what air I had, but bubbles trickled out of my mouth. The faceplate on my mask seemed to be shrinking, the blackness closing in. The water was growing even more murky, with inky trails of darkness, and his arm still encircled me, squeezing away my life like a giant squid. My own arm reached back, more from reflex than thought, to fight, to deliver one last blow, and my elbow hit cold steel projecting out from James's left side.

It wasn't ink. It was blood, and James Long was pulling me down, wouldn't let go, and I knew for certain then I was going to die there with him in that sea of blood and money.

Out of the darkness a hand grabbed my face, pried open my mouth, and inserted a regulator. From years of dive training, I blew out the salt water before I inhaled the cold, sweet air. Neal's eyes behind the glass of his faceplate peered into mine, checking to see if I was conscious. I stared back and blinked several times, trying to say thank you with my eyes.

Then I heard the muffled *whoof*, felt the concussion through the water, and saw his face jerk and the light go out in those familiar blue eyes as his body convulsed from the blast of the bang stick. I screamed into the regulator as his face disappeared into the dusky crimson water.

XXIX

WHETHER I LOST CONSCIOUSNESS OR SIMPLY WENT to some deep, dark place inside me, I don't know, but eventually, I became aware that the grip around my waist had loosened. I pushed the arm aside and slid out of James's grasp. Through the cloudy water I could make out the rest of his body, resting on the deck of the *Bahama Belle*, his arms floating upward, head slumped forward, looking more like a resting marionette than a dead man. He would not have liked this pose. Tiny silvery fish darted in, pecking at the ragged flesh on his side. Blood continued to spiral from the wound. I fought down the urge to vomit. I was still breathing off the regulator attached to the tank on his back, and now that I was loose from his grip, I had to hang on to his backpack to keep from floating to the surface.

I heard the sound of an engine and propellers through the water. Above, the shadow of a larger hull was pulling alongside the *Gorda*. It had to be the *Hard Bottom*, with Zeke and Crystal. They would surely have dive gear aboard and be ready to splash over the side at any moment. The currents were carrying off the blood in the water around me and I could see more clearly. Neal's body was gone—drifted off or perhaps snagged somewhere on the ship out of sight. Bills continued to waft out of the anchor hold. The water all around me was littered with money.

The early morning rays of sunlight slanted down toward the depths, toward the millions of live creatures, plankton, and single-celled animals that swam in the shafts of sun. It was so peaceful down here beneath the taut dome that separated the worlds of water and air. A part of me still didn't want to return to the surface.

A shadow rising over the *Bahama Belle* caught my attention. At first I thought it might be Neal. Then it passed behind the bridge, and when it emerged on the other side, I recognized the thick-bodied profile of a bull shark. This one was an old fish, his body mottled, pockmarked, and scarred from battles, yet swimming effortlessly. A short, stocky shark, his form dense with pure muscle, he seemed to assert his dominance by actually passing through the bridge deck. They were nasty predators—I'd seen what a bull shark had done once to a wounded baby manatee that washed ashore on the beach off Lauderdale. Today there had been enough blood in the water to attract dozens of them. I could tell from the angle of his fins that he was agitated and excited.

I unlatched the bottle of air from James's backpack, tucked it under my arm, and began swimming across the bottom, in the direction of the tug's stern, slowly rising toward the surface. I hoped that what was left of James would be enough to keep the shark's attention focused below.

My face broke the surface at the corner of *Gorda's* transom. The *Hard Bottom* was rafted up to the tug's starboard side, and even with the calm seas and lots of fenders, the two boats were grinding and bumping awkwardly. Someone had let out more line on the dinghy's painter, so the Whaler now floated just off the stern of the two boats. Both the engine and the generator were running on the sportfisherman, and I could hear voices from inside the air-conditioned cabin.

I ditched the tank and let it sink slowly to the bottom. Keeping my head below the level of the gunwale, I eased forward alongside the dinghy. If I could get into the Whaler, cut myself loose from the *Gorda*, and drift off, I could probably go for help.

I lifted my body over the bow, but weighted down as I was by the big T-shirt and shorts, it seemed to take forever. My arms nearly gave out as I pulled my legs into the boat. At the same time, I heard the aft cabin door slide open on the sportfisherman. My foot slipped from the oversized fins I was wearing, and I stumbled as I grabbed at the pistol and rolled onto my back, sighting down the barrel. It nearly dropped from my wet hands, but I got my finger on the trigger and pointed it at the aft deck of the sportfisherman as a diver stepped through the door.

He moved awkwardly, lifting his knees high to flop his fins onto the outer deck. He was clad only in BC, backpack, boxers, and body hair. He pushed the blue silicon mask up to the top of his head, spit out the snorkel, and smiled, showing that huge gap between his front teeth.

"It's not real smart to go pointing guns at cops, Seychelle," Collazo said as Mike Beesting hopped out of the cabin, followed by a bandaged and grinning B.J.

XXX

I HOLED UP IN MY COTTAGE FOR DAYS, JUST SITTING ON THE couch, rubbing Abaco's belly and watching it all on the TV news. South Florida went a little crazy as hundred-dollar bills washed up on beaches from Pompano to Palm Beach. Several Haitian women got into a brawl with some blue-haired retirees. Vendors flooded the beaches hawking T-shirts with photos of hundred-dollar bills and the words Florida Sand Dollars, and the reporters were having a good time covering the little festival of greed.

They recovered both bodies eventually. There was a hell of a hole in Neal, probably from more than just the bang stick. I remembered the bull shark. On TV I saw Crystal, Cesar, and Zeke all being led into the courthouse wearing handcuffs and smirks, and the news anchors bantered back and forth wondering if this time the authorities would be able to make a good case against Benjamin Crystal. State officials raided Harbor House and seized records, then brought in a new interim staff while they tried to figure out what to do about the place.

I'd found out later that Mike had been up all night and had finally gone to the police station and raised Collazo out of bed sometime around 4 A.M. They had busted into the Larsens' house at daybreak expecting to both save me and then arrest me, but instead they'd surprised Cesar, Zeke, and Crystal preparing to board the *Hard Bottom* with Sunny. The cops had then jumped aboard the *Hard Bottom*, and refusing to be left behind, B.J. had joined them, helping them pilot the *Hard Bottom* to the *Gorda* offshore. When they found *Gorda* and the Whaler both abandoned, Collazo decided not to wait for the regular police divers who were on their way, and he put on the dive gear himself.

When Collazo took my preliminary statement the next day, he told me that once they knew what questions to ask, they had indeed found a couple of witnesses who had seen what they described as a "crazy man all wrapped up in towels" panhandling on A1A the day the *Top Ten* nearly went aground. Apparently, after swimming ashore, Neal had begged for bus fare and then ridden Broward County Transit to within walking distance of the Larsens' place.

There were reporters camped outside the gates to the estate for a couple of days, trying to get me to tell my version of what happened beneath the surface that day. I didn't even go out to pick up the newspapers or the mail. Eventually the story became old news and they left.

It had been five or six days—I'd lost count—when I heard a knock on the door, followed by Jeannie's voice hollering, "Seychelle! I know you're in there. Open this door, it's damn hot out here."

When I opened the door, she clucked, shook her head, and said, "I knew it. He wanted to come over here by himself, but I told him he'd better let me come first and talk to you. Look at you. Your hair . . . have you even bathed once this week?" She was wearing another of her muumuus, this one with maddeningly perky bright yellow daisies. She had a grocery bag under each arm.

She marched me into the shower, and when I emerged, combing out my dripping hair, she was cooking something that smelled pretty good.

"Girl, you don't have any real food in this place. What have you been eating?"

I was surprised when I managed to get down a bowl of her homemade chicken soup, along with two slices of whole-grain bread and fresh fruit salad. B.J. would have been shocked to see such healthy food pass my lips. It tasted like seaweed or old hemp rope. Nothing appealed to me anymore.

"He's going to be here in less than an hour, so we'd better talk fast," she said.

"What? Who's coming over?"

She waved her hand in the air. "Don't worry about that. Listen. While you've been in here drooping around, I've been working my tail off. Collazo said the prosecutors wanted to come talk to you right away, but I've fended them off."

"But I already gave a statement after it happened."

"Yeah, yeah, but that's just the start, honey. They have been trying to build a case against this Crystal guy for *years*, and they think that now, with your help, they can do it. The stuff they found on the hard drives at that house included at least six snuff films. It seems they solved several missing-persons cases, too. At this point they're even looking at the fire that killed Long's grandmother when he was only twenty-something. And of course, the feds are technically the owners of the *Top Ten* now, so I've been dealing with them about your salvage claim. I think I've figured out a deal that will make everybody happy, so you just give me the go-ahead, and I'll see if it will fly."

Across the room, my mother's painting of the bird-of-paradise and the dark, angry sky caught my attention. It was as though I were seeing it for the first time. My breath rasped in my throat as I choked on a chunk of bread.

"What is it? Seychelle? Are you okay?"

I now understood what she had painted, what had sent her into her "bad days." Mother had known about evil.

Still facing the painting, I asked, "I've been wondering about Sunny, Jeannie. Where is she? Is she okay?"

Jeannie chuckled. "She's great, Sey. She's with a foster family, and she's back in school, tenth grade. She asked about you, too. She'd like to see you."

"Good. I'd like that." I turned away from the painting and faced her. "Okay, what deal?"

"Well, thanks to you, the government is over four million wet dollars richer, and they've seized a multimillion-dollar yacht to boot—on top of which they got their bad guy. So I just tell them that you will be happy and cooperative as their star witness in the case against the kiddie porn king, and they will give you a very lucrative salvage settlement on the *Top Ten*. I think we could probably go for the hundred thousand figure or close to it."

"That means I have to testify?"

"You'll have to no matter what, dear. They'll just subpoena you. You might as well go to them first and get something out of the deal. So all I need is the thumbs-up from you, and I'll be on my way. What do you say?"

I pushed my fruit bowl away. I'd lost what little appetite I'd been able to muster at the thought of looking again at Zeke Moss, Cesar Esposito, and Benjamin Crystal. Yet if I could help keep them away from girls like Sunny . . . hell, yes. "Go for it, Jeannie."

She came over, bent down, and gave me a smothering hug. "Just think, honey, the *Gorda* will be all yours. You'll be able to buy your brothers out." Standing and putting her hand on one hip, she asked, "Don't you think it's time you got back to work? I think you need to get outside and get on the water again."

I nodded. "You're probably right."

She collected her things and turned toward the door.

"You want to know something really stupid, Jeannie? I don't think Patty Krix ever did double-cross Neal. I think this whole thing started to unravel because of Neal's paranoia. When Neal surfaced that day out on the *Top Ten*, Patty was talking to the Coast Guard, but Neal didn't know that—he just assumed she was calling Crystal. He didn't have to kill her."

"He didn't have to try to steal that money, either. Don't you think about him anymore. Time to move forward."

I stood in the doorway watching her walk down the brick path. She glanced back down at the river, smiled, and waved, calling, "I'm out of here. She's all yours." Jeannie turned back to me. "On second thought, Seychelle, you could probably use a few more days off." She winked and disappeared around the side of the Larsens' house.

I stepped outside and looked toward the river. There, tied to the dock, was a nearly new thirty-six-foot catamaran, and B.J. was standing in the cockpit wearing only flower-print surfer trunks and a smile.

After examining the length of the boat, I squinted at him. "You didn't steal it, did you?"

"Belongs to a lady friend of mine. She once said if I ever wanted anything, all I had to do was ask. So I asked. I'm headed down to the Keys for a few days. I sure could use a hand. You interested?"

WITH HER SHALLOW DRAFT, B.J. WAS ABLE TO TAKE THAT cat far into the backwaters of Florida Bay, anchor off little no-name keys, and zigzag back to the coast to find the few rare patches of sand along the Atlantic side of the Florida Keys. I slept in the spare cabin, alone in a queen-size bunk, and B.J. pretty much left me to my thoughts, giving me some of that infamous space he was noted for. We avoided people and civilization and ate what we caught, though my appetite for most good things seemed to have vanished. I had to admit that all that fresh food B.J. was making me eat, along with the fresh air and sun, was starting to make me want to rejoin the human race, but I just couldn't muster up the desire for much of anything. There was something, some sour taste, in the back of my throat that I could not wash away no matter how many ice-cold Coronas I swallowed.

It was that black pit, taunting me again.

One afternoon when we'd returned to the boat after an afternoon's snorkeling and B.J. was down in the galley cooking up the grouper he'd just speared with his Hawaiian sling, I rinsed off under the sun shower we had hanging on the afterdeck, then toweled off my white nylon swimsuit. I helped myself to a Corona and, on an impulse, took the two photos out of the side zipper pocket of my shoulder bag: the photo of my mother and the three of us kids, and the picture of Neal and me in the Dry Tortugas. I went up forward to sit in the netting between the pontoons. I'd thought about those photos lots of times over the last few days, after Neal was really dead and finally gone. I'd thought about him and me and Ely and my mother and the choices we'd all made. I'd come close to pulling the photos out of my purse several times, but I just hadn't felt up to looking at them yet. What was different now, I didn't know, except that I wanted to make that sour taste vanish, and maybe I had to look at the dark places to make that happen.

The sun was about thirty minutes off the horizon, and the gray-green scrub on the key looked inflamed in the golden rays. Around the south side of the island, on the ocean side, the little breakers foamed bright white, almost luminous. In close to the island, the shallows glowed pale lime, gradually deepening out in the channel between the keys to a deep cobalt blue. A little dark pointed head lifted out of the water over the seagrass beds—a sea turtle surfacing for a breath.

"Are you okay?"

B.J.'s voice startled me.

"Yeah. I was just looking at these old pictures." Actually, I hadn't looked yet, I was just holding them—clutching them so tightly, I suddenly realized, that I was bending the paper.

Around the south side of the island, the surface tension caused by the swiftly rising tide smoothed the water to a glassy sheen and was broken only occasionally by the fins of a large school of tarpon as they rolled in the pass.

"I've been thinking a lot about my past. You know, how I got here to this place, today. How things might have been different if

I'd made other choices." The school of fish moved closer to our anchorage on the inside of the pass. "My mother always wanted me to be an artist. I wasn't really all that good, though."

"Very few of us ever turn out to be what our parents want us to be," he said. "They try to do the best they can, but it's not about them in the end. It's about us." He put his hand on my shoulder and began massaging the knotted muscles in my neck, trying to knead away the tension. His voice was soothing, but I felt my stomach muscles tightening at his touch. I opened my fingers and looked at the smiling faces in my hands. In just a few years, I would be the same age as my mother when this photo was taken. For the first time, I saw the resemblance that people often remarked upon, the maple-colored skin, the same-size white tank suits, the shoulder-length sun-streaked light brown hair.

She was staring directly at the camera, and I noticed the deep lines at the corners of her eyes, the furrows in her brow. Though the weather in the photo was bright and sunny, in her eyes I saw the dark squall of her painting.

"We have expectations," he said, "but then we discover life is full of hurts and disappointments and shortcomings."

I nodded and took a swig from my beer. "Yeah, I've had a few of those lately."

"What makes you so hard on yourself?"

"Me?" I cocked my head to one side. "What do you mean?"

"You're a smart, funny, talented, beautiful woman. Aside from being a terrible cook, you've pretty much got it all."

A smile touched the corners of my mouth for a little while, but as we sat quietly watching the sky turn violet, the sour taste returned.

Neal looked so damned cocky and happy and pleased with himself in the other photo. We'd made love that morning and made pancakes for breakfast before going ashore and exploring the ruins of an old fort down in the Dry Tortugas. It was funny that I even remembered we'd eaten our last papaya that day, feeding each other spoonfuls of the juicy pink-orange flesh dripping in lime juice.

"Neal saved my life down there, B.J. He didn't have to come back and put that regulator in my mouth."

"No, he didn't."

"It's funny in a way. Crystal said he was a romantic, that he would come back for me—and he did. He died because he came back to save me."

"Yes, I know." He kissed the side of my head and smoothed back my hair. "And you should be happy for him."

I turned to face him, puzzled. "What do you mean?"

"Seychelle, do you really think Neal was all that content with who he had become? The Neal we knew back when you first met him was a guy who was struggling with lots of inner demons, but he was trying, really trying, to be good for you. I don't know all his history—I don't even know if his history would explain it—but for a while there, with you out of his life, the demons took over. He did things that he could never erase. I think he went a little crazy hiding up there in the Larsens' house watching you and thinking about all that money out there, with him the only one who knew where it was. Finally, at the end, you gave him a chance to get his senses back, to do an honorable thing."

I reached over my shoulder and stilled his hands. "So you're saying I should forgive Neal, is that it?"

He laughed softly and exhaled in a deep sigh. Before he could say anything more, I turned to him.

"Please, don't say anything for a few minutes. I want to tell you something. Just listen, okay?" I took a deep breath. "The summer when I was eleven, my mother asked me to go to the beach one day," I began.

W HEN I'D FINISHED, WE BOTH SAT IN THE NETTING, QUIET for several long moments. Finally I said, "I was just a little kid." I squinted at the horizon. "I didn't know much about who my mother was. These past few weeks I've come to see just how dark her bad days must have been. No wonder she couldn't climb out." My voice cracked, but I swallowed and licked my lips. I felt like a huge stone was pressing on my chest, preventing my lungs from inflating. Clutching the photos and knowing in my own way that I was speaking directly to them, I said, "I miss her so much." The school of tarpon had reversed their direction and were moving off, back toward the slick water of the pass. "I forgive . . ."

I couldn't get the rest of it out, but he knew what I meant. I forgave all of us.

The photos fell into the netting when I stood up and clambered out of the bow hammock and dove off the starboard hull. I had to get away, be alone. As though in one of the annual lifeguards' qualifying races, I swam the crawl stroke with everything I had, all out, feet pumping, arms arcing out of the water and slicing back in with barely a splash. Each breath felt like burning sandpaper in my throat as my head rolled out of the water, gasping out of the corner of my mouth. I was headed out to the pass, to the dark, swift-moving currents, to the blue-hole depths where shadows lurked.

When I could no longer see the bottom and the surface of the water bulged smooth and taut, I kept at it, swimming with every ounce of energy I possessed, and still I stopped making any progress through the pass. The incoming tidal current sweeping through the narrow cut was just too swift. I flailed with all my strength, but I did not move an inch over the bottom. Finally, I took several short quick breaths and dove, angling downward, ears popping, lungs straining.

I opened my eyes and saw the huge silvery silhouettes gliding around me, unafraid, oblivious to my presence. Without a mask and with very little light underwater, the enormous fish seemed to appear as if by magic, looming out of the shadows swirling and swimming around me in an underwater ballet. The tarpons' scales, great round glistening disks, shimmered in the dark water, finding and reflecting the last rays of the dying day. With their low-slung jaws and big dark eyes, the huge fish might have looked evil were it not for their total indifference.

I reached out to touch a fish as it passed so close to me, but as if with some unique schooling perception, the fish's impressive body turned just out of my reach. As he turned, so did the dozens of others around him, and I wondered if it was that primordial co-operation that we'd given up to gain our free will.

My head broke the surface, and I let out a whoop so loud, it startled the egrets nesting in the mangroves on the bayside of the key. The two birds took to the air, bouncing off the tiny elastic limbs of the tree. I floated peacefully, surrendering to the current carrying me back to the boat.

B.J. stood up forward on a pontoon, leaning out over the water, his arms wrapped about the lower shrouds. Even at this distance, silhouetted against the coral-colored sky, his white grin glowed against his dark skin. He lifted an arm in a wave and hollered that dinner was ready. I began to stroke my way back to the boat with a different sort of urgency. All my appetites had returned.